UNDERSTUDY

FORGE BOOKS BY CAROLE BELLACERA

BORDER CROSSINGS

SPOTLIGHT

EAST OF THE SUN, WEST OF THE MOON

UNDERSTUDY

UNDERSTUDY

carole bellacera

A TOM DOHERTY ASSOCIATES BOOK

NEW YORK

UNDERSTUDY

Copyright © 2003 by Carole Bellacera

This book is printed on acid-free paper.

A Forge Book
Published by Tom Doherty Associates, LLC
175 Fifth Avenue
New York, NY 10010

www.tor.com

Forge® is a registered trademark of Tom Doherty Associates, LLC.

Library of Congress Cataloging-in-Publication Data

Bellacera, Carole.
    Understudy / Carole Bellacera.—1st ed.
        p. cm.
    "A Tom Doherty Associates Book."
    ISBN 0-765-30655-7 (alk. paper)
    1. Television actors and actresses—Fiction. 2. Identity (Psychology)—
Fiction. 3. False personation—Fiction. I. Title.

    PS3552.E529U53 2003
    813'.54—dc21

                                                                2002045480

First Edition: June 2003

Printed in the United States of America

0 9 8 7 6 5 4 3 2 1

To my daughter, Leah

★

my shining star

acknowledgments

Thanks to:

Maggie Moore, student at the College of William & Mary for the informative tour of W&M. Mary O'Leary, producer, *One Life to Live*, ABC, for inviting me to the *OLTL* set. Nancy J. Sherman, publicist, *One Life to Live*, ABC, for guiding my tour of the set. Wayne Bilotti, hairdresser, Laurie Fillipi, hairdresser, Renate Long, makeup, *One Life to Live*, ABC, for entertaining me with soap opera anecdotes. Bob Woods, actor, *One Life to Live*, ABC, for making me feel right at home on the *OLTL* set. Lynda Sue Cooper for helping me liven up my football fan dialogue. John O'Connor, FBI, for answering questions on how people rebuild an identity. Cindy Luty for the Tinkerbell analogy. Barbara Marshall for researching beaches in Hawaii. Hope Tarr and Elizabeth Sommer for being awesome critique partners. Jean Singleton, RN, for unwittingly giving me the idea for *Understudy*. Gloria Fitzwater, for being the "seedling" of inspiration for Robin, whose love and vulnerability shine through her party-girl persona. Kathryn O'Sullivan for helping me "rearrange" the script for *Understudy*. Laurie Miller, RN, Grant Medical Center ER, Columbus, Ohio, for graciously answering my questions. Cindy Burks, RN, and high school buddy, for reading the ER section and giving me feedback. Regina Scott, my high school English teacher in Pittsboro, Indiana, who gave me the encouragement to become a writer. To my agent, Ethan Ellenberg, for believing in this book. To my editor, Stephanie Lane, who is always a joy to work with. To my husband, Frank, who always gives me great feedback, especially this time, with the identity-switch story line. And finally, to my children, Leah and Stephen, who have always believed in me.

prologue

The emergency room doors slid open to spill an attractive middle-aged couple into the turmoil of a crowded waiting room, hair and faces wet from the falling snow, eyes frantic. The noise inside the ER was overwhelming—overhead pages blaring incomprehensible codes, people shouting, trying to get the attention of a passing nurse or doctor, an infant screaming at the level of the most raucous heavy metal bands, gurneys clattering down crowded corridors. Non-critical patients occupied seats, some of them coughing, puking, groaning, some bloodied, others looking outwardly healthy. Medical personnel in green scrubs moved through the chaos, seemingly unruffled.

The man who'd just entered looked around, his eyes settling on the bullet-proof glass protecting the reception center. He was tall and handsome, a man in his late forties with slightly graying hair, who wore an unmistakable air of power and importance.

"Over here," he said to his elegant blond companion, striding to the reception area. The woman followed.

He spoke through a window to a petite dark-haired woman wearing a brightly patterned jacket and a badge emblazoned with a smiley face and a name—Rosemary Sethford, RN. "I'm Michael Mulcahey. My daughter was brought in from a car accident. Do you know her condition?"

The nurse glanced at the erasure board on the wall behind her. "They're working on her, sir. That's all I can tell you right now. Please take a seat, and a doctor will be with you as soon as possible."

Michael's lips tightened. "I'm former congressman Michael Mulcahey, and I demand to see a doctor *right now!*"

The nurse's eyes grew cold. "Please take a seat, sir," she repeated. "The doctor will see you as soon as he has done everything possible to save your daughter's life."

The woman at his side gently touched his arm. "Come on, Mike. Let's do what she says."

He swallowed hard and turned to her. "She's our little girl, Tammy. I need to know she's okay."

"I know," Tammy said quietly. "But there's nothing we can do except wait."

She guided him to a seat in the waiting room, and they sat, gripping each other's hands. Nothing changed in the ER. The baby still cried—horrible screeching wails. A young man vomited into an emesis basin. The nauseating stink wafted through the stale air, along with the overpowering scent of cheap perfume and rank body odor. Machines beeped and shrilled out alarms. Voices in various languages babbled in fear or anger. A woman sobbed. Another moaned in pain. A man yelled obscenities. More sirens whooped, and incoming casualties clattered through the doors on racing gurneys.

And still, they waited.

Finally, an hour later, a young resident appeared in front of them, his scrubs soaked with splotches of bright red blood. Michael paled, but Tammy sat rigidly, the only sign of her tension a slight clenching of her fist in her lap.

"Mr. and Mrs. Mulcahey?" the resident said as the couple got to their feet and faced him. "Your daughter has been stabilized, but her injuries are severe. She apparently went through the windshield in the accident, and she's suffered extensive facial trauma. Her jaw was fractured, both lower and upper. There were also fractures of the nasal passages, cheekbones, and the right eye. She has suffered various lacerations and contusions to her upper body." He took a deep breath and released it, his voice softening at the look of horror on Michael's face. "I'm sorry. I'm just telling you all this because I want you to be prepared when you see her before she's taken up to ICU. You're probably not going to recognize her."

The resident was right, Michael thought, as he peered at the young woman lying on the gurney in cubicle number five. Tammy took one glance at the unconscious figure and turned away, the blood draining from her face. Michael was stronger. He took a deep breath and touched his daughter's small, limp hand, the one that was still unbandaged. "It's okay, Cupcake. Daddy's here. Robin, sweetie, you hold on. Everything's going to be fine."

They only had a moment with their daughter before medical personnel whisked her away to the elevator. Behind him, Michael heard a soft cough and turned to see the resident.

"Mr. Mulcahey, we've called in a maxillofacial trauma specialist for your daughter. There's just one other thing . . ." The resident shifted his weight and hesitated a moment as if trying to organize his thoughts. "Your daughter wasn't alone in the car. The rescue workers brought in another young female." He paused, then said, "There was nothing we could do for her. She was killed on impact. The thing is . . . ah . . . there isn't an easy way to say this, but . . . her injuries . . . were extensive. We couldn't find any identification on her. Do you think you might be able to help us . . . um . . . determine who she is?"

Michael heard Tammy gasp. His stomach lurched. What was the doctor saying? That Robin's companion was mangled beyond recognition? Dear God, no! Michael looked at Tammy, and saw in her eyes she was thinking the same thing. "Amy?" he murmured.

"It has to be," Tammy said. "They were inseparable."

Michael closed his eyes as anguish washed over him. *Oh, poor Sunshine.* But along with the anguish, he felt something else. Something that made him a less than admirable human being. Relief. Relief that it was his daughter that had been spared, and her poor, unfortunate best friend that had died.

"Mr. Mulcahey, do you think you might know this girl? And could you give us the name of her next of kin?"

Michael looked at the resident. Suddenly he felt an overwhelming weariness. It was almost five in the morning, and they'd been up since the phone call shattered the winter silence at three. But it wasn't so much physical fatigue as emotional. And now, this added shock.

"If it is Amy, there's no one you can call," he said slowly. "Her mother is her only living relative, and she's locked away in a nursing home here in Richmond. From what I understand, she's catatonic. Hasn't spoken a word in years."

Michael and the resident stared at each other as seconds ticked by. Outside the emergency bay doors, a siren moaned, and then stopped with a burp. Eerie silence fell.

"I hate to ask you this, Mr. Mulcahey, but do you think you can identify her? We need to get the death certificate processed."

After a brief moment, Michael nodded grimly. "Where is she?"

The resident turned to lead him away, but Tammy touched his shoulder. "Mike, do you want me to come with you?"

He ran a nervous hand through his neatly trimmed graying hair. "No, Tam. I don't want you to put yourself through this. I'll be back in a few minutes, then we'll go up to ICU and see how Robin's doing."

Tammy watched her husband go with the resident. She was glad he hadn't wanted her to come with him. It was bad enough seeing her daughter all bloodied and messed up. She certainly didn't want to see Amy's mangled body. It was such a shame. Such a waste of young life. But Tammy had always known that something like this would eventually happen. Robin had been running wild since her teens. In fact, it was amazing it hadn't happened before.

The phone call had awakened them just before three o'clock in the morning. The dreaded phone call from a hospital ER telling them that their daughter had been severely injured in a car accident. Well, *of course* she hadn't been alone. Wherever Robin had gone, little Amy had followed. That's the way it had been since they'd become roommates their first year at William & Mary.

She looked up to see Michael approaching her, his face even grayer than it had been before. "Was it Amy?"

His blue eyes stark, he nodded and extended his hand toward her. "The doctor said she was wearing this."

Tammy stared at the bloodstained silver chain with its pendant in the shape of a sun. Her heart bumped when she remembered the last time she'd seen the necklace. On Christmas morning, Amy had opened their gift, holding it up for everyone to admire. Tears had shown in her blue eyes as she'd tremulously thanked them—not just for the necklace, but for treating her like part of their family. It was impossible to think that shy, sweet Amy was dead.

Tammy met Michael's eyes. "Was she really . . . ?"

He gave a terse nod. "I'm glad you didn't see her. Come on, Tam, let's go check on our daughter."

The young woman heard the voices before she could make out the faces. She felt the gentle touch of a hand clutching hers. Smelled the strong scent of a familiar perfume. Slowly, she opened her eyes and through a gauze of milky whiteness saw a woman gazing down at her. An older woman, pretty, but rather frayed around the edges. She looked familiar, but her name evaded her.

"Oh, Robin, sweetie," the woman whispered, squeezing her hand. "Thank God you're going to be okay."

Robin. There was a name she recognized. She moaned, and tried to speak but something was stuck in her mouth. Some contraption. The confusion in her brain cleared a bit, and she suddenly knew who the older woman was. Tammy.

The young woman blinked and tried again to speak. Nothing but a soft groan came out. A movement beyond Tammy's shoulder caught her eye. She recognized him, also. He was gazing at her, a tender, anxious expression on his face. An overwhelming rush of love flowed through her. They really *did* care about her. It was so wonderful to finally have a family . . . after so many years of *not* having one.

"Robin, the nurse is going to give you something now to make you sleep." Tammy squeezed her hand. "But we're going to be right here all day, okay?"

"That's right, Cupcake." Michael edged over and smiled down at her. "We're not going anywhere until we know you're out of the woods."

Dimly, she saw a woman in a brightly colored jacket inject something into the IV line that ran into her left arm. Almost immediately she felt as if she were floating away. But she struggled against it, wanting to say something . . . wanting to ask . . . *something.*

Her thoughts were all muddled. But just before the darkness closed around her, one thought rang through her consciousness with crystal clarity.

Why were they calling her *Robin?*

PART ONE

1

★ AUGUST, 1996 ★

Amy Shiley stepped into her assigned room at Yates Hall, placed her suitcase on the floor, and looked around, dismayed. If she didn't know she was standing in a dorm on the hallowed grounds of the College of William & Mary, she'd swear she was in Kansas just after the infamous tornado had sucked Dorothy and Toto into its vortex. One half of the room—the good half near the window—was a battleground of chaos—clothes flung onto the bed, framed photos, books, CDs, all tossed haphazardly on the floor, the bed, the dresser. A half-eaten pizza lay drying in a cardboard box on the desk, its cheese hardened and yellowed. Open cans of soda stood amid bottles of perfume and various cosmetics on the dresser. A chocolate-covered donut with one bite taken out held court on the mouse pad next to a computer logged onto America Online where the "You've got mail" icon flashed. The stereo was going full blast playing . . . Marilyn Manson, Amy recognized with a shudder. This didn't bode well at all.

Apparently, the owner of the computer and the stereo had been called away to something way more important. And that owner, according to the letter Amy had received a month ago, must be her roommate, Robin Mulcahey. Amy chewed her bottom lip and tugged at a strand of her long blond hair, unconsciously checking it for split ends.

I wonder if we're going to get along.

If the mess on her roommate's side of the room was any clue, Amy had her doubts. Suppressing a sigh, she grabbed her suitcase and placed it on the bed—the one that was visible. It wasn't like she'd never lived with messy people before. Jeez, Mom and Dad had both been pigs. But in college, she'd hoped . . . well . . . that she'd room with someone a little more like herself.

She turned to the door to go back downstairs to get the rest of her things, and found herself staring into the wide blue eyes of a girl with blond corn-rowed hair and more than a passing resemblance to a teenaged Heather Lock-lear. She was dressed in a sleeveless eyelet top that ended just below her midriff, denim cutoffs, and black Doc Martens with khaki army socks.

"*Omigod!*" the girl shrieked, a huge grin spreading across her pretty face. "*You must be Amy!*"

Before Amy could speak, the girl sprang across the room and enveloped her in a bear hug usually reserved for someone who'd been lost at sea for twenty years. Strangely enough, Amy didn't find it at all unpleasant. Robin rocked her back and forth, her beaded hair clicking in Amy's ear. Amy sucked in a deep breath, inhaling the girl's citrusy scent. Here she was being hugged to death by a virtual stranger, and finding it kind of nice. Then again, maybe it was because she hadn't had too many hugs in the last eighteen years.

Abruptly, Robin—of course, this *had* to be Robin—pulled away from her, and gazed into her eyes, her smile evaporating. "Promise me something, Amy," she said solemnly. "Promise me you won't hate me because I'm beautiful."

Amy opened her mouth to say . . . what, she didn't know, but Robin didn't give her the chance, anyway. A bubble of champagne laughter burst from her throat, and she hugged Amy again, jumping up and down. "Oh, I just *love* you already! Isn't this just too freakin' cool? We're in *college*, girlfriend! Four years of partying and hunky guys and keg parties and . . ."

"And exams, and studying, and papers . . ." Amy added dryly.

Robin gave a dismissive flutter of her hand. "What*ever!*" She eyed Amy, a dimple flickering at the corner of her mouth. "I can see right now I'm gonna have to loosen you up. So, I'm going to major in drama. Someday you'll be able to say 'I knew her when.' What about you?"

"Anthropology, with an emphasis on archaeological studies."

Robin shuddered theatrically. "Ugh! Oooh, boy. I have my work cut out for me. I'll bet you're smart, too, aren't you?" Amy shrugged, and Robin rolled her eyes. "I knew it! What are you, a Monroe Scholar?"

Amy didn't answer, just looked at her.

Robin frowned. "You *are*, aren't you? Just my luck. Getting a Monroe Scholar for a roommate. I suppose you'll want to just sit around and study all the time."

Great, Amy thought. *Now, she hates me.* Her heart sank. As unorthodox as Robin Mulcahey appeared to be, Amy kind of liked her. How could you *not* like someone that emanated that kind of warmth and enthusiasm?

The frown disappeared from Robin's face, and once again the sun was shin-ing. "Oh, what the hell? I love you, anyway!" She grabbed Amy again and gave her another ferocious hug. "And besides"—she drew back, blue eyes dancing—"you *can't* study all the time. You'll burn out. Stick with me, Amy, and I'll show you how to get the most out of college. Speaking of which, guess what I just found out? This is a friggin' *coed* dorm! And you've just *got* to see the two buff guys moving in down in the next wing!" She closed her eyes and swooned. "Whooo . . . *hoo*! Come on, let's go introduce ourselves before the other girls get to 'em."

Amy lay in bed, staring up at the ceiling of the unfamiliar dorm room. It was two o'clock in the morning, and she had the room to herself. She and Robin had spent the last six hours with the "two buff guys" in the male wing, drinking bottles of cold Sam Adams and trading war stories from high school. Well, Robin had drunk beer with the guys. Amy had stuck to Cokes. She couldn't bring herself to drink alcohol—not after seeing what it had done to her parents. She knew Robin probably thought she was a real slug. But if she did, she hadn't said anything. Maybe she was simply too busy flirting with the guys to notice. Of course, the three of them had done all the talking. As usual, when Amy was with guys, she couldn't think of one intelligent thing to say.

No wonder she'd never had a boyfriend. Who wanted a girl who had the personality of a doorknob? And it wasn't like she was ugly, or anything. But . . . face it . . . she'd never really learned to put herself together like other girls. The hair, the makeup. Those feminine secrets that most girls seemed to know by a process of osmosis—a secret that somehow, along the way, she'd missed out on.

Maybe the missing ingredient was a mother.

She thought of her mother, remembering the way she'd looked the last time Amy had visited her in the nursing home. Sitting in a chair in the day room, her dyed black hair lank and stringy, her blue eyes staring flatly into space. It had been almost three years since Vicky Shiley had recognized her own daughter. Three years since the day Amy, a shy fifteen-year-old, had come home from school to find her catatonic, her mind unreachable. And so, the shuttling from one foster home to another had begun.

Who knows where she'd be today if it weren't for Mrs. Scudder, her freshman English teacher. Thank God for her. Even before Mama checked out, Mrs. Scudder had taken an interest in her. The teacher had recognized her potential, and nurtured it, encouraging her to write and read well beyond her grade level. It had been Mrs. Scudder who'd first made Amy realize she could go to college, and make something of herself—break away from the self-destructive lifestyle that would surely be her heritage otherwise.

Amy's eyes welled with tears as she remembered Regina Scudder's laughing green eyes and copper hair. Of course, her hair had been gone on the day Amy showed her the acceptance letter she'd received from William & Mary. Just three months earlier, Mrs. Scudder had been diagnosed with pancreatic cancer, and she wouldn't live to see out the spring. But on that day in the hospital, her green eyes had held a spark of their earlier brilliance when she saw Amy's acceptance letter. "I knew you'd do it, Amy," she'd whispered in a heartbreakingly frail voice.

It had been the last time Amy ever saw her.

Now, she was truly on her own, in her first year of college. Now, perhaps, she could have a life like other girls. Privileged girls like Robin.

During the "getting to know you" period with the guys, Amy had learned a lot about her new roommate. Robin had grown up right here in Williamsburg; her father was a lawyer at a firm on Richmond Road. He'd been a congressman in Washington when she was little, but gave it up after two terms because he missed his family, who'd chosen to remain in Williamsburg. She had two brothers, one older and one younger. Paul, a junior at the University of Colorado, played the wide receiver position on UC's football team. And Jeff—according to Robin—was an annoying fourteen-year-old brat. Her mother, Tammy—whom Robin *called* Tammy—was a real-estate agent renowned for selling million-dollar estates along the James River.

Robin unashamedly admitted it was her father's position in the community that had helped her get into William & Mary. Her grades in high school had been average, and without the clout of her family name, she would've been lucky to get into a mediocre university. It was obvious to Amy that she felt absolutely no guilt about this free ride, though. She giggled and boasted and batted her big blue eyes at the guys, and they laughed like they thought it was the funniest thing they'd ever heard. For just a moment, Amy felt a flicker of resentment. She'd worked her butt off to get into William & Mary, and there were a lot of other students out there who probably had, too, and got turned away because Robin's dad had bought her way in. But it was impossible to stay mad at Robin. Her bubbly personality, dancing blue eyes, and dazzling smile reached out and enveloped Amy, drawing her into her magic. There was something about Robin that reminded Amy of her friend in sixth grade. Her *only* friend, Melissa. It had been years since she'd thought of her.

It had always been too painful to remember how their short-lived friendship had ended. With the moving truck driving away, and a sad-eyed Mel waving listlessly out the window of the family station wagon. For one happy year, Amy's life had been almost normal, thanks to Mel. There had been sleepovers—at Mel's house, of course—movies, popcorn, fudge-making, and séances. Under Mel's attention, Amy had flowered like a bud brought into sunlight. But then disaster struck just after the beginning of seventh grade when Mel's father died of a massive heart attack. Within weeks, her mother had moved the rest of the family back to her home state of Nebraska.

There had been no other friends. Until now. She'd only known Robin for a few hours, yet she already felt a kinship with the girl. Sure, she was a little wacky, and no doubt spoiled to death by her doting family, but she was fun. And strangely enough, Robin seemed to genuinely *like* Amy—just as Mel had.

Amy flopped onto her stomach and squeezed her eyes closed. Back in the guys' room, she'd begged off a game of strip poker, not just because there was no *way* she was going to strip down in front of complete strangers, but because she hadn't gotten much sleep the night before, and she was starting to feel it. Making her excuses, she'd left Robin with the two guys and come back to her room alone.

Now, though, she felt wide-awake. Through the thin walls of the dorm, she heard raucous laughter. Other freshmen getting acquainted, she supposed. Why was she lying here in bed? Her sleepiness had totally vanished. She wished Robin would come back to the room. If she breathed deeply, she could still smell the lingering scent of her citrus cologne. What was happening in the guys' room? Was Robin already down to her underwear? Or . . . she shuddered . . . *out* of her underwear? Amy wondered if she should've made Robin come back to the room with her. But how *could* she have forced her? She wasn't Robin's boss. She barely knew the girl! And it probably wouldn't be a good idea to start out a friendship by ordering her around like she was her mother or something. Still . . . Robin had been putting the beers away as fast as the guys. What if she got so drunk she didn't know what she was doing?

That was one thing about her new roommate that really bothered Amy. The drinking. God knows she knew what booze did to people, with both her parents being drunks. Her father had paid for it with his life, and her mother . . . well . . . look where she was right now. Amy found it ironic that after all those years of living in trailer parks and run-down houses with alcoholic parents, she would finally escape into the real world and end up in college with a beer-guzzling roommate.

The doorknob rattled, and Amy stiffened. "Hey, open up!" Fists pounded against the door. "Hey, Amy!" Robin called out again. "Why's the door locked? Let me in, huh? I'm wasted!"

Amy scrambled out of bed and crossed the bare wood floor in her socks. She opened the door, and Robin lurched in, bleary-eyed but grinning. "Hey, what's with locking the friggin' door? Nobody locks doors in Williamsburg. Help me to my bed, okay? I'm so wasted, I can't see."

Amy wrapped a supporting arm around her, and together they stumbled across the room to Robin's bed.

"Oh, no!" Amy stopped and stared at the piles of clothes, books, and CDs on the bed. "Here. You'll have to take my bed while I get this stuff moved."

"O-kay!" Robin closed her eyes and slumped onto Amy's bed. Almost before her head hit the pillow, she was out. Amy stared at her a moment, then reached down to pull the covers up around her.

In the dim glow of the streetlight shining through the window, Amy could just make out her roommate's features. Curled up in the fetal position, her hands tucked under her delicate cheeks in a curiously vulnerable way, she looked almost angelic.

Amy smiled. "Good night, roomie."

It took several minutes to move all the stuff from Robin's bed. But finally, Amy crawled under the covers and wearily closed her eyes. It had been a long day— the first of her new life. She'd been waiting so long for this new life, and whatever it brought, it would have to be better than what came before.

"Amy?"

Her eyes opened at the soft sound of Robin's voice. "Yes?"

"We're going to be best friends," Robin murmured. "I just know it."

Amy smiled into the darkness. "I think so, too."

The nightmare woke her. With a start, Robin opened her eyes and stared up at the dark ceiling, the remnants of the dream still with her, much like the stale beer coating her tongue. She could never find the words to explain the dream, even though she'd been having it since she was thirteen. It was more of a sensation than a visual thing. A throbbing dark tunnel growing bigger and bigger until she was swallowed up in it. There was never any escape from the tunnel—only darkness and the sound of her heartbeat roaring in her ears.

She always woke from it in a cold sweat. Then for fifteen minutes, sometimes more, she'd lie in bed trembling, afraid to go back to sleep. Afraid of being swallowed in the tunnel again. The only thing to do was to think of other things. Try to put the dream behind her.

So, now, she thought of Joe and Robert, the two hunks in the next wing. She smiled, remembering what had happened after Amy left. She'd beaten the pants off them. Literally. They'd all three been so drunk that stripping down after losing at poker hadn't fazed them. Robin had lost a couple of hands and ended up playing the last few games topless. She hadn't minded. The guys couldn't keep their eyes off her breasts. She liked to be admired.

And then, of course, one thing had led to another, and she'd ended up giving them both head. That was okay. They were clean guys—good-looking and young—and she was good at what she did. And why not?

She'd been taught by a master.

2

"Hold still, you idiot, or I'm going to put your eye out. Look *up* for Chrissake!"

Amy rolled her eyes upward and stared at a cobweb floating from the ceiling as Robin dabbed mascara on her lashes. The cobweb was on Robin's side of the room, of course. The girl never lifted a finger to clean anything. Looked like it was going to be up to Amy to keep their room neat.

"Don't you think that's too many coats?" she asked, as Robin continued to stroke on the mascara, wrinkling her nose. Its chemical smell made her gag.

"Hel-*lo*? If I thought that, I wouldn't be putting another one on, would I? Hold *still*!" Robin fastened her hand on top of Amy's head, imprisoning her. "Jeez! You're worse than a little kid."

"I'm just not sure this is a good idea," Amy murmured, trying hard to be still so Robin would quit torturing her.

"Well, *duh*! You would be *wrong*. I'm telling you, Amy, those Kappa Chi chicks put emphasis on looks. And if you would fix yourself up, you would be a friggin' knockout! And that's what I'm making you."

"But I'm not sure I even *want* to join a sorority. I don't fit in with those girls."

"You will. There. All done." Robin stepped back and inspected her. "Shit! You're gorgeous already. Now, let's see . . ." She whirled around to her closet and examined the rack of tightly squeezed clothing. With a grunt, she pushed some back and smiled. "Here! This one." She turned around and held out a red knit dress with short lattice-edged sleeves and a button placket. It was so tiny, it looked like it was made for a six-year-old.

"I can't wear that."

"Sure you can. It's a size five." Robin thrust it at her and turned back to her closet. "Go put it on, and when you're done, we'll take those curlers out of your hair. And for Chrissake, hurry up! We've got to be at the first rush party at seven!"

Amy dropped Robin's dress onto her bed and reached into her dresser for underwear. Turning her back to Robin, she pulled on her bikini panties before shedding her robe. Unlike Robin, she couldn't bring herself to strip naked in front of her roommate. It was just too weird. Robin, though, was totally uninhibited. She slept in the nude, and when she was just hanging out in the dorm, which wasn't often, she wore boys' boxer shorts and a sports bra. After showering in the bathroom down the hall every morning, she'd prance into the room in a skimpy satin robe, peel it off immediately, pull on a pair of bikini panties, and put on her makeup topless. Amy didn't know if she'd ever get used to it. Although she tried her best to pretend it didn't bother her, Robin seemed to take a certain delight in getting right in her face in her braless condition, and Amy would feel herself go scarlet.

But she was getting better, she thought. Now, at least, it didn't bother her too much to change clothes in front of Robin. But she'd never get completely naked.

Amy quickly fastened her bra and reached for the dress. Out of the corner of her eye, she could see a braless Robin dancing to the music of Smashing Pumpkins as she stepped into a crocheted black dress. Amy carefully slipped her dress over the twistee curlers on her head. She smoothed the soft material down, then looked into the mirror.

It fit perfectly, clinging to her curves in all the right places. Amy drew in a deep breath. She *had* curves! Well, obviously, she'd known that, but she'd never worn anything that emphasized them. And Robin was right. It looked really good! How had she known? If Amy had seen this dress in a store, she would've rejected it immediately for something more conservative. And she'd never worn red in her life! It was just too "look at me" for her.

"Well, what do you think?" she asked hesitantly.

Robin turned around and her eyes widened. "*Wow!*" She let out an approving wolf whistle. "Didn't I tell you? You're a knockout. Come on, let me fix your hair."

A few minutes later, they stood side by side, gazing into the mirror. Amy couldn't believe it. Robin looked devastating in her crocheted black dress with its deep scoop neck. It hugged her breasts and hips like a second skin, its hemline reaching midthigh. She'd released her blond hair from its cornrows, and it rippled past her shoulders in shimmering waves. But Robin Mulcahey looking gorgeous was nothing new.

Amy's eyes returned to her own reflection. She just couldn't believe it. Who *was* that beautiful blond girl in the mirror? Her hair fell to the middle of her back in glorious curls. How had Robin accomplished that miracle? Her straight hair had never been able to hold a curl before. Of course, there was a ton of hairspray on it now. The scent of it still hung heavy in the room. But her makeup! It looked awesome! Good enough to replace Nikki Taylor in a Maybelline ad. Could she learn to apply it like that? she wondered.

"Didn't I tell you?" Robin said, her dimple flickering. "You are *awesome*, girlfriend. You know . . ." Her eyes returned to the mirror. "We could be sisters, we look so much alike. Twins, even." A wistful expression crossed her face. "I've always wanted a sister. But after Mom had Jeff, she said no more kids. I guess she knew he was going to be a handful."

Amy was silent for a moment. Then, "I've always wanted a sister, too."

Robin looked at her, and for a split second, her eyes were uncharacteristically solemn. "Well, that's what we'll be then. Sisters." She smiled, and the serious moment passed. "We'll be Kappa Chi sisters! Come on, let's go. You and me are gonna charm the shit out of those prissy little girls. They're gonna love us so much, they'll be down on their knees begging us to pledge their sorority. And you know what we're gonna do after we get in?" She grinned impishly. "We're going to remove those cattle prods they have stuck up their tight little asses."

Amy sipped her Coke and gazed around the room at the chattering girls clumped in groups of three and four in the spacious living room of the Kappa Chi house. The stuffy air was thick with the clashing scents of thirty or more women mingling with the aroma of an array of food on the buffet table along one wall. The noise of conversation and laughter was deafening. And as far as Amy could tell, she was the only one standing alone in the room. Why was it so easy for everyone else to mingle with strangers and be able to talk and laugh as if they'd known each other forever? Look at Robin! There she was, surrounded by Kappa Chis, mugging and laughing and fitting in like she'd lived with these perfect white-toothed girls for the last ten years.

What confidence Amy had gained in knowing she looked great with her new hairdo and in Robin's sexy dress, she'd lost almost immediately at her first rush party of the night. As soon as they'd walked in, Robin had been swept away in the tide of welcoming sorority sisters, leaving Amy to fend for herself. At first, the almost uniformly attractive girls gathered around her, too, but as soon as the basic questions were out of the way, Amy grew silent and shy. And then the death knell sounded when she was asked the million dollar question, "What's your major?" and their eyes would glaze over when she told them it was anthropology. Soon, they would slither away one by one, leaving Amy alone and miserable.

Now they were at their third rush party of the night, and Amy just wanted to go back to the dorm, crawl into bed, and cry her heart out. Who was she trying to kid? She didn't fit in here. And she'd been stupid to allow Robin to talk her into rushing the sororities. She would never ever *ever* be pledged by any of them. Besides, it wasn't just her shyness that was the problem. There would probably be background checks into her past. Subtle inquiries as to what kind of people she came from. Once they found out about the trailer courts, the nomadic life she'd lived from Florida all the way to Newport News, it would be over. She had as much of a chance to join one of these snobbish sororities as she had of becoming the first female president of the United States. And if Robin thought differently, then she was out of her flaky little mind.

As if she were psychic, Robin suddenly appeared in front of her and took her by the elbow. "Come here, Amy. I want to introduce you to Megan. She's the president of Kappa Chi."

"Robin, can we go now? I have a terrible headache."

"Don't be an idiot. Hi, there." Robin smiled brightly at a gorgeous redhead as they nudged their way through the crowd. "We're *in* here, Amy. They love us already."

"They love *you*, you mean."

"And you're with me, so that means they love us. Megan! Here she is. This is my roommate, Amy."

A tall, svelte girl with shimmering red-gold hair gave Amy a dazzling smile. It almost seemed genuine. "Hi, Amy. Robin was telling us all about you. She's quite your champion, you know. In fact, she's already told us that you two come as a team."

Amy didn't know what to say. She just stared dumbly at the tall sorority president with the sea green eyes. Tinted contacts, surely. Nobody really had eyes that color, did they?

Megan smiled, her gaze moving from Amy to Robin. "I like that. Teamwork is important to us in Kappa Chi. And our creed is 'Love, Learning, Life, Loyalty.' I think both of you will fit in great with us. So, I want you to keep us in mind on Pledge Night, okay?"

On Pledge Day, after Robin opened up her elegant white card, she pumped her slim hand into the air and beamed at Amy. "We're *in*, girlfriend! Kappa Chi, just like I told you."

"*You're* in," Amy said, biting her lower lip. She held her envelope in her hands, her stomach churning. She was afraid to open it. Suddenly, more than anything in the world, she wanted to be in a sorority. And she wanted it to be the same one Robin pledged. For only the second time in her life, she had a friend, and she didn't want to lose her.

"Open it, idiot." Robin grinned. "We're a team, and everybody knows it. If that cards says anything besides Kappa Chi, I'll run naked through University Center."

Amy couldn't help but smile. "Like *that's* something you'd hate doing." She slid a nail under the flap of the envelope and peeled it open.

Congratulations! The sisters of Kappa Chi would like you to join our sorority.

Amy stared at the gold-embossed card, not quite believing what she was reading.

"Well?" Robin snatched it out of her hands, read it, and shrieked. "*See! I told you!* Doesn't it *rock?*" Laughing, she grabbed Amy and gave her a bear hug that threatened to cut off her circulation. "Oh, girl, we're gonna have a bitchin' year together!"

Amy smiled, feeling her heart begin to soar as realization sank in. *She'd been accepted into a sorority!* Amy Jessica Shiley, daughter of drunkards, princess of the double-wides, a sorority girl. But she didn't kid herself for a moment as to how it had happened. Robin had made it clear to every sorority they'd rushed that they came as a team. And they'd all wanted Robin. Almost all of them, anyway.

There had been one rush party where the girls had been overwhelmingly conservative. They'd taken one look at Robin's fake nose ring, and their faces had taken on the appearance of stone masks. Needless to say, Amy and Robin hadn't tarried long at that party.

"Uppity straight-assed bitches," Robin snarled, her pretty face like a thundercloud. But the storm hadn't lasted long. By the time they reached the next party, she'd regained her usual sunny personality, completely forgetting that those uppity straight-assed bitches had ever existed.

"You're coming home with me this weekend," Robin said, hanging up the phone.

Amy looked up from her desk, where she was reading from her psychology textbook. Her stomach had tightened at Robin's announcement. "Are you serious?"

"Of course." Her tone brooked no argument. "My parents can't wait to meet you. Unfortunately, The Brat will be there, too, but you might as well meet him and get it over with."

"Jeff?"

"Of *course*, Jeff! God, he's such a typical little brother! Always getting into my stuff. Tattletaling. Sneaking around and trying to catch me naked." Robin rolled her eyes heavenward. "A real pain in the ass."

Amy couldn't help but laugh. "Well, I guess he didn't have to try too hard, considering that half the time you're naked anyway."

Funny thing, too. She was finally starting to get used to it. Robin's nudity was getting to be so . . . last week. Well, almost.

Robin looked down at herself and grinned. She wore a slinky white cotton camisole lettered with the words *Naughty Angel* and matching boy shorts from Victoria's Secret. "Well, fuck a duck! He doesn't have to *look*."

"Yeah, right," Amy muttered, glancing back down at her homework. "He's what? Thirteen? You might as well tell him to stop breathing."

"Fourteen. And I don't care. He's still a brat." Robin scrambled off the bed and began doing stretching exercises.

"You're lucky you *have* a family," Amy added, her eyes on her book, but not really reading the words.

"You gonna tell me about yours someday?" Robin grunted as she stretched her arms over her head.

"Someday."

Outside in the hallway, a commotion erupted. A shrill scream of excitement and the thump of footsteps as someone ran down the hall. A door slammed. Amy and Robin ignored it, just as they ignored the constant thumping of rock music and rap that competed from various rooms, theirs included.

"And when you tell me about yours, I'll tell you about mine."

Amy looked up. "What? Is there some deep, dark family secret you have to share?"

"You never know." Robin shrugged, closing her eyes and stretching. "Sometimes things aren't the way they look." Her eyes opened. "So, you'll come this weekend, right? Don't say no, because I won't accept it."

"Well, since you give me so much of a choice, I guess I will. But . . ."

"But what?"

"Do you think they'll like me?" she asked, trying to sound offhand. But it came out sounding vulnerable. Desperate.

"Fuckin' A, they'll like you. They *have* to. You're my best friend."

Amy felt a rush of love come over her. She'd only known this crazy, nutty girl for a little over two months, but she felt like they'd been friends forever. And it was weird because they really were nothing alike. Except for appearance. Both blond, (although Robin admitted that she bleached hers every month because otherwise it would be a dingy dark blond), fair-skinned, and blue-eyed, Amy was maybe a half inch taller than Robin at five-foot-four, and both of them tipped the scales at 105, give or take a pound. No shit, they *could* pass for sisters.

But in temperament and tastes, they were almost total opposites. Where Amy was quiet, Robin was garrulous. Amy was intellectual; Robin was . . . well . . . not. They didn't even agree on movies. Robin loved action and horror. Amy adored foreign films and sad love stories like *The English Patient*. Horror movies made her want to throw up.

Books? Robin, if she read at all, liked Sandra Brown, Dean Koontz, and Stephen King. Amy's tastes leaned toward authors like Amy Tan, Ann Tyler, and Alice Hoffman. Robin was a TV addict. When she wasn't out partying, she was in the dorm watching *Melrose Place, Beverly Hills 90210, The X-Files,* and

Seinfeld. And if she couldn't watch them, she taped them. Amy didn't watch much TV because there was too much studying to do, but she did like *ER* and *Touched by an Angel.*

At first, Robin laughed at her for staying in on Sunday nights to watch that goody-goody show. But one night she stayed and watched it with her, and after that, Robin wouldn't miss it either. But she still teased Amy about "going to church" on Sunday nights. After one particularly moving episode, Amy was astonished to see tears in Robin's eyes. Embarrassed, Robin had jumped off her bed and turned the channel to watch *The X-Files,* muttering about "sentimental crap."

It had worked the other way, too, though. Before meeting Robin, Amy had listened to New Age music, artists like Enya and Loreena McKennitt. She still liked New Age, but since Robin was always playing CDs of Pearl Jam and Smashing Pumpkins, rock music had started to grow on her—although she'd never *ever* be a fan of Marilyn Manson. Natalie Merchant was another artist that Robin had turned Amy on to, and lately, she'd been listening to her CD all the time. In fact, it was playing now.

Robin jumped up and cranked the volume a couple of notches. Amy knew why. "River" was starting to play. It was a song about River Phoenix, the young actor who'd died of an overdose outside the Viper Room in Los Angeles. Robin loved the song, and always sang along with it, her eyes inevitably filling with tears.

"It's so damn unfair," she raged when the song ended. "Dying so young like that."

"Well, nobody forced him to take drugs," Amy said dryly. She liked the song, too. Natalie sang it with a lot of passion, and, of course, she felt bad that a good-looking young actor like Phoenix would die like that. But still, it wasn't as if he hadn't had a choice.

Robin gave her an appraising look. "So, what's your hang-up with drugs and alcohol, girlfriend?" She positioned herself on her bed, lotus-fashion, and reached for a bottle of psychedelic purple nail polish on her bedside table. The astringent smell immediately filled the room as she uncapped it.

Amy met her gaze. And she found herself wanting to share it with her. All of it. The years of neglect. The poverty of the trailer park life in the South. The rejection she'd suffered through all the years of school.

But instead, she only said, "I lived with drunks and drug addicts most of my life. My parents."

Robin didn't look up from painting her fingernails, but Amy sensed an unusual tension emanating from her. Finally, she spoke, "That's *so* not cool."

"Yeah. Definitely not cool."

Robin didn't speak again and Amy turned back to her textbook. Natalie Merchant's voice floated from the speakers, singing "Carnival." It wasn't until the song had ended that Robin looked up from her drying nails, and said, "You know, sometimes drinking is the only thing that helps, though." Something flickered in her deep blue eyes. A shadow of a memory, some half-forgotten pain.

Amy opened her mouth to ask . . . what, she didn't know, but in the end, it didn't matter. The phone rang, and Robin reached for it, fingers splayed so as not to ruin her freshly purpled nails. "Hel-*lo*?" Her face lit up like a candle. "*Jason!* Hey, where you *been*, Sex-Machine? When're you coming to town?" She released a seductive giggle, and with a glance toward Amy, her voice dropped to a throaty purr. "Oh, baby, I've been wanting it so *bad*!"

Amy turned away, blushing. She didn't know what demons Robin had lurking in her psyche, but whatever they were, she seemed to be able to keep them at bay with alcohol and sex.

It was her business, her life. Amy had no right to meddle. Still, she couldn't help but worry. In the two short months she'd known Robin, she'd grown to care about her. And this adoration she had for tragic figures like River Phoenix really freaked Amy out.

After her mother had gone into the nursing home for the last time, Amy had believed she could finally be responsible only for herself. She no longer had to play the caretaker for the childlike person her mother had become. Yet, here she was, already feeling kind of parental toward Robin. But it wouldn't do to let her know that. Besides, she'd learned a good lesson from living with an alcoholic mother all those years.

You couldn't stop her from drinking or from destroying herself with booze. You could only pick up the pieces afterward and hope you could glue them back together again.

But then she remembered, and a chill went through her. In the end, there hadn't been any pieces to pick up with her mother. Whatever had happened to her on that last day in that filthy trailer had obliterated her soul as if it had never existed at all.

3

"Wow! This is your house?"

Robin shrugged as she parked her cherry red Tracker beside a hunter green BMW. "Home sweet home," she said sarcastically. "It even has a name. Windsong. Doesn't that just make you want to *hurl*?"

Amy gazed at the elegant Georgian Colonial house overlooking a wide bend of the James River. With its white Corinthian portico, black-shuttered windows, and the covered porch with a balcony above, its classic lines belied its age of just eight years. Her father, Robin said, had bought the land and had the home custom built after retiring from Congress.

Amy thought it was the most beautiful home she'd ever seen.

"I hate it," Robin grumbled, turning off the ignition. "It's so goddamn pretentious."

Seagulls cawed, swooping low over the river, as Amy followed Robin out of the car and headed for the lustrous black Georgian door of the mansion. Because that's what is was to her. A mansion. Fear formed a knot in her throat. What if Robin's parents saw her for what she was? Trailer park trash. Oh sure, she *looked* like a normal college student. Thanks to Robin, she was actually pretty. But no matter how she looked on the outside, on the inside she was still that rejected little girl from the wrong side of town. The outsider. Would Robin's parents see right away that she wasn't good enough to be their daughter's friend?

Robin walked through the front door, and Amy followed, heart hammering. The first thing she noticed was how good it smelled inside. A rich scent of cinnamon hung in the air, homey and welcoming. Her eyes swept the interior, and it was all she could do to keep from gasping in delight. The foyer floor was black-and-white Italian marble, the walls hand-painted with gold and silver ornaments. An ornate white staircase trimmed in rich mahogany spiraled up to the second level, bordering an overlooking balcony on three sides. An elaborate crystal chandelier hung from the second-floor ceiling to the left of the staircase. In the corner, an elegant grandfather clock pealed out the hour of five in crystalline Westminster chimes. Amy gazed around in awe.

When she was little, on the Sundays they weren't too drunk or too hung over to get out of bed, her parents would take her to model homes that were springing up like mushrooms after a spring rain in the Virginia Beach/Newport News area. Checking out how the "haves" lived was their idea of great entertainment. Amy guessed she'd been about eight years old, young enough to dream about living in a house like that one day, but old enough—and wise beyond her years—to know it would probably never happen.

She remembered stepping into the little girl's room; there was always a little girl's room with antique white furniture and cotton-candy-hued curtains to match the bedspread on the princesslike canopy bed. Amy would pretend the room was really hers, and she was the special little girl of a mommy and daddy who adored her beyond life itself. She would walk over to the built-in bookcase, eyeing the colorfully illustrated children's books. *Charlotte's Web.* The Sweet Valley Twins series. *The Baby-Sitters Club.* Amy would pretend it was almost bedtime, and she'd go into the pretty lavender bathroom down the hall and pantomime brushing her teeth. Back in "her room," she'd curl up on the fluffy pink bed and wait for Daddy to come up and read her a story. But not her real daddy. In her child's imagination, Daddy always looked like Bill Cosby. It didn't matter that his skin was the wrong color. To Amy, Bill Cosby epitomized the perfect dad. He had just the right combination of humor and authority. Her ideal mom, though, looked like Elise Keaton from *Family Ties.* Pretty and blond and even-tempered. Always loving with a gentle touch. And never drunk.

Sometimes, Amy pretended so hard it was a shock to see her real parents. Her tall, lanky father with his cropped blond hair and scraggly beard, his brown eyes glazed by the dope he'd just smoked. And Mama, with her dyed blue-black hair hanging limply to her shoulders, her eyes rimmed with electric blue eye shadow to match the denim halter top she loved to wear because it showed off her boobs.

Amy's daydream always came to an abrupt end with her father's thick Mississippi voice summoning her, and with one last look of longing at the pretty pink bedroom, she'd slowly descend the curving lushly carpeted stairs where they waited for her in the foyer below.

Daddy always grinned at the eager salesman and speaking in a voice like slow molasses, drawled, "Well, now, this place is right nice. We're really going to give it some serious thought, right, hon?"

Mama would look at him like he'd just announced he was going to fly to the moon on a broomstick, and Amy's heart would sink. That only happened the first few times, though. Amy learned quickly it was nothing but a big game to them. They would never buy a new house. Of course, then, she'd been too young to understand that people like them would never get out of the trailer courts. And deep down, they really didn't want to. And why would they? As long as they had their booze and drugs, they were happy.

No wonder she felt like a fraud standing here in this gorgeous foyer. Amy's eyes rose upward, beyond the dramatic staircase to the balconies on the second floor. "Wow!" she breathed. "God, Robin, I didn't realize you were so rich."

Robin shrugged out of her short denim jacket, strode down the hall to a closet, and tossed it in. She held out her hand for Amy's windbreaker. "Yeah, it really reeks, doesn't it? All those homeless people starving on the streets, and Mom and Dad live in this big house with my little brother like royalty."

"I didn't know congressmen made that much."

"They don't. Mom comes from old money. But Dad isn't poor. He's made a lot in the stock market."

"Robin, is that you?" A soft Southern voice called from down the hallway stretching out to Amy's left.

"Come on. Let's go meet my mom."

Robin led Amy down a gleaming cherrywood corridor into a cherry-paneled library. French doors on three sides led out to the covered porch. Classical music played softly from hidden speakers. A slender blond woman sat at an elegant Chippendale desk, scribbling a note onto parchment paper with a slim gold pen. She looked up and smiled, her cornflower blue eyes moving from Robin to Amy.

"Well, hi there, stranger. I didn't think we were ever going to see you again. And *you* must be Amy."

Amy nodded and gave Robin's mother a shy smile. She felt as if she'd stepped under a ray of sunlight beamed directly from Heaven. Where was the subtle appraisal she'd been expecting? The "who do you think you are and why do you think you're worthy of being friends with my daughter" once-over, followed by the polite questions of her familial origins and the unspoken disapproval when they identified her as PWT—Poor White Trash.

Of course, Amy didn't kid herself. That could still happen. But right now, she basked in the warmth of Tammy Mulcahey's smile and prayed with all her heart that it was genuine.

"It's about *time* you brought her over to meet us, Robin." Tammy got up from the desk and approached Amy, enclosing her in a welcoming hug. Amy closed her eyes, breathing in the delicious scent of Fifth Avenue perfume. She recognized it because it was one of her favorites. Not that she'd ever been able to afford it. But every time she went into a department store, she took one of the sample sachets and used it over and over until it was bone dry.

Tammy released her, still smiling. "I don't know what you've done to my daughter, Amy, but every time she calls me, all I hear is 'Amy this' and 'Amy that.' She's just crazy about you!"

"*Mom!*"

Amy glanced at Robin and saw that her face was flaming. She felt another rush of warmth. Oh, she'd known that Robin liked her, but she hadn't realized how much.

"You're her first real girlfriend, you know," Tammy went on. "Robin was a tomboy before she got to high school, and she hated playing with girls."

"I did not! They hated *me!*"

Tammy shook her head, her sleek blond pageboy swinging gently. "And it got worse in high school when Robin discovered boys—or I should say, boys discovered *her*. So, as you can imagine, she wasn't too popular with the other girls."

"Mom! I didn't bring Amy here to discuss my life story. Anyway, I'm starving. What's for dinner?"

"Your father is barbecuing on the terrace."

Barbecuing? It was only about fifty degrees out there. Robin caught her puzzled glance, and the dimple flickered in her cheek. "Dad's weird. He barbecues in any weather. I think it's some masculine rite of passage for him."

"How do you like your filet, Amy?" Tammy asked.

Amy stared blankly, and Robin came to her rescue. "Steak, Amy. How do you like it cooked?"

"Oh. Well-done, I guess."

Robin gave a mock shudder. "Oh, Dad'll just *die*! Sure you don't want it a little pink?"

Amy swallowed hard, trying not to gag. "Well . . . maybe just a little." She felt like a complete geek. "I get sick if it's really pink." Her low-class roots were showing, but she was really, *really* particular about her meat.

"Then you better not watch me eat mine." Robin grinned. "I like mine *bloody!*"

"Robin!" Tammy admonished. "Look what you've done. The poor girl has gone white." She sent Amy a sympathetic smile. "She's just like her father. Loves to get a rise out of people. Just can't resist shocking them."

"I *resemble* that remark!" rumbled a deep masculine voice from the doorway behind them. The enticing aroma of mesquite wood floated into the room from outside.

Amy turned to see an attractive middle-aged man with iron gray hair and crinkling blue eyes holding a platter, which was empty except for a pool of reddish-brown liquid. She swallowed hard, feeling her stomach spasm. Robin's father eyed her up and down, an easy grin on his lean face.

"So, this must be the famous Amy Shiley. We feel like we know you already, Amy. Robin talks about you so much. And you're just as pretty as she said!"

Amy started to mumble something, but Robin didn't give her a chance. "How're the steaks doing, Dad? I'm starving."

"Just put 'em on, Cupcake. Should be ready in about ten minutes."

"Amy likes hers well-done," Robin said shortly, and Amy cringed in embarrassment. Robin grabbed her arm. "Come on, I want to show you my room before dinner."

The two of them headed toward the door of the library.

"Don't turn your music up too loud," Tammy called. "We'll be calling you for dinner, and I don't want to come up and get you."

"So use the intercom." With a toss of her blond head, Robin marched out of the room, pulling Amy with her.

It was weird, Amy thought. This was a completely new side to Robin. She seemed tense, almost angry. Almost as if she couldn't stand her family. But they seemed so nice! She followed Robin up the beautiful wood-carved stairs, thinking how sad it was that people never appreciated what they had. Probably Robin didn't even realize how very lucky she was to have such a great family.

"Asparagus, Amy?"

Amy looked up to see Michael Mulcahey holding out a crystal dish filled with asparagus. Blushing, she shook her head. "No, thank you. I'm not much of a vegetable eater."

"I'll take some." Robin reached for the dish and helped herself to a huge portion of the disgusting-looking green vegetable. Everything else looked delicious, though. Michael had cooked her steak exactly how she liked it, she saw as she began cutting it. Not even the tiniest hint of pink. And the baked potato on her plate, oozing with real butter and sour cream, was big enough to feed six people.

"Why are you cutting your meat like that?" Jeff, Robin's fourteen-year-old brother, spoke in a horrified voice.

Amy looked across the table at him and saw that his blue eyes were fastened on her plate. Her hands stilled on the knife as she felt her face grow hotter. *What am I doing wrong?*

"Shut up, Jeff," Robin growled.

"But she's cutting her meat like she's gonna feed it to a baby or something."

Amy wanted to die. She wanted to just keel over in her chair and die.

"Jeffrey, you may leave the table right now if you're going to continue being rude." Michael's eyes impaled his son's.

"But Dad! You always told me I had to cut one bite at a time, not cut it all up at once!"

"*Jeffrey!*" Michael's voice was gruff.

Amy carefully placed her knife on the edge of her plate like Robin had done and slipped a small piece of steak into her mouth. She kept her eyes fastened to her plate as she chewed the tender morsel. But it might as well have been cardboard. That's how much she was enjoying this dinner at Robin's family home.

She was ashamed to admit she'd never eaten steak like this before. On the rare times her parents had taken her out to dinner, it had been to places like Western Steakhouse or Sizzler, and they'd only allowed her to order a hamburger. At home, they'd had round steak occasionally. Her parents had always cut theirs into tiny, bite-size pieces before eating it, and she'd followed suit.

Obviously, that hadn't been correct etiquette. And here, she'd shown just how low-class she was.

But one thing was for sure. She'd file this mistake away into the recesses of her brain and never make it again. Staring down at her plate, she continued with her meal, concentrating on the classical music playing in the background. She didn't know what it was, but she liked its lively violins . . . at least, that's what she thought the instrument was.

"I want a beer," Robin said suddenly, pushing away from the table. "Amy, you want one?" She was already heading out of the dining room on her way to the kitchen.

"N . . . no, thank you. My Coke is fine."

"Robin, you're too young to drink!" Tammy called after her. She glanced at her husband. He shrugged and looked away.

A moment later, Robin returned to the room with a bottle of Heineken. She took a swig and placed it on the table.

"Michael!" Tammy demanded. "Are you just going to let her get away with this?"

He sighed. "Tammy, there's nothing wrong with her drinking a beer in our own home. She's going to do it anyway, so I don't see any point in making a big deal about it."

Robin looked across the table at Amy and gave her a catlike smile. *You see how easy it is wrapping them around my little finger,* it seemed to say. Oh, Robin was truly a lucky girl. Amy couldn't imagine in a million years having the guts to pull something like this with her own parents. Then again, would they have even cared? Would they have even noticed?

Amy had finally started to relax a bit, thanks to the casual dinner conversation in which everyone but Robin participated in. For some reason, she seemed rather subdued, but by now, Amy was used to her changeable moods.

Dinner was drawing to a close. *Thank God,* Amy thought. She'd got through it with only that one gaffe. But in that, she was wrong, she realized, when Stella brought in a tray of butter-rich ice-cream sundaes topped with crushed pineapple and raspberries.

"Ah, good!" Michael said, rubbing his hands together in delight. "The traditional Mulcahey late-summer dessert." He grinned at Tammy. "Should I tell Amy why?"

Stella placed a sundae in front of Amy, and moved on. Amy eyed it, her stomach beginning to churn. Was it fresh or canned? And how could she gracefully find out?

"This is very special pineapple, Amy," Michael went on. "Comes straight from the pineapple fields of Oahu. Thanks to my good buddy, Senator Oshi Mitsuki. A little Super Bowl bet where he foolishly promised me an annual lifetime supply of fresh pineapple if the Washington Redskins beat the Denver Broncos." He chuckled. "Well, we all know what happened in that game, don't we?"

There was her answer. *Fresh* pineapple. She felt her cheeks warm with embarrassment as everyone dug into their desserts, and she just sat there, looking at the pretty mound of ice cream generously covered with pineapple and pureed raspberries.

"Something wrong, Amy?" Tammy asked.

Her face grew warmer as she looked up and met Tammy's curious gaze. She cleared her throat, and managed to reply. "I'm sorry. I'm . . . uh . . . allergic to fresh pineapple. It gives me kind of a . . . serious reaction." She touched the hollow of her throat. "My throat swells and . . . uh . . . it's kind of scary. I'm sorry," she said again, gazing down at the dessert miserably.

"No need to apologize, Amy," Tammy said briskly. *"Stella!"*

The housekeeper appeared at the door of the kitchen. "Yes, ma'am?"

"Bring Amy another ice cream. No pineapple. Would you like it topped with raspberries, Amy?"

"Yes, thank you," Amy said softly, her face still on fire.

And a moment later, Stella placed a new dessert in front of her, and the mortifying moment was over. The Mulcaheys began talking about Jeff's science project, and Amy ate her dessert in silence.

After dinner, Robin got up from the table and nudged Amy's shoulder. "Come on. Let's go to my room and watch some movies."

Amy looked around anxiously. "But don't we need to help clean up?" she asked hesitantly.

Tammy smiled but didn't speak.

Robin tossed her blond head and strode toward the door. "Stella will do it."

Another screwup, Amy thought, her face coloring. "Thank you for a lovely dinner," she mumbled, pushing back her chair.

Michael's blue eyes crinkled as he smiled. "Thank *you* for joining us, Sunshine." At her puzzled look, he winked at her. "Did you know you have a smile like a roomful of sunshine, Amy?"

She felt her face growing even warmer. Her eyes dropped bashfully from his. "Thanks."

"Amy! You coming?"

At Robin's impatient query, Amy murmured an "excuse me" and hurried out of the dining room. Despite the high color on her cheeks and her feeling of inadequacy, Amy felt a warmth growing inside her. She liked Robin's parents! And strangely enough, she thought maybe they liked her, too.

"Wow! This room is big enough for a *half dozen* people!"

Amy looked around the huge bedroom Robin had assigned her for the weekend. It was as big . . . no, bigger . . . than the master bedrooms in the model homes. A sitting area took up one side, and Amy was delighted to see a cherry bookcase filled to capacity lining a wall. Next to it, two satin-upholstered chairs in colors of cream and amethyst nestled around a cherry-wood reading table with an elegant brass claw-foot lamp. In the sleeping area, a king-size cherry bed dominated the room, a tiered amethyst bed curtain draping from the painted silk wall above it. Delicate crystal bowls of pot-pourri in the cinnamon scent she'd noticed in the foyer were placed in various spots around the room. It looked like a French country retreat, almost as if she'd stepped through a magic mirror into the seventeenth century.

She was still lost in admiration when an orange tabby padded through the door and jumped onto the bed like it was her anointed throne.

Amy smiled in delight. "Oh! Who's this?"

"That's just Ruby Two-Shoes." Robin shrugged. "Paul found her in the bushes last summer when he was home from college. For some harebrained reason, he called her Reuben. Then we found out she was a girl, so he changed her name to Ruby Two-Shoes. I'm not really a cat person, though. I've always wanted a dog, but Mom doesn't want dog hair all over the house."

"But cat hair is okay, huh? She's beautiful." Amy watched the cat curl up on the bed and begin to groom herself. She'd never been allowed a pet in the trailer, but if she could have, it would've been a cat.

"The bathroom is down the hall," Robin said. "Sorry. But you know, if you'd like, you can stay in Paul's room. He has his own bathroom."

"Don't be ridiculous! I think I can walk down the hall to go to the bathroom. Besides . . ." Her eyes scanned the bookcase. "I'd love to just sit here and read. I don't feel at all sleepy." And it was almost one in the morning.

Robin yawned. "Whatever. But just so you know, Brat uses that bathroom."

"You mean Jeff?"

"That's what I said. Brat."

"Well, I assume it has locks, doesn't it?"

"Yeah, but take my advice. Wear your robe in the hall. Jeff's hormones are in overdrive. 'Night."

Robin disappeared down the massive hall toward her own room. Amy undressed and slipped into her soft knit pajamas, then, remembering Robin's words, pulled on a navy terry robe and stepped out into the hallway. She'd just reached the bathroom door when another door opened down the hall. Jeff stuck his blond head into the corridor.

"Hey, Amy!"

She looked at him.

He stepped out of his room and sauntered toward her. "Hey, I just wanted to say . . . I'm sorry about that scene at dinner. I didn't mean to like, embarrass you or anything."

"Don't worry about it," Amy said, feeling embarrassed all over again. She turned back to the bathroom.

"I just wanted to make sure we're cool." He was gazing at her solemnly, blue eyes hopeful. Kind of like a scolded puppy waiting to be forgiven.

She smiled at him. "Yes, Jeff, we're cool."

He gave her a thumbs-up, his face lighting in a grin. "All right!" Then he turned and strolled back to his room. Amy grinned. That guy was going to be a real heartbreaker one day. Maybe sooner than anyone expected.

She stepped into the bathroom and stopped short, her mouth gaping. *This* was her bathroom? It was *incredible*! A jetted tub encased in elegant hunter green marble took up nearly one side of the room. Cater-cornered to it was a dressing table in the same green marble and a chair upholstered in cream-colored brocade. To the right of the tub was a three-cornered glass shower, also trimmed in green marble. And on the remaining wall was a gorgeous honey-colored cabinet with double sinks and counters of, yes, that same rich-looking green marble topped with scented candles in several colors and shapes. In its own alcove stood an ivory porcelain toilet with a hunter green lid.

If this was the guest bathroom, Amy wondered what the master bath looked like. She used the toilet, then brushed her teeth, spitting carefully into the marbled sink and rinsing it out carefully afterward. It looked like it had never been used before. How many maids did the Mulcaheys employ to keep this huge place looking so spick-and-span?

Back in her room, Amy crawled onto the massive king-size bed and gazed up at the moonlight shadow-dancing on the cathedral ceiling. She'd never in her life been in a bed this big. Even with Ruby Two-Shoes taking up a portion of it, it felt huge. And wonderful! Except . . . she was wide-awake. It was so quiet in the room, with just the muted roar of Ruby's purring engine breaking the silence. She could almost believe she was all alone in the big house.

It had been an exciting, but not altogether great day. She'd been too tense, too afraid of doing something wrong—and she had, of course. The meat. Even in the dark shelter of the bedroom, she felt her cheeks grow hot. God! That had been humiliating.

With a soft groan, Amy threw back the down comforter and slipped out of bed. Maybe she'd read for a while in the sitting room. She'd brought along a novel, but was almost finished with it. There were plenty of books on the bookshelf, and she was sure no one would mind if she borrowed one of them.

She turned on the reading light and sat down in one of the satin chairs. Immediately Ruby Two-Shoes jumped into her lap and settled down. Stroking her soft orange fur, Amy began to read. Moments later, she was lost in her book.

Footsteps in the hall.

Robin stiffened, her eyes fastening on her door, visible in the pale wash of the full moon beaming in through Palladian windows. The footsteps halted outside her room. Robin lay rigidly, waiting, barely breathing. She listened for the sound of the door handle turning. Trying to turn, anyway. It wouldn't. She'd made sure of that. Not that locked doors had stopped him in the past.

But nothing happened. No sound outside her door. Not even his breathing. Just a watchful silence.

He wouldn't dare. He wouldn't. Not after what had happened last time. She still had the knife in her room, and she'd use it. She'd cut his goddamn balls off just like she'd told him she would. He'd believed her then. She just hoped he still believed it. Sweat pooled under her arms, and she could smell the scent of her own fear as the moments ticked by.

The footsteps moved on, and Robin relaxed. She forced herself to stay awake a few minutes longer, just in case he changed his mind and decided to return. But finally, when the hall outside her room remained silent, she turned on her side, made sure her night-light was still glowing, and closed her eyes, falling immediately into a deep, dreamless sleep.

A soft tap on Amy's door made her look up from her book.

"Uh . . . yes?"

The door opened, and Michael stuck his head in. "I saw your light on. Is everything okay?"

"Oh, yeah. I just couldn't sleep, so I thought I'd read for a while."

"Well, I was just on my way down to the kitchen for a cup of hot chocolate. Ninety-nine percent decaf. Care to join me?"

It was on the tip of her tongue to refuse. After all, how weird would it be to be alone with Robin's father, and both of them in their nightclothes? Not that he was half-dressed or anything. She could see he was wearing pajamas under his thick black robe. Still . . .

He gave her a crooked grin. "I'd love the company."

Funny how much he looked like Jeff right now. He had that same hopeful look in his blue eyes, the one when the teenager asked if they were cool. And Amy felt herself responding to it. Anyway, a cup of hot chocolate *did* sound good.

She smiled. "Okay. Since it's decaf."

"You know, I think it's really great that Robby has found herself a girlfriend."

Amy and Michael sat at the cherry island bar, sipping hot chocolate from

Mexican ceramic mugs. Amy swept her fingers over the smooth Corian countertop, delighted with the cool clean texture. What a gorgeous kitchen! She was blown away by the state-of-the-art chrome stove and side-by-side refrigerator with icemaker capable of producing three kinds of ice. And the rest of the kitchen was simply breathtaking, too. The burnished cabinetry with built-in wine racks. A built-in wall oven combination, double chrome sinks with a water purifier, a dishwasher made out of the same cherrywood, which made it almost disappear into the wall. And a Jenn-Aire cooktop on the island along with another built-in wine rack. Oh, how she'd love to be let loose in here.

With Mama in her cups as she'd usually been, Amy had done most of the cooking back when Dad was still alive. Nothing fancy, of course. Dad had been a meat-and-potatoes man. Cooking was one of the few chores Amy had actually enjoyed. Especially desserts. She'd scoured all the women's magazines she could find in the giveaway bin at the local library and tried out the recipes.

"Hello? Sunshine? You still with me?"

Amy glanced over at Robin's father. He sat next to her on a stool at the counter, close enough that she could smell his pleasant woodsy cologne. "I'm sorry. I was just daydreaming. I do that a lot." To her irritation, she felt herself blushing. God, how she wished she could control that annoying habit.

"Not a thing wrong with a little daydreaming now and then," Michael said, lifting his cup to his mouth. "Listen, I'm sorry if Jeff made you feel uncomfortable at dinner. He's at an obnoxious age."

"I think he's sweet. He apologized to me already. Not that he really had anything to apologize for." Amy stared down into the milky chocolate in her cup. "There's a lot of things I probably don't do right. My parents weren't the greatest role models." Oh, God! Had she really said that?

Michael was silent for a moment, then, "Well, now, Sunshine, life is a learning experience. Lord knows when I first met Tammy I was nothing but a farm boy from the boondocks of southwest Virginia. You remember that scene in the movie *Big*, where Tom Hanks picks up that little itty-bitty corncob and starts eating it like it was a real corn on the cob? Well, that was me."

Was it her imagination or had his down-home accent thickened into a country twang? She looked at him. He grinned. "Yep! I was at a party at Tammy's family home, and I picked one of those suckers up and began to eat it just like that. Tammy had to pull me aside and tell me you were supposed to eat the whole damn thing. And then there was the time at a fancy restaurant I tried to stuff a whole cherry tomato in my mouth, and this thing was a big sucker, and when I bit into it, the juice flew out of my mouth and down my white shirt, leaving a trail of seeds and red stuff you could see a mile away." He laughed. "Lord! I felt like an idiot."

Amy smiled. "Believe me, I understand."

"And you know what, Sunshine? It wasn't so long ago that I made an utter fool of myself at a reception in a fancy-pantsy hotel in Washington, DC. I was a U.S. congressman, no less, and I *still* made a big fool of myself. Do you know what I did?"

Amy shook her head, smiling.

He smiled back, his blue eyes gentle. "Well, I went over to the dessert table, and helped myself to a piece of this gorgeous chocolate-filled cake with all these layers of whipped cream. Well, first of all, I couldn't find a serving spoon anywhere, so I walked over to this other dessert table and found one. I came back and started to slice through this cake, and I thought it was kind of odd that it seemed a lot denser than it looked, but I kept sawing through it. Finally, this waiter came over. He was all dressed to the nines in a black tux, and had that hoity-toity look . . . you know, sort of like he had a garden tool stuck up where the sun don't shine . . . and he said . . ." Michael straightened in his chair, and his face took on a snobbish nose-in-the-air expression, and mimicking a haughty British accent, he said, " 'I'm sorry, sir, but this is just a display, made of shortening and food color. The dessert table is over there.' Well, Sunshine, I just wanted the floor to open up and swallow me. I glanced over at the table where my party was sitting, and sure enough, a few of them were watching me with these sly smiles, and I knew they'd seen it all."

"Oh, God! What did you do, Mr. Mulcahey?" Amy asked, her eyes widening.

"Michael." His hand covered hers. "I *insist* you call me Michael. Or I won't tell you any more of my embarrassing stories."

"Okay, Michael. So, what did you do?"

"I just took a deep breath, thanked the waiter for the information, lifted my head high, walked over to the real dessert table, and helped myself to the first thing I saw. I went back to my table and pretended it never happened. That's what you've got to do, Amy. You've got to store away the information, lift that pretty head, and go on about your business."

"It's not always easy to do that," Amy said softly.

"Damn right, it's not. But that's the difference between the winners and the losers in this world. You make a mistake, you learn from it, and you move on. You see, Amy, there's a big difference between ignorance and stupidity. Lots of people are ignorant, but the stupid ones don't learn from their ignorance. The smart ones do. And you're smart, Sunshine." He patted her hand. "Something tells me you've got a bright and shining future in front of you." He stood up and yawned. "Well, I guess I'm going to head on to bed. Can you find your way back to your room?"

"I'd better come with you," Amy said, standing. "This place is huge."

He led her back to her room. Outside her door, he touched her head, and then leaned down to plant a kiss on her forehead. "Sleep tight, Sunshine."

Amy smiled up at him. "Thanks. Oh, and Mr. Mul . . . I mean . . . Michael, I enjoyed our talk."

He grinned at her and gave her a wink. "See you in the morning."

Smiling, Amy stepped into her room. Her heart felt light and full of an unaccustomed emotion. Happiness? Joy? She really, *really* liked Robin's family. They were so real and down-to-earth.

How lucky Robin was. To be born into a family like this. How very, very lucky. And she probably didn't even realize it.

4

"Robin, I really don't think I want to do this."

"You've *got* to! Think of it as a rite of passage. Shhh. Here he comes. Just sit still and be brave. It won't hurt." Robin's lips twitched, and her blue eyes danced. *"Much."*

Amy watched with dread as the burly T-shirted black man picked up the tattoo needle. "You want the same thing?"

"Yep," Robin answered for her. "A ladybug. Right above the ankle . . . just like mine."

The man grinned and reached down to adjust Amy's ankle. She flinched. "Easy, now, hon. This'll sting just a bit. What's with the ladybugs, anyway?"

"It's the symbol for our sorority," Robin said brightly.

Amy squeezed her eyes shut as she felt an intense burning sensation on her left ankle. Oh, wow! Robin was wrong. It *did* hurt. Like, a *lot*! And was that the smell of her *flesh* burning? She forced herself not to pull her ankle out of the man's grasp, afraid a sudden movement would inflict worse damage. Oh, *why* had she let Robin talk her into this lame idea? One minute they'd been walking down the street, and the next, Robin had pulled her into this tattoo parlor and gotten the ladybug emblazoned on her inner ankle. That had been incredible enough. But what was *really* incredible . . . no, what was *unbelievable* was that now, she was getting the same thing done to herself.

"All done. What do you think?"

The worst of the pain had ended, but she still felt some stinging. She kept her eyes tightly shut. "I'm afraid to look."

"Hey, it looks great," Robin said. "Look at it, Amy."

Cautiously, Amy opened her eyes and leaned forward. A cute little ladybug perched on her ankle in the exact same spot as Robin's. Okay. It wasn't so bad. In fact, it was kind of exotic-looking. There was only a bit of redness around it, and the tattoo artist assured her that would go away within hours.

Robin stuck out her own ankle so Amy could see it. "See? Now, we're twins."

Out on the street, heading back toward the campus into a bracing autumn wind, Robin practically skipped with happiness. "Mom is going to be *so* pissed when she sees this! She freaked during my senior year in high school when I got a *labret* put into my bottom lip." She giggled. "God, did it gall her when I had it in for my prom picture. She went on for hours about kids who pierce and burn their bodies. 'How can you kids mutilate yourself like that?'" Robin parodied. "I kept it in a month longer than I wanted to just to piss her off."

"So . . . is that why we had these ladybugs burned into our ankles?" Amy asked ruefully.

Robin released a peal of joyful laughter. "Yeah! Partly, anyway. But I think they look cool, don't you?"

"Well, it doesn't look as bad as I imagined it would." Amy thought about it a moment, then admitted, "Actually, yeah, they *do* look kind of cool."

"Damn right! You just wait. The other Kappa Chis will be making a beeline for that tattoo parlor before the weekend is out. You wanta bet?" Robin grinned, delighted with herself. "But we'll always be the first. And that makes *us* the coolest!"

Back in their dorm room, Robin hit the button on the answering machine to listen to her multitude of messages. There were never any for Amy. Of course, the invitations that flowed in from the other sorority girls always included her, but they were directed at Robin.

"I'll be right back." Amy stepped out of the room and walked down the hall toward the communal bathroom. Her ankle was still stinging, and the tattoo guy had told her cold compresses would soothe the area. When she walked back into the room a moment later with a wet washcloth, a new message was just starting.

"Hi, Rob. It's me, Paul." A pause, then a short laugh, and, "Your big bro."

Robin, who was stripping off her clothes to change for a date, squealed and a huge smile lit up her face. "Oh, *damn*! Why do I always miss his calls?"

". . . be coming into Richmond on the nineteenth so I was thinking maybe you could come to the airport and pick me up. Give us a chance to get caught up without everybody else around? Let me know, okay?"

Nice voice, Amy thought. Rich-toned and warm. She remembered Robin showing her a photo of Paul when she visited their house. He'd been in his football uniform, and was all smudged with dirt and grass, but his dark hair had been attractively ruffled and his blue eyes glowing with happiness. Apparently, they'd just won a big game. He'd played wide receiver in high school, and now played for the University of Colorado's Buffaloes. He was destined for the pros, Robin said. Not that she knew anything about football, except that the guys playing it were sometimes hunks. The sport itself totally sucked, she declared, but it was cool having a big brother who might be famous someday.

"Oh, Amy! You've *got* to go with me to pick Paul up," Robin said, after the message ended. "I can't wait 'til you meet him. He is *so* cool! I keep telling him he was switched at birth. He's not at all like Mom or Dad."

"But you just heard him say he wanted to be alone with you."

Robin slithered into a skintight black leather bustier dress and turned her back to Amy. "Zip me. Oh, he won't mind if you come along. He just means he doesn't want the whole family to pick him up."

Amy zipped up her dress. "I don't know, Rob. I think I'll feel like a third wheel."

"Don't be an idiot." She whirled away and peered into the mirror, grabbing a mascara tube from the dressing table. "I *insist* you come. I don't want to drive all the way to Richmond by myself. So . . ." She dabbed the mascara on her eyelashes. "What're you doing tonight?"

"Um . . . well, I've got this paper to write for English."

"Well, fuck that! It's Saturday night, girl. You need to get out of this room and go party!"

"Yeah, like, with *who*?"

Robin rolled her eyes and pulled the elastic band from her hair. Her blond locks tumbled around her shoulders. "Jeez, Amy! You're really hot! How come you don't have guys falling all over themselves to take you out?"

"I don't know," Amy said miserably. "I guess I bore them to death. They seem interested until I open my mouth and start to talk."

"Well, maybe if you'd talk about something other than mummified bodies and pieces of china they dig up in Jamestown, you might get a little more attention."

"But that's what I'm interested in!" Amy protested. "What am I supposed to do? Pretend to be something I'm not?"

Robin ran a brush through her hair. Tonight she was wearing it straight; that's how Jason liked it. "Hey, you do what you gotta do when you're dealing with frat boys who have two things on their dopey little minds. Beer and sex. Tell you what I'll do. When I'm out with Jason tonight, I'll see if he has a friend he can fix you up with, okay?"

"Hel-*lo*! I've seen Jason, remember? I don't think he'll have any friends that'll find *me* appealing." *Or that I'll find appealing.* Oh, Jason wasn't bad-looking. In fact, he was gorgeous, with shoulder-length golden brown hair that a supermodel would kill to have, sexy green eyes, and sensuous lips that immediately made you wonder how he kissed. But he was a total loser! A rock star wanna-be who came into town once or twice a month for the sole purpose of getting laid by his former high school girlfriend. Robin was completely up front about it, and treated it as casually as he did. And, of course, she knew

Jason wasn't the only guy Robin was sleeping with, so it was no big deal. Still, Amy didn't like him. She suspected he was stoned most of the time. There was something about that sleepy, yet sexy, look in his eyes that screamed out "drugs." God knows she'd seen that dazed look in her parents' eyes through most of her childhood, so she should know.

"Look, Rob. Don't worry about me. I'll meet a guy when the time is right. I'm not going to stress out about it."

Robin placed her brush on the dressing table and turned. Her blue eyes speared Amy. "You're a virgin, aren't you?"

Amy felt her face go scarlet. She sat down at her desk and reached for her notebook. "Of course I am," she murmured. "I've never even had a boyfriend."

Silence. Amy stared down at her notebook. How galling to have to admit that! Especially to someone like Robin, who'd probably had the boys competing for her in nursery school. She felt Robin's approach. "Hey?" Her hand rested lighted on Amy's shoulder. She turned and looked up.

Robin gazed down at her, her blue eyes serious for once. "There's nothing wrong with that, Amy. Save yourself for the right guy." She bit her bottom lip. "I wish I had."

"Come on, baby . . . let me . . ."

Jason's erection prodded against Robin's thigh as she squirmed from beneath him. "Jason, no! You know I don't do that!"

With a groan, Jason rolled over onto his back and glared up at the textured ceiling of the motel room off Route 60. "*Christ*, Robin! You let me do everything except fuck you. I don't get it."

"Well, tough. Take it or leave it." Robin scrambled out of the rumpled bed and strode, naked, into the bathroom, slamming the door behind her. After peeing, she washed her hands and stared into the mirror over the sink. Her blond hair was tangled and matted from writhing on the bed like an alley cat in heat. Oh, that Jason. Did he ever know how to go down on a girl! Must be that sexy mouth of his, and boy, did he know how to use it. Her eyes dropped to her small breasts, the pink-tipped nipples still hardened in arousal. She saw a tiny love bite on her left one and touched it tentatively.

Poor Jason. He was a sensual guy. The kind of guy her favorite romance authors liked to write about. A virtual lovemaking machine. Not into anything real kinky, but just down-home all-American shit-kickin' sex. And it frustrated the hell out of him that she wouldn't let him do it all. Always had, and always would.

But if it *could* happen . . . if she could let it happen, it would probably be Jason she'd do it with. He was a sweet guy. And she was pretty sure he loved her. Oh, that didn't mean he didn't screw groupies while he was out on the road. Hell, he'd be insane to turn down free sex. Besides, they understood each other. No bonds. No commitment. No complications.

Robin left the bathroom and slipped back into bed, breathing in the smell of Jason's musky maleness mingled with the smoke of the cigarette he'd just put out. She snuggled against his masculine body, her hand tracing slow circles on his flat stomach, still tanned from hot afternoons lazing on Virginia Beach. "I'm sorry, Jase, but you know my rules."

"Yeah . . . you've made 'em clear enough. I just don't get it."

As her hand moved lower, she sensed his penis jutting to attention. She moved closer and licked a line from his neck to his beard-studded jaw. "Isn't it good with us? Didn't I give you the best blow job you ever had a little while ago?"

He moaned, and turned toward her, his mouth anchoring against hers in a heated kiss. Robin threaded her fingers through his glossy long brown hair and returned his kiss greedily. Slipping her tongue into his mouth, she enclosed his hard-on in her hand, stroking confidently. She would make him forget he couldn't have everything he wanted from her. And when she was done with him, he'd be so exhausted, and so sated from their love play that it wouldn't matter that she would never allow him—or any man—to fuck her.

"So, is Paul in a fraternity?" Amy asked as Robin maneuvered her Tracker into a parking space in Lot A of the airport.

"Nah. Hasn't got time for that stuff. Not with being on the football team and carrying a full shitload of classes." She switched off the ignition and opened the door.

Amy stepped out of the Tracker into an icy November wind. Menacing gray clouds scudded low across the sky, hinting at an early snow. She shivered and pulled her faux-fur animal-print coat, a Robin hand-me-down, closer around her. Robin circled around from the car, and they headed toward the terminal.

Glancing up at the arrival board, Robin grimaced. "Ah, shit! We're late."

Wonder why, Amy thought, forcing herself to remain silent. Robin had impulsively decided to drive into Lightfoot and stop at the Pottery Factory outlets to buy a pair of sterling silver earrings she'd spied in a New Age shop the week before. For some reason, she'd decided she simply couldn't live without them *another day,* so they'd just "pop in" on the way to the airport and pick them up. Of course, you could never just "pop in" at the Pottery Factory. Amy had learned that the first time she and Robin had gone shopping there. Well, *Robin* had done the shopping while Amy just looked. But it was an all-day thing.

Needless to say, they'd spent more than a few minutes in a shop that specialized in crystals and New Age jewelry, and Robin had not only bought herself the earrings, she'd insisted on buying a slightly different pair for Amy—against her protestations, of course. But Amy had learned in the few months she'd been living with her roommate that what Robin wanted, Robin got. Finally, just to get her out of the shop, Amy had agreed to accept the earrings. They *were* beautiful, with their leverback design and small garnet stones. But pricey at forty dollars! She couldn't imagine spending so much money for a pair of earrings. Robin had paid sixty for hers without batting an eyelash, and the only difference Amy could see was that Robin's garnets were slightly larger.

"Come on." Robin grabbed her arm. "Let's go to baggage claim. He'll be there."

Amy saw Paul first. Because he was staring right at her. He was tall, definitely over six feet, yet he had the lean, muscular build of the athlete he was. He stood by the baggage carousel, dressed in faded jeans and a white turtleneck sweater and holding a down-lined jacket. A weather-beaten backpack rested on his broad shoulders. His black hair looked as if it had been ruffled by a light breeze, and his lean jaw was covered with a five o'clock shadow. But it was his eyes that caught and held her attention. A deep ocean blue, solemn and hypnotic.

In retrospect, Amy realized it could only have been a couple of seconds that their gazes held. But it might as well have been a lifetime. Her heart skipped a beat, and the blood in her veins slowed as if it had suddenly become a viscous river of warm honey. She felt this stranger's eyes upon her, and it was as if he read her very soul . . . every secret, every humiliation, every sad moment of her pathetic childhood. And then, he smiled. A slow, sweet smile, and Amy felt her heartbeat accelerate, and miracle of all miracles, she found herself smiling back. Without a trace of awkwardness or shyness, but with a naturalness that came from the very soul he recognized.

"*Paul!*" Robin shrieked, and bolted toward him.

Paul's eyes darted from Amy to Robin and widened as he realized the truth—that they were together. The smile—the one he'd held for Amy—widened and lost that secret something—that knowledge—of a moment before and became the delighted grin of a brother greeting his younger sister after a long separation. Robin threw herself into his arms, laughing. He hugged her tightly, then drew away to look at her.

"Hey, Robby! What's with your hair?" He grasped a beaded cornrow strand in each hand and held it out to the sides of her head.

She giggled. "Cornrows, asshole! What do you think?"

He leaned down, and with a devilish grin, whispered into her ear, "I don't know how to break this to you, Rob, but guess what? You're *not* black!"

"Idiot!" She gave him a push. "Don't tell me Colorado has turned you into a hick! Don't you know *anything* about style?"

"I know what I like," Paul said, his blue eyes sparkling. "And I don't like hair that clicks and clacks when you move."

"Tough! Like I *care* what you think." Robin gave a mock pout. She turned and beckoned to Amy. "Amy, come and meet my brother. He's a straight-ass conservative, but I love him anyway. Paul, this is my roommate, Amy."

Amy's customary shyness returned. She gazed up at him and tried to find that natural smile again. "Hi."

His blue eyes wrapped her in warmth. "I'm only conservative by Rob's measure," he said. "Like about 99 percent of the population. Nice to meet you, Amy." He held out his hand.

She took it, and from that moment, she was lost. *This feels amazing*, she thought dreamily. *I could look at him forever. Is this what being in love feels like?* But how could it happen just like that? She knew almost nothing about Paul Mulcahey. Only that he was a junior in college, he played football, he maintained a B+ GPA, he was Robin's older brother and . . . he was the most beautiful, charismatic man she'd ever met. Goose pimples rose on her arms as he held her hand. She caught a subtle hint of sandalwood. His aftershave?

Paul smiled down at her. "Rob tells me you're an archaeology major."

Amy dropped her eyes, blushing. "Uh-huh."

"And she studies all the time," Robin said with a grimace. "I've been trying to break her of that annoying habit, but it's not been easy."

Paul released Amy's hand, but kept his eyes centered on her. "Nothing wrong with hard work, right, Amy? You might want to follow her example, Rob . . . that is, if you plan to major in something other than boys and beer-guzzling."

"Fuck off," Robin said cheerfully, and led the way to the exit.

Amy's thoughts spun in confusion as the three of them passed through the terminal doors and headed for the parking lot. The wind whipped her hair around her face, and she grinned, feeling giddy and happy and excited all at the same time. She couldn't think past the next five days. The five days that Paul Mulcahey would be in town. Tomorrow after their last class, she and Robin would drive out to Windsong, where they'd spend Thanksgiving weekend. It would be her first Thanksgiving with a real family.

Amy scrambled into the backseat of the Tracker so Paul could sit with his sister in the front. He turned around and smiled at her. "Now, *that's* the kind of hair I like on a woman," he said. "Windblown and natural."

Blushing, Amy smoothed her hair away from her face and tried to think of a Robin-like response. But of course, her mind refused to cooperate, so she settled for "thanks," and focused on fastening her seat belt.

Robin gave her own Robin-like response. She stuck her tongue out at her brother, and said cheerfully, "Eat shit and die."

Paul looked back at Amy and winked, grinning. "That's what I love about my sister. She's a woman of few words, and most of them are made up of four letters."

Amy's heart spasmed. He was so good-looking it almost hurt to look at him.

"Admit it, Paul. You're just jealous," Robin chided.

"Is that so?" Paul's hand closed on one of her clacking cornrows and gave it an affectionate tug. It was an endearing gesture, one that filled Amy with renewed warmth. Robin looked over and gave him a heart-melting smile. Starting up the Tracker, she jerked the gear into reverse and peeled out of the parking space, tires squealing. Still grinning, she shifted gears and roared out of the airport lot, heading toward Williamsburg and home.

5

"What are you reading?"

Startled, Amy looked up, and felt her face immediately grow hot. Paul, still looking rumpled from sleep, stood in the doorway of the sunroom, wearing gray sweatpants and a navy UC sweatshirt. He apparently hadn't shaved yet because his jaw was studded with dark bristles of hair.

She thought he was the most beautiful sight she'd ever seen.

He smiled at her, a question in his eyes.

"Oh!" She looked at the paperback in her hand. *Civil War Ghosts of Virginia.* Why couldn't she be reading something more literary? What would impress an upperclassman who also happened to be an athlete? *War and Peace?* Or the latest John Grisham novel?

He stepped into the room. "Oh, one of L. B. Taylor's books? Is that his new one?"

"I don't know how new it is." Amy thumbed down a corner of the page and closed the book. "I got this at a used bookstore a few days ago. It's just down the street from the coffee shop where I work." Damn! Was she rambling on? Had he *asked* her for her life story?

Paul sat down in a cushioned wicker rocker across from her. Ruby Two-Shoes padded into the room, and without preamble, jumped into his lap, purring. He stroked her fur, smiling at Amy. "Looks like we're the only ones up this early. But I guess we'll hear Stella getting started with the turkey pretty soon. So . . . how come you're not home with your family for Thanksgiving?"

The dreaded question. And Amy hadn't been prepared for it at all. He was waiting for her answer, a genuinely interested expression on his lean, handsome face. For a moment, she considered making up a huge lie.

Oh, my parents are on holiday in the Caribbean. Or . . . they're skiing in Gstaad. They asked me to come along during their jaunt through Europe, but you know . . . I'd rather be in America for Thanksgiving. Europe is just so . . . old, you know. A true Robinism.

Trouble was, she wasn't Robin.

"I don't have any family," Amy said quietly. "Except for my mom . . . and she's been in a nursing home for the last three years. She's . . . well . . . kind of out of it. Catatonic, they call it."

To his credit, Paul didn't reveal any shock or revulsion at her confession. Or, in fact, any of the reactions Amy had half expected. Horror. Disdain. And worst of all, pity.

"That sucks," he said briefly. And it sounded like he meant it.

Something about his easy acceptance made her want to open up to him. Tell him things she'd never told anyone, even his sister. This feeling was *so* not like her, and it made her infatuation for him grow even stronger.

"Nowadays, they call my parents *dysfunctional*," Amy said. "But I only knew it was royally screwed up. Both of them were alcoholics. My father committed suicide when I was thirteen." *Oh, God! Why had she said that? She never told anyone about that horrible part of her life.* She waited for his sharp breath, his shocked murmur of sympathy, but he said nothing. Only gazed at her with compassionate blue eyes. She went on, her voice soft, "You can't imagine what it's like for me to be invited to your home for Thanksgiving."

His gaze was penetrating, but strangely, it didn't make her feel uncomfortable. At least she wasn't squirming in embarrassment as she would've expected.

"I'm glad you're here," he said quietly. "I just hope it'll live up to your expectations."

"Just being with a normal family on Thanksgiving *surpasses* my expectations."

"Well, we have our shortcomings like everyone else." Paul ran a strong, square hand through his rumpled black hair. "Robby and Jeff fight like cats and dogs over the TV remote, and Mom freaks out when she has a bad hair day. Dad goes berserk when he finds something out of place, or worse, when he *can't* find it at all. If you ask me, Dad's growing more anal-retentive every year." His voice lowered and he gave her a conspiratorial grin. "I'm the only normal one around here."

Amy smiled. "And Robin's just the opposite of your dad, isn't she? Anything goes."

His smile dimmed. "Yeah. I worry about Robby, though. Sometimes she needs to be reined in, or she'll get into all kinds of trouble." He studied her. "But I have a feeling you're good for her. Maybe you can get her to calm down a bit and take life more seriously."

"Sometimes, I think *I* need to be the one taking lessons from *her*," Amy said slowly. "She's so . . . *alive,* you know? She throws herself into the thick of things while I stand with my nose pressed up against the glass just looking in."

He didn't answer immediately. Then, "Well, maybe you two can learn something from each other. Can I see your book?" He leaned forward and reached for the book in her lap. Irritated at being disrupted, Ruby Two-Shoes sprang off his lap and stalked from the room. Paul frowned after her. "Well, *excuse* me!"

Amy smiled and passed the book over to him. He leafed through it, a wry smile on his lips. "I know this sounds kind of girly, but I think ghost stories are cool. Most guys won't admit there's anything to them. But I've always kind of believed in ghosts, you know. After all, I've seen the mystery light at Cohoke Crossing. Have you got to that part yet?"

Amy shook her head. "No, but I grew up in Newport News. I've probably heard about it. Refresh my memory."

"Here it is." He found the page he was searching for and looked up, grinning. "It's out near West Point. About a half hour's drive from here. When we were teenagers, a bunch of us used to go out there on summer nights and wait for the ghost light. There'd be carloads of kids doing the same thing."

"So, what causes it?"

He shrugged. "Nobody knows. It just appears down the railroad tracks and grows bigger as it gets to the crossing. Thousands of people have seen it. Including me and Robby."

"Really?"

"Yep." He grinned and waited.

"Well?" Amy found herself grinning back at him. "Are you going to tell me about it, or are you going to keep me in suspense?"

He laughed. "Not much to tell, really. It was dark, about eleven o'clock, and we saw this light heading toward us down the tracks. Looked like a train light, but there was no sound. Robby was about fourteen. I know that because I'd just got my driver's license." He shook his head and gave another short laugh. "When she saw that light, her nails just about punctured me to the bone, and every drop of blood in her face drained out. I could see how white she was by the glow of the ghost light. And then it was gone. Just like that."

"And *no one's* been able to figure out what it is?"

"There's all kinds of theories. Marsh gas. Pranksters. Lots of people say it's a product of wild imagination tempered with too much beer. But I hadn't been drinking that night, and I know what I saw. It wasn't marsh gas."

He fell silent. The sudden rattle of rain pelted against the white Palladian windows, and Amy glanced out to see the early-morning gray had darkened to an ominous gloom. She shivered, glad she was wearing her warmest fleece sweats.

"So, you think it's a ghost train?"

"I don't know what it is. But they say a trainload of wounded Confederate soldiers boarded a train in Richmond after the battle of Cold Harbor and headed for West Point. They never reached their destination, and no one ever figured out what happened to them. So, who knows?"

Amy felt a delicious shiver crawl up her spine. "I'd love to go see it," she said, then cringed, her face burning. Oh, God! He'd think that was a hint for him to take her. But then . . . *wasn't it?*

"We could go tonight." Paul glanced out the window at the streaking rain. "In fact, tonight's perfect. They say the light most often appears on gloomy nights. But it'll just be the two of us. You can't get Robby within five miles of Cohoke Crossing after that first time."

"That's okay," Amy said lightly, already imagining what it would be like to be in a car with Paul, separated only by a few inches. Close enough that she could breathe in his intoxicating masculine scent. Just the two of them.

"Okay." Paul stood and passed the book back to Amy. "We'll go after dark. How about seven-thirty?"

"Sure."

He flashed her his engaging smile, and Amy felt her heart skip.

"It was great talking with you, Amy. I guess I'll go head for the shower before Robby gets up and uses all the hot water." He turned to leave the sunroom, but paused at the window and gazed out. "Wow! Look at it coming down. Guess we're going to have a rainy Thanksgiving. But you know what? I'm glad. We don't get many rainy autumn days out in Colorado. I miss it."

"I've always loved rainy days," Amy murmured. "Guess it's my Celtic heritage coming out."

"Oh, is that what it is?" He gave her another lopsided smile. "Guess that explains why I like rainy days, too. Later, okay?"

After he'd gone, Amy gazed down at the book in her lap, her pulse erratic. She'd lost all interest in reading about ghosts. Her mind . . . her entire being . . . was consumed with Paul.

"More mashed potatoes, Amy?" Tammy smiled across the Italian mahogany dining table, holding a crystal bowl filled with fluffy mashed potatoes. The enticing aroma of a traditional Thanksgiving Day banquet still hung in the air, even though most everyone was already on their second helpings.

"Oh, *no*, Mrs. Mulcahey." Amy clutched her stomach in protest. "If I eat another bite, I'll explode."

One professionally shaped eyebrow rose. "Amy Shiley, if you don't quit calling me 'Mrs. Mulcahey,' I swear, I'm going to have to take you over my knee. And just ask these three kids of mine, and you'll know I mean business. I *insist* you call me Tammy!"

"Better listen to her, Sunshine." Michael gave Amy a wink. "You *don't* want to cross a Southern belle with a temper as mean as a Tasmanian devil."

"Oh, *hush*, Michael! I'm not *that* bad." Tammy pouted.

"Yeah, *right*, Mom." Jeff grinned, blue eyes impish. "Remember that time I cut myself a big piece of that lemon cake Stella made for your women's club meeting? I thought you were going to shit a brick!"

Tammy glared at her youngest son. "Jeff Mulcahey! We don't use language like that at the table! *Especially* in front of your grandparents!"

Jeff looked contrite. "Sorry, Grandma. Grandpa. Could someone pass the sweet potatoes, please?"

Alice McKinney, a petite blue-haired woman in her late sixties, reached for the bowl of candied sweet potatoes and, glowering, passed them to her grandson. "I think he does it on purpose just to shock me. But it's not going to work, young man. I've heard that word once or twice in my lifetime."

"Even *used* it once or twice," said her husband, Jimmy. He was a tall, dapper man with snow-white hair and an irreverent twinkle in his blue eyes. Amy wondered if this would be how Paul would look in his seventies. Jimmy McKinney was quite a handsome man, even at the age of seventy-two. No wonder Tammy—and Robin—were so beautiful; it was in their genes.

Everybody laughed at Jimmy's wry remark, and a lovely blush crept over Alice's delicately lined face. "Oh, *you rascal*! Quit making smart remarks and pass me some more of that stuffing. Tammy, Stella has outdone herself this year."

That was the truth, Amy thought. Not that she was a big expert on Thanksgiving dinners, but somehow, she'd expected a family as rich as the Mulcaheys to have a nontraditional Thanksgiving menu—weird things like prune and raisin stuffing, artichoke hearts filled with caviar . . . and—horrible thought— maybe not even a turkey, but some exotic bird that only rich people ate. But she'd been wrong. It had been turkey and all the trimmings, and she'd bet her scholarship there'd be plenty of pumpkin pie for dessert. *Real* pumpkin pie, not the cold custard stuff with graham cracker crust that hadn't even been baked. There had also been a brown-sugar-glazed Virginia ham, made especially for Robin because—and this, Amy just couldn't believe—she didn't like turkey! Amy had never heard of anyone who didn't like turkey. But after trying the melt-in-your-mouth ham, she had to admit it ran a close second.

Paul and Jeff didn't have any trouble putting both meats away, along with everything else on the table. They were both on their third helpings when Amy had barely been able to finish her first.

Before dinner, the entire family had gathered in the family room to watch the Lions-Bears game. Nobody really cared who won, but the guys got into the spirit of it just the same. Bored by it all, but sticking around "because that's what we do on Thanksgiving," Robin did her nails and flipped through the

December issue of *Cosmopolitan*. Amy, who'd never paid attention to football, feigned an interest, because, after all, Paul was really into it. To her surprise, she found herself not only understanding the game but enjoying it. Now, if only she could see Paul playing it, she'd *really* enjoy it.

When Stella stepped into the room to announce that dinner was ready, Amy felt butterflies in her stomach. She still wasn't quite used to eating dinner with the Mulcaheys and was always afraid she'd commit some horrible gaffe. Her nervousness stayed with her for a few minutes after she first sat down at the table in the elegant dining room decorated with antiques from Europe. But as the meal progressed, she found herself relaxing. The Mulcaheys were just so down-to-earth, so accepting and . . . *warm*. Like she *was* a part of their family. Every time Michael Mulcahey called her Sunshine, she felt herself practically glow as if she *were* sunshine.

And Paul. Several times during dinner, she'd caught him gazing at her. Each time, he'd smiled, sending a flood of heat through her body all the way down to her toes.

Cohoke Crossing, she thought. *Tonight*. She couldn't wait!

Almost as if he read her thoughts, Paul looked across the table to Robin on Amy's right. "Hey, Robby! Amy and I are driving down to Cohoke Crossing tonight to see the ghost light. Want to come?"

Robin gave him a baleful glare. "Yeah, like I want to be locked in a padded cell and force-fed Celine Dion for the rest of my life."

Tammy frowned at her eldest son. "You're not going to Cohoke Crossing tonight, Paul."

Amy's heart almost stopped beating.

Paul gave his mother a quizzical look. "Why not? We don't have any plans tonight, do we?"

"Have you looked out the window in the last hour? That's freezing rain, my dear. *No way* am I allowing you to get on those icy roads tonight. I don't care if you *are* a junior in college. I'm putting my foot down on this one, Paul."

Amy's eyes flashed to the windows. *Oh, no!* It was all she could do to hold in a frustrated groan. From where she sat, she could see the rain falling in a dismal gray curtain, but if Tammy said it was freezing rain, then it probably was. What rotten luck!

Robin rolled her eyes. "*Mom!* Paul lives in Colorado, for Chrissake! Like, he doesn't know how to drive on icy roads?"

Tammy's eyes shot daggers at her daughter. "Listen, you. I'm still *very* angry about the way you've mutilated your ankle with that tattoo. So, I'd advise you to keep your mouth zipped."

Amy crossed her legs at the ankle, remembering that Tammy hadn't seen *her* tattoo yet, and judging by her reaction when Robin had showed hers off, she didn't ever plan to tell her she'd done it, too.

"Mom's right, Rob," Paul said. "I don't want to screw around with freezing rain. Snow is one thing, but this shit is lethal." His eyes darted to his grandparents. "Sorry." He turned to Amy. "Sorry, Amy. We were all set to go ghost hunting, weren't we?"

She gave him a shy smile and nodded, wishing she weren't so bitterly disappointed.

"Well, maybe we'll work it in before I leave on Sunday," he added.

Her heart began to soar again.

Tammy pushed back her chair. "Well, if that's settled, and if everyone's finished eating, I'll have Stella clear the table. Shall we have coffee and pie in the family room later? Mike will get a nice fire going, won't you, darling?"

They all moved into the family room. Michael "got a nice fire going" by flicking a switch, and the gas logs began to burn brightly. Tammy drew out a Monopoly game from a shelf in the entertainment center, and everyone gathered around the game table, reaching for their token of choice—a pewter shoe or a hat or a dog. Two hours later, Michael was the first to go bankrupt, followed in short order by Amy, Jeff, and Paul. A few minutes later, Alice and Jimmy had to throw in the towel, leaving just Tammy and Robin to play. They were ruthless competitors, which really surprised Amy because it didn't seem to fit either of their personalities. Then again, perhaps that was why Tammy was such a highly successful real-estate agent.

Amy found herself engulfed in giggles as mother and daughter wheeled and dealed and tried to take each for everything they had without the slightest twinge of regret. Finally, after several turns of bad luck and too many IRS payments, Tammy was forced to turn over all her paper money to her daughter, declaring herself bankrupt.

"*Yes!*" Robin stood up and solemnly punched her fist into the air. "I proclaim myself the Mulcahey Queen of Mo-nop-o-ly!"

Tammy glared at her daughter. "Who raised you to be so ruthless? Taking your poor old mother for everything she's got?"

"*You* did," Robin shot back. "And you know it."

Paul glanced over at Amy. "It's always these two at the end. We call it the McKinney mean streak, right, Grandpa?"

Jimmy's eyes twinkled. "Don't you blame the McKinneys for it, son. It comes from your *grandmother's* side of the family. Her ancestors came over on the *Mayflower*, and I heard tell they were so stingy, they'd skin a flea for its hide!"

"Jimmy McKinney, you rascal." Alice playfully slapped his knee. "Stop talking bad about my folks. You'd do better to look to your own if you're talking about orneriness. Your own great-granddad was a bootlegger in the hills of Kentucky, and that's where your folks got their money."

Jimmy threw back his head and brayed. "Lord, woman! Over fifty years married, and I *still* hear that about once a week!"

Amy looked from one face to another, her heart brimming with joy. *This* was the way it was supposed to be. Family life. It was just like a WASP version of *The Cosby Show*.

As if on cue, Stella stepped into the room, rolling a mahogany cart laden with a stack of china plates and cups, a silver pot of coffee, a huge, delectable-looking pumpkin pie, and a crystal bowl of real whipped cream.

As the housekeeper served generous slices of pie, Robin slipped a tape into the VCR and hit the remote's power button. "Another Mulcahey tradition," she whispered, rolling her eyes. But it was clear to Amy that she wouldn't have skipped it for the world.

Amy was ashamed to admit she'd never seen *Miracle on 34th Street*. Her family had never owned a VCR, and the TV reception they'd received on a cheap Kmart portable had been intermittent at best.

As she slipped a forkful of creamy pumpkin pie into her mouth, Amy became lost in the magic of an irresistibly young Natalie Wood in her pursuit of a father, a real home, and a family. And she realized she was very much like that little girl. She, too, was looking for a family. And speaking of miracles, she thought perhaps she'd finally found one in the Mulcaheys.

The freezing rain turned to snow in the middle of the night, and the Williamsburg area was blanketed in one of the earliest snowstorms on record, receiving a whopping sixteen inches.

Which was fine with Amy. Of course, she was disappointed that she and Paul couldn't go to Cohoke Crossing, but if she had to be snowed in, she couldn't think of a better place to be than with the Mulcaheys—especially with Paul home.

The family spent Friday relaxing, either with solitary pursuits like reading or napping—or gathering together to watch taped movies on the VCR, play board games, and of course, eat Thanksgiving leftovers. Both Robin and Tammy grumbled about missing the "after Thanksgiving Day" sales, but their griping sounded halfhearted to Amy.

On Friday afternoon, the house was exceptionally quiet as the snow continued to fall. Amy, Paul, Jeff, and Robin had spent an hour outside, building a snowman on the high bank overlooking the James. When a mischievous Jeff shoved a handful of icy snow into the back of Amy's parka, a ferocious snowball fight broke out between the sexes. A half hour later, exhausted, giggling, and half-frozen, they stomped into the mudroom, shedding coats, gloves, and boots, before trooping into the kitchen and putting water on to boil for hot chocolate.

Amy couldn't keep her eyes off Paul's wind-reddened face. His blue eyes were sparkling with humor as he teased his younger brother about his "girly" snowball-throwing technique. Jeff took the gibing in his usual good-natured way, and it was apparent to Amy that the two brothers enjoyed each other's company. Robin, too, seemed to glow like a candle around her older brother.

After the teapot began to whistle, she prepared the mugs of hot chocolate, and she and Amy brought them to the counter.

"Oh, cool!" Robin's eyes lit up as she spied a plastic-wrapped plate of cookies on the counter. "Stella made her special chewy ginger cookies for us. Amy, wait'll you try these. They're to die for."

Robin was right, Amy realized as she bit into the sugar-crusted ginger cookie. Scrumptious! She took a sip of the rich, creamy hot chocolate, and watched the interplay among the three siblings, her heart lifting with happiness. This was what she'd always dreamed of. Being a part of a warm, happy family like this. Her eyes moved again to Paul, who was grinning at his younger brother affectionately. She felt her blood quicken. And it wasn't the hot chocolate warming it. Feeling her gaze, Paul looked at her. Her cheeks grew warm. Damn! He'd caught her staring at him like he was the main course on a banquet table. He smiled and gave her a wink. She returned his smile shyly, then averted her gaze, reaching for a second cookie. God, did he realize the power of his smile?

"Okay." Robin finished her hot chocolate and stood. "I'm gonna get in the tub and try to warm up. Catch you guys later."

Jeff reached out and rumpled Paul's hair. "Pretty boy's hair's messed up!" He jumped off his stool, dodging Paul's exaggerated lunge at him, and laughing, headed for the door. "I'm gonna go check my e-mail." Still, grinning, he ambled out of the room after Robin.

Amy watched them go, and her heart began drumming. She was alone with Paul. Taking another sip of her hot chocolate, she tried to calm her nerves. When she looked up from her mug, he was watching her, an amused light in his eyes. Lifting his arm, he took an exaggerated sniff of his armpit. "Has my deodorant stopped working?" he asked in the rich tone of an actor in a television commercial.

Amy laughed. Could this guy be any more perfect? He was good-looking, had a great personality and a sense of humor.

Lifting his arms above his head, he stretched, groaning. "Man! That felt good out there, didn't it? Running around. Working off some of those calories we took in yesterday." He dropped his arms and frowned. "But I really should go hit the books. I've got a geology exam to take when I get back." But he didn't move to go.

Amy smiled at him. "Hmmm. That's sound like an interesting course. Does it cover volcanoes and stuff?" Here was something she could discuss half-intelligently. School and classes.

"I wish." Paul sighed. "Right now, it's just all about rocks and minerals. You interested in volcanoes, Amy?"

"Oh, yeah." She nodded. "I saw a PBS special about volcanoes once, and I've been fascinated ever since. There's two places in the world I'd like to go to someday. One is Ireland because that's my heritage. And the other is the Big Island in Hawaii. I'd love to see Kilauea."

"Yeah, that would be cool," Paul said. "You know where I'd like to go? Scandinavia. I saw something on a bulletin board at school about a trip there next summer, and I just might look into it."

"You should," Amy said. "I'd travel if I could. The anthropology department at William & Mary sponsors a trip somewhere every year, but I'm not eligible to go until I'm sophomore. I think it's going to be Israel next year, but . . ." She shrugged. "I'd never be able to afford it, so no use even thinking about it." All the extra money she made at the coffee shop went to pay sorority dues.

Paul gazed at her. "Well, you never know what can happen between now and next year, Amy. Maybe you can work something out."

Just as she started to reply, the phone rang, and Paul got up to answer it. A grin crossed his face as he apparently recognized the voice of the caller. "Hey! What's happening? Yeah, the timing was great. I just hope the roads are clear by Sunday so I can get to the airport."

Amy slipped off her stool and took their empty mugs to the dishwasher. When she left the kitchen, Paul was still talking to whoever it was on the phone.

By Saturday afternoon, the roads were clear, and Amy felt her hopes rise again for a trip to Cohoke Crossing. But Paul didn't bring it up, and *she* sure wasn't going to. She hated herself for that. Robin would've marched right up to him, and said, "Hey, you taking me to Cohoke Crossing tonight or not?" Even if he *weren't* her brother.

But Amy, being Amy, could only wait and hope. Everyone was on their own for dinner, Robin informed her. Stella had left for Washington, DC, to visit her daughter, and besides, she never cooked on Saturdays anyway.

"How about pizza?" Robin suggested. "We can drive into town and bring one back."

"Maybe we should get two?" Amy said. Then added nonchalantly, "You know how Jeff and Paul can put food away."

Robin shook her head, sending her cornrows clacking. "Paul's going into town to see his old girlfriend from high school. Hey, why don't we go to The Library for gyros? Maybe there'll be a couple of buff guys there to pick up."

Amy tried to swallow her disappointment. What a complete *ass* she was! To think that the trip to Cohoke Crossing meant as much to Paul as it did to her.

"Yeah," she said, trying to smile. "Let's go to The Library."

"Okay. Meet you downstairs in fifteen minutes."

Amy was ready and waiting ten minutes later when Robin ran down the stairs. She halted abruptly on the marble floor in the foyer, the smile leaving her face. "What's with the suitcase?"

"I want you to drop me off at the dorm after we eat," Amy said quietly.

"*Why?*"

"Because I've imposed long enough on your family. You need some time alone . . . without an outsider."

Robin snorted. "Well, fuck *that!*"

Amy's jaw tightened stubbornly. She picked up her suitcase and turned to the door. "I've made up my mind, and I'm not going to change it."

"We'll *see* about that," Robin said confidently, following her out the front door.

For once, Amy held up against Robin. As they ate tender lamb gyros at The Library Tavern, Robin pleaded with her to change her mind. But Amy could be stubborn when she wanted to be. Nothing on earth was going to get her to go back to the Mulcaheys' this weekend. Just the thought of facing Paul, knowing how she'd read too much into their Thanksgiving morning conversation, made her cringe. No way could she face him again. At least not until she'd built up her defenses. She felt too raw, too . . . exposed . . . to talk to him again. He would be able to see everything on her face. The hurt, the sense of betrayal, and, worse, the need for his attention. And that she wouldn't thrust upon him.

In the end, Robin had no choice but to give in. She bitched all the way to the dorm about having to go back to Windsong alone.

"What am I going to do tomorrow? Everybody is taking Paul to the airport, and I just can't stand the drive back alone with my parents. God! My life sucks! Paul gets to go to Vail for Christmas with all his college friends. Who knows when he'll be back in Williamsburg! If I were him, I'd never come back to this hellhole!"

Amy suppressed a sigh. Much as she loved Robin, for a split second, she felt like slapping her silly. She had such a great life, and all she could do was bitch about it. And hearing that Paul wouldn't be home for Christmas wasn't improving her own mood. Jeez, life *did* suck.

So, she just remained silent and allowed Robin to vent. Surely, though, Paul would come home next summer. And surely by that time she'd have rebuilt the protective armor that he had somehow managed to put a chink into during his four-day visit home.

After Robin dropped her off at the dorm, Amy slipped into her room and crawled into bed. It was early, not even nine o'clock, and the building was eerily quiet. Of course, everyone was still at home with their families. Everyone who *had* families, anyway. Amy felt the familiar ache of loneliness sweep through her. For just a few hours this holiday weekend, she'd felt almost normal. Like she really fit in somewhere. But it had just been a facade. This was reality. Being alone. Why couldn't she just accept that?

She stared, dry-eyed, up at the dark ceiling, and her thoughts returned to Paul. Their conversations echoed in her mind. Like a tongue probing a sore tooth, her brain kept replaying their moments together over and over, every word he'd spoken, every inflection of his voice. The expression on his face. His smile. His eyes, so steadfast and compelling.

And then, it was Robin's voice she heard. "Paul's going into town to see his old girlfriend from high school."

Robin had no idea how much those words had hurt.

It was silly. She knew that. Paul owed her nothing. He was just being nice to the orphan girl. The little nobody who roomed with his sister. But she couldn't help how she felt. Her heart was as heavy as a boulder at the bottom of the James River.

She wished she could cry. But she couldn't. She *wouldn't*.

Crying had never helped. She'd learned that lesson a long time ago. There was nothing to do but swallow her pain, and go on.

No matter how bad it tasted.

6

Amy yawned and stretched her legs, blinking sleep from her eyes. It was moving day. The spring semester was over, and she and Robin had to vacate the dorm for the summer. She turned on her left side to see if her roommate was awake yet, and found herself staring at the tanned, naked body of a young man with long tangled brown hair.

Jason Barelli.

Amy squeezed her eyes shut, and waited for her heartbeat to resume. *What on earth was he doing in Robin's bed?* Well, it didn't take a rocket scientist to figure that one out. But *why* in their dorm room? Didn't Robin have any shame? Having sex in her room just a foot away from her?

Curiosity got the better of her, and Amy opened her eyes again and glanced over to make sure they *were* still sleeping. They were. At least, *he* was. All she could see of Robin was one bare, shapely leg wrapped around his lean hip, obscuring, thankfully, his private parts.

But the rest of him . . . oh, my God . . . was beautiful. No wonder Robin always dropped everything when he was in town. The sex must be mindblowing. In fact, she could almost smell it permeating the room.

Amy felt the heat rush to her face as she realized where her thoughts had traveled. This was *so* not like her. But she couldn't stop herself from admiring Jason's firm muscled chest, dusted with just the right amount of light brown hair. And God! Check out those defined, solid biceps. She felt a delicious warmth curl up from her belly as she imagined what it would be like to touch such a gorgeous male.

Suddenly Jason moved one of those beautifully muscled arms, and Robin moaned softly, drawing her leg off his hip. Suppressing a gasp, Amy flopped over onto her right side and stared rigidly at the wall. For a long moment, she lay frozen, waiting for a sound from the other bed. Nothing. Just the sound of Jason's deep, even breathing. Still asleep, thank God.

She had to pee. But nothing on earth was going to get her out of this bed in front of him. Even if he *was* asleep. It would be just her luck that he'd wake up the moment she got out of bed. And she was wearing only a skimpy tank top and bikini panties. It had been an unusually hot May, and Amy had followed Robin's lead and started sleeping, not in the nude, but in as little as possible. She simply could not bring herself to get out of bed and traipse across the room like this in front of Robin's sex-crazy boyfriend.

An agonizing hour later, she was starting to rethink things. Her back teeth were *floating*! Finally, she knew she couldn't stand it another moment. Quietly, cautiously, she eased onto her back and listened. No rustle of movement from the other bed. Not even any breathing sounds now. Oh, God! *Her bladder was aching!*

She drew back the covers and took a deep breath. Then quickly, before she could change her mind, she sat up and swung her legs over the side of the bed. Her eyes darted to Robin's bed—and froze.

Jason Barelli was awake and watching her with appraising green eyes.

Amy felt her entire body flush crimson. He saw it, too, giving her a slow, sexy smile, followed by a sly wink. Her stomach plunged. She jumped off the bed like a shot and hurled herself at her closet, grabbing the first thing she found, a thick velour robe Robin had bought her for Christmas. Thrusting one arm into the sleeve, Amy flew to the door. Behind her, she heard Jason's chuckle, followed by a low murmur from Robin.

"Just checking out your roomie, Rob," Jason said, not even bothering to lower his voice. "You never told me she was such a piece of ass. *Ouch!* Hey, what'd you do that for?"

Amy hurried down the corridor toward the bathroom, cheeks burning. Not entirely with humiliation, either. She knew it was wrong—that Jason was a sexist pig, and what he'd said was a sexist pig remark—but she couldn't help but feel secretly pleased.

No one had ever called her a piece of ass before. And this from a fledgling rock star who, Robin had told her, had his pick of groupies anytime he wanted. Flustered, she stepped into the bathroom and peered into the mirror over the sink, thankful that no one else was around.

Her blond hair was tangled from sleep, her cheeks heightened with color, and her blue eyes sparkling. She opened her robe and gazed at her body clad in its white tank top and red bikini panties. After a moment, she met her eyes in the mirror and smiled. Damn it, *she was a piece of ass*! Jason said so. And maybe it was time *she* started to believe it.

★ ★ ★

"It's safe to come back into the room now. Jason's gone."

Amy looked up at the doorway of the dorm lounge and saw Robin dressed in a skimpy silk kimono. Almost an hour had passed since Amy had been driven from her room. There'd been *no way* she was going back in there, so after she'd emptied her bladder, she'd curled up in an uncomfortable vinyl chair and, still wearing the thick velour robe, began to sweat her way through stupid Saturday morning cartoons.

"Sorry," Robin said. "He showed up at our door in the middle of the night, and I told him we couldn't but . . . well, Jason can be pretty . . . you know . . . persuasive."

"How did he get past security?" Amy asked.

"Oh, we have this friend who does fake ID cards. I just had him copy my student ID, and put Jason's photo on it. That way, he can go wherever he wants on campus. God, Amy! He's really something!" She fanned herself dramatically. "I swear, he can make me come just by licking my earlobe."

Amy blushed. "God, Robin! I don't need to know that!"

"No, what you need is a good fuck. Hey, want to borrow Jason for a night? He's already told me he thinks you're a piece of ass. I'm sure he'd love to be your first screw. And hey, that's okay with me. You might as well learn from the best."

Amy scrambled up from her seat, her face on fire. "Robin, you talk such garbage sometimes. I'm going to take a shower."

Under the pulsating hot spray of the shower, Amy found herself fantasizing about Jason. Eyes closed, she slid her soapy fingers over her sensitive nipples, imagining what it would be like to have him touch her there. But every time she tried to summon Jason's face, to feel his lips pressed to hers, his hands molding her wet, naked body against his, he would disappear—and it would be Paul doing those things to her.

She wanted Paul to be the first. It had been months since she'd seen him over Thanksgiving, yet, she couldn't get him out of her mind. Crazy as it seemed, she'd fallen hard for him. Only with Paul could she imagine making love. She *needed* it to be him. And if it wasn't, then she just might have to stay a virgin for the rest of her life.

When Robin had discovered that Amy was looking for a roommate to share a tiny apartment for the summer, she was horrified. "But you *can't*! You'll come and stay with me this summer."

Amy's heart jumped. Paul! He'd be home for the summer, wouldn't he? But no, she couldn't do it. No family could be expected to take in an outsider for the whole summer.

"I couldn't impose," Amy said firmly.

Robin's brows lowered. "*Bullshit!* Where do you think you can afford to stay working that two-bit job at the coffee shop?"

"I'll be working full-time," Amy reminded her. "And they gave me a raise, you know. If I can get someone to go in with me, I'm sure I can find a place I can afford."

"Hel-*lo*? You're not going to find a decent apartment in Williamsburg on six bucks an hour. I guaran-fucking-tee it!"

Amy hesitated. "Well, I guess I can go back to my old foster parents in Newport News."

Robin grabbed her shoulders and glared at her. "Is that what you want to do?"

Amy gazed back at her and tried to lie convincingly. "It wouldn't be so bad." A moment passed as she unflinchingly met Robin's furious gaze.

"*Suck my nonexistent dick!*" Robin released her and turned away, disgusted.

Amy felt a sick wave of fear. Was she *really* mad? All these months living together in the dorm, and Robin had never once gotten *really* mad at her.

Robin whirled, her cornrow beads clacking. "You're staying with me this summer, girlfriend. I won't take no for an answer. Got *that*?"

Amy swallowed hard. "But . . . what if your parents . . . how can you . . ."

"Don't worry about them. I'll tell it like it is. Anyway, Amy, don't you know yet where my parents are concerned, you're part of the family? Hey, you keep me entertained and out of their hair. How could they not love you? And I'll be *goddamned* if I'm going to let you go spend the summer with some friggin' foster parents who don't give *jack shit* about you!"

Amy felt tears well up in her eyes, and she turned away so Robin wouldn't see. She tried to speak, but her throat had closed up with emotion. Robin sidled up next to her and wrapped her arms around her.

"I love you, Amy," she said, her voice uncharacteristically solemn. "You're my best friend . . . no, more than that. You're like a sister to me. Don't you know that? I just couldn't get through the summer without you."

"I'll still have to work," Amy murmured.

"Only part-time. Hey, it's summer, girlfriend." Robin smiled. "And we've got some serious partying to do!"

This time, Amy couldn't hold back her tears. She clutched Robin, and for a long moment, they hugged each other silently. It was then that Amy realized Robin needed her just as much as she needed Robin.

To Amy's surprise and delight, Tammy and Michael appeared genuinely thrilled to have her in their home for the summer. When she first arrived a couple of days after school was out, she nearly tripped over herself thanking them for their generosity. Tammy put a quick end to that.

"All right. That's enough of that, Amy Shiley. From this day forward, I want you to think of yourself as a member of this family. Robin told us you're all alone in the world, but I'm here to tell you you're not. You've got *us*. And anytime Robin comes home, I expect you to be with her. I want you to consider *our* home *your* home, is that clear, young lady?"

Amy swallowed hard. She nodded.

"Okay, then," Tammy said briskly. "Go upstairs and get your swimsuit on. Stella is serving lunch out by the pool."

An hour later, Amy and Robin were lying in lounge chairs by the pool. Robin's entire lithe body gleamed with coconut oil, and she smelled like a human piña colada. Amy had diligently covered herself in sunblock with a 30 SPF because she knew from experience that without protection, her fair skin would turn lobster red within a half hour.

"Aren't you worried about burning?" she asked Robin, applying another coat of sunblock to her face.

Robin's mirrored sunglasses shot her reflection back at her. "Hell, no! I never burn. I always get this gorgeous golden tan that most people would kill for." She giggled gleefully. "If you ask me, there was some hanky-panky going on back in my great-great-great-grandfather's day. I mean, after all, if Thomas Jefferson paid some visits to the slave quarters, why not good old Grandpappy Mulcahey, huh?"

"Shhh!" Amy glanced past Robin to the back terrace. "Here comes your mom."

"Oh, shit. What does *she* want?"

Tammy had appeared on the deck dressed immaculately in a sea foam rayon sheath with a matching jacket. Holding an alligator briefcase in one slender diamond-decked hand, she walked over to them. "I have a showing this afternoon," she announced, then turned to Robin, her eyes invisible behind dark sunglasses. "Tell your father I don't know if I'll be home for dinner or not." She turned to go, but then hesitated, her gaze fixed on Amy.

"Amy Shiley, what *is* that on your ankle, young lady?"

Amy's stomach dipped, and hot color flooded her face. She quickly covered the ladybug tattoo with her other ankle, even though she knew it was too late.

Robin answered for her, a smirk on her sunblock-slathered face. "It's a *lady-bug*, Mom. You've never seen one before?"

Slowly, Tammy lifted her sunglasses and stared at Amy, her blue eyes sparkling with amusement. "You little imp," she said with a mock frown. "How long have you had that?"

Amy shrugged and cast her eyes on an orange butterfly flitting around the pink azalea bush bordering the deck. It suddenly seemed too quiet out here. There was just the sound of cicadas humming and the hiss of the sprinkler watering the lawn that stretched down to the James River. Amy looked at Robin, who rolled her eyes and released an exasperated sigh.

"She got it at the same time I got mine, Mom," Robin said. A smug smile crept over her face. "But she didn't tell you after you freaked out about mine. Who could blame her? You acted like I cut off my right tit or something."

Tammy dropped her sunglasses back in place and glared at her daughter. "You'd better watch your mouth, missy. You're not too big for me to take a switch to you. Listen, I'm running late, so I've got to go." She turned and headed back to the house, high heels clicking on the stone walkway.

Robin scowled after her. "Bitch," she muttered.

"Hey!" Amy admonished. "Don't be so hard on her. I think she took it pretty well. Considering how she reacted when you showed her yours."

Robin swung her tanned legs off the lounge chair and stood, her bikini-clad body gleaming with suntan oil. "You see only the Tammy she wants you to see," she said shortly, before stalking off and diving into the deep end of the pool.

That night in Robin's room, the two of them sprawled on her massive king-size bed with Ruby Two-Shoes curled between them, and for the first time, Amy found herself opening up about her mother's psychotic breaks. About the drinking and the drugs. The years of neglect and poverty. And she even managed to tell her about the worst day of her life.

"I was thirteen," Amy said slowly, tracing a line in the leopard-print suede-like comforter covering the bed. "I came home from school one day and found my mother passed out in the living room. The floor was covered with liquor bottles, and the place looked like a friggin' tornado had hit it. Nothing new about that. But then I . . . went into the bathroom and found . . ." She stopped, seeing the horror all over again in her mind. She shook her head, trying to dispel the image of her father sitting on the toilet stool, eyes staring, half of his skull shattered, and blood everywhere.

". . . my father," she said softly. "He'd shot himself with the army-issue gun he'd had in Vietnam."

Robin drew in a sharp breath of dismay, her blue eyes huge in her suddenly pale face. "Oh, Amy! Jesus, that's awful."

"Yeah. Pretty awful. That's why I don't talk about them much. Or myself. My childhood was really . . . well . . . let's just say it sucked." She looked at her friend. "I wanted to tell you about it because I want you to know just how much your friendship . . . and the acceptance of your family . . . means to me. This is all I've ever wanted in my life. A normal family, and . . . I just . . ." Her voice broke, and she bit her bottom lip, unable to continue.

"I catch your drift," Robin said, her own eyes misty. She reached over and gave Amy a short, hard hug. "And damn it, I'm glad you're here, too. I wouldn't have it any other way." She released Amy and pulled a protesting Ruby Two-Shoes onto her lap. "So, do you ever go see your mom?"

Amy took a deep trembling breath. "I always go on her birthday. August 18. I do it for myself rather than for her. It's guilt, I guess. Or a sense of obligation. There's really not much point in it, though. She never recognizes me. She's been in a catatonic state for the last three years. If there's ever any change in her condition, the hospital would notify me."

Robin was silent for a moment, her eyes downcast as she stroked the cat's orange fur. Ruby gave a soft yowl of protest and twitched her tail. "Why do you *hate* me? Just go, then!" Robin scowled, pushing the cat off her lap. Ruby jumped off the bed and stalked to the door, then turned and mewed imperiously. Grumbling, Robin let her out. She closed the door, then turned. "You say it's a sense of obligation, but you know what? I think it's more than that. You love her, don't you? Despite all she's done to you."

Amy met Robin's gaze. "I guess so. Isn't that weird? I can only remember a couple of times she ever hugged me or tucked me into bed when I was little. Mostly, she just ignored me. But yes, I suppose I *do* still love her. I guess that's why they say 'blood is thicker than water,' huh?"

Robin's eyes fell. "I wish I could love *my* mother like that," she murmured.

Amy couldn't believe she'd heard her right. Was she talking about *Tammy*? What was not to love? "Robin, how can you say such a thing?"

Robin's eyes met hers, and Amy saw something flicker deep in their depths. Pain . . . disillusionment? Robin shook her head slightly. "Someday, Amy, I'll tell you about *my* childhood. Not now. You couldn't handle it now. But promise me something." Her hand reached out and covered Amy's. "Don't get too close to my parents. I don't want you to get hurt."

The summer at Windsong began with lazy days reading juicy romances by the rock-edged pool with its waterfall and adjoining hot tub, and summer evenings hanging out in Williamsburg, drinking and partying into the wee hours. Well, Robin was the one drinking. As always, Amy willingly played the part of designated driver. She did it so often she almost began to think of Robin's Tracker as hers. Robin even insisted Amy drive it on the two or three days a week she had to work at the coffee shop near campus.

On her days off, there were trips to Virginia Beach and Busch Gardens. Amy couldn't bring herself to admit that she'd never been to an amusement park before, just to a couple of those shopping center carnival setups that traveled across country. Once, when she was eleven, Melissa had invited her to go with her family to King's Dominion. But when her friend's parents found out that Amy couldn't pay her own way, they'd gently told her that maybe she could come along some other time. It had been a crushing humiliation, one that Amy had never forgotten. She'd just assumed they were offering to pay when she'd accepted the invitation.

That's why it bothered her when Robin presented her with a summer pass to Busch Gardens; she'd bought it without even asking. After a futile argument, Amy had accepted it, but promised to pay her back out of her paychecks from the coffee shop.

And the first time they went to Busch Gardens, it had been an absolute blast. Of course, Robin, being the exuberant person that she was, insisted on going on every ride—the more terrifying, the better. Knowing there was no point in arguing with her, Amy, her heart pounding, had joined her on the Alpengeist, an inverted coaster which took the rider upside down six times— and through a freakin' corkscrew. She'd not only survived the ride, but had discovered she could well become a roller-coaster junkie. After that, Amy and Robin spent the rest of the day going from one coaster to another.

On the way home, Robin had pleaded with her to quit her job for the summer, so they'd have more time to have fun, but that was one thing Amy refused to do. She needed that job, especially when next semester started. So on the days or occasional evenings that she worked at the coffee shop, Robin usually rode into town with her and spent the time hanging out with their few friends from college who'd stayed in Williamsburg for the summer.

It was all working out. Amy felt like she'd died and gone to heaven. It had never been like this with the foster families she'd lived with. There'd never been this sense of belonging, of real acceptance. Although Amy had tried to get Robin to explain her strange words of caution about her parents, she'd refused to elaborate, and finally, Amy had just dismissed it. Robin could be so overdramatic. She liked being the center of attention. And truth to tell, these off-the-wall comments about Michael and Tammy kind of bugged Amy. It was almost as if Robin, upon hearing about Amy's tough childhood, felt the need to compete with her so she made these vague comments hinting at less-than-perfect parents. As *if*! It was pathetic, really. But then, that was Robin. Always had to be in the spotlight.

But Amy wasn't about to let Robin's vague comments affect the way she felt about Michael and Tammy. She loved being here with the Mulcaheys, and truly felt a part of them. There were family barbecues in the evenings, sitting out on the stone pool deck, drinking in the sweet fragrance of blue Chinese wisteria from the nearby trellis walkway mingling with the hickory wood chips Michael had placed in the gas grill to barbecue thick sirloins. The splash of water as Jeff cannonballed into the cool green depths of the pool. The chirp of crickets and the twitter of birds settling down for the evening. It was almost perfect.

Except . . . Paul wasn't there.

He'd gone to Europe for the summer. An opportunity had come up for him to join students from other countries on an educational tour of Scandinavia. And he'd jumped at it, as Amy had urged him to do back when they'd talked about the places they wanted to go someday. Robin had offhandedly given her the news on the day they moved out of the dorm. She'd had no idea of the impact of her words. He wouldn't be coming home until the first of August, and then only for two weeks before heading back to UC for his last year of college.

Two weeks. That's all she'd have with him. What would it be like to see him again? Would he even remember her? Would he remember their plans to go to Cohoke Crossing? She was doing it again. Hoping. Dreaming. Putting way too much importance on an offhand invitation he'd probably never thought of again after Thanksgiving night. Why did she do this to herself?

Because she loved him. Crazy as it seemed, she loved a guy who barely knew she existed. It was as simple as that.

★ ★ ★

The Mulcaheys threw a huge barbecue on July 4, inviting over fifty guests to swim, eat, and celebrate the nation's birthday. Michael had ordered fresh crabs from Maryland and cooked them in giant vats set up in the backyard and fired by great piles of wood. Along with the tender white crabmeat, there were platters stacked high with roasted corn on the cob dripping with melted butter, Crockpots of baked beans, and for the rambunctious kids, hamburgers and hot dogs. Dessert had been fresh-churned peach ice cream and later, as the fireworks exploded over the James River—courtesy of Mike Mulcahey—marshmallows toasted over a bonfire for S'mores.

It had been a sweltering day, with temperatures reaching nearly one hundred. After the last of the fireworks lit up the sky, and the last of the guests departed, Jeff jumped into the pool where he'd spent most of the day, and coaxed Robin and Amy to join him. Most of the grown-ups, including Amy and Robin, had resisted going into the pool earlier. Robin loved swimming, but not with "a bunch of obnoxious brats whose favorite game is to plunge underwater and pinch your nipples." She spoke like she knew what she was talking about, so any inclination Amy had had for going swimming quickly evaporated. But once the guests left, they reconsidered the idea. Amy and Robin raced up to their rooms to don their swimsuits, and when they stepped back onto the torchlit stone patio, they saw Jeff and Mike in the pool, fighting over possession of a small rubber ball.

Robin stopped short, frowning. "Oh, shit!"

"What?"

She exhaled a disgusted breath. "I might've known. You go ahead and get in if you want, but I'm going into the hot tub."

Amy stared at her, aghast. "It's ninety degrees out here. And you want to cook yourself?"

Robin stalked over to the hot tub section of the pool area. "If it's between that and sharing the pool with those two, *yes.*"

Amy shrugged and headed for the steps leading into the shallow end of the pool. The water felt blessedly cool around her ankles.

"Hey!" Jeff called out, his adolescent face lighting up in a grin. "Don't be such a wimp! Dive in."

"I don't know *how* to dive," Amy said. "Or swim, for that matter."

"No *way*! I thought you grew up near the ocean."

Amy held her breath as the water rose around her waist. It had gone from cool to cold. She shook her head, breathing in the strong scent of chlorine. "Not close enough. And my parents never got around to giving me swimming lessons." Or *any* lessons.

Jeff dived into the water and surfaced next to her. His freckled face gleamed in the light of the torches, his Paul-like smile flashing engagingly. "I'll teach you. Tomorrow, okay?"

"I have to work tomorrow."

"What about Sunday? Or Monday? How about it, huh? I can teach you to swim on Monday."

Amy smiled at him. She knew he had a crush on her. And even though he was only fifteen, it was good for her ego. It was nice to be appreciated by the male sex. Besides, she *liked* Jeff. He was funny and cute and kind. To her, at least. Robin thought he was one of those obnoxious brats.

"Okay, Jeff. It's a deal. Swimming lessons on Monday."

"*All right!* Cool."

"Sunshine, *catch!*"

Amy turned just in time to see Mike toss the rubber ball at her. She grabbed it, laughing. "What are we playing? Keep away?"

"Yeah, from Jeff! Throw it to me."

Jeff jumped up, trying to reach the ball but it went over his head. Mike caught it and threw it back. The game grew progressively rough, until finally, Jeff caught the ball, and Amy found herself in the middle, trying to capture it.

"Hey, Cupcake," Mike called over to Robin, who was sitting in the hot tub gazing blankly into one of the flaming torches. "Quit being so stuck-up and come over here and play with us."

Robin threw them a bored look. "I'm fine right here."

"Awww, *come on!*"

She hunched a shoulder and turned away. "*Piss off!*"

Amy caught her breath and waited for Mike to explode. She knew Robin was a firecracker, but she couldn't believe even *she* would have the nerve to talk to her father like that. But amazingly, Mike didn't get angry. He just shrugged and gave Jeff a wink. "Must be that time of the month."

Jeff snickered. "It's *always* that time of the month with her."

Mike laughed and dived toward his son, surfacing in front of him and reaching out to dunk him under the water. "Gotcha!" The two of them struggled playfully.

Amy looked back toward the trellised walkway leading to the screened-in porch. "How come Tammy's not out here with us?"

Mike bobbed up in front of her, grinning. "Have you ever seen Tammy with her hair messed up? No? That's why you never see her in the pool."

"How can she *not* want to get in? It feels wonderful!"

Jeff floated by on his back. "You want to know why? Because the chlorine turns her hair green. It doesn't mix well with the dye she uses." Then, laughing, he turned over and dived under. He surfaced a moment later, swam to the edge of the pool and pushed himself onto the deck. "I'm gonna go get some watermelon. Anybody else want any?"

"Not me, thanks." Amy looked over at Mike. "I wish I could float like that. Do you think that'll be part of the swimming lesson?"

"I'll teach you." Without waiting for a reply, Mike swam over and grabbed her around the waist, towing her to the deeper end.

"Oh, no! Mike, I'm not ready!"

"Nothing to be scared of. I've got you."

Suddenly he picked her up, cupping his arm under her knees. Amy's heart jumped. She really *was* afraid of deep water.

"Just relax now," Mike said, holding her securely in his arms. "I won't let go."

"You sure?"

He grinned down at her, blue eyes dancing. Amy tried to relax. Somehow, Mike reminded her of Paul tonight. Maybe it was something to do with his wet hair being slicked back or the bone structure of his face. He really was a handsome man, she thought. In fact, the whole Mulcahey clan looked like they'd come from central casting.

"Okay, this is what I want you to do," Mike said. "Remember . . . I've got hold of you, and I'm not going to let you go. I want you to lean back so the back of your head is in the water."

"Oh, no!"

"Yes. I promise I won't let you go. Not until you're ready."

Amy glanced over at Robin to see her staring at them intently. "Can I trust him, Robin?"

Robin didn't speak immediately. Then she shrugged. "He's a man. What do *you* think?"

"Hey, I taught *her* to swim," Mike said with a grin. "And she didn't drown, did she?"

"Okay. I'll try it. I guess."

"Good. Now, lean back."

Heart pounding, Amy did as Mike instructed. She could feel his strong arms holding her securely, and after a moment, she relaxed a bit and felt her head touching the water.

"Now, stretch out your legs. That's it. Make your body a straight line like you're lying on a bed."

"You've got me?"

"I've got you. That's it! That's perfect, Sunshine. Okay . . . you feel my hands under the small of your back?"

"Uh-huh." The water felt delicious all around her, caressing her skin like cool lotion.

"Well, they're there, but they're not keeping you afloat. You're doing it all by yourself."

Amy felt herself tense. "I am?"

"Relax, now. Thatta girl. Okay. I want to let you go now. Is that okay?"

"*No!*" Amy felt herself starting to sink.

"*Relax!* Just feel the water around you. As long as you keep your head back, and your legs stretched out, you're going to float."

"You're sure?"

"I'm sure." He paused a moment, then said, "You know how I know I'm sure?"

Amy shook her head, keeping her eyes closed.

"Because I'm not holding you. You're floating by yourself."

Amy lifted her head in panic and immediately began to sink.

"Put your head back. Stretch your legs out. That's it. Now, extend your arms. You're doing it, Sunshine. You're floating."

After her initial fear passed, she relished in the wonderful weightlessness of her body, the cool caress of the water cradling her. She even got the nerve to paddle her hands through the water and move from one spot to another.

"So, how do I stop when I'm tired?" she called over to Mike.

"Just put your feet down."

She tried it, and it worked. Scooping her wet hair back from her face, she moved through the water toward the shallow end. "Wow! Thanks! But that did me in. Maybe I'll have some watermelon now." She looked over at the hot tub and saw it was empty. Her eyes moved to Mike. "Where did Robin go?"

"Inside." He was gazing at her with a strange look on his face. One she'd never seen before. His expression was solemn, but his eyes were bright. It was almost as if he were admiring her, yet, it was something else, too. Something that made her feel weird and uncomfortable. But in a second, the look was gone. He smiled, and Amy began to think maybe she'd imagined that strange expression. Maybe it was just distortion caused by the light of the flickering torches.

"Hey, I have an idea," Mike said. He swam to the edge of the pool and pushed himself out, then reached for a robe and donned it. The clatter of fire-crackers somewhere in the distance broke the stillness. He turned around, tying the belt of his robe. "Come on, Sunshine. I'll make you a Mike Mulcahey special."

Amy climbed the steps of the pool onto the deck. Mike was waiting with a towel. He wrapped it around her, his hands pressing into her shoulders. For a moment, it was like a caress, almost a hug, then he released her.

He led her into the kitchen and opened the freezer door, drawing out a quart of Häagen-Dazs vanilla ice cream. Amy took a seat on one of the barstools, drawing her huge terry beach towel closer around her. It was chilly in the air-conditioned room. She'd been in such a rush to get into the pool, she hadn't thought to bring down a cover-up with her. Mike whistled as he opened cabinet doors, bringing out a bottle of coconut rum. Amy's stomach tightened.

"You're what, nineteen?" Mike asked.

Amy nodded.

"Then this'll be *our* secret. Yours and mine." He filled a blender jar with ice cream, took two cans of Hawaiian Punch out of the refrigerator, and poured it into the blender. Then he reached for the coconut rum.

Amy took a deep breath, and said, "Mike, I don't drink."

He turned and looked at her. Then he grinned. "This is a joke, right? You're best friends with my daughter, and you're telling me you don't *drink*?"

Amy shook her head, and the grin disappeared from his face. "You're serious. You really don't drink?"

"My parents were alcoholics. I've seen what booze does to people."

He put the cap back on the rum bottle. "Well, then . . . we'll just have to
have virgin Mike Mulcahey Specials."

"*You* don't have to."

He shrugged, shoving the rum bottle back into the cabinet. "Hey, Mike
Mulcahey Specials are so great, they don't *need* booze." He looked over his
shoulder and winked at her, grinning. "Right, Sunshine?"

"If you say so." Amy smiled back, relieved she hadn't offended him.

He punched the button of the blender, and it roared to life. As its contents
whirred to a creamy slush, Mike stuck a small bowl under the crushed ice dis-
penser of the refrigerator, and filled it. He stopped the blender, dropped in the
ice, and hit the button again. Another thirty seconds in the blender, and it was
done.

"All right! You ready for the taste sensation of your life, Sunshine?" He
filled two tall glasses with the creamy pink mixture and passed one across the
bar to Amy.

She tasted it. "Mmmm . . . it *is* good."

"The ice cream is my secret ingredient."

"Aha!" Amy grinned at him. "Now that I know your secret, maybe I'll start
marketing these myself." Funny, how comfortable she felt with Mike. This was
probably the first time in her life she'd ever actually bantered with someone of
the opposite sex. But then, again, this was Robin's *father*, so it didn't count.

He laughed and took a sip. "Maybe we should go into business together.
My recipe, and your business savvy?"

Amy grinned at him. "How do you know I *have* business savvy?"

"*What's going on in here?*"

Amy knew it was Robin's voice she heard, even though it didn't sound anything like her. It was too angry . . . and there was something else. Was it *fear*?
Amy turned to see her standing in the doorway of the kitchen, wearing a thick
white terry-cloth robe. Her hair was slicked back as if she'd just gotten out of
the shower. But it was the expression on her face that really caught Amy's
attention. It was a pinched, totally stressed-out look as she stared at her
father—one that Amy had never seen on her friend's face before. And was it
her imagination or did she look pale?

Amy opened her mouth to ask her what was wrong, but before she could
speak, Mike said, "We're just having a conversation about going into business
together. Making my special Hawaiian Punch slushes."

Robin's eyes didn't veer from her father's. "You're not getting her drunk,
are you?"

The beat of a moment went by as father and daughter eyed each other. The
tension in the room was palpable as some kind of secret message seemed to

pass between them. Amy squirmed on her stool. It was as if she were witness-
ing a private moment that she had no business being a part of. But the moment
passed, and Mike gave Robin his usual easy grin.

"Keep your shorts on, Cupcake. Amy told me she doesn't drink, so I made
both of us virgin piña coladas. What's with you, anyway? You've suddenly
appointed yourself the family vice officer?"

Robin didn't return his smile, but some of the tension appeared to leave
her body. She looked at Amy, and summoned a smile. It seemed forced,
though. "Hey, girlfriend. I just put *Pretty Woman* in the VCR. Come watch it
with me?"

Amy shrugged and slid off the stool, then remembered to grab her drink.
"Sure, why not? We've only seen it, what? A hundred times?"

She really couldn't understand Robin's fascination with a gorgeous prosti-
tute who somehow manages to get a handsome billionaire to sweep her off in
his limo for a happily-ever-after, but hey, a girl's gotta have her dreams.

Amy was halfway to the door of the kitchen before she stopped abruptly
and turned back to Mike. "Oh! Thanks for teaching me how to float, Mist . . . I
mean . . . Mike." She grinned and raised her drink into the air. "*And* for the
Mike Mulcahey Special."

He winked at her and toasted her with his own drink. "Anytime, Sunshine.
Just say the word."

Amy smiled, thinking how much he reminded her of Paul.

Robin was waiting at the doorway, and even though her face revealed nothing, Amy sensed she was still angry . . . or whatever it was that was wrong with
her. *Something* was definitely bothering her. Maybe when the movie was over,
she'd open up.

But she didn't. She didn't say a word about her moodiness or her father. Or
anything. Once the credits rolled, she simply said she was tired and wanted to
go to sleep. Amy stared at her, thinking how it was so *not* like Robin to want to
go to bed before midnight.

"Robin . . ." She started to ask her what was wrong. But when she saw the
closed look on her friend's face, she couldn't bring herself to say more. Quietly,
Amy slipped off the bed and headed for the door. She looked back to see that
Robin had turned onto her side, curling up into a tight ball. Vulnerable-looking,
Amy thought. Something she'd never dreamed Robin could be.

"Good night," Amy said softly.

But Robin didn't answer. She didn't say anything at all.

7

August 10. That was the day Paul's flight got into Dulles from Stockholm. The whole family planned to drive up to northern Virginia to pick him up. They'd make a day of it, Mike suggested, because Paul's connecting flight from New York didn't get in until evening. Maybe they'd spend the day on the Mall, tour the Smithsonian museums, the National Gallery of Art. Have lunch at the Hard Rock Cafe or maybe Planet Hollywood. Amy had never been to either place, or, for that matter, to Washington, DC. The U.S. government wasn't something her parents had exactly rejoiced in. So, Amy had been thrilled by the plan to spend a day in the nation's capital. Still, the excitement of exploring Washington paled in comparison to how she felt about Paul's return.

He'd be home for almost two weeks before returning to school in Colorado on the twenty-second. Amy's heart jolted as the date sank in. Oh, God! She'd forgotten about her mother's birthday. It was the eighteenth. Ever since Mama had been admitted to the rest home, Amy had made a point of visiting her on her birthday. Not, that she even noticed. Year after year, she just sat there like a moss-covered rock, dead-eyed, her beautiful hands plucking listlessly at the blanket that covered her bony legs. What she was trying so desperately to rid herself of, Amy didn't know. Her mother would never miss her if she decided not to show. Undoubtedly, she didn't have the vaguest idea that the day was special at all.

Amy knew it was, though. And she knew that something deep inside her—some vestige of love and loyalty—compelled her to be there. She wouldn't be able to live with herself if she didn't visit her mother on this one special day of the year. No big deal. She'd just get up early on that Monday morning and borrow Robin's Tracker for the drive to Richmond. She'd spend the day with Mama and come home that evening, family duty completed.

But with one phone call, her plan was shot to hell. It was Paul, calling from Oslo. He'd hooked up with a friend on the Scandinavian trip, and they were going to San Francisco for a week. He'd be home late on the seventeenth.

Amy got the news from Tammy at breakfast on a Saturday morning in early August. She'd just taken a bite of a buttery croissant topped with strawberry jam, and when Tammy announced the disappointing news, the roll became as tasteless and unappealing as stale wheat bread. *Four days instead of the eleven she'd counted on.* And one of those days, she'd be spending with her mother.

Well, she just wouldn't go this year. Mama didn't know she was there anyway, so what did it matter? She just wouldn't go!

Tammy set her china cup into its saucer and frowned at Mike across the table. "I just don't understand Paul sometimes. We haven't seen him since Thanksgiving. First, he goes to Vail for Christmas and then to San Padre Island for spring break. Now, he's in Norway. And instead of coming home for two weeks like he said, he's only going to be here four days. Maybe I'm too sensitive, but I'm kind of hurt. Doesn't he care about us at all?"

Mike buttered a warm blueberry muffin and tossed a consoling smile to his wife. "Oh, now, don't start feeling sorry for yourself, Mommy. You've got to remember your firstborn is a man now. Don't you remember what it's like to be twenty-one? The *last* thing on his mind is going to be his parents and how much they miss him."

Tammy sighed and took a sip of the rich Kona coffee Stella had just poured. "I suppose you're right, but that doesn't make it any easier. I miss him!"

"Miss who?"

Amy turned to see Robin in the threshold of the dining room. She wore a floor-length silk robe in hues of emerald green and teal, and her blond hair was still tangled from sleep. Funny, how decorous she was at home, Amy thought. No prancing around in skimpy underwear in the hallowed halls of Windsong.

"Your brother," Tammy answered glumly. "He just called from Oslo to tell us he won't be home on the tenth, after all. He's going to San Francisco with a friend."

"Bummer." Robin shrugged, plopping into a chair and in the same movement, reaching for the crystal pitcher of freshly squeezed orange juice. It was her "must have" morning beverage. Amy, who was addicted to coffee, couldn't understand how Robin managed to function early in the morning with only vitamin C to take the place of caffeine. But thinking of Robin's energy, Amy couldn't imagine what caffeine would do to her, so perhaps nature was on the right track.

Amy reached for her near-empty cup of coffee just as Stella materialized at her side to pour her another. She smiled her thanks and was rewarded with a wink from the congenial middle-aged housekeeper. Or was Stella the cook? Come to think of it, Amy had never heard the Mulcaheys refer to her position at all. She was simply Stella. Whatever, Amy had grown close to the woman, thanks to a rainy Saturday afternoon when she'd helped Stella make peanut butter cookies while Robin slept off a Friday night binge.

"So, is he not coming home at all?" Robin asked after gulping down her orange juice.

"He's coming home, Cupcake," Mike said. "A week later. But only for a few days."

Robin rolled her eyes. "Gee, I can't imagine why he'd rather jet-set around the world than spend the summer in the jewel of the Mid-Atlantic. I mean, where else can you walk into an un-air-conditioned courthouse and listen to ugly white-wigged men in hosiery spout off about church taxes and stupid old proclamations that nobody understands, anyway? Who in their right mind would choose Norway over that?"

"We get your point," Mike said dryly.

Tammy glared at her daughter. "There are thousands of tourists who pay good money to come to Williamsburg in the summer. And I'll have you know that you're very lucky to have grown up here. You think you have it bad? Well, you saw where I grew up. Out in the country, miles from everywhere. And believe me, my parents were a lot stricter than we are. I wasn't allowed to gallivant around like you do, missy."

Stricter than they are? Amy's lips twitched as she stared down at the flaky bits of croissant littering her elegant Noritake plate. The Mulcaheys really didn't consider themselves strict parents, did they?

Robin's amused blue eyes met hers across the table. Amy could practically read her mind.

Here we go. Mom is going to go off on one of her "you had it easy, wait 'til I tell you what kind of childhood I had to put up with" tirades.

Apparently, it was something she'd heard before. Many times before.

Amy reached for her coffee as Tammy droned on about her privileged but boring life in the Tidewater mansion, as Mike's eyes sparkled with amused tolerance. Robin reached for a box of Froot Loops and filled her china bowl to the brim. Amy got the distinct feeling she'd already tuned her mother out, and was thinking about the day's plan to head for the beach.

It was obvious that Paul's late arrival didn't bother her in the least. But why should it? She wasn't in love with him. What would she think if she knew of Amy's feelings for her brother? Would she approve? Or would she be horrified? Even worse, what if she laughed at the impossibility of it all? Or . . . cringing thought . . . what if her only reaction was to show pity to her deranged wallflower friend who thought that someone like Paul could ever be attracted to her?

She wouldn't tell her. Not ever. This was one secret she'd have to keep to herself. At least until she could laugh at it with her.

Amy had finally decided not to go to Richmond. But when it came right down to it, she felt terribly guilty. On the morning of the seventeenth, she awoke with the fragment of a dream still hovering in her mind. A birthday party, complete with balloons, swags of crepe paper, and even a decorated cake. *Happy Birthday, Mama!* And there they were, the two of them, eating cake and opening presents. It was not the mother she knew, though, not the sallow-faced alcohol-ravaged mother of her teens. Nor the empty-eyed, vacant stranger she'd visited in the nursing home for the last four years. It was a fresh-faced beautiful young woman with golden brown hair and sparkling blue eyes, the way she'd looked in a photograph taken years before she'd had Amy. Years before she'd taken to dyeing her hair black and rimming her eyes with thick liner that gave her the look of a motorcycle moll. Years before she'd hooked up with her drug-addicted husband and become a slave to her own addiction. It was a mother Amy had never known, but had only imagined in late-night fantasies and afternoon daydreams.

But in this dream, her mother smiled at her, eyes warm with love and tenderness. And as the remnants of the dream faded, Amy awoke, knowing she had to go to Richmond. She had to be there for her mother on this one day of the year. Maybe this would be the day she'd look at her, and Amy would see recognition in her blank blue eyes.

"I'm here to see Vicky Shiley," Amy told the nurse at the workstation on the fourth floor of the nursing home. Since Amy had been only fifteen when Vicky's psyche disappeared into the black hole of nothingness, and there had been no insurance, no money, and no known relatives, her mother had been made a ward of the state and relegated to this bleak place on the outskirts of Richmond. But Amy figured it could be worse. At least the nurses were nice.

This one, a pretty redhead, looked up and gave her a brilliant smile. "Oh, you're her daughter, aren't you?" At Amy's nod, she went on, "They're finishing up her bath right now, but it shouldn't be too long before you can go in and see her."

"It's her birthday today," Amy said, wondering if they knew.

"Oh, yes, we know! We've got her room all decorated. Wait 'til you see it. Balloons and everything."

"She's going to be thirty-seven."

"Really? She looks much younger."

That's the great irony, Amy thought. While Mom had been boozing it up, she'd looked twice her age. The blue-black-dyed hair, the heavy eyeliner, and the drugs and alcohol had hardened her, adding years to her features. Now that she was living . . . existing . . . in some faraway land locked deep inside her mind, she looked almost childlike in her innocence.

Amy took a deep breath and asked, "Is she . . . I mean . . . has there been any change?"

The nurse's smile dimmed. "I'm afraid not. I'm sorry."

Every year it was the same. Even though she knew in her heart what the answer would be, she kept asking the same question. And every year, she'd wilt in disappointment at the reply. Of course, if there had been a change, they would have notified her. So why did she always have that tiniest scrap of hope when she asked the question?

Amy took a seat in the lounge and reached for a *People* magazine on the end table. She gazed down at the photo of a glowing Princess Di taken at the auction of her gowns in Washington, DC. Maybe if she looked like *her*, she'd get Paul's attention.

He'd come in late last night, eyes etched with fatigue and clothes rumpled from the long flight from San Francisco. He'd barely spoken to his family, much less to Amy, before stumbling up to his room and falling into bed, exhausted. Apparently, his new friend in California had kept him busy the week he'd spent there. He was still asleep when Amy got up early this morning and left for Richmond.

"Amy?" The red-haired nurse popped her head into the lounge. "You can go see your mother now."

"Thanks."

Amy's footsteps slowed as she approached her mother's room. As usual, being here in this awful place brought depression descending upon her like an unwelcome cloak. The pitiful scraps of humanity that dwelled in this building seemed to reach out and grasp her as she passed their rooms. A grizzled old lady with a walker, her stringy gray hair tied back in a youthful ponytail, glared at her as she approached. "Where is my Jimmy?" she snarled. "What did you do with him?"

Amy looked away and hurried past her.

"Jimmy!" The woman called querulously. "Where are you?"

Mama's room smelled of Ivory soap and baby powder, evidence that they'd just finished with her bath. Mama's roommate occupied the bed closest to the door. She appeared to be asleep, her open mouth and beaked nose just visible above the covers.

As the nurse had mentioned, Mama's side of the room was decorated with balloons and streamers. A few greeting cards straddled her bedside table, the flowery ones that always had some corny poem in them. From the nurses, probably. God knows nobody else would send them to her. Poor Mama. Her own family had disowned her when she'd taken off with Amy's father at the age of sixteen. Amy had never met her grandparents on either side. Her parents had been rebels, needing no one but each other. A recipe for disaster when it came to their lone offspring—and for themselves, for that matter. God, in his wisdom, must have realized his mistake, and made sure that Vicky and Ray Shiley brought only *one* child into the world.

Mama sat in a chair by the window, hands in her lap, and they were still for once. She wore a pretty pink cotton nightgown and a matching robe. They looked new. Amy wondered where they'd come from. Her long hair, light brown now except for the dyed black ends, looked freshly brushed and was drawn back from her face and fastened with gold barrettes. Someone, the nurses, perhaps, had applied a bit of blush to her high cheekbones and tinged her lips with a pink gloss to match her robe.

"We prettied her up for her birthday," a nurse said as she changed the sheets on the bed.

Amy smiled. "I can see that. She is beautiful, isn't she?"

"Oh, lord, yes," said the chubby nurse with a pretty smile. She wore a name tag on her bright flowered jacket that said Cheryl. "Especially since that old black stuff is growing out, and she's getting her natural color back. Why on earth did she color it black, anyway? When she's got that gorgeous golden brown color?"

Only one of the mysteries of Vicky Shiley that would never be revealed to the general public, Amy realized.

"The only thing I can guess is because Mama had this thing about *Charlie's Angels*," Amy said. "She must've thought dyeing her hair made her look like Jaclyn Smith or Kate Jackson. She probably would've looked better if Farrah had been her heroine."

The nurse eyed her. "You take after her, you know. You've got her eyes and that pretty peaches-and-cream skin."

"Do I?" Amy looked at her mother's dead eyes. Hopefully, hers had more life. "Where did she get the pretty nightgown set?"

"Oh, some of us nurses went in together and got it for her. She's been here four years now, and we've become quite attached to her."

Attached, how? How could anyone get attached to an empty shell, a full-size lifeless Barbie doll that did nothing but sit and stare into space all day? But Amy sensed the sincerity in the nurse's voice, and she admired her for her kindness. They were a breed apart, these kind souls who took care of people like her mother. She knew she could never do it.

"That was very kind of you all," she murmured. "Thank you. I brought her one, too." She placed a wrapped box on the bed tray. She'd stopped in at the Maidenform outlet last week and found a nightgown off the clearance rack. It was silly to spend her hard-earned money on something her mother would never notice, but it was her birthday, and birthdays required gifts. Amy loved wrapping gifts, even though this time she knew it wouldn't be her mother who opened it. "I also brought her some flowers. Where should I put them?" She held out a mixture of wildflowers.

"I'll put 'em in a vase for you. There, now." She gave the bed a final smoothing and reached for the flowers. "I'll bring these right back, and then leave you two to visit a while."

As the nurse padded out of the room, Amy turned to her mother. "Happy birthday, Mama. It's me, Amy." Not a flicker of recognition, nothing. Amy leaned down to kiss her smooth baby-powder-scented cheek. She was rewarded with a blink and nothing else.

Amy drew a chair over and sat down. God, this was getting harder every year. Trying to act normal, carrying on a one-sided conversation with someone who might as well be in a deep coma for all the response she gave. But the doctors said this was the thing to do. It was possible, they said, that she actually did hear Amy's voice. Maybe even saw her, but because her soul was locked away in some secret compartment of her shut-down brain, she had no way of letting anyone know she was aware of their presence. So Amy talked. And talked. Catching her mother up on her life as if she was an eager listener, hanging upon her every word.

The plump nurse—Cheryl—returned to the room with the flowers in a pretty cut-glass vase. "Here you are, Vicky," she spoke jovially, flashing a bright smile at Amy's mother. "Aren't these the prettiest flowers your daughter brought you?" She adjusted a few in the vase and stepped back to admire her handiwork. "There, now!" Her eyes returned to Amy. "You know, speaking of your mama's hair. My sister is a beautician, and I'll just bet if I called her and told her it's your mama's birthday, she'd come right over and trim those black ends off. And then your mama will look just as pretty as a picture. What do you say?"

What's the point, Amy wondered. *Who's going to see her in here? But it would be nice to see what Mama looks like with that ugly black stuff cut off.* "Well . . . I don't have a lot of money with me," Amy said hesitantly.

"Oh, don't you worry about that. Charlene will do it for free. We'll just call it my special birthday gift to your mom. Okay?"

Amy smiled back at the kind nurse. "That's very nice of you. Okay. But I insist on giving your sister a tip."

"All right! It's a deal. I'll go call her right now."

The nurse bustled out. Amy turned back to her mother.

"What do you think about that, Mama? You're going to get a haircut today."

Vicky stared into space. Amy searched her mind for something else to say. And of course, it was Paul who came to the forefront. Paul, who was never far from her waking—or sleeping—thoughts. So, she began telling her about him. Describing his dark good looks, his mesmerizing blue eyes. His sweet smile.

"I think I'm in love, Mama," Amy murmured. "Only problem is . . . he thinks of me just as Robin's little friend. I wish you could tell me how to get him to wake up and notice me. Get him to see me as a woman instead of an immature teenager."

Of course, there was no advice forthcoming. No motherly encouragement or reassuring hugs. Amy hadn't expected any. She just continued to talk, telling her mother about the summer at the Mulcaheys', and how wonderful they all were. She talked about Jeff teaching her how to swim, about riding the Alpengeist at Busch Gardens, the barbecues, and boating trips they took on the James River in the twenty-foot sailboat the Mulcaheys moored at their dock. All the Mulcaheys were skilled sailors, and they were trying to turn her into one, too.

Amy wrinkled her nose as a horrible stench invaded the room. The woman in the other bed began to moan softly, and Amy realized what the smell was. Oh, God! She stood and went to the call button on her mother's bed. "Uh . . . I think . . . the lady in the other bed may have had an accident."

"Did she fall out of bed?" a disembodied voice asked.

"Not that kind of accident. I mean she . . . uh . . . you know, messed up her bed."

"Someone will be right down," the voice said with a weary tone.

Amy sat back down and tried to pick up where she'd left off, describing one of their jaunts down the James River. It was hard to concentrate, though, because the moans of Mama's roommate were growing increasingly louder. And the smell! It was making Amy gag. Finally, a nurse bustled into the room.

"Agnes, have you dirtied your diaper again, you naughty girl?"

The elderly woman began to talk in a foreign language that Amy didn't recognize. Italian, maybe. Her heart gave a pang. So sad, to live the last days of a long life in a place like this, reduced to shitting in a diaper like a newborn. Amy shuddered, hoping she'd never live to be so old and helpless.

A movement from her mother caught Amy's eyes, and her heart lurched. Nothing in her expression had changed, but her hands had begun to move. They plucked at her robe, as if she were trying to rid herself of annoying pieces of lint. Amy fell silent and watched her. Was this Mama's way of letting her know she was agitated? Was Amy boring her? Annoying her with her prattle?

"There, now!" said the nurse from the other side of the curtain. "Better now, Agnes?"

Amy heard a fizzing sound, and then, the sweet smell of lilacs floated through the room, but it didn't completely cover the underlying stench. Amy looked back at her mother. She stared into space, still methodically plucking at her nightclothes. Amy felt her heart twinge with pity. *Are you in there somewhere, Mama? Or has your soul long departed?*

She heard a footfall behind her, and turned to see Cheryl stepping past the drawn curtain with a tray. "Lunchtime," she trilled, beaming. "You want to feed your mother, Amy?"

Lunchtime, already? It was only eleven-thirty. The nurse placed the food on Vicky's tray table and rolled it over to where Amy sat. Amy lifted the white plastic cover and peered down into the lumps of warm food in the divided plate. Something white, something green, and something an unappetizing grayish brown. She wrinkled her nose as the moist, cloying aroma of bland hospital food wafted around her. Why did all hospital food smell the same? Like the inside of someone's raunchy gym shoes?

"Still getting baby food, I see."

"Well, it's not really baby food. We just puree it up in the blender because she still won't chew."

"Potatoes and green beans?" Amy guessed aloud, peering into the plate. "But what's the brown stuff?"

"Pork chop. She loves it, too."

Amy shrugged and ladled a bit of the pureed pork onto a spoon. *If you say so.* But when she lifted the spoon to her mother's mouth, her lips parted obligingly. Perhaps her taste buds weren't as dead as her emotions.

"Charlene said she can come over about four," the nurse said. "Will you still be here then?"

Amy had been planning to head back to Williamsburg about three. But Cheryl waited expectantly, and there was no way she could tell her that. She forced a smile to her face. "You think I'd miss seeing my mom get a new hairdo?"

Cheryl beamed. "Charlene will have some great ideas. I just know it."

After Amy finished feeding her mother—to her great surprise, she'd finished every spoonful—she noticed that her hands had stopped plucking at her robe, and now lay still in her lap. Was it hunger that had prompted the strange ritual?

Amy peered at her. "Mama, you look like you're about to fall asleep. You want to get into bed?"

No answer, of course. But her eyes were half-closed. Amy wondered what to do. Another nurse squeaked in on rubber soles, smiled at her, and looked at her mother.

"Vicky, are you enjoying spending your birthday with your daughter?" She walked over to Vicky's chair and placed a gentle hand on her elbow. "Well, it's time for your nap now. Come on, let's get you into bed."

Her mother stood up, and walked with the nurse to the bed. A moment later, she was snuggled in, the covers tucked up around her. Amy let out an explosive breath, staring in amazement.

"*She understood you!*"

The lanky blond nurse met her astonished gaze. "We don't know if it's that, or if it's just habit. Routine. She's used to taking a nap after lunch. She'll sleep for about an hour. You might want to head down to the cafeteria and get yourself some lunch." She walked to the door and dimmed the lights.

Amy followed her out, still thinking about the way Mama had so compliantly followed the nurse's orders. Wasn't it possible that she actually understood everything going on around her, but simply chose not to interact? Of course, the doctors had always said that might be the case, but Amy had never really believed it. Until now.

The thought filled her with an emotion that took her a moment to identify. *Anger.* Sheer, unadulterated anger. Because if her mother understood things, and deliberately chose not to be a part of the world, that meant she was *choosing* to reject her own daughter. She was *choosing* not to be there for her.

But then . . .

The anger left her as quickly as it had arrived. If that were the case . . . if Mama was choosing to live her life locked inside the prison of her mind, then that, in itself, was a symptom of mental illness. And she was no more responsible for it than she'd have been if her body was invaded by a deadly cancer.

Amy took the elevator down to the cafeteria and, just outside the double doors, stopped at a pay phone and dialed the Mulcaheys' 800 number. Robin answered on the third ring, her voice breathless as if she'd run in from outside.

"Hey, Robin, it's me. What's up?"

"Oh, girl, you gotta get home. Steve Chatham just called, and he's having one *hell* of a party in his parents' beach house in Virginia Beach tonight. I told him if he's got the keg and lots of buff guys, we'll round up the girls."

Just hearing Robin's vivacious voice reminded Amy that there was another world outside this depressing prison, and soon—thank God—she'd be rejoining it. As if reading her mind, Robin asked, "When are you coming home?"

"I'm not sure," Amy said. "The nurses have this hairdresser coming in to give my mom a cut. I said I'd stick around and see how it turns out. What time do we have to leave for the party?"

"Oh, hell, it won't get going 'til probably ten o'clock. Let's say we'll leave about nine? You'll drive, right? I mean, I plan to get *plastered* tonight."

Amy grinned. So, what *else* was new? "Yeah, I'll drive. I should be home long before nine. Uh . . . How's Paul? You think he might like to come to the party with us?" Amy waited for Robin's answer, every muscle in her body on alert.

Robin guffawed. "Shit! You think he'd be caught dead at an underclassmen party? I don't *think* so! Besides . . . guess what?" Her voice lowered, and Amy could almost see the devilish look on her face. "Paul is in *love!*"

Amy's smile froze, and her heart almost stopped beating. "With who?"

"That girl he went to San Francisco with. Yeah, it was a *girl*! He neglected to tell us that. He met her on that trip to Scandinavia. She's a college student from Berkeley. God, he won't stop talking about her. Monica *this* and Monica *that* . . . it's all we hear! And get this, Amy, she's a violinist! Monica Ashton. I'll bet she's a snob. Don't you think? I mean, a *violin*, for God's sake!"

For a long moment, Amy couldn't speak because of the lump growing in her throat. Finally, she said quietly, "Is she pretty?"

"Yeah, I guess so. Paul showed us some photos from Norway. She's tiny . . . maybe five-foot-one. Long black hair, straight as a stick. Blue eyes. High cheekbones. Yeah, she's pretty, I guess. If you like skinny, stuck-up intellectuals."

"So . . . it's really serious, huh? Paul and . . . Monica?" She hated saying her name. Hated the fact that it was paired with Paul's.

"Who knows? But I'll tell you this. I've never heard Paul talk about somebody so much. Oh! The other line's beeping. I'll see you when you get here, okay? Bye."

She hung up before Amy could say good-bye. Biting her lower lip, Amy replaced the phone in its cradle and turned toward the cafeteria doors. Her stomach growled in hunger, but she knew she couldn't eat. Not after hearing Robin's offhand announcement.

Paul is in love. Paul and Monica.

Tears misted her eyes. *It's not fair,* she wanted to scream. *I love him!* Holding back a sob, Amy stumbled into the ladies' room and locked herself into a stall. Sitting on the toilet, she buried her face in her hands and gave in to a silent crying jag. For a girl who'd vowed never to cry, she'd been doing a lot of it lately. Ever since she'd met Paul.

How ironic that at the happiest time in her life, with school and a brand-new family who seemed to cherish her as much as she did them, she felt so achingly miserable. *Is that what love does to you?* she wondered. *Tears up your insides and mangles your heart and emotions as if they were made of wet tissue paper?*

But sitting here crying wasn't going to change a thing. Wiping away her tears, she stepped out of the stall and went to the sink to splash cold water on her face. For a long moment, she gazed into the mirror. The makeup she'd applied that morning had all been washed away. Her blue eyes, streaked with mascara, stared back at her, bereft.

"You didn't lose him, you idiot," she whispered. "You never had him."

Abruptly she turned back to the stall and unwound a length of toilet paper to dab at the smudges of mascara. Oh, how she wished she'd had the foresight to bring an emergency bag of makeup with her. But what did it matter if she looked like a pale rag doll? The nurses didn't care, and God knew Mama didn't even see her.

Mama. Amy glanced at the silver-and-gold-toned Timex on her left wrist, and saw that it had been almost an hour since she'd left her room. The nurses had mentioned something about bringing in a birthday cake. Could Mama *eat* cake? After all, it couldn't be pureed, could it?

As it turned out, the nurses didn't serve any cake to Amy's mother, but they did feed her spoonfuls of icing, which she seemed to enjoy. The whole thing was rather pathetic, Amy thought. The forced gaiety—at least, it seemed forced to her. The singing of "Happy birthday, dear Vicky." The unwrapping of her one present—the nightgown Amy had bought—by the plump, smiling nurse, Cheryl, as the three others oohed and aahed around her. Amy tried not to let her pity show. After all, the nurses were good-hearted souls who, presumably, chose this profession because they cared about people. But she couldn't stop the uncharitable thought fluttering through her mind that the "birthday party" was more for them than it was for her mother. They certainly seemed to enjoy the cake they gobbled down.

Cake that *they* had bought, Amy reminded herself with a flood of guilt. She put down her own sugary-iced square, her stomach souring at the meanness of her thoughts. Why did this always happen? Every time she came here to visit her mother, she felt like a different person. An angry, vengeful person. And she didn't like it at all. She was an intelligent person; she'd maintained a 4.0 GPA in her first year at William & Mary. She understood that her mother couldn't help being the way she was.

Then why was she so furious at her?

"Oh, *here* she is!" Cheryl smiled at someone at the door. "You're early, Charlene!"

Even plumper than her sister, the pretty strawberry blond stepped into the room, carrying a case labeled Charlene's House of Beauty. "I don't usually make house calls, you know," she said in a thick, syrupy drawl. "Except for birthdays. Is this the birthday girl?"

The nurses dived into action, clearing away the cake and paper plates. Charlene fastened a drape around Vicky's shoulders and took a plastic bottle out of her case and began to spray down her hair. A moment later, her scissors began clipping and snipping, and long strands of black-tipped brown hair dropped to the plastic drape.

"Something short and sassy, you think?" Charlene glanced at Amy, acknowledging her as the decision maker in the room. "Something that can fall right into place after a shampoo without a lot of fuss?"

"Sounds good to me," Amy said.

"You think it'll be okay with her?"

Amy resisted the urge to roll her eyes, or worse, groan out loud. "I don't think she'll mind." As *if*!

"Okay, then."

Ten minutes later, the room smelled like a hair salon, and Vicky Shiley had become a new woman. Her hair—completely golden brown now—had been cut in a layered style, short but classy. Charlene had moussed and blow-dried it, but insisted that it would look almost as good if it was air-dried into place and then fluffed out with a pick. *That's what they always say.* Amy thought with amusement. But Mama really did look good. Amy wondered if she had any idea what had just happened. It certainly wasn't evident by her expression; it was the same as always.

Amazing, though, how something as insignificant as a haircut could totally change one's appearance. Too bad there wasn't such a quick fix to change the inner person, as well. Mama may look more like a normal person, but she was as messed up psychologically as ever.

And her hands were moving again. Doing that weird plucking thing. Surely she wasn't hungry again already? She'd just had a ton of icing from her cake.

Suddenly Vicky's right hand moved upward and clutched at her nightgown over her left breast. Amy watched her. She'd never seen that particular movement before. Cheryl noticed it, too.

"Vicky, hon? What's wrong? You don't like your new hairdo?"

Vicky began to tug violently at her nightgown. Amy stood up, her heart freezing. *Something was very wrong!* Vicky opened her mouth, and deep, guttural grunts erupted from her throat. Cheryl's face paled.

"What is it?" Amy asked, moving toward her mother. "What's wrong with her?"

Cheryl lurched for the call button above Vicky's bed. "We need a crash cart in 416," she yelled, all businesslike now. "I think she's having a heart attack."

A bell dinged out in the hall, and over it, came the mechanical voice of a recording, "Code Blue, Room. 416. Code Blue, 416."

Then all hell broke loose.

8

Amy punched out the 800 number to the Mulcaheys with trembling fingers. Robin answered on the first ring, and when Amy identified herself, she snarled, "Where the *hell* are you?"

Tears blurred Amy's eyes. "I'm at a hospital in Richmond. My . . . mu . . . mu . . . mother had a heart attack. She's in intensive care."

Silence. Then, her voice subdued, Robin said, "Is she going to be okay?"

"I don't know. *They* don't know." Amy bit hard on her lip. "It's touch-and-go, they say. It could be days before they know what's going to happen. Oh, Robin! I'm so scared. I don't know what to do!"

"Where are you? What hospital?"

Amy told her.

"Give me an hour." The line went dead.

True to her word, fifty minutes later, Robin stepped into the intensive care lounge. The moment Amy saw her concerned face, she burst into tears. Robin flew across the room and took her into her arms.

"Shhhh . . . she's going to be fine, Amy." Robin stroked her hair, holding her in her arms as if she were the mother and Amy the child.

"She's all I have, Robin," Amy sobbed. "She's all that's left of me in this world. Once she's gone, I won't have anybody!"

"That's not true," Robin murmured, holding her tight. "You have me, Amy. You'll always have me."

Robin checked them into a Holiday Inn near the hospital. Amy had protested, not wanting her to put such an expense on her charge card. Who knew how many days they'd have to stay?

"Don't be an idiot, Idiot," Robin said offhandedly. "We've got to sleep, don't we? And I don't know about you, but I damn well can't sleep on those plastic chairs in that waiting room. And I don't intend to try!"

But even though they'd stayed at the hospital well after visiting hours, and it was almost midnight by the time they'd undressed and gone to bed, they lay in the dark in separate full-size beds and talked for hours.

"I don't want her to die," Amy murmured. "I guess that's selfish. Maybe she'd be better off if she did. I mean, what kind of quality of life does she have now? But . . . for whatever reason . . . I'm just not ready to let her go. Does that make any sense, Robin?"

Robin was silent for so long that Amy began to think she'd fallen asleep. But then out of the darkness, she spoke, "I guess it does. After all, she's your only living relative . . . that you know of, right?"

Amy blinked back tears, staring up at the dark ceiling. "Yeah. All I know is . . . my mother never told me she loved me. She barely touched me with any kind of affection. Yet, for some reason I'll never understand . . . I still love her. I guess that *does* make me an idiot, doesn't it?"

"No, it just means you're human," Robin's voice was subdued. Or maybe just sleepy. "I love my mom, too. And sometimes, I hate her."

Oh, here we go again. Amy felt a ripple of irritation run through her. Most of the time, she maintained a sense of humor about Robin and her dramatic innuendos, but this time, she just couldn't. Why did everything always have to be about *her?*

Amy turned over on her side and peered through the semidarkness at the curled-up lump on the next bed. "I can't understand why you're always saying things like that about Tammy. She's wonderful! You should feel lucky you have a mother like her."

"Yeah, *right!*" Robin shot back. "You can say that because you don't know the real Tammy Mulcahey."

Amy's voice rose in exasperation. "Well, *tell* me! Who is the 'real Tammy Mulcahey,' and why is she such a bad person that you actually hate her sometimes?"

Robin flopped over onto her side, facing the wall. "It's late. We'd better get some sleep so we can get over to the hospital early tomorrow. Today, I mean."

Amy felt like groaning in frustration. She wished Robin would just quit saying stupid things like that if she wouldn't elaborate on them. She turned over with a sigh. Well . . . whatever it was, it could never be as bad as the situation in which she'd grown up. Whatever the faults of Tammy and Mike Mulcahey in raising their children—and, of course, every parent had faults—at least their kids were always loved, and they knew it. Wasn't that the most important gift a parent could give their child?

With that thought ringing through her mind, Amy fell into a troubled sleep.

★ ★ ★

On Wednesday morning, Vicky underwent an angioplasty to open up the blocked blood vessel that had caused the heart attack. After the three-hour procedure, the surgeon proclaimed it a complete success and if her recovery was routine, as expected, she could go back to the nursing home on Saturday morning.

"Not Friday?" Amy asked hopefully. She was being selfish again, thinking that Paul's flight to Denver left on Friday afternoon, and she would miss him completely if she wanted to accompany her mother back to the nursing home. Which, of course, she had to do. It would look weird if she didn't.

The surgeon shook his sandy head. "I'm afraid not. We want to make sure she's stable before we send her back."

So, that was that. She wouldn't see Paul this time. Then she remembered Monica, and realized it was probably a good thing. The more distance between them, the better. It would give her time to get him out of her system. Maybe she should take Robin up on her outrageous idea to have Jason sleep with her. After all, she couldn't stay a virgin forever, could she? She vowed to bring up the subject with Robin that very night.

It was harder than she thought it was going to be, she discovered.

She finally got up the nerve after they turned out the lights and got into their beds. "Remember that day in the dorm when I woke up and saw . . . you know . . . you and Jason?"

Robin yawned loudly. "Yeah. What about it?"

"Remember what he said . . . uh . . . about me? You know . . . he called me . . ." She felt her face grow hot in the darkness.

"A nice piece of ass. Yeah, I remember."

"You remember what else you said?" Amy asked hesitantly. "You know . . . about him and me . . . uh . . . well, you know . . ."

"Fucking? You can say it, Amy. You're not gonna go to hell for saying the word *fuck*." Her voice was laced with humor. "Yeah, I remember. Why? Have you changed your mind? You want me to set something up?"

"*No!* I mean . . . I don't know." She took a deep breath and released it. "Maybe."

Robin sat up in her bed, and even in the green glow from the bathroom's ultramodern night-light, Amy saw her grin. "No shit?"

"I said *maybe*. I'm not really sure . . ." Amy's face burned.

"You *go*, girl," Robin exploded, delighted with the idea. "I'll call Jason as soon as we get home. When do you want to do it?" She scratched at her head, mulling it over. "Let's see . . . he's doing a gig in Myrtle Beach for the next couple of weeks, but I think he said he'd be back the middle of September. I know! We'll arrange a camping trip to . . . *yes!* We'll go to Assateague. We'll set up tents on the beach, far enough away from each other so you and Jason can have some privacy, and I'll invite . . . let's see . . . who do I know who has a suckable dick?"

"Robin!"

"Well, hey! I want to have some fun, too. I know. I'll bring along that football player I went out with last fall. What was his name . . . Jess?"

"Jack."

"Whatever. Hey, that's cool, isn't it? You'll do Jason and I'll do Jack. J & J!"

Amy drew the covers up over her head, her entire body flooded with heat. "God, you are *so* gross!"

"And you love it. Admit it, Amy. You love me to death, and I'm the best thing that ever happened to you, right?"

Amy came up for air. "No one ever said you had a self-confidence problem, but yes, Robin, you're right. You're the best thing that ever happened to me."

"And you love me, right?" Her tone was teasing, but Amy sensed an underlying note of insecurity.

"Of *course* I love you, idiot! You know that. And you *are* the best thing that ever happened to me."

Robin didn't respond. Had she fallen asleep?

But as Amy's eyes closed and she began to drift into sleep, she heard Robin's soft voice. "You're the best thing that ever happened to me, too."

Just as the cardiologist had promised, Amy's mother was released from the hospital on Saturday morning. Amy and Robin drove her back to the nursing home in the Mulcaheys' Mercedes, and within the hour, Vicky Shiley was ensconced in her old room. The other bed in the room was empty, and more disconcerting, neatly made up. Had that old woman died? Amy decided not to ask anyone. She didn't really want to know.

Gazing at her mother in the chair by the window, Amy wondered if she had any idea how close she'd come to death a few days ago. Maybe it would've been better if . . .

Amy shook the thought away. No. She wouldn't think like that. It was wrong.

"Mama?" She glanced over her shoulder at Robin waiting in the doorway, then approached her mother. "We have to go now, okay? Back to Williamsburg." She brushed a kiss against Vicky's soft peach-scented cheek. "I'll see you again . . ."

Next year? She couldn't bring herself to say that, even if it was probably true. ". . . in a few months, okay?"

What did it matter, anyway? A few months, a year. Two years? Her mother had no comprehension of the passage of time. It probably wouldn't matter if Amy never showed up again. Vicky wouldn't even miss her.

So, why did she feel so guilty as she paused at the doorway for one last glance? Her heart ached at the vacant, soulless look on her mother's face.

"Bye, Mama." *Or whoever you are. Wherever you are.*

She closed the door and followed Robin out into the vicious August heat. It would be a long, boring drive back to Williamsburg in their separate vehicles, but there was nothing they could do about that. Following behind Robin's Mercedes heading east on I-64, Amy turned up the volume on the radio and began to sing along with Sarah McLachlan's "Sweet Surrender."

By the end of the second verse, she was back in the real world, having thankfully left her mother's depressing one behind.

Amy stood in front of the huge mirror that took up the width of an entire wall in the guest bathroom and dabbed mascara onto her lashes. On the green-marbled countertop, a portable CD player blasted out Sheryl Crow's "Change Would Do You Good."

Twisting her hips to the beat of the music, Amy plunged the mascara wand into the tube a couple of times and sang along with Sheryl. *"Scully and angel on the kitchen floor and I'm calling Buddy on the Ouija board . . ."*

A movement at the opened door distracted her. She turned to see Robin standing in the corridor, wearing nothing but a pair of teeny-tiny panties and a Wonderbra, her hair in hot curlers. Which was odd because Robin, unlike at the dorm, usually wore a robe here, and never, ever pranced around half-dressed. Not only that, but her face was sheet white, her mouth opened in shock.

Something about her expression reminded Amy of Munch's painting, *The Scream.* She'd seen it in a coffee table book downstairs, and it had given her the creeps. The way Robin's expression was doing now.

Amy reached for the volume knob and turned Sheryl off in midtaunt. "What's wrong?" Her stomach took a sickening dive. *Had something happened to Paul?* "Oh, God, Robin! What's *wrong?*"

"Princess Di has been in a car accident," Robin said slowly. "It just came over the radio. Amy, they say she's seriously injured."

Amy's first reaction was relief. It wasn't Paul or any of the other Mulcaheys. But as her words sank in, her heart kicked painfully. Like everybody else, she felt a certain kinship to the sad-eyed blond princess. Her fairy tale had been one that many teenage girls identified with—the regal prince riding in on his white horse to sweep the ordinary girl out of an everyday life of obscurity and into the spotlight of instant fame and celebrity. Not that anyone truly believed Lady Diana Spencer was an ordinary girl, but she had the right girl-next-door image. Now, to think that England's shining star could be dying at this very moment, or already dead, was simply incomprehensible.

"Her boyfriend is dead," Robin went on. "They say their car was being chased by paparazzi. Oh, Amy! She *can't* die!"

And to Amy's complete amazement, Robin—trash-mouthed, tough-as-nails Robin—burst into tears.

★ ★ ★

They'd planned to go out that night. One of the Kappa Chis was having a big end-of-summer barbecue at her parents' oceanfront cottage in Virginia Beach, and even Amy had been looking forward to it. But all the networks were broadcasting continuous updates—and lots of speculative filler—about the accident, and Robin was glued to the TV. She'd drawn on a silk robe over her underwear and taken the hot rollers out of her hair, but hadn't bothered to run a brush through her blond locks. The thick curls tumbled around her shoulders in golden disarray, framing her bloodless face.

Amy was still rather amazed by Robin's anxiety, and she wasn't sure she quite understood it. Sure, *she* was sad and concerned about this tragedy in the making, and yes, it would be a great loss to the world if Diana died, but Robin needed to get a grip. Amy had reasoned with her that they should stick to their plans and go to the beach party, but Robin looked at her as if she'd just suggested swabbing themselves with fish guts and jumping into shark-infested waters.

"How can you even think of partying. Don't you get it, Amy? Princess Di could be *dying!*" And she turned her brimming eyes back to the wide-screen TV.

Amy gave up and accepted that here was yet another facet to Robin's increasingly complex personality. And to think, when she'd first met the kooky girl that day in their dorm room, her first thought had been "Airhead Alert!" Robin was obviously deeper than Amy had given her credit for.

Just before midnight, unconfirmed reports from Paris newsmen began to come into the networks' newsrooms that Diana had died. Robin stiffened in the white leather love seat, absorbing the news, her eyes staring in horror at the screen.

"Oh, no," Amy whispered, her heart giving that unpleasant kick again. She looked at Robin, expecting an outburst even worse than the one that had erupted at the first news from Paris. But for a moment, nothing happened.

Finally, Robin moved, rubbing her hands up and down her upper arms as if she were freezing. Then she slowly unfolded her legs from the love seat, stood up, and plodded toward the door.

"This world sucks," she said quietly. "It really sucks."

And she left the room.

For the next week, Robin sat in front of the TV, grieving with the world for Diana. She just couldn't seem to get enough of it. Amy was mystified. She'd had no idea that Robin had been such a big fan. Up until now, she couldn't recall Robin ever talking much about Princess Di. Oh, she'd mentioned something back in July when the princess had been in Washington to auction off her old gowns. Amy seemed to recall her saying something about going up to the Smithsonian and "getting a little number to wear to one of the Kappa Chi dances." She'd been joking, of course. Spendthrift that she was, even *she* couldn't afford $10,000 for one of Princess Di's discarded gowns.

No matter what Amy suggested—going to the beach, a last day at Busch Gardens before school started—Robin shook her head. She just wanted to sit and watch another installment of *Death of a Princess*. Amy was actually relieved when Saturday arrived, and the funeral was televised from London. Amy and Robin sat with Tammy in the family room and watched the whole thing. Mike and Jeff were understandably absent. Men hated stuff like that, Amy knew. At least her dad had.

Tears streaked down Robin's face, almost from the beginning, and even Tammy was blurry-eyed. It wasn't until Elton John sang his tribute that Amy began to lose it, and by the end, she was sobbing along with everyone else. It was just so sad. And those poor boys, losing their mother like that.

Robin was right. This world really *did* suck.

When the funeral was finally over, Robin hit the power button on the remote control and the TV set blinked off. She turned to Amy, her eyes red-rimmed. "I don't know about you, but I'm ready to go out and get drunker than a friggin' skunk."

Tammy opened her mouth as if to reprimand her, but then closed it, her eyes resigned.

And that's exactly what Robin did. By the time Amy drove the Tracker into the driveway at Windsong that night, it was two in the morning, and Robin was passed out in the seat next to her. She was so blitzed that Amy had to get Jeff out of bed to help get his sister out of the car and into her room. With that accomplished, Amy dropped wearily into her bed and rubbed her tired eyes.

For good or bad, the old Robin was back.

"There you are! I've been looking all over for you!"

Amy looked up from the bench where she'd been sitting outside of Ewell Hall trying to figure out her fall schedule. Robin loped across the lawn, her backpack slung over one shoulder, wide-legged jeans trailing the ground. Amy hoped their illustrious sorority sisters didn't catch her wearing the latest in slacker wear, to which she'd taken a sudden liking in the past weeks. Her hair, too, had undergone a transformation; instead of the usual corkscrew curls or the beaded cornrows, she was wearing Pocahontas braids, which combined with a sudden aversion to cosmetics of any kind, made her look like she was about twelve years old. But darned if she wasn't as beautiful as ever!

Amy tucked a strand of hair behind her right ear and squinted up at Robin. The afternoon sun slanted golden rays over her newly bleached blond hair, making her look more radiant than usual. "Hey. What's up?"

Robin flopped onto the bench beside her and shrugged off her backpack. "Christ! These friggin' books get heavier every semester. Guess what?"

"Hmmm?" Amy glanced down at her schedule again. She wanted to apply for an internship with the Archaeology Department, and was trying to figure out where she could work it in between classes and her job at the coffee shop—and still maintain some kind of social life with Robin.

"We're in."

"In where?" Amy's index finger moved down her list of classes. If she could get Wednesday afternoons and Friday mornings off from the coffee shop, she could probably get the required ten hours per week at the archaeology center. That might work.

"Amy! I'm talking to you!"

Amy looked up at Robin and saw that she was smiling like the proverbial cat who'd just chowed down on the canary. "I'm listening."

"No, you're not, you're looking at your schedule. And this is *important*!" She grabbed Amy's arm and squeezed. "I got us into the Kappa Chi house!"

Amy stared at her. "But I thought only juniors and seniors could live in the sorority house."

Robin grinned. "Connections, baby. I've got connections. And you and I are sharing a room, of course. It's the cutest house, Amy. All blue and white with a screened-in porch in the front. Looks like it should be at the beach. And it's just down on Cary Street. We can move in tomorrow if we want."

"Wow! I don't know how you swung it, and I don't think I *want* to know how you swung it, but it'll be nice getting out of the dorm. I just hope the girls who didn't get in won't hate us."

"You worry too much, you know that? Oh, and guess what else? Jason is back in town."

Amy's heart gave a sickening lurch, and she could feel the blood draining from her face. "But you said the middle of September! That's a week away."

She shrugged. "Oh, the Sands Ocean Club fired the band because the drummer showed up drunk, so he's back. And I told him about how you want to have sex with him and—"

"Jeez, Robin! You didn't say it like that, did you?" Her cheeks were on fire.

Robin unzipped her book bag and began rifling through it. "What difference does it make how I said it? The bottom line is he's cool with it. In fact, he's *quite* cool with it because he thinks you're hot. Those were his exact words, by the way, and so I told him we're on for this weekend. He's going to take care of the camping permits and get the tents and everything. I just have to call Jake and see if he's up for it." She wriggled her eyebrows and grinned. "Literally speaking, of course."

"Jack," Amy muttered, and tried to fight the sudden nausea twisting in her gut.

"Whatever." Robin found what she was looking for and drew it out of her backpack. A sheet of paper. She unfolded it and began to read.

Amy bit her bottom lip. She felt cold inside, yet, strangely, as if she were burning up with fever. This weekend? But that was so soon! She thought of Jason, thought of what they were going to do. And goose pimples rose on her arms despite the warmth of the afternoon sun.

I can't go through with it.

This wasn't the way she'd imagined it would be. When she'd thought of making love for the first time, she'd just assumed it would be with someone she loved. Not a complete stranger. Even if that complete stranger happened to be a hunk. It wasn't right, and she couldn't do it.

She opened her mouth to say just that, but before she could get the words out, Robin released an ear-piercing shriek.

"Oh, my *God*!" She began to laugh. "I don't fucking *believe* this!"

"What?"

"Check out this e-mail I just got from Paul! That dickhead is *engaged*! To Monica, the San Francisco deb!"

Amy was rendered speechless by the horror that flooded through her at Robin's offhand words.

"Je-*sus*! How long has he known her? Three months? God, he must have it worse than I thought." A thoughtful look crossed her face. "Hmmm . . . you don't suppose he's got her pregnant, do you?"

Amy finally found her voice. "Paul is getting married?"

Robin folded up the e-mail and stuffed it back into her bag. "Oh, not until after they graduate, he says. They're talking about setting a date for next July. But hell! A lot can happen between now and then. If you ask me, it won't last. Christ, she's hundreds of miles away at Berkeley. What relationship can last with that kind of distance between them? He probably only asked her to marry him because he's in withdrawal from all the hot sex they had over the whole goddamn summer! Give him a few weeks, and when some lush Colorado beauty makes goo-goo eyes at him, it'll be all over. And it'll be the same thing for Little Miss Society Girl. Wait and see!"

Amy stared across the green expanse of lawn incongruously called Sunken Garden, focusing her gaze upon the stately brick of Tucker Hall. The Department of English building was reputed to be haunted by the ghost of a young woman who threw herself out of a second-floor window because a love affair had gone sour. Hearing the news about Paul made Amy identify with the poor girl.

She took a deep breath and turned to Robin. "Go ahead and tell Jason we're on for this weekend. And tell him . . . I hope he lives up to his impressive reputation."

A delighted grin crossed Robin's face. She reached out and squeezed Amy's knee. "You *go*, girlfriend!"

9

Moonlight glimmered, silvering the rolling waves pounding onto Assateague's shore. The salty tang of the sea mixed with the scent of woodsmoke and marsh grass, and underlying it was the lingering aroma of grilled hot dogs. Over the music of the surf, a dove cooed from the scrub pines behind the dunes. A lonely sound, thought Amy, as she sat cross-legged on a blanket, roasting a marshmallow over the crackling bonfire. She wasn't hungry for the S'more she intended to eat, but it would serve to postpone going into the tent with Jason, so it was all good.

Even though she hadn't looked at him directly all evening, and had barely spoken to him since they'd arrived at the campsite, she was uncomfortably aware of him sitting next to her, roasting his own marshmallow. Her first furtive glance had assured her that he looked more gorgeous than ever in his tight faded jeans and purple Pearl Jam T-shirt. His long, golden brown hair was tied back in a ponytail accentuating his carved cheekbones and piercing green eyes. If she peered out of the corner of her eye, she could see one perfectly shaped forearm as it rested on his raised knee, so close she could almost make out every golden hair, every freckle. His hands were nice, too. Slender and long-fingered. Guitarist's fingers. He had a thing for silver rings and leather bracelets. Which made him all the sexier.

She looked again at his hand turning the stick with the toasting marshmallow, and shivered. What would his hands feel like touching her body? Her cheeks grew hot. She would soon find out.

Across the bonfire, Robin cuddled with Jack. Like Amy, she was dressed in jeans, T-shirt, and an Ocean City sweatshirt to protect against the cool ocean breeze. But from the looks of things, she wouldn't be wearing all those clothes for long. Jack had his tongue stuck halfway down her throat, and she had one hand under his shirt, stroking his stomach. Amy wished they'd just go into their tent a few feet down the beach and do what they had to do; but then again, she didn't want to be left alone here with Jason. Because that would mean they would have to go into their tent, and she wasn't sure she was ready for that. In fact, she was quite sure she wasn't ready at all.

With a sudden giggle, Robin ripped herself away from Jack and pushed him with such force that he toppled backward onto the sand. "You are *bad*, Jack Malloy! Making me forget we have an audience." She leisurely got to her feet, brushed the sand from her butt, and extended a slender hand down to Jack, smiling seductively. "Come on, you bad boy. Let's go see what you've got for me under those tight jeans."

Jason looked up from his marshmallow and watched Robin pull Jack to his feet. Amy wondered how he felt about seeing his girlfriend lead another guy to her tent so she could make love to him. But his expression was inscrutable.

Robin snaked her arm around Jack's waist and snuggled her body up close to his. She gave Jason a saucy smile. "Remember what I said. Be gentle with her."

"You can count on it." Jason smiled and turned to level his gaze at Amy.

She felt her entire body go white-hot as all three of them looked at her. Jesus! Why didn't Robin just get on the Internet and tell the entire world that Amy Shiley was about to lose her virginity! Blushing furiously, Amy pulled the toasted marshmallow off the stick, burning her fingers in the process, and stuck it on a graham cracker. She reached for a square of Hershey's chocolate and pushed it into the hot marshmallow, keeping her eyes averted.

"You sure are a quiet one, aren't you?" Jason said.

She looked up to see him gazing at her, an appraising look in his eyes. Was he this close a moment ago? She forced a shrug. "I talk when I have something to say."

Two dim shapes disappeared into the darkness. Robin and Jack making their way to their tent. Amy's pulse skipped a beat, then began to race. She was alone with Jason. For a moment, she fought panic. Her breathing shallowed, and her heart began stomping so hard, it felt like it was auditioning for River-dance. *Oh, God! I'm going to hyperventilate!*

Jason leaned toward her, and she swallowed hard. He was going to kiss her! Instinct took over. She thrust the S'more into her mouth—the whole thing. It was a huge mouthful, and the melted chocolate didn't quite make it in. She felt it oozing down her chin.

"Mmmm," she mumbled, struggling to chew and swallow all at once. "This is . . . *so* yummy!"

He scooted closer, his eyes on her mouth. His scent embraced her—something crisp, cool, and woodsy. "Yeah, it looks inviting."

Before she could think of a response, he leaned toward her, and this time, there was nothing she could do to avoid his kiss. But to her amazement, he didn't kiss her. Instead, she felt the touch of his warm, wet tongue as it licked the chocolate from her chin. Her insides turned to jelly, and a deep warmth radiated from the pit of her stomach downward. She tensed, her hand clutching the roasting stick, as Jason's tongue worked its way up to her mouth, licking and tasting and caressing.

Her lips parted under his exploration, and she let out a soft gasp of delight. It was enough for him. His mouth closed upon hers, his tongue seeking gentle entry. The heat between her legs blossomed, grew demanding, and unconsciously, she thrust herself toward him, her mouth opening, taking him in. His hands grasped her head, entwining in her hair, and with a soft growl in his throat, he deepened the kiss, stoking her senses and sending her into a dizzy dive of mindless want.

Finally, Jason pulled away and gazed at her, surprise flickering in the depths of his green eyes. Reeling from his kiss, Amy stared back, heart drumming. She was shocked to find her fingers locked in the strands of his long ponytail.

"Wow!" Jason whispered.

Wow was right. It had been one *hell* of a kiss. And she wanted more. *Damned* if she didn't want a *lot* more. Her eyes dropped from his, and she felt herself blushing. His finger nudged her chin upward so she was forced to meet his gaze.

"You really *are* shy, aren't you?" he whispered.

She nodded. He smiled, his eyes soft. "But you know what?" His thumb traced over her swollen lips. "I'll just bet underneath that shyness, you're one hot little biscuit. And baby, if you want it, I'm going to melt your butter."

The line was corny, she knew that. But somehow, incredibly sexy.

He reached over and took the roasting stick from her. "See what you do to me?"

He pressed her hand against his bulging erection. Amy drew in a sharp breath. She liked the feel of him under her palm. The unleashed power of his male sex. She felt heady at the thought that she—*she*—had brought him to this state. That kissing her had turned him on. For the first time in her life, she knew what it meant to be a woman desired.

"You want to go into the tent?" Jason asked.

Amy caught her breath and stared into his eyes; they were cloudy with arousal. Slowly, she nodded.

Bare-chested, Jason lay on his side next to her, one hand stroking the nub of her left nipple. She wasn't naked. Not yet. In fact, she still wore her T-shirt and jeans, but his hand had slipped under her shirt to deftly unhook the front-closure bra that Robin had insisted she wear "for better access." As his talented fingers drove her to distraction, his mouth worked its magic on hers, delivering deep, drugging kisses that kept her brain spinning as if she were riding an even more exhilarating version of the Alpengeist. Robin was right, she thought—when she *could* think—Jason's mouth was to die for. Not that she had a lot of experience, but *God,* he could kiss!

Jason drew away from her, his breathing ragged. "Jesus! You're hot, Amy. You're driving me crazy."

Amy smiled up at him. He made her feel so . . . so seductive. Like she was someone else entirely. Her hand reached for his ponytail.

"Take it down," she whispered.

He didn't waste any time in doing what she requested. A split second later, he'd ripped the elastic band from his hair, and it spilled down around his shoulders. *Oooh, nice. Very nice.* Gazing into her eyes, he took her chin in his hand and lowered his mouth to hers again in a slow, soul-stirring melding. She laced her fingers through his hair, opening her mouth under the pressure of his.

His hands tugged at her T-shirt, pushing it up. She felt cool air whisper against her bare breasts, and her nipples hardened. His hand covered one breast, then the other, warming them. He began to kiss his way down her neck. A moment later, she felt his hot, wet tongue licking at her nipples, teasing and tugging with his lips.

"Oh . . ." she gasped, and the warmth between her legs became molten fire.

He moved from one breast to the other, leisurely feasting. She writhed under him, her head rolling back and forth, her hands threaded through his long, silky hair.

"Oh, God . . . please . . ."

He raised his head. "Please what, Amy?"

She moaned, not knowing how to ask for what she wanted.

But he read her mind. "You want me to touch you, Amy?" The palm of his hand cupped her swollen mons, pressing against her heat. "You want me to touch you here?"

Her head thrashed. Her pelvis pushed against his hand. "Ye . . . *yes!*"

His hands moved to her zipper, and in the quiet of the tent, there was only the sound of their heavy breathing, the muted roar of the ocean, then finally, the whisper of her zipper parting.

"Lift your hips, Amy," Jason urged in a ragged voice.

She mindlessly obeyed, so crazy with desire that she would've agreed to almost anything as long as he would put out the raging fire he'd ignited.

She felt him sliding her jeans down her hips, and the kiss of the cool night air on her naked limbs. She imagined what she must look like, lying on the floor of the tent, her blond hair tangled, her T-shirt pushed up above her exposed breasts—and below the waist, wearing nothing but skimpy bikini panties. Wanton, she supposed. But she didn't care. She didn't care about anything except his touch.

And his touch was driving her out of her mind. His fingers pressed against the moist crotch of her panties. The intimacy sent a new level of heat through her. But she wanted more. Again, he sensed her thoughts, and with one easy movement, he slid her panties off, tossing them over his shoulder. Lying on his side, he watched her face as his hand slid between her legs, slipping inside her wetness, exploring.

Amy thought she was dying. Blissfully dying. But when his fingers found her sensitive nub and began to gently massage it, she saw heaven. Stars exploded in a myriad of colors, and she cried out, shuddering, and still, his fingers didn't cease their magic, until finally, shattered and trembling, she returned to earth. Jason's mouth settled on hers in a sweet, succulent kiss.

He drew away, watching her. "Did you like it?"

She nodded, unable to speak. He kissed her again, tongue probing. Amy enjoyed it, but found herself wanting to push him away. Couldn't he give her some time to recover?

In the quiet, she heard the sound of a zipper.

"My turn," Jason said. He reached out and took her hand. "Touch me."

He drew her hand to him. She gasped as it came in contact with something hot, hard and huge. She knew what it was, of course. But she'd never felt a penis before. At her touch, it seemed to grow even bigger and more powerful. It scared her. How on *earth* was he going to get that huge thing inside her? She'd heard stories about how it hurt the first time a girl had sex— and that was with guys of ordinary size. Surely, Jason was bigger than most.

His hands covered hers as he showed her how to stroke him, and Amy was dismayed to find that he seemed to be growing.

"Did Robin ever give you any tips on giving a guy a blow job?" Jason asked huskily. "She gives really good head. Why don't you give me a little, Amy-doll? I won't blow my load in your mouth. I promised Robin I'd give you a good fuck, and that's what I'll do, but I'd really like your mouth on me for a minute."

Amy's hand stilled on his erection as a shudder of revulsion swept through her. Oh, God, this wasn't the way it was supposed to be. He was so crass, so trash-mouth! Yes, she'd been turned on by his kisses, and he'd brought her to climax with his touch, but did she really want her first time to be with an aspiring rock star/gigolo who was fucking her because he was doing a favor for his on-again, off-again girlfriend? And that's what it *would* be. Fucking. Not making love.

She pulled her hand away from him and got up on her knees, searching for her panties. Jason blinked and stared at her. "What are you doing?"

She found her panties balled up in the corner of the tent. Grabbing them, she turned them right side out, hands trembling.

"I'm leaving." She didn't know where she'd go, but she was damn sure she wasn't staying here with him.

"What do you mean, you're leaving?"

She drew on her panties and reached for her jeans. "I've changed my mind, Jason. I don't want my first time to be with you. It was a mistake, and I'm sorry."

Even in the near darkness of the tent, she could see his face fill with color.

"Are you fucking out of your mind? You get me in this condition, and then you tell me you're *changing your mind*? What the fuck are you? A goddamn cocktease?"

Amy felt the blood drain from her face. "I'm sorry. I just . . . can't go through with it."

He stared at her, his green eyes sparking fire. "You . . . little . . . *bitch*!" He tugged his jeans up, and with an effort, zipped them. "You got what *you* wanted, didn't you? Yeah, you just took and took, and now that it's time to give, you've decided to become the prim and proper little church girl, and fuck *me* over! Well, there's a name for girls like you, honey, and it ain't pretty." He grabbed his T-shirt and tugged it over his head. "And just let me give you a word of warning, sweetheart, you do this with the wrong guy, you're gonna find yourself tied up and raped brainless! Hey, you don't have to leave. *I'm* leaving. I've got a little problem I need taken care of, and you're not woman enough to do it."

Jason unzipped the flap opening of the tent and crawled out into the night. Amy heard the sound of his footsteps plodding away.

Slowly, she got up on her knees and scooted over to zip the tent. Then she fell back to the ground and stared up at the canvas roof of the tent, dry-eyed and miserable. *Paul,* she thought, *it should have been you.*

It has to be you.

Even though it was still dark inside the tent, Amy knew it was morning. Maybe it was the sound of the seagulls squawking as they dived for breakfast or maybe it was just a sixth sense. Whatever, she was glad the long night was over, and soon, please God, they'd be on their way back to campus. She hadn't slept well, probably not more than a couple of hours. Not so much because the sand was hard beneath the floor of the tent, or because the autumn night had grown uncomfortably cool towards daybreak, but because her thoughts were in turmoil after the fiasco with Jason. She knew she'd been insensitive and selfish, and she certainly understood his anger, but the whole thing had been a horrible mistake. And if she'd gone through with it, the mistake would've been compounded. She didn't regret the decision she'd made, but perhaps she could've handled it better. Perhaps if she'd tried to explain how she felt, that she was hopelessly in love with someone else, he would've understood. But somehow, she didn't think he'd been in an understanding mood.

Her full bladder protested as she turned over, and she knew she couldn't put off a trip to the rest room any longer. She unzipped the tent and stuck her head out. Early-morning fog swirled low on the beach, making it almost impossible to tell the gray breakers from the sky. Amy crawled out and stood, shivering. Summer was definitely on its way out.

Through the swirling gray fog, something moved near a dune, and her heart jolted. Then she realized it was just one of the wild ponies that roamed all over the island. Through a momentary thinning of the fog, she made out two more ponies, two dark ones and one multicolored. She watched them until the mist closed around them once more, then headed toward the Porta-Johns.

They were a short walk away behind the dunes in a shelter of scrub pines. Getting there would take her past Robin's tent, and as she headed in that direction, she saw the single pair of footprints in the sand. Jason's, she supposed. She remembered his last derisive comment to her before he'd stormed out.

I've got a little problem I need taken care of, and you're not woman enough to do it.

The only other woman in the vicinity was Robin, but she'd been occupied with Jack. Surely Jason hadn't.

Amy stared at the silent tent as she walked by. God, even Robin wouldn't have participated in a threesome, would she? But she knew the answer to that. If the opportunity presented itself, she would. And Jason knew that as well as she did.

Sick. It was so sick. Amy blushed as she imagined Robin with the two guys. She remembered one day last winter when Robin had brought a *Penthouse* magazine into their room and they'd read the letters in "Forum." Amy had been horribly embarrassed, yet, fascinated, and, yes, even turned on by them. But those were stories probably made up by people with wishful imaginations. The thought of Robin actually participating in something like that was positively *vile*!

After using the toilet, Amy stepped out of the Porta-John, and froze. Robin stood outside, waiting for her. Her hair was loose and tangled, her eye makeup, which she'd taken to wearing again, smudged. She was barefooted and wearing only an oversize T-shirt that reached just past her upper thighs. Jack's or Jason's? She looked as if she hadn't slept at all. She looked . . . well fucked.

But she was scowling, her blue eyes glittering with anger. "Do you have any idea what a shit-for-brains you are? Jason told me what happened."

Something snapped inside Amy. Maybe it was the sanctimonious look on Robin's pretty face. How *dare* she look like that after spending the night screwing two guys!

"Lay off, Robin. I'm not in the mood."

"Hel-*lo*? That's part of the problem, isn't it? But Jason tells me you were *quite* in the mood in the beginning. At least until after he made you come."

Hot blood rushed to Amy's face. Embarrassment, humiliation, anger. The emotions roiled through her, one after the other. Her hands clenched into fists. "Well," she said emphatically, "I guess I'm just not a *slut*."

Robin's face paled. She sucked in a deep, shocked breath, staring at Amy with stricken eyes. Then she turned and stalked off, disappearing from view behind the dunes.

10

Robin didn't speak to her for three days. Back in their room at the sorority house, the atmosphere was so cold, Amy thought she'd have to dig out her winter sweaters early just to survive it. Like a stone carving, Robin sat on her bed, scribbling in her journal, and Amy knew exactly who she was writing about. No matter how hard Amy tried to get her to talk to her, it just wasn't happening. And instead of looking at her, Robin looked through her. It was as if a wicked fairy godmother had come out of nowhere and rendered Amy invisible.

The first time she tried to apologize, several hours after they'd returned to Williamsburg, Robin had refused to listen. When Amy stepped into their room, Robin looked up from her journal, her face darkening. She slammed the notebook shut, locked it away in a cedar box, and pushed it under her bed.

"Robin, I'm sorry," Amy began. "I didn't mean what I said."

Robin just glared at her, and with a toss of her disheveled blond locks, she strutted out of the room, slamming the door behind her. Amy heard her knocking on Karen Upperman and Marcia Mason's door across the hall. She didn't return to their room until long after Amy had gone to bed.

Amy tried to apologize again the next morning, and this time, Robin at least looked, at her. The expression on her face was noncommittal as Amy listed her reasons for being so bitchy that morning at Assateague.

"I was probably PMS-ing. My period started last night, and also, I was feeling guilty for the way I treated Jason. I know it wasn't cool to get him all excited like that and then just stop . . ." Her face flamed, but she kept going. "And you know, maybe I said that horrible thing to you because I'm a little jealous of . . . well . . . the way you're so at ease with . . . you know, your sexuality." As she stammered through her apology, she kept hoping Robin's blue eyes would warm, but they remained cool. Amy didn't know what else to say, so she paused and waited for Robin to speak.

Robin stared at her a moment, then rolled her eyes. "Whatever. I've got to get to class." She whirled and strode out the door.

For the second night in a row, Robin didn't return to the room until late, long after Amy had gone to bed. Amy was miserable, but she didn't know what to do. Their friendship couldn't be ending over something she'd said in the heat of the moment, could it? Even though, admittedly, it had been a really awful thing to say. But surely Robin would forgive her! She had to! Wasn't that what friendship was all about?

By the time Amy got out of the shower the next morning, Robin had left for her first class. Tuesday was Robin's busy day; she had classes straight through until four-thirty, with barely enough time to squeeze in lunch. But when Amy returned to the sorority house after her eleven o'clock anthropology class, she was stunned to see Robin curled up in her bed, facing the wall.

"Robin, what's wrong? Are you sick?" Alarmed, Amy approached her.

"Yes," she mumbled.

Amy touched her shoulder gently. "What can I do to help?"

Robin turned over and peered up at her, her eyes puffy, the track of tears still evident on her pale face. "You can be my friend again," she said in a heart-breakingly vulnerable voice.

"Oh, Robin!" Amy sat on the side of her bed and took her roommate into her arms.

Robin clutched her and began to cry. "I don't want you to hate me, Amy. I don't know what I'd do if I lost you."

Amy stroked her tangled blond hair, feeling her own tears pricking her eyelids. "Don't cry, Robby. I don't hate you. I could never hate you. You're my best friend, don't you know that? My only real friend."

"Am I?" Robin drew away to gaze at her, her eyes shimmering with tears.

"You know that. I told you, I lost my temper on Sunday. It's something I inherited from my mother, I guess. It takes a lot to make me mad, but when I do, I explode. And you just happened to be in the line of fire. I *am* sorry, Robin. I didn't mean what I said."

Robin leaned her head back onto Amy's shoulder. For a long moment, they held each other, silently. Then, Robin spoke again, her voice muffled against Amy's shirt. "I'm not a bad person, Amy. I'm not a slut. I'm really not."

"I know." Amy stroked her damp hair, her heart twisting in pity. "I know you're not."

The fall semester was flying by at the speed of summer. On October 12, Amy celebrated her nineteenth birthday at the Trellis in Merchants Square with a group of friends that Robin had gathered for the occasion. There were twelve of them, and Robin footed the bill, much to Amy's discomfort. Especially since it really wasn't Robin who'd be paying the VISA bill, but Mike. Still, it was the first birthday Amy could remember that she was surrounded by friends who really seemed to care about her. It was a good feeling.

Later that night after they'd returned to the sorority house, Robin gave Amy a two-hundred-dollar gift certificate for the Gap outlet store on Richmond Road. Amy tried to refuse it, protesting that it was way too much, but Robin insisted she keep it.

"We wear the same size, so I'll go shopping with you, and we can buy things we both like, and that way, double our wardrobe." Robin had an answer for everything, and a way of making it sound like it made perfect sense.

Halloween arrived, and one of the Kappa Chis, Sue Moore, threw a costume party at her family's supposedly haunted three-hundred-year-old plantation home near Yorktown. At first, Robin didn't want to go because of her fear of anything ghostly, but Amy talked her into it by promising to stay at her side all night and vowing to keep her furnished with lots of booze. They went, dressed as two of the Spice Girls, Amy as Posh (with a black wig), and Robin as Baby. They didn't see one ghost, much to Amy's disappointment and Robin's relief.

Thanksgiving approached, and Amy began to think about Paul coming home. It had been an entire year since she'd seen him . . . well . . . if she didn't count those two minutes in which she'd seen him in August when he'd been dead on his feet from jet lag. How much had he changed? And would he bring Monica with him? Horrible thought! How would she be able to get through the weekend, watching them together? Of course, she could simply choose not to go to the Mulcaheys' for Thanksgiving. Even though she knew they expected her. She was treated like part of the family, and it thrilled her to be thought of that way. But if she didn't go, what would she do? Stay in the empty sorority house? Go spend the weekend with her mother in the nursing home? She shuddered, the thought too depressing to contemplate. No, she'd simply have to go through with it. Be strong. Be an adult. Besides, maybe once she saw Paul again, especially if he was drooling all over his fiancée, she could put her infatuation in perspective. Maybe even get over it altogether. She had to believe that was possible because she didn't want to go through her entire life as a virgin.

Robin confirmed her worst fear on Sunday night before Thanksgiving. Paul was flying in on Wednesday, and bringing Monica with him. With relief, Amy turned down Robin's invitation to go to the airport with her and Tammy to pick them up. It was her late night at the coffee shop; she didn't get off work until ten. She really hoped that by the time she drove out to the Mulcaheys' it would be so late that she wouldn't have to face either of them until the next day.

But luck wasn't with her. It was just past ten-thirty when she drove Robin's Tracker around to the rear of Windsong and came into the kitchen through the mudroom. She stopped short when she saw Paul sitting at the breakfast bar, sipping a cup of coffee and reading from a textbook.

The air left her lungs. How was it possible that he looked even better than he had the last time she'd seen him? His glossy black head was bent over the book, one square hand wrapped around his mug. He wore a black turtleneck sweater and black jeans. The heels of his cowboy boots—mandatory Colorado wear, Amy suspected—were hooked on the bottom rung of the stool. He was apparently so absorbed in his book that he didn't hear her come in. For a fleeting second, Amy considered trying to slip past him unnoticed. But if he should look up and catch her, she'd be mortified. Besides, here was her chance to practice some of the feminine wiles Robin had been trying to teach her.

"That must be awfully exciting reading. What is it? The latest John Grisham novel?"

Paul looked up, and his blue eyes crinkled as a smile spread over his face. "Better than that," he said, turning back the cover so she could see it. "*CGI Programming with Perl 5*. Fascinating title, isn't it?"

"I didn't know you were into computers."

He closed the book and sighed. "Well, I figure I'd better have a backup just in case I don't get that call from the NFL in February."

Amy shrugged out of her fleece-lined jacket and draped it over her arm. "Robin seems to think you're a shoo-in."

"Robin is my little sister. She thinks I walk on water."

Amy grinned. "You *don't*?"

His smile widened. "I can part the Red Sea, but the walking-on-water thing is still a challenge."

Amy laughed. "I think you have your Bible stories mixed up. Moses parted the Red Sea, not Jesus."

He shrugged and flicked a dark strand of hair away from his eyes. "Guess I've forgotten everything I learned in religion classes. Hey, want some coffee? I just brewed a fresh pot."

Oh, yes. She recognized the smell. Probably because she'd been surrounded by it for the past eight hours. Coffee was the last thing she wanted to drink now. "Yeah, sure." She placed her jacket on a barstool, topped it with her purse, and went to the coffeemaker. As she poured a cup, she asked herself why she was doing it. Why did she feel such a need to be close to Paul when she knew that days later, she'd be reliving every moment and fighting back the pain?

His brilliant blue eyes swept over her. "You're looking good, Amy. You've grown up a lot over the last year."

Amy stirred cream into her coffee. "Has it been a year?" *Exactly 365 days, six hours, and seven minutes.*

"Yeah. Last Thanksgiving, remember? I was sorry to hear about your mom's heart attack. How's she doing?"

She brought her mug of coffee over to the breakfast bar and slid onto the stool next to Paul. "Okay. Her heart seems to be fine now, but . . . otherwise, she's just as unresponsive as ever." She didn't add that she hadn't been back to see her mother since summer. The pang of guilt she felt every time she thought of her was punishment enough.

"Sorry to hear that." Paul gazed down at his coffee. "I was also sorry I didn't get to see you when I was here in August. I'd hoped we could do that trip to Cohoke Crossing."

Amy's heart jolted. She didn't know what to say.

"So . . ." Paul eyed her, smiling. "Have you got a boyfriend, Amy?"

"No!" Amy felt her face redden as images of that night with Jason flashed through her mind. "I mean . . . not really."

"Well, you've got plenty of time. Don't rush it. I guess Robin told you about Monica?"

Yes, and I hate her! "Uh-huh. She said you're engaged."

"Yeah, well . . . we haven't set a date yet. We're thinking about next July."

"Is she a senior, too?" *As well as being an A-number-one bitch?*

"Yeah, she's a music major at Berkeley. In fact, she's already been offered a position in the Nob Hill Chamber Orchestra."

"That'll make for an interesting marriage if you get drafted by the Denver Broncos," Amy said dryly. "Or worse yet, an East Coast team."

Paul stared at her, his lips quirking in amusement. "I can see Robin's been rubbing off on you. You've perfected the art of sarcasm, haven't you?"

Amy blushed. It was true. She'd come out of her shell in more ways than one in the last year—thanks to Robin.

"But you're right," Paul said. "And we've talked about the possibility of a long-distance marriage, but we're hoping it won't come to that. I've got a couple of 49er scouts giving me a hard look, and I'm hoping I'll be one of their first draft choices. And if not that, maybe Oakland will draft me."

Robin had been keeping her abreast of Paul's football career. He'd been playing well, having caught a total of eleven touchdown passes since the beginning of the season.

"Well, I hope it all works out for you, Paul." *Not! I hope you get drafted by the Miami Dolphins, and Monica stays in California, and you fall out of love with her, and realize I'm the only girl you can ever love.*

"I think you're really going to like Monica, Amy. She's quiet and serious and intellectual—a lot like you are—but once you get to know her, I'll bet you two really hit it off. It's Robin I'm worried about. Christ! I hope she doesn't say anything to offend her."

Amy felt her hackles rise. "Well, Robin isn't going to change her personality for anyone."

"Hey, I'm not putting her down. But you know how she is. She speaks before she thinks, and I'm afraid she just might say something that'll shock Monica. Her family is . . . well . . . pretty conservative. Nob Hill society, you know."

"Prissy snobs, you mean?"

He looked startled, then grinned. "Yeah. Guess you could say that. But trust me, you'll like Monica."

Trust me. I won't.

"Hey, maybe we could check out Cohoke Crossing this weekend. You up for it?"

Amy's heart fluttered. Calm down, she told herself, taking a sip of coffee. *Don't let him see your eagerness.* From somewhere upstairs, there was a loud thump, followed by a yell of frustration. Jeff, of course. He was always going off about something.

Paul grinned. "I can see nothing much has changed around here. But about Cohoke Crossing, I know we can't convince Robin to come along, but Monica would love it. She's real adventurous."

Amy swallowed the suddenly bitter-tasting coffee, and placed her mug down on the counter. "I'd like to, but you know that 'not really' boyfriend I have? Well, he's got me pretty booked up all weekend." She slid off the stool, grabbed her coffee mug, and dumped its contents into the sink. "Speaking of which, I told him I'd call after I got here, so I'm going up to my room." She placed the mug in the dishwasher and closed the door. "Good night, Paul. Great seeing you again."

Great, bullshit! Great like a root canal. Great like a catastrophic earthquake.

He smiled at her, eyes radiating warmth. "'Night, Amy. See you at breakfast."

Fuck you, Paul. I hate you. And I detest Monica.

Amy smiled at him sweetly. "Good night."

As soon as she left the kitchen, her smile disappeared. It was going to be a long, torturous weekend.

She was wrong. She didn't detest Monica. She *abhorred* her. And it was obvious that Robin felt the same way. Amy could tell by the amused look Robin threw her right after Paul introduced Monica to her at breakfast the next morning.

"So, you're the adopted Mulcahey," Monica said as she extended a slender hand bedecked with a huge garnet ring and a smaller diamond. Paul's engagement ring, Amy supposed, her heart aching. "Paul has told me about you."

Amy shot him a questioning look. What had he told her? He didn't meet her eyes, so she guessed the beautiful Monica knew everything about her. How galling!

The petite elegant young woman was smiling, but her beautiful blue eyes remained cool. Her expression was about as warm as a Macy's window mannequin. *The ultimate ice princess,* Amy thought.

Monica wore her shoulder-length hair in a sleek black curtain. It was thick and gleaming, the kind of luxuriously rich hair that might've been featured in a Pantene ad. She wore an expensive scent, Amy noted. Estée Lauder, she guessed. Nothing overpowering, but just enough to make a statement.

And her clothing! While everyone else was dressed casually in jeans and sweaters, Monica had chosen a camel pin-striped dress and matching long jacket paired with plain brown suede pumps. Amy didn't know about designer wear, but she'd bet her next paycheck Monica's shoes probably cost more than the grant she'd received for the fall semester. And even though Monica was the one who was overdressed at breakfast, somehow, her attitude conveyed that it was everyone else who looked out of place.

They sat down to a sumptuous breakfast of French toast, crisp bacon, and lean Virginia ham, with fresh-squeezed orange juice and Stella's delightful hazelnut coffee. As the platters were passed around, Amy noticed that Monica took only one slice of French toast and a small glass of orange juice. What was she? Anorexic? She *was* awfully slender. But her breasts were big enough. At least a C cup. One more reason to hate her, Amy thought. Both she and Robin had to resort to Wonderbras to get any hint of cleavage—not that Miss Priss would ever *show* any cleavage. Not to the general public, anyway.

Amy's eyes settled on Paul as she took a sip of coffee. From the moment Monica had walked into the room, he'd acted like a man hypnotized. He couldn't keep his eyes off his girlfriend. Everyone else in the room might as well have been invisible. And seeing the way he looked at Monica made Amy's heart throb with pain.

"Oh, guess what, Mom?" Paul said, helping himself to more French toast. "Monica's family has invited me to go to Gstaad with them over Christmas break, and I said I would. I've never skied the Alps before."

Tammy stiffened, the smile leaving her face. "But you went skiing over Christmas last year. I thought you'd be home this year."

Paul shifted in his chair and started to speak, but Mike cut him off. "It's Switzerland, Tammy! No man in his right mind would turn down a trip like that, right, Paul?" He looked across the table at Monica as he transferred a slice of tender pink ham from the platter to his plate. "Monica, you should try some of this. It's a Virginia specialty."

Monica paused in cutting into her French toast, her manicured shell pink nails glinting in a ray of sunshine coming through the dining room skylight. It also caught the light from her diamond engagement ring, making it sparkle. Amy's depression deepened.

"Oh, I don't eat meat, Mike," Monica said. To Amy's ears, it sounded like a reprimand.

Mike? She'd picked that up fast enough. She said his name like they were old buddies.

She gave him an apologetic smile. "I guess Paul didn't tell you I'm a vegetarian." Her slim shoulders lifted in a little shrug. "But I try not to be a fanatic. And one must eat, right?"

Everyone stared at her in silence. Paul gazed down at his plate as if he'd found something of enormous interest there. Tammy plastered a smile on her face and looked at Monica, her eyes cool.

"Oh, dear. I *do* hope you'll find something you can eat at dinner. I'm afraid we're quite the traditionalists. Turkey and all the trimmings, you know. The kids would revolt if we changed the menu."

It was then that Amy realized Tammy disliked Monica just as much as she and Robin did. Her spirits lifted. Maybe if Paul saw that the entire family couldn't stand his fiancée, he'd reconsider things.

Monica's smile seemed forced. "That's perfectly fine, Mrs. Mulcahey. I wouldn't dream of asking you to change the menu for me."

Mrs. Mulcahey. No first-name basis with Paul's mom. *Definitely* a good sign!

"As a matter of fact, Paul and I were hoping we could take over part of the kitchen for a little while and prepare one of my specialties. I brought the ingredients from California."

Uh-oh. Stella was going to love having her kitchen invaded during her Thanksgiving Day preparations!

To her credit, Tammy managed to keep a smile on her face. "I suppose that would be okay. You'll have to check with Stella, of course. The kitchen is her territory, not mine."

"Really?" Monica's plucked brow furrowed. "But she's the help, right? You surely don't have to ask *her* permission?"

Tammy's eyes grew frosty. "Stella is part of our family. She's been with us for years. But I'm sure she won't mind sharing her kitchen with you. Will you, Stella?"

The plump gray-haired housekeeper had come into the room with another platter piled high with golden French toast. "Will I what, Mrs. Mike?" She beamed at her employer, her cheeks rosy from the warmth of the kitchen.

"Paul's guest wants to know if she could share the kitchen with you this afternoon while she prepares a special dish for us?"

If Amy hadn't been watching Stella closely, she might've missed the subtle tension around her mouth. But she recovered quickly, summoning a smile. "I suppose the kitchen is big enough for both of us." Her dark eyes settled on Monica. "Feel free to come in whenever you're ready, miss."

"Thank you," Monica said with a brittle smile. Her eyes moved past the housekeeper dismissively. "May I have another glass of juice, please?"

Paul reached for the crystal pitcher and filled her glass. Amy watched him. It was easy to see who was in charge of this relationship. God! What did he *see* in her?

Jeff shoveled a huge bite of syrup-drenched French toast into his mouth and mumbled, "So, what's the specialty, Monica?"

Monica turned her cool gaze to Jeff. "Oh, just a little something I dreamed up for a vegetarian Thanksgiving. I hollow out a small pumpkin and stuff it with a mixture of nuts and wild rice, then I bake it. It's delicious!"

After a moment of awkward silence, Mike grinned, and said brightly, "Well! I, for one, can't wait to try it."

Robin giggled, then tried to cover it by turning it into a cough. "Excuse me," she mumbled, dropping her napkin onto her plate and scrambling up from her chair. Holding a hand over her mouth, she ran out of the room. Amy watched her go, amazed at her restraint. It was so unlike her.

Amy took a last sip of coffee and pushed back from her chair. "Breakfast was delicious. Will you excuse me, please?"

She found Robin in the sunroom, laughing her guts out. When she saw Amy, she laughed harder. "Can you believe it? *Stuffed pumpkin!* God, if Paul eats it with her, I'll absolutely shit a brick!"

Amy grinned. "I hope she doesn't expect us all to try it. So . . . what do you think of her?"

Robin shook her head, her smile widening. "I think . . . the sex must be *phenomenal!*"

The stuffed baked pumpkin sat on the laden table with all the other dishes, looking like a dehydrated jack-o'-lantern that had been left out on someone's doorstep three weeks past Halloween. The filling didn't look much more appetizing. But everyone politely took a spoonful, except for Monica and Paul, who not only filled their plates with the stuffing, but took a portion of the soggy baked pumpkin as well.

Amy had watched Paul fill his plate and wondered if that was all he was going to eat. Last year, like everyone else, he'd eaten his fill of turkey, stuffing, and mashed potatoes, and had done so with relish. Surely he hadn't become a vegetarian just because his girlfriend was?

If he has turkey, there's still a chance that he's not totally lost to her.

Although he gazed longingly at the tender slices of turkey breast, he didn't take any. Amy's heart deflated. But then Tammy came to the rescue.

"Paul, aren't you going to have any turkey?"

He looked at his mother and then at the tempting platter of meat. "Well, I . . ."

"I've been trying to teach him a healthier way to eat, Mrs. Mulcahey," Monica broke in, holding a pumpkin-laden fork. "And he's been doing quite well. Since he cut out meat from his diet, he's been playing much better on the field, haven't you, Paul?"

Paul's lean face filled with color. "I've been doing okay."

Liar, Amy thought. She'd bet her last dollar he hadn't been sticking to a meat-free diet while he was in Colorado. Probably only when *she* was around.

Monica's eyes speared him. "So, you wouldn't want to ruin it now, Paul. Have some more stuffed pumpkin."

It was an order, plain and simple, and everyone at the table knew it. Outrage flared in Tammy's pale blue eyes. There was an obvious edge to her voice when she spoke, "It's Thanksgiving, Paul. Surely you can bend your rules for one day. Have some turkey."

War had been declared. Robin and Jeff leaned forward, eyes gleaming in anticipation of the coming battle. Tammy and Monica exchanged glances, Tammy's challenging, Monica's coolly assessing. Mike's knife paused as he sliced into his turkey, and a grin flickered at his lips. Alice, Tammy's mother, touched a cloth napkin to her fuchsia lips, her bright blue eyes darting from Tammy to Monica like an inquisitive bird. Her husband, Jimmy, calmly continued with his dinner, eyes sparkling. Amy watched Paul, and waited to see what he'd do. Like a condemned prisoner asked to choose between hanging and the firing squad, his gaze swung between his mother and his girlfriend.

The moment of truth. What would he do? Turkey or no turkey? Mother or Monica? Amy found herself praying for turkey and Tammy.

Finally, Paul shrugged. "Maybe just a little white meat."

Amy's shoulders slumped in relief. Tammy's face lit in a radiant smile as she reached for the platter and, with a grandiose flare, passed it to her eldest son. "That's my boy."

Monica's lips tightened, but she remained silent. Amy suspected that poor Paul would catch hell for this little drama later. And that thought thrilled her. If he realized what a shrew his bride-to-be was, surely he'd end the relationship.

Paul took a bite of turkey, and closed his eyes in ecstacy. "Oh, yes! This is delicious." Without a glance toward his fiancée, he reached for the gravy boat and poured a generous amount onto his turkey.

Monica's eyes glittered. "I'll have some more of my stuffed pumpkin, if you don't mind. Would someone pass it to me, please?"

Jeff grabbed it and grinning brightly, passed it over. "You're in luck, Monica. There's plenty left."

She shot him a murderous glance and took the platter. Amy looked down at her half-finished plate, trying desperately to hold back a smile.

This was turning out to be a very good Thanksgiving, after all.

11

Amy dribbled caramel syrup into an oversize coffee mug, then topped the steaming beverage with a generous dollop of canned chemicals labeled whipped cream. She slid the concoction across the counter to the dapper elderly man engrossed in his newspaper. "Here you are, Dr. Johnston. Your caramel deluxe."

"Thank you, Amy." His brown eyes gleamed at her under bushy gray eyebrows. "So, how goes it with your internship?"

"Great! I really enjoy working in the lab." She opened the glass case and drew out a platter of sticky buns. "Want one with lots of nuts?"

He gave her a wink and a crooked smile. "Oh, why not? Can't make me any nuttier."

Amy selected the gooiest, nuttiest bun, placed it on a colonial blue plate, and slid it in front of him. "Here you go. Yeah, it's really cool examining all those old pieces of pottery and wondering about the people who used them."

"You should think about signing up for that trip to Israel next summer." He took a noisy slurp of his coffee. When he looked up, his bushy moustache was flecked with foam.

Amy hid a smile and resisted the urge to grab a napkin and dab it off for him. Dr. Johnston was her archaeology professor, and he was a sweet old man who wore a perpetually bemused expression that made him the target of student mockery all over campus. One class with him, and it was obvious why he was the object of ridicule by the more insensitive students. Amy had to admit he was a little "out there," often lapsing into a daydream right in the middle of a lecture, but she liked him. A creature of habit, he came into the coffee shop for a caramel deluxe coffee and a pastry every day before his eleven o'clock class, and although he wasn't the most talkative man in the world, he always spent a few minutes chatting about his favorite subject—archaeology. When he was a young man, he'd worked at digs all over the world, including Egypt and the Mayan civilization in Mexico. But ill health had brought him back to Virginia in his midforties, and he'd been at William & Mary ever since. Amy hoped that one of these days, she could get him to open up and tell her more about his adventures. It was a good bet he had some fascinating stories to tell.

She grabbed a sponge and began to wipe down the counter. "I'd love to go to Israel, and I would if I could afford it." She shrugged. "Unfortunately, I just can't swing the tuition, and my scholarship doesn't cover educational travel."

Dr. Johnston tore off a portion of his sticky bun and popped it into his mouth. "Well, Miss Shiley, you should go talk to Bobby Marino in Student Affairs. Tell him Jimmy Johnston sent you, and that you need to find a way to finance that trip. He'll be able to work something out. A bright girl like you, with the kind of GPA you've got. Should be no problem at all. I'll call him myself and tell him you're coming."

Amy felt her hopes rising. Was it possible? "Thanks, Dr. Johnston." Amy beamed at him. "I hadn't even seriously considered going because of the money. But it would be a dream come true! I've never even been out of the state of Virginia . . . well, not since I was five years old, anyway."

A bell dinged as the front door opened, and a gust of unseasonably cold air blew in along with a pretty blond girl dressed in the colonial wear of a bar-maid. At first, Amy just assumed she was one of Colonial Williamsburg's reen-actors, perhaps a tour guide for one of the taverns. Until she spoke.

"Hey, Amy! Do I not look *hot* or what?"

Amy focused on the girl's face—her sparkling blue eyes, the dimple flash-ing as she grinned. "Robin! What's with the tavern wench outfit?"

"It's my uniform," she said brightly. "I got a job over at Chowning's Tavern. Three nights a week, I'm going to be doing 'Gambols.' " She giggled. "And wait 'til you see the act! It's *so* naughty!"

Amy's eyes fastened upon her friend's cleavage swelling above her low-cut bodice. "Yeah, I can imagine what the jokes are going to be about." She low-ered her voice and leaned toward Robin. "What did you do? Get implants?"

"Of course not, silly! It's called stays, and it's the forerunner of today's Won-derbra, but a hell of a lot more uncomfortable!" She didn't bother to lower her voice, apparently unconcerned that the few customers in the coffee shop were watching her with amusement. Their attention was all the encouragement Robin needed to milk it for all it was worth. She cupped her breasts and flaunted them to the entire room, grinning broadly. "Whatta ya'all think?"

A young man sitting in the corner applauded and was joined by a couple of others. Professor Johnston flushed bright red and gazed down at his half-empty coffee cup as if its contents held the answer to the world's most puzzling prob-lems. Amy shook her head, but couldn't help grinning at Robin's antics.

Robin winked at her. "I think I just figured out Victoria's secret."

"So, what's with the job?" Amy asked as Robin slid onto a stool at the counter. "You're the one who's always complaining because *I* have to work."

"It's an acting job. It'll look good on my résumé when I go to New York. Can you get me one of those slushy fruit drinks? The pineapple-orange one."

Amy dropped ice into the blender, poured in a measure of pineapple-orange juice and a scoop of vanilla ice cream, then hit the button. Ice clattered for a couple of seconds before it blended into a slushy light orange purée.

Sometime after the fall semester started, Robin had decided she was serious about becoming an actress. It was her life's calling, she declared, throwing herself into her acting classes with gusto. It was no surprise to Amy that Robin was a natural at acting. After all, she was an extrovert who enjoyed being the center of attention. Auditions for the spring opening of *Cat on a Hot Tin Roof* were being held on the last week before Christmas break, and Robin was determined to win the female lead of Maggie. It didn't matter that everyone told her it was unusual for underclassmen to win meaty starring roles like that.

"I'll win it," she'd told anyone who had the nerve to challenge her. "Because I *am* Maggie."

Amy hoped she would. In the last year of living with her, she'd learned a lot about her best friend. For one thing, Robin wasn't as emotionally strong as everyone seemed to think she was. She fought a lot of demons, and even Amy hadn't been able to draw her out about them. She remembered the two times Robin had fallen apart on her—when Princess Di was killed, and after their first argument. If she was counting on getting the part of Maggie, and didn't, would she be crushed? Amy hoped it wouldn't come to that. For the first time, Robin was channeling her energy into something positive rather than destructive.

Amy poured the orange drink into an old-fashioned soda glass, topped it with a spear of pineapple and a cherry, and placed it in front of Robin.

"Oh, guess what?" Robin stuck a straw into her drink and took a long slurp. "I got an e-mail from Paul this morning."

Amy's heart bumped, as it always did at the mention of Paul's name. She ran her hands under the faucet and hit the plunger of the liquid soap container a couple of times to wash off the pineapple residue before her fingers started to itch. "Yeah? How's he doing?"

She grinned, eyes dancing. "Not good. Miss Nob Hill broke up with him. Didn't I tell you it wouldn't last?"

The room brightened. And was it her imagination, or could she actually hear the birds singing from the trees along Duke of Gloucester Street? Why, suddenly, did the world seem a better place, a place where dreams came true, where one's most desired wish would be granted, where bad things never, *ever* happened to good people and where anyone, absolutely *anyone,* could eat fresh pineapple without the slightest allergic reaction?

For decorum's sake, Amy tried not to look too happy. "Oh, that's too bad. Is he really torn up?"

Robin didn't even try to hide her delight. "Oh, it's hard to say with Paul," she said breezily. "If you just go by his e-mail, it sounds like it's no big deal. He just said she sent him a 'Dear John' letter after she got back to Berkeley. Something about different goals and lifestyles . . . some bullshit like that."

"It's the turkey," Amy murmured.

Robin burst out laughing. "You know, you're probably right! She struck me as the type who would drop somebody because he wouldn't follow her 'rules.' God! He's better off, believe me! Can you imagine what she'd be like after a few years of marriage?" She placed an index finger above her top lip and stuck a straight arm into the air. "You *vill* do vot I say, mein husband, or I vill be forced to turn you in to the Gestapo!"

"Shhhh, Robin." Amy grabbed her arm, glancing around to see if the owner was anywhere within earshot. "You want to bring a lawsuit on the coffee shop?"

Robin rolled her eyes. "Oh, screw 'em if they can't take a joke. God! We live in such an uptight society. Makes me sick." She lowered her mouth to the straw and took another slurp.

A sudden thought struck Amy. "Does this mean Paul will be home for Christmas, after all?"

"I guess so! God knows he won't be welcome in Gstaad." She released a joyous laugh. "Jesus, I'm glad they broke up. I couldn't stand the bitch! And I certainly wouldn't want *her* as a sister-in-law." Her blue eyes focused on Amy and lit up. "You know what? I should fix *you* up with Paul! Just think, if you married him, we'd be sisters for real!"

Amy felt the blood rush to her face, and she turned away, searching for something to do. "Oh, you're nuts."

"Why not? You two would be perfect for each other. You even like to watch football, don't you? The most boring sport on God's green earth. You even *understand* it! I'll bet the Dragon Lady didn't know a tight end from a fleaflicker." She let loose a giggle. "Not that *I* do. But I'll bet you do, huh, Amy?"

Amy felt herself blushing. "Like that would impress Paul!" She grabbed a sponge and concentrated on scrubbing a nonexistent stain on the counter. Was Robin teasing her? Or did she really think she and Paul would be a good match?

Robin's eyes lit up. "Aha! So, you *are* interested in my brother?"

"I didn't say that." Amy dumped the dregs from a coffeepot and began to ladle coffee grounds into a paper liner.

It was true she'd developed an interest in football once she knew Paul played, but a relationship would have to be built upon more than a shared interest in a sport. She could see the gears turning in Robin's mind as she chewed over this new possibility. Here was the time to admit her interest.

Interest? Who was she kidding? Here was the time to admit her *love* for Paul. Who knew? Maybe Robin could give her some advice on how she could get him to reciprocate that love. God knows she was an expert in attracting males. Could some of that rub off on *her?*

Amy turned around, fixed her gaze upon Robin, and took a deep breath. But before she could speak, the front door opened and a group of students burst in, cheeks reddened by the gusty wind. For the next ten minutes, Amy was occupied with preparing their convoluted orders.

"Hey, Amy. I'll catch you later, okay?"

Amy looked up to see Robin at the door, waving. She gave her a harried smile and nodded. "Okay!"

The door closed behind her. The moment of truth had come and gone. Amy wasn't sure if she felt relieved or disappointed. But then, it really didn't matter. She'd have plenty of other opportunities to talk to Robin.

What did matter was that the engagement was broken. Paul was free! Amy grinned and added an extra dollop of canned chemicals to the top of a Cafe Vienna.

It was the Christmas morning Amy had always imagined. Well, almost. The house of her imagination had never been this big or grand. It had been more like the model home they'd visited when she was a child. Everything in her fantasies had been of a smaller scale. Like a regular six-foot Christmas tree decorated with multicolored lights and ornaments from Sears in front of the window in the family room and a nice, but small, brick hearth burning a cozy wood fire. A loving family gathered together, excitedly opening gifts and exclaiming in surprise. But her imagination could never have dreamed up what she was experiencing right now. She sat in the library of Windsong where a twelve-foot Christmas tree soared to the ceiling, twinkling with white fairy lights, swagged in white and salmon ribbons and hung with delicate crystal ornaments; it was the kind of tree usually seen only in elegant hotel lobbies or celebrity homes. A gas fire burned merrily in the ornate marble fireplace. The Mulcaheys, wearing thick winter robes, were settled comfortably on sofas and chairs, mugs of coffee—and hot chocolate for Robin—nearby, as they finished opening the last of the gifts. At first, Amy had felt awkward because she'd had so little money to spend on presents. It had been almost impossible to shop for the Mulcaheys, but Robin had helped her, and they'd found something for everyone—a small crystal votive cup for Tammy, a pair of leather driving gloves for Michael, a book on John Elway for Paul, and a computer game for Jeff. As for Robin, Amy had bought her a new diary bound in a gorgeous blue-and-gold fabric with a celestial design. She'd nervously watched everyone open their gifts, and sighed in relief when they each seemed pleased with her choice.

Paul, seeing the John Elway book, looked at her from across the room and gave her a smile that made her toes curl in the warm fleece slippers Jeff had given her. "Who told you John Elway was my hero?" he asked.

Amy blushed, and murmured, "I think you may have mentioned it once or twice."

"Open mine next," Robin said, dropping a wrapped box on Amy's lap. "Hurry up, because I can't wait to borrow it," she added with an impish grin.

The box was heavy, and Amy knew even as she opened it that Robin had spent way too much money on her. As usual. It was sure to make the sweater she'd bought for her at 50 percent off at Express look really cheap and ordinary. "Oh, Robin!" she sighed, gazing at the gorgeous black leather jacket nestled in tissue paper. "Oh, this is too much."

Robin's eyes danced. "Don't you just love it? You're going to look so awesome in it."

Amy opened her mouth to protest the expense, but before she could say anything, Michael handed her a small wrapped box. "And this is just a little something from Tammy and me," he said with a smile. "I was the one who picked it out, though. So, if you don't like it, I'll take you shopping so you can find something else."

Amy took the box, feeling a lump rising in her throat. She hadn't expected a gift from Robin's parents. Or from any of her family, really. Yet, they were treating her like she was one of them. And that was a better gift than anything they could give her in a festively wrapped box.

"You didn't have to get me anything," she murmured, staring down at the gift.

"Sure we did," Michael replied. "You're like another daughter to us, Sunshine. Go ahead. Open it."

Amy drew in a sharp breath, gazing down at the fragile silver chain with its pendant in the shape of a sun. "Oh, it's beautiful!"

Michael grinned. "As soon as I saw it, I knew it was perfect for you. Because you've got a smile like a sunbeam."

"Thank you, Michael . . . Tammy." Amy smiled at Robin's parents. "I can't tell you how much this means to me."

Robin leaned closer to examine the necklace. Moments before, she'd opened a gift from her parents that had also been jewelry—a gold heart pendant with an off-center diamond.

"I like yours better," she whispered now. "Can I borrow it sometime?"

"Sure," Amy whispered back.

"There's just one more gift under the tree," Michael announced, reaching for a small box. "Let's see . . . who is this one for? Oh! It says Robin. Here you go, Cupcake." He tossed it to her.

"Who is it from?" Robin asked, unwrapping it.

"Santa." Michael grinned.

She opened the box and pulled out a key ring with two keys dangling from it. "What's this?"

"Why don't you go look out on the driveway and see?"

Robin stared from Michael to Tammy, her eyes huge. Then she jumped up from her chair and raced out of the room. Everyone followed. Amy had just reached the foyer when she heard Robin's delighted scream. "*Omigod! It's a Camaro!*"

Amy watched as Robin wrenched open the front door and bounded down the steps. By the time Amy stepped out after the rest of the family, everyone had gathered around the new black Camaro.

Robin was jumping up and down in excitement. "Is it really mine? No shit? It's really *mine*?"

"It's a combination Christmas and birthday present," Tammy said. "So, don't expect anything when March rolls around."

"Oh, my *God*!" Robin shrieked, looking torn between wanting to hug her parents or wanting to jump into the car and drive away. The hugging won out. She went to her mother first and embraced her. "Thanks, Mom. I love it!" Then she turned to her father.

Amy, watching, sensed some tension as they stared at each other. Then, after a moment of hesitation, Robin approached Michael and gave him a brief hug. "Thanks, Dad. It's the coolest present ever." Then she turned back to her mother. "Can I take it for a drive now? Me and Amy?"

Tammy frowned. "I think Stella has breakfast ready. Why don't you wait until later?"

As they headed back into the house, Amy felt a tap on her shoulder. She turned and saw Paul behind her. Her heart skipped a beat.

"Hey, Amy. I have a little something for you." He handed her a rectangular package.

She felt her cheeks grow hot. "Oh, you didn't . . ."

"I know," he said, his lips quirking in a wry grin. "I didn't have to get you anything. That's what you've said every time someone gave you a gift. I know I didn't have to, but I wanted to. I saw this in the bookstore in Merchants Square, and thought of you."

Amy unwrapped the gift and stared down at the book. It was the new ghost story release by L. B. Taylor. She smiled and met Paul's eyes. "You remembered!"

He nodded, smiling. "Of course. Let me know if it's any good, okay? And by the way, we never did get out to Cohoke Crossing, did we?"

Amy shook her head.

Paul held the door open for her, and as she passed him, he added, "Well, maybe we can find time to do that while I'm home."

"*Ohhhh, servant boy!*" Robin trilled, a come-hither smile on her face.

Dressed in her low-cut barmaid outfit, she winked and smiled saucily at a handsome ponytailed young man clad in the colonial wear of a servant. She crooked an enticing finger at him. "'Tis said in the market square that your sweet mother has run off with the town drunkard, and left her poor son to make his way alone in this cruel world. Come, dear boy, and bury your sorrow in the bosom of motherly comfort."

The servant "boy" turned to the audience in the tavern, lifted his eyebrows, and a slow, delighted smile crossed his face. The crowd clapped and hooted. He turned back to Robin, his eyes having grown mournful and his expression taking on the appearance of a butt-kicked hound dog. Robin crooked her finger again, giving him another lascivious wink. Tongue lolling, he loped over and gleefully buried his face in the lush fullness of her breasts. The crowd howled with laughter as Robin grabbed his head and pushed his face closer, her eyes rolling with orgiastic delight.

Blushing, Amy laughed and glanced over at Paul. Her heart did a belly flop as she caught his blue gaze upon her. She couldn't be sure in the glow from the candlelight, but she thought his color was heightened. Was he embarrassed by the ribald antics of his sister? But surely he'd been to "Gambols" before and knew the humor often got a bit raunchy? And he knew Robin well enough to know she'd be smack in the middle of any opportunity that arose to cross the line between racy and raunchy.

No, she didn't think he was at all concerned with Robin and her naughty act. In fact, she got the feeling he wasn't even really paying that much attention to the entertainment in the popular tavern. Amy felt the heat on her face intensify. Why was he looking at her like that? It was almost as if he was really seeing her for the first time.

Disconcerted, she glanced down at her wristwatch. Almost ten o'clock. Just two hours left of 1997. A thrill of anticipation swept through her. What would 1998 bring? Love, she hoped. Love with someone special. She chanced another glance at Paul and saw he had turned his attention back to Robin. He wore an amused smile on his handsome face, yet Amy saw something else in his expression. Was it sadness? God, he looked so good in that hunter green sweater and the brown suede jacket he hadn't bothered to take off after they'd settled at their table in the crowded tavern. His black hair was tousled by the capricious wind of an unseasonably mild winter night. Amy loved it like that. It made her want to thread her fingers through its ebony satin texture, press her lips to his sensuous mouth, and touch the bristled black hairs that shadowed his lean jaw. . . .

Horrified at the direction of her thoughts, Amy fastened her gaze on Robin and tried to forget Paul's disturbing proximity. It was Robin's idea that they gather a group together and come to the last "Gambols" of the year. They'd called some of the Kappa Chis, and the sorority girls had brought their dates. To Amy's delight—and disquiet—Robin had roped Paul into coming along to round out the group. Of course, since Amy and Paul were the only singles of the group, for the night, at least, they would be a couple.

Amy realized that Robin intended to play matchmaker when she showed up in her room that afternoon and immediately vetoed the dress she'd chosen to wear. "Not that one." She grabbed the simple black chiffon dress edged with tiny pink primroses and placed it back in her closet. "What do you want to look like? Rebecca of Fucking Sunnybrook Farm?" She raked through Amy's closet, rejecting one dress after another. "Oh, God! It's impossible!" With an explosive sigh, she stalked out of the room and returned a moment later with a tiny spandex number in red jacquard. She held it up by its spaghetti straps. "I ordered it from Victoria's Secret for Valentine's Day, but it'll be perfect for you tonight." Amy had protested, but it had been wasted breath.

A moment later, Amy stood in front of the mirror, encased in the body-hugging slip of a dress. God, she looked like a two-bit hooker! No, that wasn't exactly true. The dress was slinky and sexy, but not slutty. Granted, it revealed more of her breasts than she was used to, but the strapless Wonderbra lived up to its name in giving her some *ooomph*. Maybe that was why Paul kept looking at her all evening. He was probably wondering where her C-cup boobs had materialized from.

"At least you've got bigger tits than me," Robin mocked, eyeing her bosom. "Jason calls mine his little crab apples. Maybe we should both think about implants. I'd at least like to have grapefruits, wouldn't you?"

Amy had worn her hair down, the way she knew Paul liked it, swinging free and casual. And for sure, her appearance had made an impact on him when she'd descended the stairs to the foyer where he and Robin waited. With a delighted grin, Robin, already dressed in her barmaid outfit, snapped a photo of Amy with her digital camera. Then she turned quickly and got one of Paul's dumbfounded expression. Amy saw it for herself, but she couldn't wait until Robin downloaded the photo onto her computer so she could make sure he really looked as blown away as she'd thought he had. But remembering how he kept looking at her tonight—how she could feel him looking at her right now—she didn't think she'd need the photo as proof.

The vignette of the randy servant boy and the obliging barmaid ended, and the audience showed their approval with wolf whistles and applause. Dimple flashing, Robin curtsied to the crowd and tripped out of the room.

Amy jumped when Paul's hand touched her arm. He leaned in close, his warm breath tickling her ear. "I think my sister has finally found her calling."

"You seem surprised she's so good." With an effort, she drew her eyes away from his and took a sip of her Coke.

"No way! I've always thought Robby could do anything she put her mind to." His square hands wrapped around the pewter stein of beer in front of him. Eyes pensive, he added, "I wish I could be here to see her play Maggie next spring."

"Yeah, she wishes you could, too. Oh, Paul, you should see her. She's already learned all the lines, and rehearsals don't even start until mid-January."

Robin had done exactly what she'd set out to do. She'd won the role of Maggie hands down, blowing out the competition—even a senior with credits a mile long, one of them a CBS soap opera. With her passionate, angst-filled audition, she'd left the director reeling, and as she exited the stage, there'd been no doubt in anyone's mind—especially Amy's—that she had the part sewn up.

Amy was thrilled for her. Maybe this was exactly what Robin needed to get her on the right track. Lately, Amy had been worried more than ever about her drinking and near-manic partying. Robin's behavior was reminding her just a little too much of her mother's in the early days before she'd finally checked out of reality. Maybe it was time to encourage her to get help. Then again, now that she had this play to prepare for—and it would definitely take up a lot of her time—maybe she'd cut back on the drinking on her own.

A serving girl in colonial dress appeared at their table to replenish their drinks. Paul smiled up at her, and immediately a becoming blush heightened her pretty face. Amy's heart sank. How did she ever stand a chance with a guy like Paul when every girl within spitting distance blossomed like a spring crocus under his gaze? She could only imagine what it was like in Colorado. The charismatic, not to mention, good-looking football player surrounded by gorgeous nubile coeds. Why on earth would he want anything to do with a boring little virgin like Amy Shiley?

"The check, please," Paul said to the waitress.

As soon as Robin changed clothes, they were heading for a New Year's Eve party at Joni Einer's house in Lightfoot. Robin appeared moments later, wearing a slinky thigh-length black dress with a scooped back cut so low it might have been a swimsuit. Her hand was wrapped around the firm bicep of the ponytailed man who'd played the servant boy.

"I've talked Justin into going to the party with us," she announced, reaching down for Paul's beer stein. "You don't mind, do you? Yeccch! It's warm!" But she drained it anyway. Winking at Amy, she added, "You guys got a head start on me, so I'll have to catch up. Ready to go?"

Paul stood and held Amy's black velvet coat for her. The night air was mild as they stepped out of the tavern into the dimly lit Duke of Gloucester Street and turned right to walk the few blocks to the parking lot where Robin's new Camaro was parked. Robin held Justin's hand and practically skipped ahead, so anxious she was to get to the party. Amy and Paul walked at a slower pace, enjoying the December night masquerading as October, and the utter stillness of Colonial Williamsburg after most of the tourists had left. From behind them, the clop of hooves on cobblestones approached, and a carriage rattled by, lit by a single lantern to guide its way. The driver touched his tricorn in silent greeting, and Paul and Amy waved back. For a moment, it almost seemed as if they'd taken a step back in time.

"What a great night. You cold?" Amy jumped slightly as Paul's arm draped around her shoulder.

"Uh . . . no, I'm okay." Stupid, she admonished herself. Now, he'd take his arm away. But he didn't. In fact, it seemed to tighten around her.

"You know, as much as I like Colorado, there's no place like Williamsburg. I forget how much I love it until I come back."

"Me too. I was just thinking that. About how much I love it here."

She looked up at him, saw the way the light wind tossed his black hair. A sliver of moon slipped out behind a cloud, illuminating him. He looked up at the sky, his face euphoric. Feeling her gaze, his eyes met hers. He smiled, and her heartbeat faltered.

To cover up her nervousness, she spoke in a rush, "You can just feel it, can't you? The history? The people who walked this very street, who loved and hated . . . realized dreams, and suffered horrible tragedies."

Paul smiled. "You're so awesome, Amy. Most girls your age are bored to death by history."

Amy felt her cheeks grow hot. "I guess I'm just a romantic at heart. Maybe I was born in the wrong time period."

His arm tightened around her shoulders. "Don't change. I like you just the way you are. So . . . what do you think the chances are that I can get the Redskins to draft me?"

The thought made her heady. Washington was only two hours away.

"I think they'd be crazy not to."

His hand squeezed her shoulder. "How about moving to Colorado and becoming my personal cheerleader?"

How about falling in love with me and making me your personal cheerleader for life?

If she were Robin, that's what she'd say. She'd turn this into the moment of truth. *Love me or don't love me. Let's just get on with it.*

But she wasn't Robin, so she just blushed and remained silent.

"Looks like whatever team I go with, it's going to be the wide receiver position," Paul said. "So much for wanting to play quarterback."

"You're lucky you have a talent for both," Amy said, feeling more confident now that they were discussing something she understood. "But you've got great speed. That's why they'll want you as a wide receiver. You can probably beat any cornerback in the pros."

He squeezed her shoulder and pulled her closer. Her heart lurched with joy.

"I think you already *are* my personal cheerleader," he said, a smile in his voice.

Amy felt as if she were floating on air. "Maybe I am."

Robin and Justin were waiting at the Camaro, but they'd found something to do to pass the time. He had her up against the car and was in the middle of a thorough tonsil examination, using his tongue as an instrument. When she heard their approach, Robin ripped away from him, laughing.

"About time! Jeez, we'll be lucky to get there before the friggin' New Year."

"Hey, just enjoying the night, sis," Paul said with a shrug. "You should try it some time. Slow down and enjoy the moment."

Robin rolled her eyes and aimed her remote entry at the car. The power locks opened with a click. "You sound like a freakin' hippie."

Paul held the front seat back for Amy as she slipped into the close confines of the backseat, then he crawled in after her. She felt warm all over at being so close to him, close enough to breathe in his musky sandalwood scent, so uniquely his own. She was glad that the drive to Lightfoot would take a good twenty minutes; she wished it would take forever. Justin got into the front seat next to Robin. She started the ignition, and the CD player began blaring out Alanis Morissette's "Ironic."

Paul looked over at Amy and grinned. He began to sing along with Alanis. Robin joined in, and finally, so did Justin and Amy. By the time they reached Route 60, they were competing to drown each other out. After the song ended, Paul, laughing and out of breath, reached over and took Amy's hand.

He held it all the way to Lightfoot.

The New Year was over an hour old, and Robin was shit-faced. Pretty much the way she'd started out the year before.

Paul spoke in a raised whisper. "Okay, I've got her. You go ahead and get the door."

Amy hurried to the back door of Windsong and unlocked it. She held it open as Paul strode up the walkway, cradling Robin in his arms.

After they arrived at the party, Robin had started downing beers, and then had had the bad sense to switch to vodka. By midnight, she'd been totally out of it, and with Robin, the drunker she got, the more uninhibited she became. When she'd climbed onto the kitchen table at twelve-fifteen and began to strip the slinky dress off her shoulders, Paul had grabbed her and hustled her out of the house, much to the disappointment of every horny male in the kitchen, Justin included. She'd fought him all the way like a wildcat, screaming obscenities. He wore a half-inch scratch just below his left eye to prove it. *Robin will be horrified when she sees it tomorrow,* Amy thought.

Damn her, anyway! Here it was a new year, and Amy was spending it with the guy she was crazy about. But this wasn't the romantic end of the evening she'd envisioned. Here she was playing nursemaid to Robin. Again.

She slipped ahead of him to run up the stairs and open the door to Robin's room. By the time he stepped inside, Amy had tossed the shams onto a chair and thrown back the thick leopard-print comforter. Paul settled Robin's body onto the coordinated sateen sheet and stepped back.

"You want to get her out of that dress?"

Amy nodded. "If she pukes all over it, I'll never hear the end of it."

"I'll be downstairs."

"Uh . . . Paul? I know this is awkward, but . . . I can't get her out of that by myself. It's practically glued to her body."

He blushed, his gaze sweeping over his stuporous sister. "How can I help?"

Amy gazed at Robin, thinking. "Let me get the skirt up past her hips, then maybe you can hold her in a sitting position while I tug it off over her head."

"Sounds like a plan." But he looked dubious. Or maybe just embarrassed.

It got worse, Amy realized a moment later as she saw that Robin wasn't wearing panties under her panty hose. Paul averted his eyes, his face turning even ruddier.

"Okay. Prop her up."

Paul took a deep breath and slipped his arm under Robin's shoulders, forcing her into a sitting position. Her blond hair fell forward, obscuring her face. She moaned an unintelligible protest and lapsed back into dreamland. Amy tugged her dress up over her breasts, not at all surprised to find she wasn't wearing a bra. But apparently Paul was horrified at the discovery.

"Oh, jeez," he murmured, planting his gaze on a poster of three hard-hatted male models sporting tight jeans, bare chests, and granite jaws.

Amy had to grin. "Oh, come on, Paul. Surely this isn't the first time you've seen a pair of naked boobs." Amazing how comfortable she felt with him after spending the evening together. Yesterday, she couldn't have imagined saying something so flippant to him.

"Not my *sister's*!" Paul retorted, keeping his eyes firmly on the poster of the construction hunks.

"Okay. Can you hold her arms up? There!"

The dress was off. After Paul eased Robin back to the bed, Amy pulled the comforter over her. Releasing a sigh of relief, she said, "We'll just let her sleep in the panty hose."

Downstairs in the foyer, Amy glanced at Paul, feeling her shyness return. She didn't want the night to end. All too soon, he would be returning to Colorado, and she didn't want to waste a moment of her precious time with him. She wanted to stay up with him all night. Watch the sun come up on the first day of 1998. But could she tell him that?

She took a deep breath and opened her mouth to do just that, but before she could speak, he smiled and held out his hand. Amy's heart skipped a beat. "What?"

He nudged his head toward the door. "Come on."

e looked at his outstretched hand, then trustingly put hers into it. "Where going?"

His smile widened. "Cohoke Crossing."

Robin's Camaro was parked on a bluff overlooking the railroad tracks. On the CD player, Jewel plaintively sang "Foolish Games." It was a song that always brought tears to Amy's eyes when she was alone, so anguished was the singer's love for a guy who apparently didn't love her back. But now, crazy as it seemed, she didn't feel so hopeless about Paul. He was here with her, wasn't he? Monica was no longer in the picture. And there was no doubt he'd been looking at her differently all night. Why *wasn't* it possible there could be something more than friendship between them?

He'd been quiet during the half hour drive to Cohoke Crossing. Now, he sat, staring into the darkness, moonlight washing over the pensive look on his lean, handsome face. She wondered if he was lost in the sadness of Jewel's song, or was he simply staring intently at the railroad tracks, hoping to catch the first glimpse of the ghostly light?

"Does she do that often?" Paul asked when Jewel's song came to an end. "Get that drunk?"

"More often than she should," Amy said quietly. How much should she tell him? Would she be betraying a confidence if she admitted how often Robin got trashed? "I worry about her."

"So do I. She was pretty wild in high school. I'd hoped college would calm her down some." He shook his head. "I've never understood her, you know. I love her with all my heart, but I don't understand why she has to act out like that. Does she open up to you?"

Amy shrugged and gazed down at the dark railroad tracks. Was this why Paul had brought her here? To discuss Robin? And she'd so hoped he was finally seeing her as a woman in her own right, and not just Robin's best friend. "Not really. Sometimes, I think she wants to, but if I ask too many questions, she withdraws."

"She's always been like that. You know, I don't think I've ever seen her cry. Even that time she fell out of a tree and broke her arm, she didn't cry, and God knows she had to be in agony."

A memory of Robin's tear-streaked face after the announcement of Princess Di's death flashed in Amy's mind. The only other time she'd seen Robin cry was when they'd made up after their one and only argument. "She's a tough cookie, all right. But you know, I think being in this play is really going to turn things around for her. It's like, all of a sudden, she has a career plan. And you know, once rehearsals start, she's going to be so busy, she's not going to have time to drink." Her words sounded hollow, even to herself. But Paul seemed to take them at face value.

He looked at her and smiled. "You know what? I'm really glad she has you." He reached out and took her hand, sending Amy's heart bumping. "You're good for her. In fact, I think you're good for all of us. You're so quiet and calm—kind of like the eye in the middle of a storm." His thumb stroked the indentation between her thumb and forefinger.

Amy caught her breath. She smiled, meeting his gaze. "But isn't the eye of the storm the most dangerous place to be?"

His eyes locked with hers, and his smile faded. "I'm beginning to think it is."

Amy had to look away. She loved the way he was looking at her; it was thrilling, yet, frightening. Her heart raced beneath the lace texture of her dress. For a moment, everything felt surreal, dreamlike. Was that it? Was this one of her wild fantasies? Or could it possibly be real? Being here with Paul, feeling this strong current of electricity crackling between them? She couldn't blame it on liquor. Paul had had one beer at the tavern, and at the party, after seeing the way Robin was putting it away, he'd switched to soda. No, the heated look in his eyes couldn't be blamed on booze.

"So, how's it going with your boyfriend?" he asked.

Amy swallowed hard. "My boyfriend?" She grabbed a strand of her hair and eyed it for split ends. Even though it was almost impossible to see anything in the near dark.

Paul reached out and grabbed her hand, pulling it away from her hair. "Stop that. You're going to make yourself go cross-eyed. And yeah, your boyfriend. The one you had at Thanksgiving. Remember? You were anxious to get up to your room so you could call him."

"Oh, him." Jolted, Amy searched her mind for something plausible. She didn't want to admit she'd been lying. "I'm not seeing him anymore." She thought of Jason and blushed. "It was a short relationship." *Like about fifteen minutes.*

"Well, I know how that goes. I guess you heard Monica broke up with me?"

"Yeah. Sorry about that." *Sorry, my ass.* But what else could she say?

He released her hand and combed his through his shiny black hair. "It was a shock. I thought everything was cool between us when she flew back to San Francisco, but I guess it wasn't."

Amy didn't know what to say. Politeness required her to make some sort of sympathetic response, but she just couldn't bring herself to say she was sorry. She wasn't. She was glad, *ecstatic* Monica was no longer in the picture. Silence stretched out between them, broken only by the sound of the rising wind whistling through the bare tree branches and the hoot of a lone owl. It went on so long she felt like she had to break it, say something. "It was the turkey, wasn't it?"

Her face flamed. Dumb, stupid, *idiotic* thing to say!

Paul looked at her, then he laughed. Laughed hard. She grinned, and a giggle escaped her.

"Yeah! It was the turkey!" Paul shook his head, grinning as if he couldn't believe it hadn't occurred to him before. "It was the goddamn *turkey*!"

More laughter. When they finally got their mirth under control, Paul realized the Jewel CD had ended. He reached for the leather-bound CD album on the backseat. "What else has she got in here?" Switching on an interior light, he flipped through it. "Melissa Etheridge . . . Sheryl Crow . . . Alanis Morissette. God! Doesn't Rob have anything but pissed-off female singers? I'm in the mood for something a little more mellow."

Amy selected a CD and handed it to him. "Here. Play this one."

He squinted at the title. "*Songs from a Secret Garden?*" He leveled his gaze at her. "What's this? Some New Age mystic crap?"

She grinned at him. "Just put it in. You'll love it. The first song is my favorite. It's called 'Nocturne.'"

A female voice issued from the CD player, a voice clear and pure as Waterford crystal followed by a haunting violin. Paul sat silently, listening, until the song ended.

In the quiet before the next song, Paul rubbed his hands over his suede-jacketed arms. "Christ! It gave me chills."

"Good ones, right?"

"Oh, yeah. Her voice! The music. It . . ." He shook his head.

"Leaves you speechless."

"Yeah. Wow! Is the rest of the CD this good?"

"I love it. And Robin does, too, even though she won't admit it. She calls it my New Age shit."

He laughed. "Robby has a way with words, doesn't she?" He glanced out toward the railroad tracks. "Looks like we're not going to see our ghost light tonight."

Amy felt a lurch in her heart. Was he about to suggest they leave? She wanted to hold on to this night—this moment—forever. It was perfection. Just sitting here in the dark car with him, listening to soft, romantic music. He was so close, she could smell his sandalwood scent. Feel the warmth of his body.

"Oh, look! The moon's going behind a cloud." She pointed out her window, trying to distract herself from the suddenly uncomfortable track of her thoughts. But it backfired on her.

He leaned close, scrunching his head near hers so he could see. Her heart almost stopped beating as she felt his warm breath on her cheek.

"Mmmm." He leaned closer, turning his face into her hair. "Your hair smells so good. What is it, peach? I noticed it before when we were putting Robby to bed."

Her heartbeat had resumed at the pace of a stampeding horse. She sat still, afraid to move. Afraid to break the spell. "It's my shampoo," she said softly. "Tropical coconut."

He chuckled. "Peach, coconut? What's the difference? I like it." He reached out and grasped a lock of her hair, stroking it between thumb and forefinger. "You've got really nice hair, Amy. I've always thought that. And it's natural blond, isn't it?"

A delicious shiver rippled up her back as he continued to play with her hair, sliding it through his fingers. "Yeah, I think it's the only thing about me that Robin is envious of."

"Amy?"

"Yeah?"

"Look at me." He reached out and touched the side of her jaw, turning her to face him. Amy caught her breath at the soft look in his blue eyes. "Don't sell yourself short, okay? You're a beautiful, sweet girl."

Amy smiled, and for a moment, she felt ridiculously close to tears. She'd waited so long to hear Paul say something like this to her. "You really think so?" she whispered.

He nodded, and taking his thumb, traced it along the line of her bottom lip. She gazed at him, breathless. *Kiss me! Oh, Paul, kiss me.* "You're going to make some lucky guy really happy one of these days."

She stiffened.

"What? What's wrong?"

Biting back tears, she turned away and stared out the window. "I think you should take me home."

"Amy?" His hand pressed on her shoulder. "What did I say?"

Finally, she turned back to him, and it was impossible to hold in the anger. "You know, I understand now why Monica broke up with you. You're an *idiot*, you know that?"

He stared at her. "*Why?*" She didn't answer, and a moment later, she saw realization dawn on his face. "Oh, Amy. I *am* an idiot. Are you trying to tell me you have a crush on me?"

Crush? He was even more of an idiot than she'd thought. "Let's just go home."

"No, let's talk about this. Look at me."

When she did, she was horrified to see pity on his face. Oh, God! How could she have been so mistaken to believe he was actually seeing her as an attractive woman tonight? But how to explain those looks he'd been giving her? Smoldering, contemplative stares at the tavern? She might be naive and inexperienced, but she damn well recognized a look of appreciation in a man's eyes, and she'd seen it in Paul's tonight.

"It's just that . . . I guess I've always thought of you as . . . you know, a younger sister," Paul said, choosing his words carefully. "You're like part of the family, you know."

"*Bullshit!*"

The caustic word hung in the air between them. Amy saw shock in Paul's eyes, and felt it shuddering through her. *Had she really said that?* Yes, she had, and she knew she couldn't leave it at that. It was almost as if she could hear Robin egging her on. *You've gone too far now to turn back, girl. Go for it.*

"That was no brotherly look you were giving me when I came down those stairs tonight," Amy said quietly. Slowly, she shrugged out of the black velvet coat Robin had loaned her. As his eyes swept over her low-cut dress molding to her breasts, she felt her shyness evaporate. Like the time she'd been with Jason in the tent, she felt that magic power come over her, that secret feminine power that turned men to weak-kneed slaves. She smiled at him, her heart thudding. "And that's no brotherly look you're giving me right now."

"Oh, Christ, Amy!" He moved toward her.

His hands twined into her hair, and drawing her to him, his mouth settled onto hers. Warm, so warm and sweet. Amy nestled against him, opening her mouth, allowing all her pent-up longing to emerge in one heated kiss. Her hands slipped inside his jacket, pressing urgently against the warmth of his chest. Oh, God, she'd never known kisses could be this sweet. His tongue tangled with hers, tantalizing, questioning. Her nipples hardened. She felt a delicious warm wetness between her legs.

In the back of her mind, she heard the music playing and the sounds of their staggered breathing, the rustling of their hands against each other's clothing. His palm cupped her breast, and against his mouth, she released a startled, rapturous sigh. He drew away, his eyes questioning. She reached out and brushed a hand down his face, carefully avoiding the ugly scratch Robin had inflicted on him. Oh, how could she explain to him how much she wanted him? She covered his hand with hers, pressing it to her breast. His mouth returned for another kiss, more urgent this time.

She grew daring, dropping her hand to the crotch of his black jeans, delighted to feel the bulge there. Just a little touch, pressing just *here*, and he groaned, dragging his mouth from hers. "Oh, Amy. You don't know what you're doing to me."

"Yes, I do," she whispered. Her fingers threaded through his hair as she guided his head back to hers, fastening her parted lips on his. She explored his lips with her tongue, nibbling, drawing him in. Her hand returned to his erection, pressing and stroking. She felt his hands at the spaghetti straps of her dress, tugging them down over her shoulders. The bodice fell, revealing her lacy strapless Wonderbra. Paul drew away, his eyes drinking her in. Even in the darkness of the car, she could see he was flushed, excited. And knowing that she was the cause of his excitement thrilled her. Made her bolder. She drew away from him, and reaching behind her, unfastened her bra. It fell to her lap. He sat motionless, his eyes locked with hers. Then, slowly, his gaze moved to her breasts. She could see in his eyes that she was beautiful, and she loved him for it. Never again would she feel like she wasn't pretty enough.

He reached out and palmed her breasts as if he were holding a priceless, precious work of art. She closed her eyes, shuddering with pleasure. His hands were warm on her skin, and again, she wanted to freeze time. Hold this moment of pure perfection, put it away in a locked box, so it would never truly be over. He leaned forward, nuzzling her neck, trailing kisses down her shoulder blade to the swell of her breast. She drew in a sharp breath as he hesitated, his thumb rolling over her crested nipple. Then slowly he dropped his head, his silky black hair skimming her skin, and suckled at her breast. Liquid fire shot through her. She squirmed against him, her skirt riding up high on her thighs.

"Oh, Paul," she murmured, throwing her head back in ecstasy as his tongue flicked at her nipple. "Oh, yes! I . . . want you . . . I want you . . . to be the first."

He stiffened and drew his lips away from her breast. It was quiet inside the car. Only the sound of their ragged breathing. Even the CD had stopped sometime ago. Slowly, Paul drew away from her and awkwardly tugged at the bodice of her dress, pulling it up so it covered her breasts. He turned away, refusing to meet her eyes.

"We can't do this." He started the ignition, his face expressionless. "I'm taking you home."

12

Amy stared at him, holding her dress tightly against her breasts. "But *why*? Paul, I *want* to. I want you to be the first." *Oh, God. That sounded so pathetic. So desperate.*

He backed the car up, his face expressionless. "Because it's not right like this. Here. In a car like two horny teenagers. You're not Robin, and I'm not Jason Barelli."

Her heart froze. Oh, God! Had Robin told him about that night at Assateague with Jason? With trembling fingers, she tugged the straps of her dress back onto her shoulders and pulled on her velvet coat, stuffing her bra inside it. She felt cold and sick. Paul pulled onto the highway and headed toward Williamsburg. Raindrops splattered onto the windshield; the weather had changed. A cold front moving in?

The silence between them was heavy, charged. In the illumination of the instrument panel, Amy saw the *Secret Garden* CD sticking halfway out of the CD player. She thought about pushing it in. Anything to drown out the deafening quiet in the car. But she felt frozen, unable to move. Paul switched on the windshield wipers as the rain grew heavier, and the rhythmic swishing of the blades seemed to add to the tension between them.

She bit her bottom lip and stared out into the darkness, fighting back tears. What had she done wrong? She'd practically begged him to make love to her. Like a common whore, she'd stripped in front of him, practically offered herself on a silver platter. Why didn't he want her?

She thought she knew. He'd remembered who she was. Or rather, *what* she was. A girl from the wrong side of the tracks. Poor white trash. The heir to the Mulcahey fortune couldn't risk it all by getting tangled up with a girl from her social class, no matter how pretty or sexy he found her. And he *did* find her sexy. She knew she hadn't imagined his erection. He'd wanted her, all right. Just not enough.

By the time they reached Lightfoot, the rain was driving down so hard Amy wondered how Paul could possibly see the road. It thundered against the windshield, obliterating the earlier silence. Paul drove slowly, his hands clenched on the steering wheel, his face a mask of concentration. The visibility was so bad that she had stopped obsessing about his rejection and was now seriously wondering if their first day of 1998 would turn out to be their last. Suddenly Paul flicked on his blinker and turned into the parking lot of a 7-Eleven.

He put the gearshift in park and turned to her. "You want anything?"

She shook her head, huddling in her coat. It *was* getting colder. Paul noticed her shiver and turned the heat up a notch. "I'll be right back."

He opened the door and slammed it behind him. And even though he was gone, his scent lingered, and a fresh wash of pain swept through her. She sat, staring at the rivulets of rain streaming down the windshield between the swish of the blades. She wished they were back at Windsong. She wished she could just crawl into her beautiful king-size bed in her lovely big bedroom and cover up with the lush satin comforter. She'd listen to the rain beating against the window and let herself cry. Maybe Ruby Two-Shoes would mew at the door, and she'd let the big orange tabby in so she could curl up on the bed with her. She'd stroke her soft, clean fur, bask in her aloof but unconditional love, and try not to think about how very horribly 1998 had started.

The door opened, and Paul scrambled into the car, his hair shiny with beads of rain. Amy looked away, fastening her gaze on the red, green, and white trim of the convenience store. She heard the rustle of paper as Paul took something out of a package.

"Here."

She glanced over and saw that he was holding out a small box. Her eyes dropped to it, and her stomach tightened as she recognized the name. Trojans. Her gaze lifted slowly to his. His face was solemn, his eyes questioning.

"Are you sure this is what you want?" he asked softly.

She looked at the box again, and saw that his hand was trembling, ever so slightly. Her heart began to pound. She reached out and took the box out of his hand, dropped it into her lap, then took his hand in hers. She met his eyes, moistened her bottom lip with her tongue, and whispered, "It's what I've wanted since the very first day I met you."

Windsong was quiet when they slipped inside. Only the sound of the rain beating down in a deafening tattoo. It was three-forty-five in the morning. Hand in hand, Amy and Paul climbed the stairs and crept down the hall toward her bedroom. She stepped inside, and he followed, closing the door behind them.

In the darkness, Amy turned to him and slipped the coat off her shoulders. Paul shrugged out of his suede jacket. She couldn't see him well, but she felt his intense gaze. His fragrance of sandalwood mixed with rain drifted over her as he reached out and cupped the back of her head in his hands. She gasped, and before she could take in a breath, his mouth clamped down on hers.

Slipping her hands under his sweater, her palms pressed against his cotton shirt, warm from his skin. His hands tightened on her shoulders, toying with the straps of her dress. Pressing against him, she moaned, tasting his tongue, exploring. The straps slipped from her shoulders, and he peeled her dress down. He ripped his mouth away from hers and kissed a trail down her neck to her shoulder blades. Cupping her breasts in both hands, he began kissing and licking his way down. Her knees grew weak and unsteady.

"I want you, Amy," he whispered against her skin.

Amy's heart melted. No one had ever wanted her before. Not her parents. Not even Jason, really. But Paul did. Paul wanted her.

"Yes," she whispered. "Make love to me."

He scooped her into his arms and carried her to the bed. His eyes blazed at her as he drew the sweater over his head and unbuttoned his shirt. While he was occupied with undressing, she quickly stripped off her panty hose, tossing them onto the floor. A moment later, Paul was naked and lying beside her, his big square hands caressing and infinitely tender as they roamed over her body. His mouth seized hers again.

He drew away, gazing into her eyes. "Are you afraid?"

She shook her head. "Not with you. I know you would never hurt me."

He frowned. "It might hurt. They say it does the first time."

Was he having second thoughts? Oh, dear God, she'd curl up and die if he stopped now. *She couldn't let that happen!*

Surprising even herself, she took his hand and gently guided it to the moist center between her legs. "I'm wet for you, Paul. You won't hurt me."

He touched her then, his fingers gentle and exquisitely knowing. His mouth plundered hers with long, drugging kisses that left her breathless and wanting more. He drew his mouth away from hers and began to paint her neck and shoulders with hot, wet kisses, forging a trail down the valley between her breasts. His hands cupped them, and beneath his touch, she felt her nipples harden into small round pebbles. The delicious ache between her legs intensified. She writhed under him, biting her lower lip, her fingers laced in his silky hair. His mouth closed over one peaked nipple, hot and urgent. She gasped with pleasure. Finally, after long moments of sweet torture, he released it and captured the other between his lips. As he suckled her, Amy trailed a hand down his neck onto his shoulder, skimming his sculptured biceps.

She couldn't believe she was touching him so intimately. That he—Paul!—

was lying here naked with her, tonguing her breasts, driving her crazy with need. His mouth nuzzled its way down her rib cage onto the flat of her stomach. She tensed, even though the ache between her legs had become an inferno. His hands caressed her thighs, urging her legs apart.

"Paul," she murmured, unsure.

"Shhh. Trust me, Amy."

His fingers slipped inside her, gently plundering.

"Oh, God!"

Then, she felt it. Hot, wet electricity. Joltingly erotic. His tongue delved into her, tender but relentless. She arched her head, struggling for breath. One hand clenched the sheets, the other grasped his hair. She bucked against him as the river of heat turned to flowing lava, and finally, with a soft cry, she surrendered to him, quaking and shuddering. Only then did he draw away to slide up her body, cradling her to him, cementing his mouth to hers in gentle communion.

"Oh, Paul," she whispered shakily when he drew away. "Oh . . . God . . . I . . ."

"Shhhh." He touched her trembling lips with an index finger, his eyes gazing into hers. "You're so beautiful, and so very sweet." His lips flickered in a smile. "You even taste like tropical coconut."

Amy's hands slid down his sculptured chest, lightly covered with black hair. She shook her head, gazing at him in wonder, still trembling from the emotion he'd wrought in her. "Not . . . coconut," she whispered. "Peach . . . shower gel."

He smiled. "Whatever." His mouth covered hers again, this time more urgently.

Amy felt the fires begin to burn again. She wanted to do something for him. Make him feel the way he'd made her feel. She reached out and touched him, drawing in a sharp breath at the heat and power of his hard length.

He gave a soft moan at her touch, and she felt intoxicated by his delight. He was large, but not so massive and frightening as Jason. She touched him tentatively, but with a sense of growing fascination. So soft, yet deliciously hard. Like silk over steel.

So, this was what it was all about—this sex thing. This, and what had just happened a moment before. For the first time in her life, she was beginning to understand just what the big deal was.

Paul's breathing grew ragged as she caressed him, and finally he covered her hand with his own and stopped her. His mouth lowered upon hers, sensuously exploring, as his hand snaked down her body, finally sliding into her wet center.

"Amy," he whispered. "Are you ready? I don't think I can hold on much longer."

She nodded, unable to find her voice.

He reached over to the bedside table where he'd placed a foil-wrapped condom. Moments ticked by. Amy watched him slide the condom on. Outside, the rain drummed on the roof. It seemed to be keeping time with the drumming of her heart. Beside her, Paul moved. He cupped her chin in his hand, and turning her face toward him, his mouth covered hers, and slowly, cautiously, he eased himself on top of her. She returned his kisses eagerly, thrilling to the weight of his warm male body. Yes, she was a little scared, but she knew, with every fiber of her being, that this was right. She loved Paul with all her heart, and this moment was one she'd been waiting for since she'd first seen him in the airport lounge.

Gazing into her eyes, he held his body poised over hers. "Amy? Are you sure?"

Her answer was to guide his head down to hers and open her mouth to his kiss. She felt him prod against her, and she couldn't help but tense. Paul's mouth feathered across hers in butterfly kisses. His hand slipped down between their bodies and slid into her wetness. She gasped as a shiver of pleasure pulsed through her. With one smooth drive, he broke through.

He held himself, motionless, his eyes locked upon her face, waiting. Amy set her jaw, her nails digging into his back. Pleasure had turned to burning pain, radiating between her legs and up through her womb. Paul's eyes glimmered with concern. His hand cradled her chin. Tenderly, lovingly, he brought his mouth to hers. As the waves of pain began to subside, Amy kissed him back. He drew away, stared down at her.

"Okay?"

She nodded, one hand traveling down to his smooth buttock as she arched against him. He began to move. Slowly, cautiously. Amy caught her breath. The pain was no longer pain at all, but something entirely different. Something . . . oh, God! Something delicious! Her nails scraped his back as he plunged into her, faster now. She met his every thrust, moaning out her delight.

"Oh, God! Paul! I . . ." The orgasm rocked through her.

His hands clenched into her hair as he came, calling out her name. For a long moment they lay bonded together, hearts pounding, eyes closed. Then Paul untangled his hands from her damp hair, kissed her lips gently, and turned over on his side, bringing her with him. Her breath ragged, she clung to him, kissing the hollow of his throat, her hand clamped around his firm biceps. He stroked her back, nuzzling his face in her hair.

She felt a wetness on her cheeks and realized she was crying. "I love you," she whispered. "I love you so much." Whether he heard or not, she didn't know. But his arms tightened around her, and, breathing in his male scent, she fell asleep.

It was still raining. A feeble morning light washed the bedroom in tones of gray. Amy gazed out the window at the beadlets of water streaking the glass.

The nature-sounds clock on her bedside table—one of Robin's Christmas gifts—showed 5:47, whispering its song of a rain forest waterfall. She lay on her side in the fetal position, Paul nudged up behind her, cradling her. She felt his arms encircling her, his lean stomach pressed against her back, and was afraid to move, afraid that her slightest adjustment would wake him, and then he'd leave.

She'd been wrong about those other moments, she realized. *This* was the moment she wanted to preserve. Lying here in this bed with the man she loved, the man who'd made her a woman. And who'd done it so tenderly, so completely. There could be no more perfect moment than this, she thought. This was the ultimate.

Oh, God, she loved him! Every part of him. She smiled. Especially that part she felt even now, nestling up against the roundness of her bottom. She'd never dreamed that sex could be so wonderful. Oh, she'd hoped it would be. What girl didn't? But she'd heard that the first time was often disappointing, that things didn't get really good until you'd done it a few times. Oh, that hadn't been true for her. Just thinking about how he'd made love to her—the touch of his hands, the feel of his mouth—made her all hot and achy down there.

It was a moment before she realized what she was doing. But when she felt his warm penis stir and thicken, she caught herself subtly—or maybe, not so subtly—pushing her buttocks against him. With a soft moan, he rubbed up against her, his arms tightening. Then he lifted his head, and she felt his tongue teasing at her earlobe.

"What are you trying to do, Amy?" he whispered. "Drive me crazy?"

She turned in his arms and fused her naked body against his. "That's *exactly* what I'm trying to do," she said saucily, smiling. "Is it working?"

"Oh, yeah." His mouth closed upon hers in a voracious tongue-tangling kiss.

Robin swung her legs over the edge of the bed and sat up. "Oh, shit."

Her head felt as if it had been bludgeoned with a sledgehammer; the inside of her mouth might as well have been lined with flypaper. She tried to swallow, but couldn't produce enough spit to do so. On trembling legs, she stood and stumbled to the bathroom, trying to decide the order of her most pressing needs. A drink of water first, then a good, long piss. She turned the gold-fixtured spigot to the right and, clutching the smooth white Corian basin, waited for the water to run cold. But the sound of running water, and perhaps the rain beating against the huge bay window over the Jacuzzi, was too much for her, and peeing won out over drinking. She pulled down her panty hose—*why the* fuck *am I still wearing them?*—and sat on the toilet, dropping her throbbing head to her knees as she thankfully emptied her bladder.

Afterward, she stripped off her panty hose and, naked, walked back to the sink, where the water was still running. She filled a paper cup and drank it thirstily, but even after a second cup, her mouth still felt like it was coated with mouse fur. Maybe some juice would help.

She staggered back into her room and drew on her long fleece robe. The digital clock on the VCR showed 11:15. Everyone was probably still sleeping. Mom and Dad had gone to a New Year's Eve party on Capitol Hill, and had planned to stay the night at the Four Seasons. They probably wouldn't be back until early afternoon.

Walking slowly on tentative legs, Robin made her way downstairs and into the kitchen. She wondered how Paul and Amy had made out the night before. If she found out they'd called it a night after bringing her home, she was going to knock them upside the head. She'd done her best to play matchmaker, and if they were too stupid to figure out they were perfect for each other, then screw 'em. Opening the refrigerator door, she pulled out a container of orange juice and poured herself a big glass.

"Well, you're up awfully early, considering how wasted you were last night."

Robin held a trembling hand to her aching forehead and grimaced. "Please, Paul. Not so loud!"

"I barely spoke above a whisper." He stepped around the island and opened the cabinet to take a glass from it. "Any of that orange juice left?" He lifted the carton, shook it, and poured himself a glass.

Robin eyed him. "You're still wearing what you had on last night. You just get home?"

He shrugged. "Maybe."

"Where's Amy?"

"Upstairs asleep, I guess."

Robin sat down at the breakfast bar, cradling her head between her hands. "Jesus! What's wrong with you two? You didn't hang out after you brought me home? Christ! You're both hopeless." A needle-sharp pain shot through her head. "*Ouch!* Remind me not to mix beer and vodka in the future, okay? It sucks."

Paul just stared at her.

She ignored him and took a long swallow of juice. Then she carefully set the glass on the counter and turned to defiantly meet his gaze. "*What?*"

"You know."

She rolled her eyes and turned away. "Oh, fuck. Don't start with me."

"Don't start with you?" Paul's eyes blazed. "What if I finish with you, huh? What if I just wash my hands of you . . . walk away and just let you go on destroying yourself, piece by piece. Drink by drink. What if I do that, Robin?"

She stared down at the gray Corian countertop. "Who gives a fuck what you do?" she muttered. "It's my life."

His hand clamped on her arm. "And you're my sister. I care about you, you stubborn little twit, and I don't like what I see happening here. You see this scratch on my face? You did that when I dragged you off that kitchen table. What were you doing on the kitchen table, you ask? You don't even remember, do you? Well, let me fill you in. You were doing a striptease in front of a roomful of horny frat boys. What do you think would've happened if big brother hadn't been there, huh? Do you think Amy could have rescued you? Hell, no! You would've been gang-banged right there on the kitchen floor! And when they were done with you, they might've taken Amy next."

Robin shook off his hand, picked up her glass, and drained the last of her juice. Then she turned and grinned at him. "Well, you have to admit, that would've been one hell of a way to start the new year."

He stared at her, pity in his eyes. "I know you think you're cool, Robby. All this rough talk and slutty behavior. But it's not you. Not the real you."

Robin stared at the empty juice glass, trying to hold back the wall of anger threatening to engulf her. She didn't want to hurt Paul; she loved him. But he didn't understand, he didn't know how very stupid he sounded. "You don't *know* the real me," she said quietly. "No one knows the real me."

"I know you're not a slut."

She lurched up from the breakfast bar, her head spinning. With one sweep of her hand, she knocked the juice glass to the beige Mexican tile floor where it shattered. "Well, that's where you're wrong, Paul. *I am a slut!*" She screamed it into his shocked face. "And guess who I have to thank for it? Here's a news flash for you! The honorable former congressman Michael G. Mulcahey!" She watched the blood drain from his face and gave him a cold grin. "That's right, Paul. Our wonderful, upstanding, right-wing, family-values father taught me, oh, so very *thoroughly* taught me, how to be the perfect slut that I am today!" Even though her head throbbed as if it were being jabbed with an ice pick, she managed to hold it high as she hobbled toward the door. Turning, she gave him another cool smile. "And you wonder why I drink?"

Paul knelt on the floor, cautiously gathering up the shards of orange-juice-splattered glass. *Christ! Robin was more messed up than he'd realized.*

What was all that garbage about Dad? *Our wonderful, upstanding, right-wing, family-values father taught me, oh, so very thoroughly taught me, how to be the perfect slut that I am today!*

Jesus, it sounded like . . . Paul shook his head. No fucking way. Robin was just trying to shock him. God knew why she always felt the need to draw attention to herself by uttering the most vile things her dizzy little brain could spew out. But to start in on family members. That was a new low, even for Robin.

Paul stood and dumped the shattered glass into the trash basket in the mudroom. Then he set about cleaning the orange juice from the tile with a paper towel. One thing was for sure. Robin needed some kind of therapy. She was consumed with anger. Before he left for Colorado, he'd have a talk with Mom and Dad, telling them of his concern. Maybe they could figure out how to get her to see a therapist.

But now . . . now, there was a sweet, beautiful young woman upstairs, waiting for him. Last night had been incredible—almost as if it had been a first time for him, as well. Every time he thought of Amy—of her sweetness, the soft look in her blue eyes as she gazed into his, he felt dizzy with desire. How incredible was that?

Before last night, Amy had been just Robin's best friend. A cute girl, for sure. And smart and fun to be with. But up until she descended the stairs in that sexy red dress last night, he hadn't thought of her as more than that. And he definitely hadn't planned on anything happening between them. Yet . . . now that it *had*, he couldn't wait to get back to her. He'd be leaving for Colorado tomorrow. And he didn't want to waste another moment without Amy in his arms.

Amy twirled a few strands of spaghetti around her fork and tried to keep her eyes from wandering to Paul. She knew he was trying to avoid her gaze as well, but like her, was having a difficult time of it. They'd agreed to keep their relationship secret for the time being—Amy's idea. It was too new and fragile, too special and pure to be shared with others right now. It wasn't that she thought the Mulcaheys would disapprove . . . no, that wasn't exactly true. She *did* worry that they would disapprove. Maybe it was okay for her to be a friend of their daughter's, but to be a love interest of their elder son, now, that might be a different story.

There was an odd tension at the table tonight, Amy realized. As usual, Stella was visiting her daughter for the holidays, so Michael had cooked dinner. Spaghetti and meatballs, one of his specialties. She'd noticed that Tammy and Michael were barely speaking. Had they gotten into a fight at the New Year's Eve party the night before? Come to think of it, she'd been reading in the sunroom when they'd come in this afternoon and had been startled by the slamming of the front door and the angry clicking of Tammy's heels as she stomped up the stairs. But Amy had been so consumed with thoughts of Paul that she hadn't paid much attention to it.

Robin, too, was acting really weird tonight. She'd barely said a word since she sat down at the dining room table. Then again, she was nursing one of the worst hangovers she'd ever had, or so she'd said. Only Jeff was his usual outgoing, talkative self, bubbling over about a new computer game he'd received for Christmas. Poor kid! No one appeared to be listening to him, judging by the lack of response. Paul was quiet, too. Amy hoped it was because he was mooning over her like she was him. She blushed, thinking of their early-morning lovemaking, and how sweet it had been. They'd made love three times now, and it had been better each time. Would he come to her room to-night? It would have to be tonight. He was leaving early the next morning. Her smile faded. So little time left! When would she see him again? At the very earliest, spring break. Oh, God! How could she wait until then? She suddenly felt like crying.

As if reading her thoughts, Paul turned to his father, and said, "Oh, by the way. You don't have to leave early to take me to the airport tomorrow. Amy said she'll drive me." Startled, Amy looked over at him. His eyes met hers calmly. "Right, Amy?"

She swallowed the bite of meatball in her mouth and nodded. "Right."

Michael shrugged and continued with his meal. Jeff resumed his mono-logue about the cool computer game he was mastering, while Tammy tried to look interested. A pale and silent Robin gazed out the window at the drizzling rain, ignoring everyone. Amy stabbed another meatball with her fork and again wondered if Paul would come to her room tonight.

"Amy and I will take care of the dishes, Mom," Paul said when everyone had finished dinner.

This got Robin's attention. Her gaze skewered him. "What is she? Your personal slave? 'Amy's taking me to the airport.' 'Amy and I will take care of the dishes.' What's up with that?"

Amy could see by the flustered look on his face that her barb had hit home. She spoke up quickly, "It's no big deal, Robin. We decided earlier that since Stella is gone, we'd help Tammy out and do the dishes, and as for the airport, I have the early-morning shift at the coffee shop tomorrow, so I don't mind dropping him off on my way."

Michael beamed at her. "Appreciate that, Sunshine. Truth is, I'm going to be a little strapped for time tomorrow."

"On your way?" Robin muttered. "Last time I checked, Richmond was in the other direction." She shrugged and pushed away from the table. "I'm going back to bed. This friggin' headache has turned into a goddamn migraine."

Tammy winced at her language but remained silent. Robin's exit seemed to be the cue for everyone else to get up from the table and amble off. Paul waited until they left, then slowly, he stood and came toward Amy. Her heart skipped a beat at the turbulent look in his eyes. He took her hand and drew her out of her chair and into the dark kitchen. She felt the smooth, rounded edge of the island behind her as he backed her up. His hand crept under her hair to the base of her skull, cradling it.

A thrill of excitement zipped through her as his hard-on pressed against her, bulging through his jeans. "Paul," she said shakily. "I thought we're supposed to be doing the dishes."

"We are," he said. And she could hear the smile in his voice. "But first, we're going to do *this*." His mouth captured hers, and with a sigh of surrender, she gave herself up to his kiss.

The dishes would have to wait.

"Remember what I did to you last night . . . how I made you come the first time?"

"Mmmmm?" Her eyes were half-closed, and she was lost in the sensation of his hand playing with her nipple.

They were lying naked on her bed, sated by another thorough session of lovemaking. It was almost midnight. His flight left at six-thirty. They still had a few hours left.

"You're falling asleep on me, aren't you?" He kissed her neck. "We said we were going to make love all night."

Amy smiled, her eyes still closed. "We will. I'm just taking a little break." Her eyes opened. "You're not ready again, are you? So soon?"

He chuckled. "Babe, I'm almost twenty-two. What do *you* think?" His nimble fingers moved to her other breast, and she smiled. Equal opportunity, she supposed. His index finger brushed a small, crescent-shaped mark on the slope of her left breast. "This a birthmark?"

She shrugged. "I guess so."

"It looks like a crescent moon." He leaned over and kissed it gently.

"So . . . what is it you want me to remember about last night?" she asked. "I remember it all." She stretched, feeling like a sleek, contented cat. "It was wonderful. Fantastic! Better than I ever imagined it could be!"

He traced an index finger down between her breasts and onto her stomach, toying with her belly button. "You liked it when I went down on you, didn't you?"

"Uh-huh," she murmured, blushing. "I liked it a lot."

"Well, guys like it, too. You know . . . when you do it to them." He hesitated, his fingers moving in a slow circle over her stomach. "You want me to show you . . . how to pleasure me like that?"

She turned over on her side, sliding her body up against his. "Yes," she whispered, her mouth brushing his. "I want to learn everything I can about pleasuring you. Just let me know when you're ready." In answer, he grabbed her bottom and crushed her up against him. She gave a little laugh. "Oh! You *are* ready, aren't you?"

And he began to teach her.

The digital clock showed 4:18. Amy saw it through glazed eyes. Somewhere in the recesses of her brain, she knew there wasn't much time left. But there was enough.

She faced Paul, sitting astride him, their eyes locked as she rode him slowly, savoring him. Her hands were clenched in his black, disheveled hair. His grasped her waist. She felt as if he were gazing into her very soul. Knew her innermost secrets and fears. Her essence. As his strokes intensified, grew faster, she bit her bottom lip. The peak was close, but she didn't want to go over. She wanted to freeze-frame the moment. Keep him here inside her forever. But there was no way to stop the winds of a hurricane. To hold back the force of an earthquake. With a gasp and a sharp cry, she shuddered and dropped over the edge. A moment later, his hands tightened on her, and he closed his eyes as a slight grimace crossed his face. She watched him come, thinking the expression he wore was the most beautiful she'd ever seen. Finally, he grew still and opened his eyes. They gazed at each other, frozen. She moved her hand up his jaw to his cheekbone, lingering on the fading scratch made by Robin's nail. He grabbed her hand, kissed it, his eyes still glued to hers.

It was a tender, sweet gesture, and it brought tears to her eyes. An emotion flickered in the depths of his, something she couldn't identify. Sadness? Uncertainty? His hand brushed a strand of damp hair from her face. Her bottom lip trembled, and she had to blink quickly to hold back her tears.

"I don't want you to go," she whispered.

He nodded. "I know. I don't want to go either. These last two days with you . . ." He shook his head. "They've been incredible. I wish . . ."

Whatever it was he wished, she would never know. The alarm clock's tropical bird cawed its raucous tone. She'd set it the night before for four-thirty, just in case they fell asleep.

She slipped off him and rolled over to the side of the bed to turn it off. When she turned back to him, he was already sitting up and reaching for his clothes. Her hand trailed lovingly up his back.

"You wish what, Paul?"

He stood up, pulling Jockey shorts over his lean buttocks, and turned to her. "I wish we had another night," he said with a sad smile.

Somehow, she knew that wasn't what he'd planned to say before the alarm clock went off. Summoning a light tone and a smile, she said, "You mean there's *more* you'd like to teach me?"

He winked at her and reached for his jeans. "I think there's plenty more we could teach each other."

When, she wanted to ask. *When, Paul?* But she couldn't. She *wouldn't* put any pressure on him.

He zipped his jeans, his gaze roving over her. "You are so beautiful."

She blushed, and reached for the sheet. "You're embarrassing me."

"And still so shy," he added. "I like that about you. It makes it even better when . . . you know."

Her face was on fire, but she had to smile. "What you're trying to say is underneath all this shyness, I'm just a wanton slut, right?"

He shook his head, smiling. "Not you." He crawled across the bed and bent over her, capturing her chin in his hand. His lips brushed hers tenderly. "Never a slut, Amy. Just a very sexy lady."

"Only with you, Paul," she whispered, drawing his head down again for another long, deep kiss.

After a few moments, he drew reluctantly away. "I've got to go take a shower. Meet you downstairs in forty-five minutes?"

There was nothing she could do but nod.

"That's my flight. I'd better go." Paul's eyes scanned her face, almost as if he were trying to imprint her features on his brain. "Amy, I . . ." He shook his head. "I don't know how to put into words what this time with you meant to me. I feel so honored that you . . ." His voice trailed away.

"You don't have to say anything." Her arms were laced around his neck, her fingers playing with the satiny black hair at his nape. "Just . . . come back soon, okay?"

He bent his head and kissed her. It was a sad kiss, one of longing and regret. He drew away, and cupping her chin with one hand, he traced her bottom lip with his thumb. "I'm going to be dreaming of this mouth for many nights to come."

She trembled, her eyes drinking him in. *When would she see him again?* "You'd better go," she whispered. "Everyone else has already boarded."

"Okay." He kissed her again, this time hard and passionately. Then, for a long moment, he held her silently. She pressed her face against his chest, fighting to hold back tears. God, he smelled so good. She'd never ever forget his scent, even if she never saw him again. He released her. Eyes somber, he pressed a kiss on her forehead, then turned and walked away.

She waited until he'd reached the gate, then with a note of desperation, called out his name. He turned. She knew she'd never forget this image of him. Standing there at the gate in his faded jeans, a red and navy Norwegian sweater and his opened suede jacket. His freshly washed black hair gleamed under the fluorescent lights. Even from the few feet that separated them, she could see the blazing blue intensity of his eyes.

"Write me," she said softly. "And call, okay?"

He nodded, and with a wave of his hand, he was gone.

13

Amy cut across the southwest corner of Barksdale Playing Field, taking a well-used shortcut to get to Cary Street and the sorority house. The field was empty of any athletic events on this dreary January afternoon. No lacrosse or field hockey. No soccer or outdoor track. Only students bundled up against the aching cold, making their way to and from classes, or if they were fortunate like Amy, heading home after their last class of the day. It was Friday afternoon, and despite the bleakness of the winter day, most of the students Amy met were in good spirits, looking forward, she supposed, to a fun-filled weekend.

Not her. It stretched out in front of her, two days and three nights of loneliness. Nothing new, of course. She'd been lonely before. But that had been nothing compared to the gnawing ache she felt now, yearning for Paul and wondering why he hadn't written in the three weeks since she'd seen him off at the airport. She still could hardly believe it. She'd been so sure, so *positive* that after the magic they'd shared, there would be long, romantic love letters. Hushed, secretive phone calls late at night. Maybe a delivery of flowers. And daily e-mails, of course. But there had been . . . nothing.

He'd arrived in Colorado safely. She knew that because she'd heard Tammy talking to him on the phone when she returned to Windsong that evening after working her shift at the coffee shop. Her heart had lifted in anticipation, and she'd slumped into a chair in the family room, sure he would ask to speak to her. And then she'd watched, dumbfounded, as Tammy told him to take care of himself and said good-bye.

She smiled over at Amy as she hung up the phone. "Paul made it back okay. It was so sweet of you to take him to the airport, Amy. I would've done it, but you know, I had that breakfast appointment with clients."

"No problem." Amy summoned a nonchalant tone. "So . . . did Paul have a good flight?"

"I guess so. He really didn't say." Tammy picked up a Merchants Square flyer and began to leaf through it. "Oh, my! These after-Christmas sales are unbelievable!" She looked up and flashed a radiant smile. "That's what we women should do tomorrow. We'll spend the day shopping."

But even shopping couldn't keep Amy's mind off Paul. As the three of them roamed the stores—Robin and Tammy buying, and Amy just looking—she kept wondering when she'd hear from him, and tried not to obsess on why he hadn't asked to speak to her. Of course, he wouldn't want his mother to know about them. They'd agreed upon that, hadn't they? That being the case, she probably wouldn't hear from him at Windsong at all. Classes didn't start again until the nineteenth but Amy decided to return to the sorority house early so she'd be there to get Paul's first letter or phone call. Robin was more than ready to return, too. After a few days at Windsong she was always in a lather to get back to campus life and freedom.

But as the days passed, Amy's mail slot at the Kappa Chi house remained empty, and the answering machine she shared with Robin held only calls from a variety of males, all for her popular roomie. Of course, Paul knew Robin would hear any messages he left, and then their secret would be out. But that didn't explain why there were no letters, no e-mails. From the beginning of their freshman year, Robin had shared her computer with Amy, and she used the Internet under her own screen name, *DiggerA*. She'd made sure to give Paul her e-mail address, thinking how great it would be to keep in daily contact with him. For the first few days after returning to the Kappa Chi house, she'd downloaded her e-mail, her heart beating fast with anticipation, her eyes scanning the list of messages for his screen name, *Buff28@hotmail.com*. She'd thought it was so cute. And apt, because he certainly *was* buff. But she knew it was in honor of UC's football team, the Golden Buffaloes, and 28 was his jersey number.

Her heart fell each day, though, as she saw her e-mail download. No *Buff28*. Just the names of the archaeology club loop she belonged to, and a few other students she shared classes with. A couple of times, she'd actually gone so far as to write Paul an e-mail. *Dear Paul. How you doing? I guess you're busy with classes and whatever you have to do to keep in shape for football. I'd love to hear from you, though. Just to know you're okay. Love, Amy.* But each time, as she moved her mouse to the Send button, she simply couldn't bring herself to click it. Maybe it was pride, or maybe it was just fear. Whatever, she couldn't do it. If she sent it, and he *still* didn't answer, she'd have to face the fact that their two nights together meant nothing to him. And how could she bear that?

She turned the corner onto Cary Street and a sudden burst of frigid air redolent with the pleasant scent of woodsmoke sent her cornrow braids clacking.

On a whim the other night, Robin had insisted on cornrowing Amy's hair. "We'll be twins," she'd chortled, dimple flashing. When she was done, Amy had stared into the mirror, amazed. They didn't look like identical twins, but no one would argue that they weren't sisters. Of course, the next day, Robin had impulsively removed her own cornrows and returned to her satin-straight Pocahontas look. But Amy had decided to keep hers for a while. Maybe it was because she felt like the new style gave her some of Robin's innate sexiness.

Not that it mattered. There was no one here in Virginia she cared to have sex with.

She hurried up the brick steps of the blue sorority house and through the door to the front screened porch. A moment later, she was unlocking the door of her room and stepping inside. As usual, it looked as if a tornado had blown through, demolishing exactly half of the room, and leaving the other half—Amy's—as pristine as a recently cleaned room in a swanky hotel. She deposited her book bag on the chair at her desk and walked over to Robin's side of the room, bypassing discarded clothes, underwear, and damp towels from who knew how many days to get to her desk. Moving aside textbooks, notebooks, a couple of CD cases, and a half-empty can of Diet Coke from the chair, she sat down and clicked the mouse onto the triangular America Online icon.

Her pulse accelerated as she clicked on a "flash session," and waited as AOL did its peculiar technological gibberish that culminated in the cheery male voice announcing, "You've got mail!" Her eyes fastened on the screen names downloading in the little box. There were about twenty messages. An unusually busy day. Amy supposed the cold weather was keeping people more chained to their computers than usual. "Goodbye," chirped the cheerful computer voice.

The flash session was completed. Amy clicked on Read Offline Mail, and scrolled down the messages. She froze, and her heart cranked into overdrive. *Buff28.*

"Oh, God!" She stared at the name, barely breathing. Then slowly, she closed her eyes and lifted her face heavenward. "Oh, thank you, God. Thank you!" After a long moment, she opened her eyes and looked at the screen name again. The subject heading was blank. With trembling fingers, she manipulated the mouse so that the arrow pointed to his message. She took a deep breath and double-clicked it.

It was a long message. She saw that right away. Good. That was good. The longer, the better. She resisted scrolling down to the end of it to see if he'd signed it in some sweet, sexy way. No, she'd savor it, word by word, line by line. She began to read.

Dear Amy,

I'm sorry I haven't written before now. It's been really weird since I got back, and to tell you the truth, my mind has been so messed up

*over the last couple of weeks, I knew I wouldn't be able to make any
sense if I wrote you. I'm probably not going to make any sense now,
but I have to try. I owe you that.*

Amy stopped reading, and stood, her heart bumping. The saliva in her mouth
suddenly tasted peculiar, and it took her a few seconds to recognize the taste of
fear. It burned its way up from her stomach, a cold tide of foreboding, malignant
in its daunting advance. She knew she didn't *have* to read the whole message. If
she wanted to, she could simply delete Paul's message, unread, into oblivion.

But that wouldn't change things, would it? Whatever he was going to say—
whatever he *had* said, couldn't be deleted from reality. And in the end,
wouldn't it be better to know than to always wonder?

With leaden feet, she returned to Robin's desk and started from the beginning again and this time, she kept reading.

*When I got back to Colorado, Monica was waiting for me in my
apartment. My roommate had let her in when she arrived the day
before. Amy, I'd never seen Monica like that before. So whacked out
and depressed about the way she'd dumped me. You have to realize
she's not the kind of girl that finds it easy to admit a mistake. She
begged me to take her back, and Amy, I just had to do it. She's the
first girl I've ever really been in love with, and we had something
really special last summer in Norway and . . . well, we're back
together again. We're thinking about a June wedding.*

*Amy, I know this isn't what you want to hear. I know how you feel
about me, and I'm really sorry to hurt you like this. But I want you to
know that I'll never forget those two nights with you. I meant what I
said when I told you what a beautiful, sexy, sweet girl you are, and
how someday, some guy is going to be so lucky to have you. I'll
always be glad you chose me to be your first lover. I've heard that we
never forget the first person we make love with, and I certainly hope
that's true for you. Stay sweet, Amy, and know that you'll always hold
a special place in my heart. Paul.*

Amy stared at the last line for a few minutes, her body stone cold. Her heart
still beat inside her chest; she still breathed in and out like she had for the last
twenty years. But she felt as if something had died inside her. Whatever it was,
her idealism, her innocence, her belief in happy endings . . . it had died an
ugly death the moment she'd read the sentence "We're thinking about a June
wedding."

Moving as if she were underwater, her hand manipulated the mouse's
arrow on the delete button, and she double-clicked. There. It was gone. Just
that easy. She stared at her other messages, but didn't really see them. From

the room next door, rock music thumped—Smashing Pumpkins. She'd never hear them again without feeling like throwing up. Slowly, she stood, unable to summon the energy needed to click out of her mailbox.

Funny, she thought, as she walked aimlessly to the window, then to her desk, and back to the window. *I'm really handling this okay. I'm not screaming or throwing things.* Or like Tucker Hall's famous ghost, throwing herself out the window. Maybe it was just good old-fashioned shock. It numbed your mind, froze your heart, and anesthetized your feelings. *Let's hear it for good old-fashioned shock!*

The key rattled at the door, and Amy turned to see a beaming Robin stepping into the room. "Hey, roomie! You beat me home. Listen, I heard about this new bar that's opening in Richmond tonight. You game for some hearty partying?"

Amy stared at her, then burst into sobs.

Robin grabbed the paper from the printer and began to read it. A scowl marred her pretty face, and by the time she finished it, her skin was the color of the leverback garnet earrings that shimmered on her earlobes. She crumbled the paper into a ball and threw it across the room.

"That slimy, no-good, piece-of-shit brother of mine is a fucking *loser!*" She paced the room, fists clenched. "All I can say is, he'd better make sure he doesn't step foot into this state again soon, because his ass is *mine* if he does! That *bastard!*"

Amy watched her listlessly. She lay curled up on her bed, clutching her pillow as if it were a stuffed animal. She couldn't say that the brokenhearted weeping she'd done in Robin's arms had really made her feel any better, but at least she no longer felt that deadness inside her. No, that was long gone. She felt plenty now. Pain, mostly, rocking her insides, a gnawing animal feeding on what was left of her heart.

She'd managed to sob out the entire humiliating story to Robin, leaving out the really personal stuff, but getting the gist of it across. Paul's tenderness, and her admission of how she'd been in love with him since the first time they'd met. Robin had nodded at this, unsurprised. She'd suspected it all along, she said. But she *had* been surprised about Amy losing her virginity on New Year's Day. "Why didn't you *tell* me," she exploded. But seeing the look on Amy's face, she added, "Never mind. Go on." And on Amy had gone, telling her how she'd been so sure he'd felt the same way she did. How she'd waited for the letters, the phone calls, the e-mails that had never come. Until today.

Robin, upon hearing about the e-mail, asked her permission to get on-line and retrieve the message, and Amy had consented. After all, she knew most of it, anyway; what was left to hide?

"Well, *fuck* him . . . *and* his bitch society queen!" Robin snatched up the crumpled ball from the floor and tossed it into the garbage. "You're way too good for him, anyway." She whirled, blond hair flying, and stalked to her closet. "Men are all fuckin' sleazeballs! Every last friggin' one of 'em." Her hands raked through her clothes. "Come on. Get up! We're going to Richmond tonight."

Amy buried her face in her pillow. "I don't want to go out. I just want to go to sleep."

"Oh, *that's* a brilliant idea. Just burrow there in your little bed and wallow in self-pity. *That'll* teach my moron brother a lesson."

"Don't start, Robin. I'm not in the mood."

Robin turned and glared at her, hands on hips. "If you think I'm going to allow you to waste away and die because of an insensitive, idiot, ass-hole *man*, you don't know me at all, Amy. Now, get your skinny ass up out of that bed and go take a shower. I'll find something sexy for you to wear." From the sweater bins in her closet, she drew out a cranberry cashmere turtleneck that had been a Christmas present from Tammy. "This will look *so* hot with your new boot-cut jeans. And it matches our garnet earrings perfectly!" She tossed it on the bed and turned back to the closet. "Jesus! Paul is going to rue the day he messed with my best friend! I'm going to rip his goddamn balls off next time I see him!"

"Girlfriend, you look awesome!" Robin beamed at her as they stood in front of the full-length mirror gazing at their reflections.

Amy gave her a watery smile. "For a girl who's just had her heart stomped on, you mean?" Didn't Robin see her red-rimmed eyes and puffy face? But all things considered, Amy had to admit she looked pretty decent in Robin's cashmere sweater and her own snug-fitting jeans. Tomorrow, though, she was going to get rid of the cornrows. It just wasn't her. Only someone like Robin could carry it off. Oh, God! Why couldn't she be more like Robin? No wonder Paul had dumped her for Monica. She was a dweeb. An uninteresting, socially awkward loser.

"Oh, I forgot!" Robin bounded over to her desk and began searching through the debris. "Where is that shopping bag from the Fenton Gallery? I have something for you."

"Oh, no. Robin, you've got to quit buying stuff for me."

"I can't help it! Oh, here it is." She grabbed a small bag buried under a cast-off sweatshirt and drew from it a square box. "I stopped in after class and as soon as I saw this, I knew it was perfect for you. And don't worry. I got some-thing for myself, too. See?" She stuck out a slim wrist and showed off a beaded cuff sterling silver bracelet. "Here. This will go perfectly with your outfit."

Amy took the box and opened it. "Oh, Rob!" A princess-cut garnet and onyx pendant with marcasite accents nestled on top of a square of cotton. It was exactly the kind of antique-looking jewelry Amy would've salivated over if she'd seen it in a store. How well Robin knew her taste. She just wished she'd stop spending so much money on her. It made her feel more like the poor country cousin than ever.

"Hey, if you don't like it, we can always exchange it for something else." Robin said, watching her closely.

Amy looked at her. "Of course I like it. It's gorgeous. But it's too expensive."

"How do you know how expensive it was?" Robin scoffed. "For all you know, I bought it off a street vendor for ten bucks."

"Yeah, right. You forgot. I saw the Fenton Gallery bag."

Robin laughed. "Like I wouldn't use an old bag so you'd think I got it there."

"Like you'd give a shit what anyone thinks about where you do your shopping. You're not your mother, you know."

"Thank *God*! Come on, Amy, put the freakin' necklace on so we can get outta here."

Amy knew better than to argue with her. Besides, she did love the necklace. Still, she and Robin needed to have a serious talk about all this impulsive gift-giving. There was a limit to how much charity she could accept. Birthdays and Christmas, she'd insist. She wouldn't accept any more gifts beyond that.

Robin fastened the new necklace around Amy's neck, then turned her around for inspection. "Perfect," she said. "Except that other one has got to go. It ruins the effect."

Amy touched the sun pendant that Tammy and Michael had bought her for Christmas and glanced at her reflection. "I can't wear them both?"

"No. It looks sucky. Take it off. In fact, I'll wear it tonight, okay? You know I've always liked it better than the one Mom and Dad got me."

Amy unfastened the chain of the sun pendant and handed the necklace to Robin. It was true. Robin had made it clear from the beginning that she'd much rather have the sterling silver necklace than the one they'd got her, an eighteen carat gold heart with a diamond chip just off center.

After Amy helped her with the fastener, Robin smiled at herself in the mirror, fingering the spiky rays of the sun pendant. "Yeah. This rocks. You'd think my parents would know by now that I prefer silver over gold. But that just goes to show how clueless they are."

As usual, when Robin put down her parents, Amy felt the urge to defend them. Robin just didn't realize how lucky she was to have parents who loved her, even if they didn't know what precious metal she preferred.

"There!" Robin linked her arm through Amy's and grinned into the mirror. "Don't we look hot?"

Amy tried to smile. But her eyes revealed her true feelings. "I don't know if I can do this tonight, Rob."

"Yes, you can." Robin gave her a stern look, then softened it with a brief hug. "We're going to go out and have fun tonight, girlfriend. And I don't want to hear another word about my friggin' brother, you understand? Only a doofus would choose that skinny witch over you. Come on, get your coat. It's colder than Monica's titty out there."

Gator's, the new bar in Richmond, sucked, and if it wasn't for the brawny redneck who'd parked his tight jeans–clad butt on the chair next to Robin's, Amy was sure they would've left hours ago. But he was cute, he liked to dance, and he insisted on paying for the rounds of Heineken he and Robin were putting away—assets that she found irresistible—so Amy had no choice but to settle in for the duration. While Robin and the Garth Brooks look-alike tore up the dance floor, Amy was kept company by his morose friend, a lanky black-clad guy who, if she squinted just right, bore an uncanny resemblance to Dwight Yoakam, only with a full head of hair. Maybe they'd stumbled into a country stars' impersonation club by mistake.

A waitress, dressed in fringed cowboy boots, skintight shorts, and a clinging T-shirt emblazoned with a grinning alligator drinking a beer, appeared and began to dole out drinks. She placed two brimming beers where Robin and "Garth" were sitting and a mixed drink for Dwight. Then she slid a beer in front of Amy.

She stared at it. "I didn't order this."

"I ordered it for you," the man in black said.

"I don't drink," Amy said flatly, still eyeing the bubbling golden liquid.

He shrugged and reached for the beer.

"Wait!" Amy's hands curled around the cold glass. She marveled at the wet, cool texture of it under the pads of her fingers. It felt good in the stuffy warmth of the bar. She drew the glass toward her. "Maybe it's time to change that particular policy," she murmured, lifting it to her lips. The beer was icy cold against her tongue, its scent pungent with yeast. She took a sip and swallowed, grimacing at the bitter taste. But almost immediately, she felt a warmth spread through her insides. A few more sips, and her head felt pleasantly light. By the time Robin and "Garth" returned to the table, their faces shiny with sweat, the glass of beer was half gone. Robin noticed it immediately, and her eyes lit up.

"Well, hot-*damn!* I never thought I'd live to see the day that Amy Shiley took a sip of alcohol! Hey, girl!" Grinning, she lifted her hand in a high five. "You're a *bad girl* now!"

Amy slapped her hand, and grinned back at her.

A little while later, when Dwight ordered another round, Amy didn't protest.

Amy didn't consider herself drunk. After all, if she was drunk, wouldn't she have taken Garth and Dwight up on their offer to crash at their apartment just a few streets away from the bar? Robin had been up for it; that was for sure. But Robin was always up for wild sex with guys she'd just met, especially when she had a half-dozen beers sloshing around in her stomach. Upon Garth's leering suggestion, Amy clamped a hand down on Robin's wrist, squeezing in warning, and without giving her a chance to speak, said, "No, thanks. We've got to get back to campus."

Garth—or Ray—she'd finally remembered his real name—grinned at her from across the table. "You sure you want to drive back to Williamsburg? It's snowing like a sonuvabitch out there."

Alarmed, Amy glanced over her shoulder out the window. Her heart lurched. He wasn't lying. Big clumps of snow drifted down from the black sky, yellowish in the glow of the parking lot lights. A sickening fear oozed through her as she reached for her coat on the seat behind her.

"Come on, Robin. We'd better get back before it gets too bad out there. I'll drive." She bent down to grab her purse. "Where the hell . . . ?" She looked on the other side of her feet, but didn't see it there either. "Hey, has anyone seen my purse? I can't find it."

Robin giggled. "Hello! Did one of you guys take Amy's purse? That's *so* not cool."

Panic bubbled inside of Amy as a frantic search failed to find it, and finally, she had to admit defeat. She gave the bartender her name and phone number in case someone turned it in later, but she had a feeling she'd never see it again. Luckily, she'd had very little cash in it, and it was a damn good thing she couldn't afford any credit cards. But her driver's license, ATM card, and school ID were gone. Great. Just great. She'd have to put a stop on the card tomorrow, and on Monday she'd have to find time to go to the DMV and to Admin to get a new ID. Just lovely.

Another thought occurred to her. *Shit!* "Robin, give me your driver's license. With the luck I'm having today, we'll get stopped on the way home, and they'll take me to jail for driving without a license."

For some reason, Robin found this hilarious, but she dug her wallet out of her purse and still giggling, started looking for her driver's license. Amy suppressed a sigh of impatience, and snatched the wallet out of her hands. "Just give me everything, okay? Let's go." She tucked the wallet into her parka pocket.

"Come on, girls," Ray whined. "Why don't ya'all just forget driving home now and come on over to our place? It's only a few blocks away."

"Sorry," Amy said coldly, pulling on her parka. "Let's go, Robin."

Robin impulsively threw her arms around Amy. "You're just a sweetheart, Amy. Even if you *are* a mother hen." She pressed a sloppy kiss on Amy's face, almost losing her balance in the process. "That's why I love you."

"I love you, too, Rob." Amy steadied her and then helped her pull on her coat. "Come on, now. We have a long ride home." *And five to one, you'll be passed out before we leave the parking lot.*

They stepped out of the noisy club into the quiet of the falling snow, Robin leaning against Amy as they trudged through three inches of slush. Amy stepped on an icy patch, and her foot skidded. Robin stumbled, too, and grasped at her, releasing a gale of laughter that carried on the frigid air like the joyous ringing of Christmas bells.

"Ooops . . ." She giggled, clutching Amy as she slipped again. "Guess I had too m . . . much to dr . . . drink."

"Well, *duh!*" Amy reached the passenger door of the Camaro and propped Robin against it. "Where's your keys?"

"Keys?" Robin looked up at the snow, smiling like an enchanted child. She stuck out her tongue, catching a snowflake, and another gale of laughter overtook her.

Amy gave her a gentle shake. "Hel-*lo?* Earth to Robin. I need your *keys.*"

"Oh. Okay." Robin leaned groggily against the car, digging in her oversize leather bag. "In . . . here . . . somewhere. Oh, here they are!" She dangled them in front of Amy's eyes, her goofy smile widening "Here you go, Designated Driver. Wake me up when we get back to good old William & Mary."

Suppressing a sigh, Amy took the keys, clicked the remote entry, and opened the passenger door, then waited as Robin crawled into the front seat and collapsed. She slammed the door and hurried through the snow to the driver's side. The scent of woodsmoke from the fireplace inside the pub hung in the frigid air, bringing a sense of nostalgia to Amy, warring with the tension bubbling inside her.

A burst of icy wind tugged at her sodden knit cap, sending her cornrows clicking against her numbing face. She blinked snow out of her eyes and fumbled for the door handle, hurling herself inside and slamming the door against the elements. It was hardly warmer inside, but at least it was shelter. Biting her bottom lip, she inserted the key into the ignition as a sick, liquid fear ate its way through her stomach.

Designated Driver. Like hell! She'd only had two beers. But for her, it was two beers too many. She wouldn't have had that if she'd known how the weather had turned. Who knew a freakin' blizzard would descend on Richmond?

It was almost an hour's drive to Williamsburg . . . more with the snow. But what were they supposed to do? They had to get back to the sorority house. For sure, she didn't have money for a hotel. Of course, she had Robin's credit cards, but jeez, it just didn't feel right for her to use them. Wouldn't that be fraud or something if she signed into a hotel with Robin's credit card? God! She should've followed her first instincts and stayed home tonight. What a nightmare this was turning into. *Thank you very much, Robin.*

Look at her. She was too blotto to know what was going on. Totally oblivious to their predicament. But damned if she didn't look like a sleeping angel with her long honey-blond hair framing her perfect face like a curtain. As *if!*

Robin was about as far from an angel as she could get. Even if she wasn't wasted, she would've just laughed at their situation. Nothing fazed her. Amy sighed. She wished *she* could be so cavalier about everything.

When the Camaro roared to life, she breathed a sigh of relief and switched on the windshield wipers and defroster. Slow and easy. That's how she'd take it. After all, two beers didn't make her drunk, right? Besides, the interstate would probably be pretty empty this late. It might take them a while, but they'd get back to campus in one piece. And the next time Robin decided they were going bar-hopping in Richmond in the middle of friggin' January, Amy was going to tell her to get a life.

They wouldn't be in this situation tonight if . . .

She thought of Paul, and the pain washed through her again for the millionth time that night. Oh, God. She had to stop this. It was over. She had to accept it.

"Men are scum . . ." she whispered, her gloved hands tightening on the icy steering wheel as she waited for the windshield to clear.

The defroster worked quickly, and in another minute, the windshield was clear. She put the car in reverse and backed cautiously out of the parking space. The wheels crunched on the snow, and as she shifted gears, she felt them slip, losing traction. Camaros were notoriously bad in snow. That's what Daddy had always said during the brief time he'd worked as a used car salesman in Newport News. But Robin could have cared less about practical things like reliability. She'd had her heart set on a Camaro—and that's what she'd gotten.

Amy narrowed her eyes and leaned forward, straining to see through the swirling snow as she eased onto the ramp leading to I-64. The streets had been plenty bad in town, but once on I-64, it seemed to be better. Virginia Department of Transportation trucks were out en masse, salting down major roads and keeping traffic going at a good clip. She was surprised there *was* so much traffic heading east. Where was everybody going on a Friday night— no . . . make that a Saturday morning—at two o'clock?

She felt her tension ease as the road remained in fair condition. A green sign loomed out of the snow, and she squinted to read it. Only ten miles to Williamsburg. She released a deep, tremulous sigh of relief. Soon, she'd be crawling into her nice warm bed in their room at the Kappa Chi House. After, of course, getting Robin into *her* bed. Without, she hoped, Robin puking her guts out like she had last time. God, what a mess! It had been three o'clock in the morning, and Amy had had to clean not only their room in the sorority house, but a couple of spots in the corridor outside.

A burst of wind sent the car shuddering, and Amy's heart lurched as she fought to keep control. She glanced at the speedometer and eased her foot on the accelerator. Good roads or not, sixty-five miles per hour in a snowstorm was too freakin' fast. She rounded a curve and saw brake-lights ahead. Close. *Too close.*

"Omigod!"

She slammed her foot on the brakes, and a millisecond later, realized her mistake. The Camaro fishtailed, and began to slide. Amy jerked the steering wheel to the right, but the car didn't respond. It was as if she'd driven onto a skating rink. The Camaro spun in a semi-circle, and time slowed to a teardrop.

Almost as if she were outside of her body, Amy saw herself clutching the useless steering wheel, her mouth open in a silent scream. She saw Robin's head lolling against her seat, a slight smile on her lips, blissfully unaware of what was happening. And last, just before the blackness set in, she saw the glaring lights of the eighteen-wheeler bearing down upon them.

PART TWO

14

"Robin, honey, we've got to go now." Tammy patted Amy's bandaged arm. "The nurse says you need your rest, but we'll be right outside, okay?"

Feeling panic bubble inside her, Amy watched Tammy's face draw away. It was replaced by Michael's. He smiled down at her, tears misting his crinkling blue eyes. "That's right, Cupcake. You just get some rest, and don't worry about anything. Mommy and Daddy are right here."

He, too, moved away. Amy moaned, trying to speak, but the contraption in her mouth wouldn't allow it. She moved her head back and forth on the pillow, a desperate fear gurgling its way up from her stomach.

Why are they calling me Robin? Where is Robin? Oh, dear God! What is happening here?

A woman in a brightly colored jacket appeared at her side with a syringe. "Shhh . . . hush now, hon. It's not going to do you any good to get all riled up." She inserted the needle into the IV line and pushed the plunger. "This'll make you sleep, Robin. It's what you need now. Lots of rest."

The edges of her vision darkened. Desperately, Amy clung to the sight of the nurse's round face gazing down at her compassionately.

Don't go! Her brain screamed. *You've got to tell me why you're calling me Robin!*

The nurse's face disappeared, and there was only a blessed blackness.

A stranger's voice, speaking in a low murmur. "She'll need extensive plastic surgery. Her face was . . . uh . . . destroyed when she went through the windshield."

A soft gasp. Tammy's. "Oh, dear God."

"Don't worry, Mrs. Mulcahey. Reconstructive surgery has come a long way in the last ten years. By this time next year, you'll barely be able to tell she was in an accident." A pause. "But we're getting ahead of ourselves. Right now, we have to concentrate on the next couple of days. She's stable, but guarded. We have to keep a close eye on her, and be prepared for complications."

Even in her groggy state, Amy knew they were talking about her. The airway—she'd seen enough episodes of *ER* to know that's what it must be—was still inserted in her mouth, so even if she was physically able to summon the strength to talk, she couldn't. The drugs they were giving her kept her floating in a state somewhere between consciousness and a black void. The voices faded again, and she drifted in the warm, comforting darkness.

Voices again. Closer, this time. She felt someone's presence at her bedside and tried to, but couldn't, open her eyes. It took too much energy.

"Are you gonna tell her about Amy, Mom?" That was Jeff's cracking adolescent voice.

"Not now." Tammy. Her voice sounded strained. "We'll deal with that after she gets through this crisis."

There was a snuffling sound. *God! Is Jeff crying?*

"I just can't believe she's dead," he croaked.

Retreating footsteps. Whose? A hand grasped hers and squeezed. "Oh, darling. . . ." Tammy. Her voice was a ragged whisper. "How am I going to tell you?"

I just can't believe she's dead.

Is that what Jeff had said? She felt as if someone had injected ice water into her bloodstream. They were talking about *her*! Amy.

But I'm not dead! I'm here, listening to you talk. I'm alive!

But they were calling her Robin, not Amy. Not just once, but several times. Her heart bumped.

They think I'm Robin!

Which meant . . .

Oh, God. Her heart froze as the implication sank into her brain. Amy wasn't dead, but *someone* was. Someone who looked very much like her, close enough that they'd been mistaken many times for sisters.

Amy moaned in despair. Robin. Dear, God! *Robin is dead?*

At her cry, Tammy squeezed her hand tighter, and the familiar scent of her Fifth Avenue perfume washed over her. "It's okay, Robby, honey. Mommy is with you."

With an exhausting effort, Amy managed to open her eyes. She stared up into Tammy's concerned face, saw her blue eyes swimming with tears. Amy moaned again, desperately trying to scream out the truth. *I'm not Robin, I'm Amy!*

Tammy gave her a watery smile. "It's okay, darling. Mommy is going to take good care of you. We're going to get through this together. All of us. Daddy is trying to reach Paul right now, and he'll come home, and we'll all be here together to help pull you through this. You have to be strong, okay, Robin?"

Darkness was closing in again. Tammy's face swam out of focus, and finally, Amy could fight it no longer. She gave into the sweet softness of unconsciousness.

In frustration, Paul threw back the covers on his bed, jackknifed his legs over the side, and sat up. Running both hands through his hair, he rested his elbows on his knees and released an exasperated groan. He lifted his head and peered at the clock on his bedside table—12:05.

Christ!

He stood. Wearing only a pair of Jockey shorts, he padded into the kitchen, opened the refrigerator door, and grabbed a half-gallon carton of orange juice. Took a large gulp straight from the carton and shoved it back onto the shelf.

There. His throat felt a little better. The six beers he'd had earlier had carpeted his tongue and throat with what felt like a half inch of horse manure. But it hadn't done a damn thing toward making him drunk. Which had been the ultimate objective.

Getting drunk, he'd hoped, would take his mind off Amy and that fucking e-mail he'd sent her this afternoon. Jesus Christ! *Why* had he done that? He'd regretted it as soon as he'd hit the Send button. In fact, he'd actually gone online to try to "unsend" it, but then he remembered, too late, that you couldn't "unsend" mail to other Internet users, not if they weren't with the same carrier. For a moment, he'd contemplated sending another e-mail with the header: Don't Read the First E-mail from Me. But that was stupid! Of course, she'd read it. No one could be that strong. And the truth was, he still didn't know what he wanted. *Who* he wanted. Wouldn't it be unfair to lead her on?

She was so sweet, so innocent. His heart warmed just thinking of her. He could still see her beautiful blue eyes, the way they looked deeply into his as they made love that last morning; they seemed to be gazing deep into his soul, making a connection there that, truthfully, he'd never felt with Monica. So, why was he still so undecided about his feelings for Amy?

He'd been totally unprepared to find Monica in his apartment when he returned to Colorado. And as he'd written Amy in that damn e-mail, she'd seemed like a different person. A softer, more vulnerable Monica. Tears had streaked her perfect porcelain face as she'd begged him to take her back, telling him how much she loved him and how much she regretted breaking off their engagement. As she'd kissed and held him, he'd remembered Norway, and how they'd first made love in her berth on a coastal steamer off the coast of Bergen. He'd fallen in love with her during that trip—or thought he had—and they'd planned a future together.

Now, though, the doubts were creeping in. He had taken Monica into his bed on the night he returned to Colorado, but as his body made love to her, he'd found his mind was far away in Virginia. Instead of Monica's almond-shaped eyes, he saw pure blue eyes rimmed with dark, lush lashes. Instead of Monica's firm, grapefruit-size breasts, he'd felt Amy's pert, brown-nippled peaches. Instead of Monica's expensive French perfume, he'd inhaled Amy's light scent of coconut. Or was it peach? Christ, he didn't know what it was except that it belonged to Amy. And that was enough to make him light-headed.

But Monica had returned to California two days later, confident in his love, in their future. He supposed he'd led her to believe they had one. Yes, they had, in fact, discussed a wedding date. Still, he couldn't shake Amy from his mind. Or his heart.

But he knew that's exactly what he had to do. At least, that's what he'd been telling himself for the last three weeks. But he'd kept putting it off. Amy loved him. No one could fake the kind of emotion she'd shown during those two days together. He was her first love.

But first love never lasts. Everyone knew that. She was so young, after all. Too young to tie herself down. She would find someone else eventually, and now that she'd had her first sexual experience, she'd be ready to take on something more serious.

Why, then, did the thought of Amy making love with someone else tighten his guts with jealousy? Make him want to ram his fist into the wall?

So, he'd procrastinated. Put off the ugly deed for another day. Maybe the right words would come to him if he waited. Christ! He didn't want to hurt her. She was so sweet . . . so . . . *Amy.* And God knows she'd had her share of misfortune in her young life. He hated like hell having to add to it.

He wanted to regret that anything ever happened between them. But he couldn't. Even now, thinking of her soft, slim body under his made him hard as a rock. He'd slept with only three girls before Amy. His high school girlfriend, Maggie, a one-night stand with a horny sorority girl during his freshman year at UC—and Monica. Maggie and he had lost their virginity to each other when they were juniors. They'd gone steady until they'd left for separate colleges, parting amiably, both of them ready to move on. But Paul had learned after that soulless experience with the sorority girl that he wasn't like most college guys whose primary goal was to bed as many babes as possible before their sophomore year. No doubt, he was an uptight conservative yahoo, like Robby called him, but for him, sex had to be more than just a collision of two anonymous bodies in a strange bed.

So when he'd met Monica during the Scandinavian trip, he was ready for a real relationship, and something had clicked between them. It had been her phone call today that had finally made him realize he had to tell Amy the truth. Monica told him she'd found the perfect wedding dress at an exclusive shop on Nob Hill. And what did he think about a sunset wedding at Big Sur?

He'd hung up, heart heavy, and sat down at the computer. Painstakingly, he'd typed the e-mail. Read it once, pretending he was Amy. When he'd finished, tears blurred his eyes. There was no way he could make it gentler. No way he could shield her from the pain. With a trembling finger, he'd clicked the mouse's arrow on Send.

And it was done.

Paul pulled on a pair of jeans and a sweatshirt, and walked to the sliding door that led to the balcony. Stepping outside into the clear, cold winter night, he gazed westward at the Rocky Mountains. It was just after eleven o'clock in California. What was Monica doing? On the phone, she'd said something about taking in a movie with a girlfriend.

The wind whipped around him, and he turned to the right, hugging his arms for warmth. Out there, far away to the east, was Virginia. And Amy. He glanced at his wristwatch. Twelve-fifteen. Two-fifteen Eastern time. She was probably in bed, asleep. Were tears staining her beautiful peach-tinted cheeks? Tears caused by him?

His heart twinged. He didn't want to be the cause of her tears. Christ! If any other guy had done what he'd done to that sweet, innocent girl, he'd tear him to pieces.

"What kind of fucking bastard are you, anyway?" he whispered savagely.

Breaking Amy's heart. A girl like that. A girl that any guy would be crazy not to want. He was a goddamn fool! He balled his fists under his armpits, leaning against the railing, glaring off into the flat prairie stretching eastward.

He remembered the way Amy had clung to him at the airport, her eyes luminous. Her body had trembled as he'd held her. Had Monica's body ever trembled like that at his mere touch? Amy hadn't said the words to him, not at that moment, but everything about her had exuded her love for him. No, she hadn't said it then, but that first night—that early morning—when they'd first made love, she'd said it clearly just before she'd fallen asleep.

"I love you. I love you so much."

He blinked, startled to find tears erupting in his eyes. He turned blindly and stepped back into the apartment. His heart thudded as he crossed the room to his desk and reached for the phone. He stabbed out the area code and phone number of Robin and Amy's room at the Kappa Chi house.

He raked a hand through his tangled hair as it rang once. Then twice . . . three . . . four times before the answering machine picked up, and Robin's chirpy voice rang out, "Hey, what's up? Robin and Amy aren't here right now, so you know the drill. Leave a message, and we'll call you back. Peace."

Paul didn't even consider hanging up. He'd had an epiphany out there on the balcony, and he damn sure wasn't going to fuck this up. He didn't give a damn if the whole world heard his message to Amy.

"Amy, this is Paul." He took a deep breath and went on, "That e-mail I sent you today? Forget about it. It was all lies. I don't love Monica. As soon as I get off the phone, I'm calling her to break it off. And Robin, I know you're probably hearing this, but you know what? I don't give a fuck." A slow grin came over his face, and he held the phone a few inches from his mouth and shouted, *"I love Amy Jessica Shiley!"* He brought the phone back into a normal position and lowered his voice, "I do, Amy. I love you. Call me back, okay? No matter how late it is."

He disconnected, then began to punch out Monica's number. Halfway through, he heard the call-waiting beep. His heart bumped. Was it Amy calling back so soon? Maybe she'd been there all the time, listening to his voice on the answering machine.

"Hello?" he said eagerly, unable to hold back a hopeful grin.

"Paul? It's Dad."

His smile froze. "Hey, Dad! What's up?" Something about his father's voice sent chills through Paul's body.

"There's been an accident, Paul. Robin and Amy were driving back to Williamsburg during a snowstorm, and they were hit by a semi."

Paul's head grew light. His hand tightened on the phone. "But they're okay, right? They aren't . . . they didn't . . ."

"Robin is in critical condition." His father's voice was grim. "The doctors think, though, she has a good chance of pulling through. Amy, though . . . she wasn't so lucky. She didn't make it, Paul."

Paul dropped the phone and sank into his chair. He felt as if he'd been kicked in the stomach by the Buffs' two-hundred-pound field goal kicker.

"Paul?" His father's voice came to him, tinny and faraway. "Paul? You still there, son?"

Paul dropped his head to his desk and began to sob.

How could it have happened? Why did they think she was Robin? Was it because she'd been driving Robin's car? But surely, Tammy and Michael could tell the difference between Amy and their own daughter? Yes, their bodies were similar; so were their hair and clothes. But . . .

The thought seared through her, and her stomach plunged sickeningly. Maybe there hadn't been much left to identify. *Oh, God! Oh, Robin!*

But still, why did they think . . . *wait.* It was beginning to make sense. She'd been driving Robin's car. Robin's wallet had been in her coat pocket. Another thought jolted through her. Robin had been wearing her sun necklace—the one Tammy and Michael gave her for Christmas. So many little things, but they added up to something huge. But why hadn't the hospital done a DNA test to make sure? Blood work . . . *something!*

A memory swirled through Amy's mind. Robin, lying in bed in the dorm room that first winter after they'd become best friends. Her voice coming out of the darkness, teasing, yet, curiously vulnerable. "If I were dying, Amy, would you give me one of your kidneys?"

"Well, sure," she'd responded without hesitation. "As long as we're compatible. My blood type is A-positive. What's yours?"

Robin's reply had held a satisfied smile. "I'm A-positive, too. See, I told you we're soul sisters."

A twisting pain shot through her, and it wasn't because of her injuries. She could still see her friend's laughing face. The way her cornrows twirled as she moved around their room, dimple flashing. Her familiar, sweet voice uttering profanities that from any other girl would've sounded vile and coarsely vulgar, but coming from Robin had sounded only . . . Robin-ish.

How could she be dead? How could her beautiful, trim body be destroyed so badly that her own parents couldn't recognize her? Amy shuddered. She felt as if her own body were being submerged in an ice-cold bath. Right now, at this very moment, her friend—her very best friend in all the world—was lying in a steel drawer in the morgue. Maybe at this very hospital.

Tears blurred her eyes. Robin hated to be alone. She was afraid of the dark. They'd always had to keep a night-light burning because Robin, who in daylight wasn't afraid of anything in the world, couldn't bear to be in the dark. But she was now. Down there in the cold, dark morgue, all alone.

Amy heard a rustle of movement and, through the slits in the bandage, saw the heavyset nurse approach. Something tightened on her good arm. A blood pressure cuff? There was a hiss of air, and the tightness relaxed.

The nurse made a clicking noise with her tongue. "Blood pressure's up again," she muttered.

She moved away.

Poor Tammy and Michael. They'd completely fall apart when they realized someone had made a mistake, and it wasn't Amy who'd died in the crash, but their precious daughter. It wasn't right! It *should've* been her.

After all, if she died, who would care? Who would *really* care? Oh, yes, Michael and Tammy were sad, believing that Robin's roommate had been killed. Poor Jeff had actually been crying. But underneath all that sadness, there was relief. Relief that it wasn't *their* daughter who'd died. And if she—Amy—had died, it wouldn't really affect them. Not for long. Their lives would go on as they always had. Sure, Robin would've been devastated. Amy knew Robin loved her. But Robin wasn't the kind of girl to stay down for long. Eventually, she would've found a new best friend. No, there was no one else who'd really be heartbroken over her death. Mama, cocooned in the dark sanctuary of her mind, wouldn't even understand the significance of it when they broke the news to her.

It would've been better for everyone if it *had* been her who died. Not Robin. After all, she was the one at fault. *She* had been the one to get behind the wheel after drinking. Then a thought occurred to her. She might *still* die. Sure, Mike and Tammy were telling her she was going to pull through. That everything would be all right. But didn't everybody say that to dying people? In all the movies, in the television programs like *ER*, critical patients were comforted by others. No one ever grasped the hand of a dying person, and said, "Hey, bub. Your number is up. Time to check out."

I want to die. Dying now would be better than waking up and seeing the look of horror on Mike and Tammy's face when they realized she was Amy, not Robin. Oh, God! How could she stand it . . .

The thought hit her like a lightning bolt. The voice in her room earlier. A doctor's voice, she realized now.

She'll need extensive plastic surgery.

Like Humpty Dumpty, they'd piece her together again. And to do that . . . they'd need to know how she looked before . . .

Her heart began to pound. *Is it possible?* Could it be so simple? Could this be the answer to everything? Tammy and Michael would have their daughter back. Jeff and Paul would have their sister. And she, Amy, would have the family she'd always wanted.

Paul. Oh, God, *Paul!* He didn't want her as a girlfriend. The e-mail had made that more than clear. Now that Robin was gone, there would be no reason ever to see him again. How could she bear that? Wouldn't crumbs be better than nothing? As his sister, she'd have that, at least. She'd be able to be near him for the rest of her life. It would be hard, being so close, and unable to love him the way she wanted to, but wouldn't that be better than having him walk out of her life forever?

She gasped as the enormity of the idea hit her. Once they took her off the ventilator, and she was able to talk, the Mulcaheys would discover the truth—that is, if she chose to tell them. And then what would happen? Oh, their common decency would compel them to pay her medical bills, and perhaps for a little while they'd stay in touch. Out of respect for Robin. But sooner or later, they would slip away, and once again, Amy would be all alone in the world.

Another, more horrifying, thought occurred to her, and a shudder rivered through her body. What if she was permanently disabled? What if—Oh, God!—what if her body had been damaged beyond repair, and she was forced to live out her life in a wheelchair, helpless and alone? Perhaps even relegated to a nursing home like Mama. Oh, God! She *couldn't* let that happen. She'd die first. Find a way to kill herself.

But that wouldn't happen. The Mulcaheys wouldn't allow that to happen. *Not if she became their daughter.*

Not if she became . . . Robin.

"Robby? Hey, sis . . . it's me. Paul."

Amy heard his voice coming from what seemed to be a great distance. She tried to open her eyes, but the drugs made her eyelids feel as if they were weighted by stones. His hand curled around hers—her good hand—and she felt him move closer.

Paul. *Paul!* A soft moan rumbled from her throat. They'd taken the airway out, but still, she couldn't find the energy to speak. Couldn't force her lips into the right shape. Was it because of the drugs they'd given her for her injuries? How badly had she been hurt? She felt no pain, really. Just a gnawing ache that seemed everywhere, yet, nowhere in particular. The drugs, she supposed, were keeping the pain at bay.

"Oh, Robby . . ." Paul's voice broke, and she felt a lock of his hair brush her hand as he bent his head. "Oh, God. This so sucks."

Wetness on her hand. Was he crying? Amy concentrated on opening her eyes. She had to see him. Had to!

He squeezed her hand tighter. "Robby, I asked Mom to let me be the one to tell you. She wanted to wait until you're stronger, but I know that's not what you'd want. We all know how you hate bullshit. So, I'm going to tell you the truth. Amy didn't make it, Rob. I'm sorry. She was just too badly hurt."

Through sheer force of will, Amy managed to open her eyes long enough to see Paul's ravaged face, his blue eyes moist. She moaned again, wishing she could speak. Somehow, comfort him. How strange to think he was grieving her. *Her!*

He took a deep shuddering breath. "Dad has taken care of all the funeral arrangements since Amy had no family. She's going to be buried in our family plot. I'm sorry you won't be able to go to the service . . ." He stopped and shook his head. Ran a trembling hand over his brow. "Oh, God, Rob . . . she was so special. She wasn't like any girl I'd ever met."

Amy's heart lurched. What did he mean? She willed him to say more. Give her something . . . anything . . . that would stop her from going through with this charade. It wasn't too late. Emergency surgery had wired her smashed facial bones back into place; she'd overhead a surgeon talking to Robin's parents this morning. But there would be no reconstructive surgery until later. If Paul would only give her a sign that their weekend together had meant something to him.

"You remember what Dad called her? Sunshine. It was corny, sure. But I kind of dug it, you know. That's how I felt when she smiled at me. Like the sun had just come out from behind a cloud."

Amy would've smiled if she could have. She tried again to open her eyes, to communicate to him that she understood. But what little energy she'd summoned before had slipped away. Right now, it was enough to feel Paul's hand holding hers and know that he loved her. She was sure of it now. That e-mail he'd sent? There was an explanation for it. And when she got through this, she'd ask him why he'd sent it.

She knew now she couldn't go through with it. Becoming Robin was simply a sick fantasy, an insane idea. And it would probably never work. Tammy and Mike were going to be devastated when they realized their daughter was dead, but with Paul by her side, Amy would help them get through it. And she'd play the part of a surrogate daughter as long as they needed her.

"Oh, Paul! I got here as soon as I heard!"

Whose voice was that? It sounded vaguely familiar. Amy felt her stomach tighten. Unpleasantly familiar. Again, she tried to open her eyes.

"Monica! I told you not to come."

"As *if*!" Heels clicked on the tile floor, moving closer. "Darling, what kind of woman would I be if I didn't come to my fiancé's side when he needed me?"

Finally, painstakingly, Amy managed to open her eyes and turn her head toward the voices. Through a blurry mist, she saw the raven-haired girl peering down at her, her expression a mixture of curiosity and revulsion. Turning away, Monica pressed crimson lips against Paul's stubbled jaw. Everything inside Amy froze.

"We're going to get through this, Paul. Together."

Amy closed her eyes. Paul's hand had released hers at Monica's arrival. Who was she kidding? Paul didn't love her. He never had. This was the woman he loved.

"Oh, look at her, Paul. How pitiful. She's crying. Do you suppose she's in a lot of pain?"

"I don't know, but she's conscious," Paul said quietly. "She's hearing everything we say, so maybe it's not a good idea to talk about her like she's not here. Anyway, she's probably crying because I just told her that her best friend is dead."

"Oh, you mean that little blond who was at Thanksgiving dinner with us?"

"Yeah. Amy. Her name was Amy."

He was right, Amy thought, as she slipped down once more into the soothing darkness. Amy *was* dead.

It would be the best solution for everyone.

15

Amy sat alone in the hospital room, waiting for her heartbeat to slow to a reasonably steady pace. Closing her eyes, she took a deep breath of the antiseptic hospital air and released it, willing herself to be calm for what lay ahead. Outside the corridor, orderlies and nurses bustled past, sometimes wheeling noisy gurneys and lunch tray carts. And in the lounge waited Tammy and Michael. Moments before, Dr. Ovadeerling, the plastic surgeon who'd become intimately familiar with her face during the last six surgeries, had sat across from her and unwrapped the bandages from the most recent and, hopefully, *final*, surgery.

He'd pulled away the last layer of bandage, and smiled, his eyes lighting. "Ah . . . yes . . ." Then he handed her a mirror.

She took it with a trembling hand, but when it came right down to it, she couldn't make herself look at her reflection. Instead, she put the mirror down on the bed and asked to be left alone.

The surgeon didn't seem surprised. With an affectionate pat on her knee, he rose from his stool, giving her a gentle smile. "Take your time, Robin. I know this is a big moment for you." He left the room on quiet-soled shoes, the door silently clicking shut behind him.

So, here she was. The big moment. And she was paralyzed. Gripped by a fear unlike anything she'd ever felt in her life. Yes, even more terrifying than that moment in which she'd seen the eighteen-wheeler bearing down upon them.

It felt so weird. Her face, exposed, for the first time since the accident. The feel of air currents brushing against the raw, virginlike skin, the sudden weightlessness with the bandages gone. Bandages she'd worn for the last thirteen months.

Thirteen months. It seemed more like thirteen years—this last year of her life. It had been a blur of operating suites, ICUs, and hospital rooms. Between surgeries, she'd gone home to Williamsburg—to Robin's home, of course. Living in Robin's world, but feeling relatively safe behind bandages like a caterpillar webbed by its cocoon. Allowing Tammy and Michael to take care of her, coddle her, love her back to life. There was no real playacting involved as long as her face was in the rebuilding stage. Oh, she remembered to try to eat like Robin. Which wasn't a real problem in the first few months because everything she ate was sucked through a straw until she finally graduated to strained baby food. But once she was allowed solid food, she had to remember that she hated chocolate and—hardest of all—coffee. For weeks, she'd suffered horrible headaches as her body weaned itself from caffeine addiction. But other than the food thing, she didn't really have to try hard to make sure they didn't suspect she was not Robin.

Such a horrifying accident would subdue anyone, and that was exactly what the Mulcaheys thought. The accident had been a wake-up call for their wild little Robin. As a result, she'd grown up overnight. They were not surprised that between surgeries, their daughter wanted nothing more than to stay at home, spending her days reading romance novels or watching television. And once a week, seeing a psychologist to help her deal with the tragedy.

At first the idea of psychotherapy had appalled her. Wouldn't the shrink see through her immediately? See her for the fraud she was? Her immediate impulse had been to refuse. Isn't that what Robin would have done? But Amy had to admit she wasn't sure. Surviving such a horrible accident and losing her best friend would've caused her unimaginable shock and trauma.

She knew that because losing Robin had totally messed *her* up. Over a year had passed, but Amy still missed her—still grieved for her—as much as anyone in this family. But she had no one to share her grief with. Now, here was her chance. So, Amy had agreed to therapy. After her first few sessions, her fears were allayed when Dr. Stevenson, a white-haired Southerner with a soft-spoken voice, didn't seem at all suspicious.

Now, though, the protective bandage was gone. And it was time to step into the life of Robin Mulcahey, completely exposed. Could she pull it off?

No choice. She *had* to.

Another horrible thought occurred to her. What if the surgeon had screwed up? What if he hadn't been able to reconstruct Robin's face? What if . . . oh, God . . . what if she were disfigured? That would serve her right, wouldn't it? For trying to steal her best friend's face. *I can't go through with this.* Panic welled inside her, but she fought it back.

Just do it. She took another deep, tremulous breath and stood up. Moving slowly, she walked to the bathroom, her hand reaching for the light switch. Her heart pounded; she could almost *hear* it pounding. Her throat was dry with fear. It was way too late for second thoughts. From the moment that knife had first cut into her face, there'd been no turning back. They'd taken a photo of Robin Mulcahey and put her face back together again. The nose, the mouth, the cheekbones. Painstakingly modeled in a series of surgeries. Until finally . . . the moment of truth. The masterpiece, revealed.

Amy sucked in a deep, shuddering breath and hit the light switch. Stared at her reflection in the mirror.

"Oh, God . . ." she whispered. With a shaking hand, she covered her mouth.

No. Not *her* reflection. *Robin's.*

Reddened and swollen, an angry scar still visible near her right earlobe, but unmistakably, Robin's face.

"Oh, Robin . . ." she whispered. It had been thirteen months since she'd seen this familiar face. Her best friend, gone. But her face was still eerily here. It gave her chills. But it wasn't just that which made her feel queasy. For the first time, Amy realized that she'd never see her *own* face again. Amy Shiley was gone forever, just as permanently as Robin was.

A cry of dismay escaped her throat. The door of the room opened, and footsteps approached. In midsob, Amy turned away, not ready to face anyone yet. It was too soon.

"Robin?" It was Tammy. "Oh, honey, I know it's an emotional moment. Go ahead and cry if it makes you feel better." Robin's mother appeared in the doorway of the bathroom. She reached out to stroke her hair, chin length now, since they'd had to shave her head for one of the earlier surgeries. Amy had made a point of buying lightener and pretending to use it as soon as her hair grew out. Gently, Tammy placed her hands on Amy's shoulders and turned her around.

Amy held her breath, her pulse racing, as Tammy's gaze swept over her. Would she pass inspection, or would some telltale sign reveal that she was an imposter?

Tammy smiled. "The swelling will go down, and a little makeup will take care of that paleness. But oh, darling, you're so beautiful." She hugged her close. "Robin, it's so good to have you back."

A huge lump had formed in Amy's throat. She relaxed in Tammy's embrace, giving herself up to the comfort of motherly love. It was so good to feel cherished, even if it was under false pretenses.

After a moment, Tammy drew away and gazed again into her face. Her eyes were cloudy with emotion. "Oh, poor Amy," she murmured.

Amy stiffened, and for a crazy moment, she thought the ruse was over. *Tammy knew it was her!*

"That poor girl didn't have a fair shake, did she?" Tammy squeezed her shoulders. "Coming from that dysfunctional family and shuffled around from one foster home to another. Yet, she really made something of herself, didn't she? Such a bright future ahead of her. It's just so sad . . ."

Amy had to turn away, afraid of what her expression might reveal. She slipped past Tammy and stepped out of the bathroom. "She really loved you guys, you know." She tried to control the tremor in her voice, but couldn't.

She hoped she sounded like Robin, enough so that Tammy wouldn't suspect anything. They knew her larynx had been injured in the accident, so hopefully any difference in their tone would be attributed to that. Still, she'd worked hard in trying to remember Robin's syntax and unique voice inflections, and now that she was unmuffled by bandages, it was more important than ever to talk like her. "You . . . *we* were the family she'd always dreamed of having," she added.

"I'm going to miss her," Tammy said softly, following her out of the bathroom. "She was a lovely girl." She paused, a sober look on her patrician face. "Darling, there's something I want to say to you." She took a deep breath and went on, "I know I've made some mistakes with you. I haven't always been there for you, I know that. And I've probably been harder on you than I've been with the boys, but . . . we have a second chance now, don't we? Can we start over? You and me?"

Amy hadn't the faintest idea what Tammy was talking about. She'd always thought Robin and her mother had had a pretty decent relationship . . . despite Robin's frequent snide comments. A sharp rap on the door saved her from answering.

It opened a few inches, and Michael stuck his head through. "Can I come in? I want to see that beautiful daughter of mine."

Tammy smiled and motioned him in. He stepped through the door, a broad grin on his handsome face. "Hey, there, Cupcake. Come here and let me see what you look like."

Heart pounding, Amy took a step toward him. He stared at her, his expression implacable, and she felt a lick of fear shoot through her stomach. It was as if he were looking at a stranger. But then he smiled and held out his arms. "How about a hug, beautiful?"

Amy stepped into his arms. Funny, she thought, as he held her close. She didn't remember ever seeing Robin showing affection to her father. Just flippancy and outright rudeness. But it felt good to be in his arms.

My family. This is my family.

Michael drew away and gazed into her eyes. His were suspiciously bright. "Welcome back, Cupcake. Are you ready to come home?"

So many things to learn . . . to remember. Amy knew nobody expected her to become the old Robin overnight. In fact, it wasn't inconceivable that the emotional trauma of such a horrible accident could've banished the old Robin completely. Anyone who saw the change would just chalk it up to the life-altering accident. But Amy knew that her best chance for pulling off this charade was to *become* Robin in every way she could. Oh, she had no intention of pulling out all the stops and becoming the wild, booze-guzzling girl she'd been before the accident. No, a calmer, more subdued Robin would not raise an eyebrow.

But it was the little things that Amy had to be the most careful about. Sitting in the right chair at the dinner table. Turning right into Robin's luxurious bedroom instead of going on down the hall and making a left into the guest room.

Staying in Robin's room had been even more painful than she'd imagined it would be. Everything about the room screamed Robin. The posters on the walls from high school that she'd never taken down. The half-naked construction workers. Rock groups like Smashing Pumpkins and Pearl Jam. Photos on the dresser of Robin in her cheerleader uniform and in her prom dress standing beside a younger, clearer-eyed Jason. Stuffed animals on the bed. An elaborate stereo system and a standing CD case jam-packed with CDs, presumably from her high school years. And in her huge walk-in closet, stacks of Victorian-flowered photo albums and notebooks high on the top built-in shelf. Maybe someday, when the pain of loss had eased, Amy could bring herself to look through them. Relive Robin's short life, and perhaps, come to know her better. But not now. It was too soon.

Amy scanned Robin's rows and rows of clothes, all haphazardly jumbled together with no sense of order. The closet was bigger than Amy's room in the most luxurious of all the trailers she'd lived in. Once she got over the pain of touching Robin's clothing, inhaling her zesty citrus scent, and remembering her wearing *this* skirt with *this* top, her first inclination had been to rearrange the closet. Divide it into sections and place everything together in an organized, practical way. But she knew she couldn't do that. Robin would never do that.

Food was another danger zone she skirted daily. Now that she could eat again, she had to be very careful. It was hard enough when, at breakfast, Stella poured the fragrant cups of Kona coffee for Michael and Tammy, and all Amy could do was gaze longingly and inhale its enticing aroma. Even a year without coffee had not eliminated her craving for it. What would Tammy and Michael do if one day she simply decided to try it? Would that be so unheard of that someone could suddenly change her mind about a dislike? But no, she couldn't risk it.

And then there was the time Michael barbecued steaks. He'd placed Amy's down in front of her, and she'd blanched at the slab of beef swimming in red juices. She knew there was no way in the world she'd be able to cut into that bloody steak and put it into her mouth. Tammy, noticing her white face, came to her rescue. "Michael, honey, why don't you put Robin's steak back on the grill for a few more minutes. I think it's a little *too* rare." Michael shrugged and did as requested. Amy smiled her thanks at Tammy who smiled back, and said, "Tastes change, huh?" Another disaster averted.

Chocolate was another roadblock. Robin had been the only person Amy had ever met who hated chocolate. She remembered teasing her about it. *Hey, you can't be a woman and still dislike chocolate, Rob. Don't you know that, girlfriend?*

Sometimes, though, the craving was so intense that she had to give in to it. She'd started driving again this spring—in Robin's old Tracker, which Michael had never sold. It hadn't been an easy thing to do, getting behind the wheel again, but it was something she knew she had to do if she was ever going to have a normal life. And in the fall, she'd return to college to repeat her sophomore year. A car was an essential. The first time she'd driven into town, she hadn't gone over forty miles per hour. Other cars had passed her as if she were standing still, and many of those drivers greeted her with raised middle fingers. But she got to Williamsburg in one piece.

Now, when the craving for chocolate was overpowering, she'd sneak into town and buy a couple of bars, eating them on the sly. The last time this happened, she'd wandered over to the archaeology lab building, munching on a Reese's Peanut Butter Cup, savoring each bite as if it were the last she'd ever eat. She hadn't gone into the building; now that she was Robin, she had no student intern ID that would allow her entrance, but she'd stood outside, remembering the many afternoons and evenings she'd spent in there, poring over broken pottery and other relics from colonial days.

Last summer while she'd been recuperating from surgery, the archaeology students had gone on the dig to Israel—the one Dr. Johnston had urged her not to miss. Her grant for it had come through in March, but, of course, by that time, Amy Shiley no longer existed. Where had the students gone this summer, she wondered. Greece? Egypt?

Not that it mattered to her. She'd already registered for classes in the fall, having met with Robin's guidance counselor to figure out her schedule. As a theater major, she would take courses like Speech and Diction, and Introduction to Theater Concentration, not to mention the several different acting classes that were required. All in all, though, it was an incredibly light schedule, at least compared to Amy's sophomore year. Only one math course was required—the same one Amy had taken in her freshman year and passed easily.

No, Robin's schedule was the least of her problems. The thought of getting up and acting in front of people scared the crap out of her. Unlike Robin, she wasn't an exhibitionist. She preferred staying in the background, blending in with the wallpaper, rather than being in the limelight. But what could she do? No way would Robin suddenly start taking real classes. Amy tried to visualize her as something mundane—a teacher or some kind of businesswoman, but couldn't. No, the only thing she could see Robin doing was theater . . . or maybe stand-up comedy. And Amy realized that if she was going to pull this masquerade off, she'd have to train to become an actress.

And after all, how difficult could that be? She was one, anyway, wasn't she?

The house was quiet as Amy climbed the stairs to her room. Good. Maybe she'd have the pool to herself. There were still a few hours before dinner, and she'd decided to swim a few laps and maybe work off some of her nervous energy. She'd come a long way since two summers ago when Jeff had taught her to swim. Good thing, too, since Robin had always been like a duck in water.

She was halfway to her room when she heard the roar of rage coming from Jeff's bedroom. "*Fuuuuccccckkkk!*"

Heart knocking, she ran to his room and burst through the opened door. *"Jeff! What's wrong?"* She had to shout over the pounding music of Alice in Chains.

He looked up from his computer, his attractive youthful face flushed. He glared at her, blue eyes stormy. "I hate this fuckin' thing," he growled. "It's fucking useless."

Her first inclination was to tell him to watch his tongue. But of course, *fuck* was Robin's favorite word. Which, she reminded herself, she hadn't been using much lately. She strode over to the stereo and turned down the volume to a low shriek. "What're you trying to do?" she asked.

"I'm installing this new software, but it's all fucked up. I can't get it to work right." He slid his wheeled chair back from the computer, closed his eyes, and ran his slender fingers through disheveled blond hair.

Amy's heart jolted. For a second there, Jeff had looked so much like Paul. Same mannerisms, same expression on his face. It reminded her that it had been five months since she'd seen him. He'd been home in February after the Denver Broncos had won their second Super Bowl, high on victory and still amazed that he'd actually gotten to play in the fourth quarter. He'd caught a couple of good passes, neither of them thrown by the great John Elway but by the second-string quarterback who'd been put in after the Broncos had taken a comfortable lead. Paul still couldn't quite believe he'd been lucky enough to be drafted by the Super Bowl champions, and was still living in Colorado.

He'd only been home a couple of days before flying to Honolulu with some of the other Broncos, not to play in the Pro Bowl, but to participate in an NFL-sponsored golf tournament. It had been so weird for Amy. She'd still been in bandages, and it had been almost impossible for her to look at him and remember she was supposed to be playing the part of Robin. Couldn't he *see* the love in her eyes? She'd watched him on the sly, gazing at his lips and remembering how they'd tasted. His beautiful square hands, so important for a wide receiver, the way they'd felt on her body. The memories were all she had left.

He had made no mention of Monica. All she knew was that the woman had accepted a position in the Nob Hill Chamber Orchestra. Were they still seeing each other? She'd wanted desperately to ask, but of course, she hadn't. Whatever, they hadn't married as planned after college graduation, and that was something Amy thanked God for every night. But one thing was for sure. Paul wasn't without female companionship. Michael had begun subscribing to the *Rocky Mountain News,* as Paul's photo often appeared in the society page, always with a gorgeous supermodel type on his arm. Never the same one twice. Once, it was a young starlet who owned a winter home in Aspen. Another time, a buxom blond member of the Pony Express. Amy hated them, one and all, but as long as she didn't see the same one twice, she could live with it. God help her, though, if Paul ever got serious about one of them. How on earth would she be able to handle that?

During his short visit home, he hadn't mentioned Amy at all. What did that mean? Was he trying to spare Robin from bad memories, or had he already gotten over Amy's "death"? Humbling thought, that she had mattered so little to him.

"Hey, Rob? Any of your boyfriends know anything about computers?" Jeff asked, eyes hopeful.

"I don't . . ." Amy bit her bottom lip, horrified that she'd almost admitted to not having any boyfriends. She summoned a bright smile. "Get *out*! Do I look like the kind of girl who dates computer nerds?"

"Well, *excuse* me!" Glumly, Jeff turned back to his monitor. "This really sucks! You know how much I paid for this piece of crap?"

"Hel-*lo*? You mean how much *Dad* paid for it." Amy reached over and grabbed the software box. "Did you bother to read the instructions? Tell you what. You go downstairs and get me a Coke, and I'll take a look at it."

"You?" Jeff stared at her. "What do *you* know about computers?"

Amy's grin froze as she realized she was treading in dangerous waters. "Probably more than you do, Fart-face. You want me to look at it or not?"

Shaking his head, Jeff lifted his lanky frame out of the chair. "Whatever. But if you screw it up even worse, I'm gonna tell Dad to take it out of your allowance."

"I don't get an allowance, Dork."

"Yeah, right," Jeff smirked, loping out of the room. "Whatever you want to call it. Just don't fuck up my computer."

Amy shook her head, turning to Jeff's monitor. She was beginning to understand why Robin had always called him a pain in the ass. By the time he came back up with her soda, Amy had his program running. He handed her the Diet Coke, a look of amazement on his face. "You're shittin' me! You got it working?"

Amy popped the top of the can and took a sip, grimacing at the metallic taste. God, she hated diet drinks! And of course, Robin had drunk nothing but. "No problem," she said. "If worse comes to worst, read the instructions, Jeff." She stood and headed for the door.

"When did *you* get so good with computers?" Jeff called after her.

Amy thought quickly, hesitating at his door. "Amy gave me some lessons."
Jeff's face sobered. "Amy was cool. Bet you really miss her, huh, Rob?"
Amy nodded. "Yeah, I miss her. More than you can imagine."

At dinner Amy was relieved when Jeff didn't mention how she'd fixed his computer problem. Maybe it hadn't been such a big deal, after all. After she'd changed into her swimsuit and gone down to the pool to swim laps, she'd worried about what she'd done. What if he told everyone that Robin had become a computer whiz? Surely, that would arouse suspicion. But maybe she wasn't giving Robin enough credit. She hadn't been stupid, after all. Flighty and frivolous, yes. But not stupid.

By the end of the meal, and with no mention of the computer, she'd finally started to relax. Then Stella brought in dessert. "Your favorite, Miss Robin," she said, smiling broadly. "Pineapple cheesecake."

Amy felt the blood drain from her face as the housekeeper placed the elegant cheesecake on the table and began to slice thick wedges from it. She didn't dare ask if the pineapple was fresh or canned. If it was Robin's favorite dessert, why would she care? Stella handed a plate to Amy. She stared at the thick wedge of cheesecake, inhaling the rich tropical aroma of pineapple, and immediately, her throat began to itch. There was her answer. It was *fresh* pineapple.

She stared at the dessert. It might as well have been a cobra curled up on the plate. For her, fresh pineapple was as lethal. Panic curled inside her. *What could she do?* How could she not eat Robin's favorite dessert, and have a logical explanation for it?

"What's wrong, Robin? You're white as a ghost."

Amy looked up to see Tammy gazing at her, a cheesecake-laden fork hovering near her mouth. She swallowed hard and cleared her scratchy throat. "I . . . I . . ." Her eyes darted from Tammy to Michael to Jeff. All three of them were staring at her curiously. She looked back at the chunks of golden pineapple glistening on top of the cheesecake. Now her eyes were itching and starting to tear. She coughed, hitching in a breath.

Tammy placed her fork on her plate and leaned forward. "Robin, are you *crying?*"

Amy rubbed her eyes and scraped her chair back from the table. "I can't eat pineapple," she said slowly, feeling their stares. "Not since the accident."

"I'll have yours," Jeff said through a crammed mouth. He reached for her plate.

Tammy swatted his arm. "Don't be rude, Jeff." She looked back at Amy. "What is it, darling? What does the accident have to do with you not eating pineapple?"

Amy cleared her throat again, thinking quickly. Was it too late to salvage things? She looked down at her dessert, and spoke quietly. "I was drinking piña coladas that night. I still had the taste of pineapple juice in my mouth when I came to. I just . . . can't eat pineapple now. It reminds me of . . . that night."

The room was silent, except for the music of Mozart issuing from the hidden speakers. Finally, Jeff broke it. "So, can I have hers, Mom?"

Tammy nodded. Amy pushed the plate over to him.

Michael cleared his throat. "I seem to recall that Amy was allergic to pineapple."

Amy's heart skipped a beat. Slowly, she turned her gaze to Michael, expecting to see a light of challenge in his eyes. But he looked perfectly normal, as if he was only making polite conversation.

"*Fresh* pineapple," Amy murmured. "Canned didn't bother her. You don't use fresh pineapple in piña coladas . . . not at a dive like Gator's, anyway."

"Well!" Tammy folded her arms and smiled across the table. "It's perfectly understandable that you don't like pineapple anymore. I'll make sure we don't serve it again when you're at dinner. Would you like some ice cream instead?"

Amy shook her head. "I'm stuffed. If you'll excuse me, I think I'm going to go sit out on the deck and read my book."

"Of course."

As she left the room, she heard Jeff's sarcastic comment. "Jeez! That accident must've screwed up her brain. When's the last time *she* asked to be excused?"

Amy hurried out to the deck, and only then did she allow the trembling to overtake her body.

The alarm shrilled, and Amy reached for it, eyes closed. One punch of the snooze button, and the noise stopped. She rolled onto her back and rubbed a hand over her forehead, where a headache had begun to pulse. She'd been having the headaches since the accident. They usually started before she opened her eyes in the morning and faded only after she'd been up a couple of hours.

After a moment, she opened her eyes and gazed up at the cream-colored cathedral ceiling. Sunlight speared in from a skylight, spotlighting a path to the bathroom across the room. Its angle told her she should be getting up. It was Wednesday, August 18. Mama's thirty-ninth birthday. It had been two years since she'd last seen her.

Amy thought back to that visit, and tears blurred her eyes. Robin had still been alive. Incredible how fast life can change. Last year at this time, she'd been home at the Mulcaheys', recovering from another surgery. Beneath the bandages, she'd worn a stranger's face—not her own, but not yet Robin's, either. Even if she could've somehow found her way to the nursing home, how could she walk in there like the invisible woman and face the stares, dodge the questions, and graciously accept the apologies? Besides, Vicky Shiley's daughter was dead.

So the only answer was not to go. This year, though, would be different. She had been thinking about Mama for months. One night in June, she'd awakened from a nightmare where she'd been at her mother's funeral. In the dream, she hadn't known if she looked like herself or like Robin. But it didn't matter. She'd felt the anguish of a daughter saying a final good-bye to a mother.

She'd awakened in a panic, the dream still vivid in her mind. With ice-cold fingers, she'd called information for the number of the nursing home, and then waited anxious seconds for someone to pick up the phone on her mother's ward. When a nurse finally answered, Amy's throat went dry as she searched for the right words to ask the question. They would want to know who was calling. She couldn't say it was Vicky's daughter.

"Do you have a patient there by the name of Victoria Shiley?" she asked in a breathless rush.

A pause. Then, "Yes, we do. May I say who is calling?"

Amy's heart bumped, and quickly, she hung up the phone. So, she was still alive, at least. That's when she knew she had to go see her this year. Not as Amy, of course. She could never be Amy again, but she'd go as Robin. And why not? Was it so impossible that Robin would go visit the sad shell that had been Amy's mother? Not that she planned to tell the Mulcaheys.

Amy crawled out of bed and headed for the shower. An hour later when she came downstairs, no one was around except Stella. She was in the kitchen loading the dishwasher.

"Where is everybody?" Amy asked, opening the refrigerator door and grabbing the carton of orange juice.

The housekeeper threw her a broad grin. "Just you and me, hon. Mrs. Mike has already left for a breakfast meeting with some clients, and you just missed Mr. Mike."

"Oh, yeah. And Jeff is off on his camping trip. Well, I'm heading out, too." She poured herself a large glass of juice and took a sip. "Tell Mom I'm going to spend the day shopping, and I might not be back until after dinner tonight."

"Oh, you must have some serious shopping in mind," Stella said, freckled hands propped on her ample hips. "You want me to fix you up a nice breakfast before you go? An all-day shopping spree takes plenty of energy."

The sweet, motherly look on the housekeeper's face caused Amy's heart to melt. She placed the glass of juice on the counter and on impulse, walked over to Stella and gave her a hug. "I love you, Stella."

Stella hugged her back. If she was surprised by Amy's sudden display of affection, she didn't show it. She smoothed back an errant strand of hair from

Amy's face and smiled down at her. "I love you, too, honey. Every day I thank God you're still with us."

Amy's smile froze, and she drew away from the housekeeper, turning her back so Stella couldn't see how her words had pierced her. "I'm going to pass on breakfast. I'll stop by McDonald's and grab an Egg McMuffin or something."

A few minutes later, she was in the Tracker and driving on Interstate 64 toward Richmond.

"Hi. I'm here to see Victoria Shiley." Amy tried to control the trembling that had overtaken her as soon as she'd walked into the nursing home.

The plump woman behind the nurse's station looked up. Amy looked at her name tag, wondering if she was the same nurse who'd given Mama a birthday party two years ago. *Cheryl.* She looked a little older and at least fifteen pounds heavier, but for sure, it was the same nurse. How could someone work in a place like this year after year after year?

The woman's brown eyes swept over her. "Are you a relative?"

Amy felt a flutter of panic. Was it her imagination or was the nurse looking at her suspiciously? "Uh . . . no, I'm not. I'm . . . Robin Mulcahey. Vicky's daughter, Amy, was my best friend. I guess maybe you heard that she . . . uh . . . was killed in a car accident?"

Cheryl's eyes warmed. She shook her ash blond head regretfully. "Oh, yes. That was so horrible. I was on duty the morning the police came to inform Mrs. Shiley. Of course, they didn't know about her condition beforehand. They told her anyway, even though she didn't register a word of it, poor thing." Her gaze sharpened. "Oh! Are you the friend that was . . . uh . . . in the car with her?"

"That would be me," Amy said grimly.

"Oh, honey!" The nurse reached across the counter and placed her hand on Amy's arm. "What a horrible year you must've had! It just tears my heart out."

This calls for a Robinesque response.

But she just couldn't. She felt too close to tears to pull off a flippant reply. "It's been tough, but . . . well . . . you do what you have to. Anyway, I know Amy would've wanted me to stop in and see her mother on her birthday. I know how she always used to try to be here for it."

Cheryl's face brightened. "Of course! That's so sweet of you to come, but . . ." Her voice dropped to a whisper. "But you know, don't you, there's been no improvement. Vicky still isn't responsive."

Amy felt the hope dim inside of her, and was surprised it had been there at all. She hadn't *really* believed anything had changed, had she? But as always, she had to ask. "No improvement at all?"

"I'm afraid not. Why don't you take a seat in the lounge, and I'll go see if they're done with her morning bath."

Fifteen minutes later, Cheryl appeared in the doorway of the lounge, and with a bright smile, told her she could go in. Amy stepped into the room and saw immediately that something had changed in the two years since she'd been there. Mama's elderly roommate was gone, and in her place was a young woman, probably not much older than Amy, herself, sitting in a wheelchair next to the bed. Amy averted her gaze after one swift glance, but she knew the image would be embedded on her brain for years to come. The young woman's body was horribly twisted and misshapen. She sat with her head cocked to the right, her eyes staring vacantly, her mouth slack and coated with spittle. What on earth had happened to her?

And for the first time since the accident, Amy realized that perhaps Robin's death had been a blessing. Because if she'd survived, she might have ended up like this poor girl, and that would've been an even worse tragedy. Robin would never, ever have wanted to live like this.

Amy stepped past the curtain that divided the room and saw her mother sitting in a chair by the window, wearing a pretty pale blue nightgown and matching robe. Her eyes stared into space. Her hair had grown out from the short cut and now touched her shoulders in a lank, shapeless mop. A little gray streaked the area around her temples. Weird. Mama was only thirty-nine, way too young to be going gray. But who knew what was going on with her metabolism? She'd had a heart attack when she was thirty-seven, and what were the odds of that?

A few birthday cards had been placed on her serving tray, probably from the nurses. Would they be bringing in a birthday cake like before? Amy sat down in the chair opposite her mother, placing the gift she'd brought on her lap. She glanced toward the door to make sure they were alone, then leaned forward.

"Mama?" she spoke in a whisper. Stupid, really. There was no one around to hear except for that poor thing on the other side of the curtain, and it was obvious that, like Mama, she was living in her own little world. "It's me. Amy. How are you feeling?"

No matter how hard Amy tried, she couldn't stop herself from searching for some kind of response. A twitch of her lips. A glimmer of a soul behind those empty blue eyes. But as always, there was nothing.

Amy released a sigh and looked down at the birthday card on top of her present. She opened the envelope and drew out the card, placing it with the others on the serving tray. "I got you a new nightgown, Mama. But it looks like you've already got a new one."

"All of us nurses pitched in for it."

Heart lurching, Amy looked around, feeling the blood drain from her face. Had the nurse heard her say "Mama"?

Cheryl stood there, smiling broadly. "Oh, I'm sorry! Didn't mean to scare you. I just came to ask if I could get you a glass of orange juice or something? We'll be bringing in Vicky's morning snack soon."

Amy placed a hand over her thundering heart and tried to compose herself. "Yeah, I'd love a glass of juice. Thanks." She waited for the soft padding of Cheryl's footsteps to disappear before turning back to her mother.

"Oh, God, Mama. I've got myself into one hell of a mess."

Then, in a soft, methodical voice, she told her everything, only pausing when Cheryl returned with Mama's snack and her orange juice. "I'll take care of it," Amy told the nurse, placing the tray of chocolate pudding on the serving tray and wheeling it over to her mother's chair.

Somehow, in the deep recesses of her mind, Vicky must've realized her snack had arrived. As soon as Amy lifted the pudding-laden spoon to her mouth, she opened it like an expectant bird. Amy watched her in amazement. Even though her face was still expressionless, it was obvious she enjoyed the taste of the pudding. She finished the entire bowl within a few moments.

"So, you see, Mama . . . when I realized Robin was dead, and they thought I was her, it just made perfect sense. They would have their daughter back, and I would have . . . you know . . . a family. But I hadn't counted on feeling this much guilt. Will it ever go away? Or . . . is this something I'm going to have to live with the rest of my life?"

It was cathartic, telling her the truth. She was the only person in the world Amy could confess to. Was it because she couldn't understand, couldn't blow the whistle on her?

"But if you were normal," Amy whispered, "I wouldn't be in this situation, would I?"

Vicky began plucking at her nightgown, the same way she had during her last visit. Amy's heart lurched. She'd done that right before the heart attack. Amy started to get up to call the nurse. And that's when she saw it.

Her breath left her body as her eyes connected with her mother's. *There was someone in there!* For the first time in almost five years, Amy saw a soul inside her mother.

Vicky's hands plucked restlessly at her gown. Her mouth opened, birdlike, and her vocal cords flexed. A raspy, foreign sound issued from her throat. Amy reached out and grasped her arm, stilling its agitated movement.

"*Mama?*"

Vicky's eyes held hers, desperate, struggling. A harsh croak burst from her mouth, and Amy felt the world tip upside down as she realized what her mother was trying to say.

"*Aaaaammmeeey.*"

16

Amy was still shaken as she drove back to Williamsburg. *Her mother had recognized her!*

That would've been incredible enough if she'd had her old face. But somehow, Mama had known it was she even though she looked like a complete stranger. *How?* How was it possible? And why now, after all these years?

After her mother had called out her name in that strangled, alien voice, Amy had clutched her restless hands and peered into her eyes. "Mama, do you know me?"

But then, right in front of her, Amy saw the awareness begin to fade. *"Mama, no!"* She gave her a little shake, trying to jerk her back from the edge of oblivion, but it was already too late. She was gone.

Tears of frustration blurred Amy's eyes. Trembling, she stumbled down the hall past the nurse's station to the rest room, hoping to compose herself. This was good, she reasoned. If Mama could come back once, even if it was only for a few seconds, it could happen again. And maybe next time, she'd stick around longer.

Returning to her mother's room, she felt calmer, even a little optimistic. She vowed to visit Mama more often. Maybe if she was here, actively working with her, who knew what would happen? Wasn't it possible that she could actually come out of this catatonic state altogether?

The thought was mind-blowing. And a little scary. What would happen with this masquerade Amy was living? Would her mother, with all her faculties intact, keep her secret? Probably, Amy thought ruefully. If she thought there might be something in it for her. After all, Mama had never been candidate for Mother of the Year. More often than not, she'd treated Amy as a nuisance, an annoyance that, if she allowed it, would get in the way of her love affair with the bottle.

But a tiny hope flickered inside of Amy. That with the miracle of her mother's return to reality, perhaps her personality had metamorphosed into one of a loving mother. Someone like Tammy . . . or even Stella. It was a ridiculous hope; she knew that. But one that refused to die inside of her.

She spent the rest of the afternoon talking to Mama, coaxing her to return from that wasteland in which her mind had disappeared. But there was no further spark of recognition, not a semblance of personality in that vacant stare.

She'd been a fool to hope for two miracles in one day, Amy realized as she took the exit for Williamsburg, her brows knit in concentration. She'd come back in a couple of weeks, she told herself. Maybe something would happen next time.

"Well, this is the last box, Robin."

Squatting next to the cardboard box she'd just opened, Amy looked up to see Tammy step into her room at the Kappa Chi house, carrying a medium-size box.

"Good. Just put it down anywhere." Amy pushed an errant strand of hair behind her ear and reached into her box. "I don't know where to start with all the unpacking."

Tammy set the box on top of several others on the floor, then brushed her hand across her slightly damp brow. It was ninety degrees outside, and yet, Tammy looked as fresh as a spring breeze. Her sleeveless navy short-set still retained the iron's crisp creases, and her sleek blond bob secured with a headband showed no signs of drooping. Her tanned legs were long and slender, her pedicured feet clad in fashionable slingback sandals from Ann Taylor in Georgetown. How *did* the woman do it?

"Whew! At least the hard part is over." Tammy's eyes scanned the boxes, lingering on the one she'd just brought in. "You know, darling, some of Amy's things are mixed in with yours. When Dad and I came here after the accident to pack up your stuff, we just brought it all. Since Amy didn't have any family to claim it—"

"I know." Amy spoke through the tightening in her throat that happened every time she heard her name—her *former* name—mentioned. "Don't worry. I'll go through it. I'll donate the stuff I can't use."

Tammy approached her. "It might be tough for you," she said softly. "I can help if you want."

Amy stood and wrapped her arms around Tammy. "Thanks, Mom, but I can do it. I think I *need* to do it."

For a moment, Tammy stiffened, as if she was surprised by Amy's sudden show of affection. But then she relaxed and hugged her, stroking her hair. It had grown out to just below her jawline, and she wore it in a smooth bob, much like Tammy's. "Okay, honey. I just want you to know I'm here for you if you need me. I know that hasn't always been the case, and I want to make it up to you."

Amy frowned. She had no idea what Tammy was talking about. Why the sudden guilt trip?

Tammy drew away, her brow puckered with concern. "I know it's not easy for you, coming back here to the Kappa Chi house without Amy. I think you're very brave, Robin."

"It's not bravery," Amy said soberly. "I'm just doing what I have to do to survive."

Tammy smiled, weaving her fingers through Amy's hair, gently pushing it back from her face. "In my book, that's the definition of bravery." Her gaze focused on Amy's hair. "Oh, and by the way, I've been meaning to tell you, you've been doing a great job on your hair. I like this shade. It's new, isn't it? A little more wheat-colored than usual?"

Amy's smile faltered as her heart slammed a wallop in her chest. "Yeah, I've been experimenting."

"Well, it looks great. And you've been keeping it up, too. I haven't seen any dark roots on you in ages. Do you still go to Gloria to have it done?"

Amy stepped away from Tammy and knelt beside the box, thinking furiously. "Oh, I've going to this new place one of the Kappa Chis recommended," she lied. "Only problem . . . it's halfway to Virginia Beach. And I don't think you'd like her, Mom. I mean, she's good but . . . well . . ." Amy shrugged, hoping she'd said enough to put her off.

"She's what?"

Amy carefully avoided Tammy's gaze. "She's . . . well . . . what some people might call . . . poor white trash. She works out of her home in a trailer park."

"Oh." Tammy was silent for a moment, then, "Well, I guess I should stick with Gloria, anyway. She's been doing my hair forever, and I wouldn't want to hurt her feelings."

Amy relaxed. Much as she loved Tammy, she was well aware of the importance Robin's mother placed upon being seen in the right places and patronizing the right restaurants, clothing stores, and hair salons. For example, she never shopped at the Pottery Factory or even the outlet stores that lined Route 60. Like the other women in her social circle, the only place to shop in Williamsburg was Merchants Square. But if she had serious shopping in mind, she'd drive all the way to DC and use her plastic all over Georgetown. No *way* would Tammy Mulcahey go to a trailer park to get her hair dyed.

Tammy wiped her hands down the front of her shorts and glanced around at the stacks of boxes. "Well, I don't know about you, but I'm starving. How about burgers, my treat? We can go to that library place you're always talking about."

"Sure," Amy agreed reluctantly. She hadn't been to The Library since the accident. It would be weird without Robin. But a lot of things on campus were going to be weird without her. She couldn't avoid them all.

Amy followed Tammy out the door and locked it behind her, glad to put off the daunting task of unpacking.

Tammy smiled at her as they started down the stairs. "It was so sweet of the girls to offer you a room by yourself. I guess they realized it would be impossible for you to replace Amy."

Early in the summer, Amy had received a letter from the Kappa Chis offering the single room. Although she'd had her doubts about Robin accepting it, because God knows, she'd *hated* being alone, Amy had finally decided to take them up on it. With a roommate, she'd always have to be on her toes, making sure she didn't do or say anything that would be so *not* Robin. Now, at least, behind closed doors, she could be herself. For a little while.

As they descended the stairs, they passed a couple of Kappa Chis on their way up. One of them, a petite dark-haired junior named Leah, flashed Amy a brilliant orthodontically enhanced smile.

"Oh, Robin, I'm so glad you're back. It wasn't the same here without you." Impulsively, the girl gave Amy a brief hug. She drew away, her hazel eyes darting to Tammy. "We all just love your daughter to pieces, Mrs. Mulcahey."

Tammy smiled and murmured something. Amy wasn't listening. She was too busy trying to choke down the guilt she felt. The same guilt she'd felt earlier this morning when she and Tammy arrived to find a "welcome back" party for her in the parlor of the sorority house. Most of the Kappa Chis were there, the seniors who'd been a year ahead of her and Robin, the juniors they'd pledged with during their freshman year, and the sophomores who'd been newbies last year. They'd all been so sweet and welcoming. It had warmed her heart, but she'd had to keep reminding herself that it was Robin they were welcoming back into their fold, not her. Not that they hadn't mentioned her with wistful smiles and just the right tone of sorrow in their voices. But Amy couldn't help but think if they knew the truth—that *Robin* had died—there would have been inconsolable tears and heartbreak.

Who was she kidding? There probably wouldn't even have *been* a "welcome home" party for Amy. She'd never really been one of them, after all.

But now she was. Even if it *was* a lie.

Amy sat on the floor in her room, surrounded by remnants of her life before the accident. There were the textbooks from the classes she'd been taking that spring semester. The file of papers from the archaeology internship in which she'd been involved. The novel she'd been reading, Mona Simpson's *Anywhere But Here*, the corner of page seventy-eight still turned down to mark her place. And all the other ordinary things. Brushes, hair gel, makeup. The only thing Tammy hadn't brought was Amy's clothing. Apparently, it hadn't occurred to her that since they'd been the same size, "Robin" might want to go through Amy's wardrobe and take what she wanted. Amy smiled and shook her head ruefully. Of course it made perfect sense to Tammy. Why would her daughter want any of the clothes that poor Amy had worn? It was only stuff from the cheap outlets anyway. Amy didn't have to ask to know that Tammy had given it all away to Goodwill.

A knock on the door jerked her out of her thoughts. "Hey, Robin!" A voice called out from the hallway. "We're heading out for pizza. Want to come?"

Amy opened the door. Leah and a tall auburn-haired girl she didn't recognize were standing there. "Thanks, but I'm going to pass. I've got all this unpacking to do, and to tell you the truth, I'm still stuffed from lunch."

"Okay." Leah smiled brightly. "But hey, later tonight the Kappa Delta Rho guys are having a party at their house. Lots of cool, good-looking guys and a keg. We're heading over about nine-thirty. If you want to come along with us, just be at my room about twenty after, okay?"

"Yeah, sure. I'll think about it." *Not.* Amy kept the smile glued on her face until the two girls turned and headed back down the hallway.

She closed the door, but not before she heard Leah's carrying whisper, "Robin used to be such a blast. I sure hope that accident hasn't changed her too much."

Amy slowly walked back to the box she'd been unpacking. *I sure hope that accident hasn't changed her too much.* Leah didn't realize it, but she'd just uttered the understatement of the century. Amy knelt and began to pull more items from the box. A stack of classical CDs. A cheap jewelry box from Claire's Boutique, which held her earrings and other costume jewelry. Amy tugged at the sterling garnet earring in her ear—the only good pair of earrings she had owned until now. Robin had been buried with hers, the ones that were near identical to Amy's except that the garnets were a bit larger. Thank God no one had ever noticed the difference.

She sighed, listlessly sifting a finger through the cheap jewelry. She supposed she *should* go to the frat party. No doubt, Robin would've jumped at it. But she knew she wasn't ready to throw herself into the frenzied college social life just yet. It would have to be done sooner or later, she knew. But not on her first night back on campus.

She pulled out a rectangular cedar box, recognizing it right away. Robin had kept her journal notebooks in it. It was locked, so she set it aside. There was probably a key for it somewhere. It could wait. She'd seen something else in the bottom of the big box. The answering machine. She stared at it a moment, then reached for it. It was one of those older machines that held tiny cassette tapes. Amy wasn't sure if these kinds of machines were even sold anymore. They were all electronic now. She opened the little window and stared down at the cassette tape. Her heart began to beat a little faster.

No. You shouldn't do it.

But it was a morbid compulsion she knew she couldn't control. One more time. She just wanted to hear Robin's voice one more time and remember how she'd looked when she'd made that recording. It had been on a day just like this two years ago. They'd been in another room in this very house, and Robin had sat on her bed, wearing nothing but a pair of panties and a skimpy camisole. Her blond hair had flowed down her back in rippled glory; she'd been beautiful and happy and funny—and so full of life. They'd taken turns leaving stupid greetings on the answering machine.

Hello, Losers! Robin and Amy aren't here right now because . . . hel-lo? We have a life, and you don't. So, please leave a friggin' message, and if it's interesting enough, we might call you back.

Robin's, of course. And Amy's . . .

You've reached the answering machine of Robin Mulcahey. She's not here right now. Duh! What did you expect? That she's just hanging out waiting for your phone call? Please leave a message and she'll call you back. If you're lucky, you might hear from her before the new millennium. Oh, and by the way, if you happen to be calling for Amy Shiley, please know that she is NOT interested in joining the Cosmetique Beauty Club at this time. Thank you.

That little message had earned Amy a laugh and a flying pillow from Robin. Finally, though, Robin had settled down and left a halfway-decent greeting.

Amy slowly walked over to her desk and plugged in the answering machine. Her finger hovered over the announcement button, trembling slightly. Maybe Tammy had erased it when she'd packed it up. Amy almost wished that would be the case. She feared she would fall apart when she heard Robin's voice. But even knowing this, she pushed the button, her heart in her throat.

Hey, what's up? Robin and Amy aren't here right now, so you know the drill. Leave a message and we'll call you back. Peace.

Tears blurred Amy's eyes. She pushed the button again. And again. Over and over, she listened to Robin's voice. If she closed her eyes and listened to it, she could imagine her in the room. Smiling her trademark mischievous smile, her dimple flickering. Amy played the greeting one more time, moving to the mirror and staring into Robin's face. Amy formed her mouth into a big smile— one that didn't reach her eyes—and . . . no dimple. No matter how she twisted her mouth, she couldn't find a dimple. No one had ever remarked upon its absence. This was the first time she'd ever thought of it. It was superstitious she knew, but somehow, she wondered if the absence of Robin's dimple was sym- bolic of the absence of her soul. Now, this face in the mirror—Robin's face on Amy's body—looked grotesque, alien. Because it was Robin's face, but not her essence. Not her soul.

Amy felt panic bubbling up inside her. *How on earth am I getting away with this charade? Can't they see? All these people I interact with day in and day out . . . are they blind? Or just hopelessly stupid?*

No, they weren't blind or stupid. They were simply seeing what they wanted to see, Amy realized. Not the imposter, but the girl they loved, even if she was just a shadow of the person she'd been before.

Amy closed the window of the answering machine and stared down at it. She'd save this tape with Robin's last-recorded words. Why, she didn't know. Comfort, she supposed. Just knowing it was there if she ever needed to hear her.

She opened the window again and started to take the tape out, then paused. They'd never returned to their room that night. Robin usually had had tons of messages on their machine when they'd returned from an outing. How many had called that night, maybe even after she was already dead?

It was morbid; she knew that. But like before, she couldn't seem to stop herself. She hit the PLAY button, and the machine beeped. Jason's lazy voice informing Robin he'd be in town the next weekend. Sherry, one of the sorority girls, reminding them about a Kappa Chi meeting on Sunday night. Jason again, just wanting to talk. And then, the last voice she'd been expecting. The voice that sent shivers of longing through her body.

Amy, this is Paul . . . that e-mail I left you today? Forget about it. It was all lies. I don't love Monica. As soon as I get off the phone, I'm calling her to break it off. And Robin, I know you're probably hearing this, but you know what? I don't give a fuck . . . **I love Amy Jessica Shiley!** *I do, Amy. I love you. Call me back, okay? No matter how late it is.*

Amy sank to the floor, trembling. "Oh, my God."

She knew she had to play it again to be sure of what she'd heard, but for the moment, she couldn't move, couldn't breathe. Couldn't function. She dropped her face into her hands and forced herself to take deep, cleansing breaths. *Paul loves me!* He'd said that, hadn't he? He'd shouted it. Or . . . was she finally losing it? Had this masquerade she was living finally driven her over the edge? Could it be that she'd imagined the whole thing?

Slowly, Amy got to her feet. Her legs felt curiously wooden as she walked to the desk and hit the PLAY button again. She stood there, white-knuckled hands grasping the desk edge as she listened to Paul's voice again. *Call me back, okay? No matter how late it is.* She closed her eyes and shook her head. Hot tears trickled down her face. It was too late now.

He loved her. Deep down inside, she'd never really stopped believing that. The memory of those nights together hadn't lied to her heart. The tender love-making they'd shared had been so much more than sex. She'd always known that, but she'd allowed her head to convince her heart it wasn't true.

"Oh, Paul," she murmured. "Why did you have to wait so late to call?"

If only he'd called that afternoon right after she'd gotten the e-mail. Or if she'd had the guts to call him and put him on the spot, make him tell her voice to voice that he didn't love her. Maybe he would've realized then that he couldn't say it. Maybe she and Robin wouldn't have gone to Richmond to find the new bar. Maybe Robin would be alive today if . . .

Maybes and what-ifs. Nothing but crap! You could "maybe" yourself to death, and it wouldn't change a thing.

But Paul loves me!

For an insane moment, Amy thought about calling his number in Denver. Telling him that she loved him, too, that she'd be on the next plane to Denver, that the two of them could build a life together and live happily ever after. But when she tried to imagine what his response would be, only three words came to mind.

Who is this?

And reality crashed down around her. The woman Paul Mulcahey loved was dead.

And the woman who loved him . . . was his sister.

17

Amy pulled into the long paved driveway of Windsong and parked beside a new silver blue Corvette. After turning off the ignition of the Tracker, she sat there a moment, staring at the sports car and trying to get her breathing under control. Turbulent gray skies drizzled cold rain, and rivulets of water streaked the car windows, lending a dismal mood to the afternoon. Amy shivered.

Paul was home. That had to be his rental car. Unless Michael had succumbed to midlife crisis-itis and stopped at the Chevrolet dealer on the way home from his law office. No. It was Paul, and he was home for Thanksgiving.

Amy glanced into the rearview mirror to check her hair. A small electric shock quivered through her as she saw Robin's face looking back at her. This still happened way too often. Would she ever look in the mirror again without expecting to see her old face?

She gathered her books and got out of the Tracker, hurrying up the stone walkway to the mudroom entrance. With any luck, she could get to her room before running into Paul. She needed time to prepare for that. This would be the first time she'd seen him since learning how he felt about her. About Amy, she amended. This Thanksgiving holiday was going to be a true test for her. Would she be able to remember she was supposed to be Robin when everything inside her—her emotions, her love for Paul, her very soul—was Amy Shiley?

The house was quiet when she stepped into the kitchen, fragrant with the scent of lemon oil from the freshly wiped cabinets. The appliances and counters sparkled under Stella's efficient hand. It was just after four. Michael was probably still at his office, and Jeff was surely out with his friends. That left

Tammy and Paul. They were probably in the family room, or maybe the library. Amy quickened her step, quietly pushing open the swinging door leading into the dining room.

"Hi, Robin." Tammy looked up from a vase of flowers she was arranging. "How do you like my centerpiece?"

Amy forced a smile, her heart bumping. "Nice. Um . . . did Paul make it home?"

"He did." Tammy smiled, repositioning a bloodred flower. "Didn't you see his rental car? That explains why he didn't want anyone to pick him up at the airport. Guess he's traveling in style these days."

"So, where is he?" Amy summoned a nonchalant tone, but to her, it came out sounding unnatural.

Tammy didn't seem to notice. "He's taking a nap before dinner. Seems he was up late at a party last night."

"Poor baby." Amy gave her a bright Robinesque smile. "Well, catch you later."

"Dinner's at seven," Tammy called after her as she left the room.

Amy hurried up the stairs. Good. Paul was safely in his room, and with any luck, she wouldn't have to deal with him before dinner. She would use the next couple of hours to relax and unwind, prepare herself for their meeting. Maybe she'd take a hot bath in the Jacuzzi. The chilly rain had begun falling early this morning, and her bones ached from the damp cold as she'd scurried around the campus. That bath was going to feel awesome.

She was almost to her room when Paul's door opened, and he stepped out into the hallway. Like a deer caught in the headlights, Amy stiffened, her eyes locked on his. His face lit up in a smile, and Amy felt her heart breaking as she thought about the last time they'd been together—not the time in the hospital—but the last time in this house. The way he'd smiled at her then.

"Hey, Rob!" Closing the distance between them in two long strides, he wrapped his arms around her in an affectionate hug.

Amy closed her eyes and drank in his sandalwood aftershave. Beneath her ear, she heard the soft, even thud of his heartbeat, felt the warmth of his body. For a moment, she felt almost weak with longing. It had been so long since she'd been in his arms. It was where she belonged. Right here. Enclosed in his embrace.

Not anymore. You gave up the right to be in his arms when you gave up your identity.

She took a deep, tremulous breath and drew away. Summoning a mischievous smile, she peered up at him. "Hey, you're not going all soft on me, are you, big bro? If I didn't know better, I'd say you look like you're about ready to turn on the waterworks." She wasn't kidding. His blue eyes were suspiciously bright. "You'd better not. If word gets out to those three-hundred-pound defensive ends you play against, you're dead meat."

Paul grinned and squeezed her shoulders. "Since when do *you* know the difference between a defensive end and a field goal kicker?" The smile remained on his face, but his eyes sobered. "It's just so good seeing you looking like yourself again, Robby. I'm really proud of you, you know."

"Get *out!*" Amy gave him a playful shove, then tossed an exaggerated look behind his shoulder. "So, where's Miss Nob Hill? Did she bring her own pumpkin this year?"

"Jesus, Robin! Where you been? I called it quits with Monica months ago. It didn't take us long to realize a long-distance relationship just wasn't going to work."

Amy tried to hide the elation she felt, even though it was mixed with sorrow. Where would the two of them be now if she hadn't taken over Robin's identity? "Well, it's clear you're brokenhearted about it."

"Yeah, right. No, I knew a long time ago things weren't going to work out with us. I don't know how we stayed together as long as we did . . ." His voice trailed away, and his eyes grew distant.

What was he thinking? Amy pasted another bright smile on her face and tried to insert a teasing tone into her voice. "So, you dating anybody now?"

He looked at her, seemed to recollect his thoughts, and returned her grin. "Hey, I'm twenty-three, an NFL wide receiver, not bad-looking, and I have money. What do *you* think?"

"Anyone special?"

He shook his head. "No one special." Sadness flickered in his eyes. "Not anymore, anyway."

Amy's throat tightened. Was he thinking about her? About Amy?

"I guess you could say I've become a little cynical about the whole relationship game," he added. "None of the women I meet seem . . . you know, genuine. Or maybe I'm just expecting too much . . ."

She had to get away from him. Every moment she spent near him made her want to confess it all. And she couldn't do that. His love would turn to hate— because what man could still love a woman who'd deceived not only him, but his entire family, and in the most hideous way possible? She couldn't bear his hate. If she couldn't have the romantic love she craved from him, she'd have to settle for brotherly love. That was better than indifference, and way better than hate.

Again, she summoned her false smile, and said, "Yeah, well . . . life sucks. Hey, I'll catch you later, Paul. I'm heading for a soak in the hot tub."

"Yeah. Don't fall asleep in there, Rob."

Amy turned to her door, still feeling his eyes upon her.

"Hey, Rob?" he said, just before she stepped into her room.

She turned. "Yeah?"

"Did I tell you that you look beautiful?"

Her heart melted at the sweet smile on his face. Her hands itched to run through his silky black hair the way they had before. She searched for a Robin-ish quip in response to his compliment, but nothing came. Instead, she gave him a watery smile and a murmured "thanks."

Then she stepped quickly inside her door and closed it behind her. Only then, did she allow the tears to flow.

Thanksgiving dinner was as weird as it had been last year. But only to her, she supposed. Everyone in the family was here, including Tammy's parents. Tech-nically, no one was missing, but Amy felt the yawning absence of Robin like a physical pain. As she chewed listlessly on a tender slice of ham, she realized that this, then, was her own personal hell. The price she had to pay for the masquerade she'd chosen to live.

Next to her, Grandmother Alice reached for a succulent slice of turkey breast and placed it on her china plate. Amy's mouth watered. She hadn't tasted turkey in two years, not since that last Christmas dinner she and Robin had eaten here. And God knew she'd never be able to eat it again. Not here, anyway.

Like last year, Stella had baked the ham especially for her, and she was the only one of the whole clan who had to eat it. Everyone else was stuffing them-selves with turkey. It wasn't that Amy disliked ham; she could take it or leave it. But she *loved* turkey, and seeing everyone else eating it when she couldn't, was maddening. *Damn* Robin for not liking the single most important dish on a Thanksgiving table! Immediately, she felt guilty for her mean thoughts. It wasn't Robin's fault she was sitting here lusting over turkey. She'd chosen this; she had to live with it.

"You're awfully quiet today, Robin," Grandmother Alice said, her birdlike blue eyes scanning her.

Grandfather Jimmy winked at her, his wrinkled mouth splitting in a gold-toothed grin. "The cat got your tongue, girl?"

"No." Amy grabbed her wineglass and took a sip, her cheeks warming. Damn! When was she going to learn to be more outgoing? This, by far, was the most difficult part of being Robin. And the drinking, too. Robin had been such a drinker that it would certainly raise eyebrows if she suddenly became a tee-totaler. "I was just thinking . . ."

"You, *thinking*?" Jeff snickered as he shoveled a forkful of stuffing into his mouth. "That'll be a first."

Amy threw him an evil look. "Up yours." There. That was a Robin response.

Paul laughed, and Michael grinned. Their grandparents' faces were com-placent. Only Tammy looked mildly disturbed. "Now, let's try to keep things civilized, shall we? Robin, what were you thinking about? You did look very far away."

Amy looked across the elegant table at her surrogate mother, and without

thinking, answered, "I was thinking about Amy." Her face grew hot as she realized what she'd said. "About how much I miss her not being here with us."

An awkward silence fell. Amy's heart drummed. *Oh, God! Somebody say
something.* Had they forgotten her already? Had she meant so little to them?

Michael cleared his throat. "We all miss Sunshine, honey. That's what she
was like, you know. A beam of sunshine right into our lives."

Slowly, Amy looked up and met his eyes. He gazed back at her, a solemn
look on his handsome face. She knew he meant what he said. Looking from
one face to another, she saw the sadness mirrored in their eyes. Even Jeff had
lost his usual smirk. But the somber expression Paul wore had her blinking
back tears.

Grandmother Alice reached out and placed a blue-veined hand on hers.
"We know you miss her, child. But you know what I think? I think she's right
here with us at this very moment."

Amy nodded, holding back a sudden urge to laugh hysterically.

You have no idea, Grandmother, how very right you are.

The torture went on even after coffee and pumpkin pie were served. Michael
put a videotape into the VCR, and with horror, Amy watched a young Robin—
perhaps six years old—horseplaying in the pool with Paul, who must've been
around nine, and a much younger-looking Michael. Her heart twisted in
agony. Robin, at that age, had been adorable, with a full head of blond
ringlets and huge blue eyes. She giggled and splashed in the water, dodging
out of Paul's grasp and swimming away like a small, sleek goldfish. With a
wave, she dived under, then surfaced, and whoever was filming them—
Tammy?—drew in for a close-up. Robin grinned mischievously, her dimple
flickering.

The camera moved to Paul, who'd climbed out of the pool and was making
his way to the diving board. At nine, he was tall for his age, with the slender build
of a basketball athlete, rather than the football player he'd turn out to be. His hair
was raven black and, in marked contrast, his eyes a startling blue. It was strange
seeing the man she loved as a nine-year-old; it was almost as if she were watching not Paul, but his future son. What would *their* son look like if the impossible
could happen and she could make a life with him?

Dangerous thought. She was relieved when the camera angle changed.

The Mulcaheys were at the beach. Robin, looking about the same age as in
the earlier scene, was lying asleep on her stomach on a beach towel. The camera swept away, focusing on Paul stumbling from the surf with a pail of water.
He grinned mischievously into the lens and headed toward Robin. Kneeling
next to her, he cautiously untied the strings of her swimsuit top. He stood and
reached for the pail. Eyes glittering with pure devilment, he threw the water on
her back. She yelped and jumped up from the blanket, realizing too late that

her top was undone. Howling with laughter, Paul took off running, and Robin, holding her top to her flat chest, barreled after him, screaming revenge.

Laughter exploded in the darkened family room, and Amy tried to imagine how Robin would be reacting to these movies. Arching an eyebrow, she glanced over at Paul and saw he was grinning at her sheepishly.

"Did you ever forgive me for that one, Rob?"

She shrugged and gave him a mock glower. "You were a real jerk, you know that? I hope I caught up with you and gave you what you deserved."

"Are you kidding? You almost drowned me that day."

"Good." Amy looked back at the screen.

She saw Tammy—late twenties, Amy guessed—sitting in the shade of a huge umbrella, wearing shorts and a halter top. Dark sunglasses perched on her nose, and a floppy straw hat protected her head from a stray beam of sunlight that dared to find its way through the protection of the umbrella. She seemed unaware of the camera as she scribbled notes onto a pad on the table in front of her. The camera drew back, and Amy saw a playpen under another umbrella. A plump, blond baby sat inside, contentedly stacking colorful blocks. Jeff, of course. He looked like he was about a year old. Suddenly a small body clad in a two-piece red swimsuit ran into the frame, shrieking with laughter—Robin, still wet from the pool. *"Mommy, Mommy! Paul is trying to dunk me!"*

As the little girl reached for her mother, Tammy jumped up from the table, her perfectly made-up face tightening in horror. *"Get away from me, Robin! You're all wet!"* she snapped in a shrill, furious voice.

Robin froze, the joy draining from her face, replaced by hurt bewilderment. She backed away from her mother, muttering, "Sorry."

Tammy glowered at her. "You should be. You're not acting very ladylike. Now, go back and play. I've got work to do." Suddenly Tammy's gaze locked on the camera. "Oh, really, Mike. Can't you put that thing away?" Frowning, she sat back in her chair and returned to her paperwork. The video moved on to another day in the life of the Mulcaheys.

But Amy couldn't get the look on Robin's little face out of her mind. Hadn't Tammy seen it? Hadn't she realized how her harsh rejection had hurt her daughter? It was a little thing, one moment in a little girl's life, but it was a telling moment. There had been no affection in Tammy's face, no warmth in her voice. Amy remembered all those times Robin had criticized her mother without going into any detail. Maybe this was a small sample of why she'd felt the way she had.

A new scene started. A birthday party. Robin, wearing a lacy pink dress, her hair a mass of curls, blowing out eight candles on an elaborately decorated cake. Amy stood. She couldn't take any more of this. It just hurt too much to watch a young Robin, alive and vibrant, on videotape. She pleaded her old standby excuse—a headache—and said good night to everyone, her eyes lingering on Paul for a moment. She knew he was leaving early the next morning; he had to be at practice on Saturday to prepare for the upcoming game against the Kansas City Chiefs. Who knew when she'd see him again?

Although she was physically exhausted, she didn't feel at all sleepy, so when she got to her room, she started filling the tub. Maybe a hot bath would relax her. A bubble bath, she decided. She wasn't in the mood for the frenzy and noise of the jets. She poured in some peach shower gel, hoping it would produce bubbles, and it did. Moments later, she climbed into the tub, sinking gratefully into the froth of bubbles until her body was enclosed in the soothing hot water. From her bedroom, the gentle strains of a Celtic harp issued from the CD player. Candlelight flickered around the tub, casting dancing shadows on the marbled walls. She stretched out, resting her head on the inflatable bath pillow, and closing her eyes, released a sigh of pure delight.

She must've dozed off. Lifting her head, she gazed around in confusion. The noise came again. Someone knocking at her bedroom door.

"Just a minute!" She sat up and reached for the bath towel on the ledge of the tub.

"Hey, Rob! You aren't asleep, are you?"

Her heart jumped. It was Paul. "No! Hold on! I'm just getting out of the tub." She wrapped the lush oversize towel around her and stepped out. Casting a glance in the mirror, she dried off and slipped into a thick, white terry-cloth robe. Her face was flushed with the heat of the bath, and with her hair pulled back in a haphazard ponytail, it was like staring into Robin's beautiful likeness. That was one good thing about this situation. She'd never have to worry about her looks again, because Robin had always been gorgeous.

So why was it she often found herself missing her old face?

She opened the door to find Paul holding a tray with two cans of ginger ale and a couple of sandwiches. He was dressed in comfortable sweatpants and a Denver Broncos sweatshirt. "How's your headache?"

She shrugged. "The bath helped."

"Good. Thanksgiving wouldn't be the same without our ritual." He grinned and nodded toward the tray. "You didn't think I'd forgotten, did you?"

"Forgot?" Amy echoed, shaking her head.

"Yeah, ginger ale and Fluffernutters." Paul stepped into the room and placed the tray down on her dresser. "Go get your pajamas on. I promise I won't eat your sandwich."

Still flustered by his appearance, Amy opened a dresser drawer and pulled out the first garments she saw—a pair of soft cotton leopard-print pajamas that looked very much like the comforter on her bed. Excusing herself, she went into the bathroom and closed the door.

She slipped out of the robe and drew on the pajamas, buttoning the top with clumsy fingers. Her heart was racing at the thought of being alone with Paul in an intimate environment like her bedroom. She hadn't been with him like this since . . . *no!* She had to stop thinking like that. He was her brother now, for God's sake!

When she stepped into the bedroom, she was shocked to see him sitting on the king-size bed, his back against the headboard, cradling a can of ginger ale in his hands. The cat, Ruby Two-Shoes, was curled up next to him. Smiling nervously, Amy grabbed her own can and sat down on her desk chair.

Paul looked up at her. "What's Ruby doing hanging out in here? I thought you didn't like her. And why are you all the way over there?" He patted the bed beside him. "Come on. How can we share confidences when you're all the way across the room?"

Amy felt her face grow hot. "Hey, I never said I didn't like Ruby. I just like dogs better." She'd always preferred cats, but of course, Robin had pretty much ignored Ruby. She stood up, but instead of approaching Paul, went to the tray and grabbed a sandwich. "Fluffernutter, huh?" Peanut butter and marshmallow creme welled from the edges of soft white bread.

"Sure. Would I change tradition? Bring me one, will you? It's been hours since dinner."

Amy grabbed the plate of sandwiches and went to the bed. "Are you sure you're allowed to eat stuff like this? Coach Shanahan will have your hide if you put on too much weight." She deposited the plate between them and crawled onto the bed, arranging a couple of giraffe-appliquéd pillows at her back. Ruby stood up, stretched, and crawled into her lap.

Paul took a bite of his sandwich and winked. "What Coach doesn't know won't hurt me. How do you know so much about Coach Shanahan, anyway? Have you suddenly become a football fan?"

Amy shrugged and took the other sandwich from the plate. "Well, I've got to watch my big brother's games, don't I? What kind of sister would I be if I didn't give you some support?"

"Will wonders never cease," Paul murmured, swallowing another bite of his sandwich. "Never thought I'd see the day when anyone could get *you* interested in football."

"I like watching you," Amy admitted. Was that so weird? Surely if Robin had lived, she would've watched Paul play pro football. "You're really starting to carve out a name for yourself, aren't you?"

He shrugged, finishing off his sandwich and taking a sip of ginger ale. "I can't complain. Except for the fact that we aren't winning much this year. But I guess that's to be expected, with John gone, and Terrell out for the season. I guess we just have to call it a rebuilding year and leave it at that."

Amy took another bite of her Fluffernutter. It was really tasty. The only other time she'd had one was at her childhood friend's house. Melissa. Strange. She hadn't thought of her in years. Where was she now? It had broken Amy's heart when she'd moved away. Now, here she was, trying to adjust to the loss of another best friend.

"So, Rob. How are things with you?" Paul's blue eyes held hers. "I mean, *really?*"

Amy looked away from him, lifting a shoulder in a slight shrug. "Okay." She finished her sandwich and began stroking Ruby's soft orange fur.

"Don't bullshit me. You can't fool me, and you know it. You haven't been yourself since the accident."

Amy's heart plunged sickeningly. Her mouth grew dry with fear.

His hand reached out and enclosed hers, his warmth radiating up her arm. "Robby," he said gently, "talk to me, babe. I know it's been a tough couple of years for you. Are you still going to therapy?"

Amy nodded.

"Good. That's good. You don't get over something like this overnight, you know. What about the drinking? How are you doing with that?"

"I've cut down a lot." *Understatement. I never drink anymore, except for an occasional glass of wine with the family. And then, only when it would look odd not to have one, like this afternoon at the Thanksgiving meal.*

Paul smiled, squeezing her hand. "Glad to hear that. I know that hasn't been easy for you to do. Before the accident, I was really starting to worry you had a serious drinking problem."

He was right. Robin had been well on her way to becoming an alcoholic, if she hadn't already been one. Amy thought back to that last night at the hick bar in Richmond. Robin had been downing beers like a chocoholic devoured M&Ms. If only Amy had known what was in store for them hours later. How she wished she could go back in time and stop her. But then, *she* had been the one to have two beers. *She* had been the one at the wheel.

She was the one responsible for killing her best friend.

Amy stared down at the leopard-print comforter, her eyes blurring with tears. "I miss her," she whispered. "I still miss her so much."

"Me too."

Something in his voice made her look up at him. She caught her breath at the anguished look in his eyes.

"You know what I don't get?" he said. "Why were you driving that night? Let's face it, Rob. You were the one who was always trashed."

Amy felt the blood drain from her face.

Frantically, she searched for an intelligent response, but before she could come up with anything, Paul went on, "Hey, I know Dad managed to pull some strings and make sure you weren't charged for DWI, but . . . come on, Rob. You were wasted, weren't you? Why wasn't Amy driving?"

Remembering that night, remembering the e-mail that had led to the horrifying chain of events, Amy felt a ripple of anger shoot through her. "I guess you didn't know Amy as well as you thought you did, Paul. She *had* been drinking that night, and you know why, don't you?"

Paul glanced away, his face flooding with color. "Oh. So, you know about that?"

The obvious misery on his face went a long way in cooling her anger. "Amy and I didn't have any secrets."

He turned to her, his blue eyes glimmering with pain. "I'll never forgive myself for hurting her like I did."

Amy looked away from him, unable to watch his anguish. She concentrated on stroking Ruby's orange fur. "Anyway, it's all in the past, and we just need to move on."

Paul fell silent for a moment, and then said softly, "You smell like her." He leaned toward her, closed his eyes and inhaled. Amy almost stopped breathing. He was so close, his mouth just inches from her neck. What if she turned and kissed him? What would he do?

Draw back in horror, of course. Like any decent brother would do. Then he would leave her room in disgust and never be able to look at her again without revulsion.

"Coconut," he said, drawing away from her, eyes still glimmering with sadness. "That's the shower gel she used. You use it, too, don't you?"

Amy nodded. "Actually, it's peach. We did a lot of shopping together. Bought the same things. Shared everything." Not true. Robin had always gone for citrus scents. But would Paul know that?

His eyes were far away. Suddenly he shivered.

"What's wrong?"

He shook his head. "Nothing. Just a *déjà vu*. I feel like we've had this conversation before." He looked over at the stereo. "Your CD has stopped."

He slid his legs over the side of the bed and stood up. Ruby protested at the movement with a soft yowl and jumped off the bed. Paul strode to the door and let her out. Amy tried to keep her eyes from sweeping his sculpted body. Football had kept him in great shape, beefing up his chest and arms, but keeping his buttocks lean and firm. In his tight sweatpants, his butt was gloriously defined. After closing the door behind the cat, he knelt in front of her CD case, eyes scanning. He pulled out a CD and studied it a moment, frowning. Then slowly, he opened the case, took out the disc, and slid it into the player.

Goose pimples prickled her arms as the opening track from *Songs from a Secret Garden* began to play—the clear, sweet soprano of "Nocturne." Amy began to tremble. For a moment, she was back in Robin's Camaro with him, parked at Cohoke Crossing, listening to the music. Instead of crawling back onto the bed where he'd been before, Paul sat on the edge, his back to her, as the song went on. Neither of them spoke.

When it finished, he turned to look at her, and she was shocked to see tears in his eyes.

"I was in love with her," he said softly.

Amy didn't speak. Couldn't speak.

"It wasn't just sex. I fell in love with her that weekend, but I was too stupid to realize it. Then I broke her heart. Stomped on it like it was nothing."

"I was such a bastard. But Rob, when I realized what I was throwing away, I called her to tell her I loved her. But you know what? It was too late. It was too fucking *late!*"

Amy stared at him, wanting so much to reach out and touch his bristled jaw. His eyes were wounded, angry. He turned around and faced her. "You asked me yesterday if I had a girlfriend. Yeah, I have lots of girlfriends. I sleep with them, and I leave them. You know why? I keep looking for Amy. I know she's gone, but I keep looking for her anyway. Is that fucked up or what?"

"Oh, Paul."

I'm not gone. I'm here. Can't you feel me?

He reached out and hugged her. She felt his tears wet against her neck.

"Oh, Robby," he whispered. "How am I ever going to get over her?"

Amy held him in her arms, rocking him as if he were a child. Her own tears streamed down her face. His plaintive question rang in her brain, and was answered by her own.

How am I ever going to get over you?

Paul stepped into his room and closed the door. For a long moment, he stood in the dark, his brain awash in memories of Amy. Why was it that she felt so close whenever he was around Robin? It was too weird. It was almost as if some of her soul had entwined with Robin's, crazy as that sounded. But so many things about his sister reminded him of Amy. It was uncanny. The way she cocked her head when she was listening to conversation. How she sat so still at dinner tonight, almost as if she were trying to be invisible. And then later, when they were watching the home movies, she hadn't realized he'd been watching her. The way she played with her hair just like Amy used to.

Damn! He shook his head. *You're losing it, buddy. Looking for ghosts when everyone knows they don't exist.*

It was just wishful thinking, of course. Amy was dead. And no amount of wishing would bring her back.

Amy came downstairs to breakfast on Sunday morning, anxious to be on her way back to campus. Since Paul had left early on Friday, there seemed no reason to stay any longer at Windsong. In fact, in the ultimate of ironies, she was beginning to find that she felt more and more uncomfortable

around the Mulcaheys the more time she spent with them. Funny, a family
was all she'd ever wanted, and now that she had one, she just wanted to get
away from them.

Tammy and Michael were the only ones at the table, both of them
engrossed in the Sunday paper.

"Good morning." Amy went into the kitchen and opened the fridge to get
the orange juice. Her gaze rested momentarily on the fresh pot of coffee on
the counter. She wished she had the nerve to pour herself half a cup and drink
it quickly here in the kitchen. But it was just too risky.

Back in the dining room, she settled into one of the empty chairs and
reached for the basket of muffins Stella had baked on Friday before she left on
a three-day holiday.

"You want part of the paper, Cupcake?" Michael asked.

"The Style section, please."

He passed it over. Amy buttered a muffin and began to read a review of a
new movie. She was glad the Mulcaheys weren't talkative in the mornings. At
least that was something she had in common with them. Of course, being
able to drink the forbidden coffee would've helped get her into a more socia-
ble mood.

"Oh, dear," Tammy said suddenly.

Something in her tone made Amy and Michael look up at her.

"What?" he asked, his eyes shifting to the newspaper section in her hands.

Probably wondering if some of their investments had taken a dive, Amy
thought.

Tammy looked over at Amy, a disconcerted expression on her face. "Robin,
did you know the name of Amy's mother?"

Amy felt a coldness invade her body, chilling her to the bone. "I think it's
Victoria. Why?"

Tammy shook her head and gave a little click of her tongue. "I was afraid
you were going to say that. Look at this. A Victoria Shiley died in a nursing
home in Richmond on Friday. Do you suppose it *is* Amy's mother?"

Amy fought back the bile that had risen in her throat. "Excuse me," she
mumbled, before lurching out of her chair and running out of the dining room.

Amy stood alone at her mother's grave. The casket, silver blue with ornate silver trim, rested on casters at the side of a green drape which, presumably, covered the yawning hole in the ground. Thanks to the Mulcaheys, her mother
wasn't going to be buried in some potter's field, but in a respectable spot in an
attractive Williamsburg cemetery near the James River, next to, of course, her
loving daughter. Amy knew she'd manipulated them into it. All it had taken
was one little sigh and a murmur about how there was no one in the world
that could give poor Vicky Shiley a proper burial, and Michael had shushed

her and immediately got on the phone to make the arrangements. Amy knew she should probably feel guilty, but she didn't. Mama's life had sucked. The least she deserved was a good ending.

Amy had gone alone to the funeral; she was glad no one had offered to go with her. She didn't think the Mulcaheys thought it was odd—that she'd attend her best friend's mother's funeral. She told them she was doing it for Amy, and they'd appeared to understand.

It had been a sad affair—the funeral. Only a few nurses from the home had shown up. A handful of people, including Amy. *So pathetic—to live thirty-nine years on this earth, and only have a few people care enough to attend your funeral.* But then, Mama hadn't exactly won any popularity contests.

Still, guilt assailed her. She'd meant to go visit more often. Especially since there had been that moment of awareness. But somehow, time had gotten away from her. With classes and the social life she'd forced herself to participate in, she hadn't managed to get back to the nursing home. Now, it was too late.

Amy had remained dry-eyed during the brief service. It was only here at the gravesite, after everyone else had ambled away, that she felt close to tears. Hard to believe she was saying good-bye. Not just to her mother, but to her former life. The last tie with Amy Shiley was about to be buried under tons of dirt.

She saw movement out of the corner of her eye—the gravediggers, most likely eager to get on with their job. Amy touched the smooth top of the casket. "Good-bye, Mama," she whispered, "I love you." *Despite everything.*

She turned and walked away. Inside the Tracker, she took the cell phone from the glove compartment and hit the speed dial. She felt numb as she listened to the phone ring at the other end. It was picked up on the fourth ring.

"Yeah?"

"Hi, Jason," Amy said. "You want to come over to my room tonight?"

Jason flopped over on his back, a contented smile on his face. *"Christ! That was good!"*

Amy snuggled against his naked body, her blood still zinging from the orgasm he'd just brought her to. *So, this was what it was like to finally make love to Jason Barelli.* No wonder Robin had kept him around for so many years. The guy knew just what to do with those sexy hands and voracious mouth. Not that she was in a position to compare. Paul had been her only lover, and of course, there was no comparison with him because she loved him. What she and Jason had just done, though, had nothing in the world to do with love. Just old-fashioned animal lust. And at that, he was A-okay.

His hand cupped her right breast. "Hey," he whispered, his breath hot against her ear, "how come you never let me do that before?"

"What?" Amy murmured, closing her eyes drowsily.

"Fuck you."

Amy opened her eyes. "What do you mean?"

"*You* know." His thumb stroked her nipple.

"*What?*" Amy tried to stifle a yawn. Sex with Jason had been awesome, but now, she just wanted to sleep. Funny, she'd never thought of him as a pillow-talk kind of guy.

He drew away from her and propped his chin on his hand, eyeing her as if he were inspecting a newly discovered species of insect. His left hand continued to caress her right breast. "You never let me fuck you before, Rob. Why tonight?"

Amy froze. Looking into his gorgeous green eyes, she saw he was telling the truth. But did he really mean what it sounded like? Robin had never actually had intercourse with him? But that was *impossible!* The way she'd always talked about her adventurous sex life, Amy had assumed she'd done . . . well . . . everything. But come to think of it, had she ever talked about doing anything except oral sex? Amy couldn't remember it if she had.

"Hey, I'm not complaining," Jason gave her a lazy smile. His hand moved to her other breast, tenderly stroking. "You don't have to tell me why you finally changed your mind. It was worth the wait."

He moved toward her and buried his face between her breasts, licking and sucking. Amy clung to him, barely breathing, as she tried to digest the startling information he'd let slip.

Suddenly he cupped the weight of her breasts in his hands, peered up at her and grinned. "Your tits are bigger, too. What's up with that?"

Heart hammering, Amy slid down his body and fastened her mouth to his. It was the only way she could shut him up.

18

Amy glanced at her wristwatch as she waited for the WALK sign on the corner of Fifty-seventh Street and Seventh Avenue, barely holding in a frustrated sigh. Almost ten minutes late for her lunch date with Ellen Aviani. Would she wait?

It was the height of the lunch hour, and the sidewalks were thronged with pedestrians trying to make their way somewhere to grab a bite to eat before heading back to their offices. As always, traffic jams snarled the streets, and the warm spring day was filled with the cacophony of honking horns, squealing brakes, and occasional sirens, not to mention the babble of various languages, boom boxes playing a mix of rap, rock, and salsa. Just another lunch hour in Manhattan.

Finally, the light changed, and after two flying taxis ran the red light to whiz past, Amy, along with the clump of pedestrians, stepped into the intersection to cross.

To her right, she felt someone watching her, and purposely kept her gaze fixed on the man's shoulders in front of her. *Oh, please! Not now. I don't have time for this now.*

A sharp gasp. "My *Lord,* Patty, *look*! It's *Carly August* from *South Riding*!"

Amy pretended not to hear, but felt her face filling with color. A couple of people in front of her glanced back, but kept walking. True New Yorkers, of course. Used to seeing familiar faces every day. Amy tried to pick up her pace, but it was impossible. Too many people.

"*Omigod!*" shrilled another voice, presumably Patty. "It *is* her. Oh, we gotta get an autograph. *Hellooo?* Excuse me. *Carly!*"

Amy knew she should keep going. She was already late, and Ellen Aviani wouldn't wait forever. But fame was still too new to her, and she just couldn't find it in her heart to ignore a fan. Maybe someday she'd become so jaded that she would be able to walk away, but not now.

She edged her way over to the entrance of the Park Central Hotel and smiled at the two women working their way toward her, grinning as if they'd just won the state lottery.

"Hi," Amy said, when they reached her.

One of them, a frizzy blond with freckles, fanned herself. "Oh, my Lord, I just can't *believe* I'm standing here looking at Carly August. Can I have your autograph? I just *love* how mean you are on that show."

The other woman, older, with graying hair and owlish glasses, cut in, "You should leave that sweet Jenny and Justin alone. They love each other, and why you want to take him away from her, I just don't know."

"Do you have something for me to sign?" Amy said, trying but not exactly succeeding at holding a natural smile.

The frizzy blond dug in her oversize handbag and finally thrust out what looked like a bill. It was addressed to Mary Monger at 161 Poplar Lane in Pittsboro, Indiana. "Sign this. My name is Mary. You know, I thought after you had that breakdown, you were going to change and become a good person. It sure seemed like it for a little while, but now, you're right back up to your old tricks. *Shame* on you!"

Patty, who apparently wasn't as enamored of Amy's character as Mary was, glowered at her. "You know, you should just leave Justin alone. You broke his poor heart without a by-your-leave, and now that he's finally found love with a sweet girl like Jenny, you want him back. You just make me so mad, I could spit fire!"

Amy managed to hold on to her smile as she scribbled her name on Mary's bill. "Well, it's good to know you feel so passionately about the story. Do you have something you'd like me to sign?"

God, she hoped Patty wasn't the kind of fan who might get violent. Hadn't Susan Lucci talked about soap fans who'd become irate, thinking she actually *was* Erica Kane?

"Well . . . all right," Patty mumbled grudgingly, drawing out an envelope from her bag.

Don't do me any favors. Amy's lips twitched as she signed her autograph for Patty. "There you are. Thank you." She gave a mental grimace. Why was she thanking these two women for interrupting her and making her even later than she already was?

"Oh, thank *you*," Mary gushed, brown eyes shining with excitement. "I just can't believe I'm standing here talking to you."

Patty glared. "Now, you remember what I said, missy. Leave that sweet Justin alone!"

"Okay." Amy brightened her fake smile. "You two take care, and enjoy your holiday. Gotta run, bye-bye." She turned and walked quickly toward Fifty-sixth Street, blending into the stream of pedestrians.

"*Bye, Carly!*" Mary shouted gleefully.

Blushing, Amy walked on. She wondered if she'd ever get used to strangers stopping her on the street and acting like they were long-lost friends.

Robin would've loved it.

She shook her head, banishing the unwelcome thought. Her therapist, Rhoda Myer, was still trying to teach her to let go of the past, and most of the time these days, she was able to do just that. Not that Rhoda knew the real story. She believed that "Robin" was still suffering from the emotional trauma caused by the accident. But no matter how hard Amy tried to forget the past, thoughts of Robin still crept in now and then. Inevitable, she supposed. After all, the past was with her every time she looked in a mirror.

Amy stepped into the Carnegie Deli and scanned the crowded lunchtime tables for Ellen Aviani. There she was in the corner, a plump middle-aged woman with a smooth dark bob and bangs. Ellen Aviani, the editor in chief of *Soap Star* magazine, a woman whose face was known by anyone involved in the soaps. To be interviewed by Ellen herself was a real coup for a soap actress. It meant you'd made it in the business.

And Amy had kept her waiting. Definitely *not* a good idea.

"I'm so sorry I'm late," Amy apologized as she reached the table. "The run-through ran long, and I couldn't find a taxi . . ."

"Don't worry about it, Robin." Ellen waved a hand bedecked with various gemstone rings. "Sit down, and let's get you a drink." She raised one black eyebrow, and a waitress immediately appeared at their table.

Amy was impressed. She'd heard Ellen Aviani had a lot of power, but hadn't realized it extended to service people in the restaurant business.

"Iced tea, please," Amy said to the waitress.

"I'll have a refill," Ellen ordered in her no-nonsense Brooklyn voice. "And since you're here, we'll go ahead and order lunch. I'd like a pastrami on rye with provolone, lettuce, tomato, and light mayo. Robin, what are you having?"

The waitress scribbled on her pad, and turned to Amy with pen poised.

"Just the iced tea."

When the waitress walked away, Ellen frowned at Amy, eyebrows raised. "No lunch? Don't tell me you're one of those anorexics?"

Amy shook her head. "No, not at all."

"Good. I hate the little bitches." Ellen's brittle brown eyes flicked up and down Amy's body. "A few extra pounds won't kill you, you know."

Amy decided to be honest. "I'm too nervous to eat. It's my first major interview, you know."

"Nervous?" Ellen let go with a belly laugh that had heads turning at nearby tables. "You're nervous about our little chat? Why, that's the silliest thing I've ever heard. I don't bite."

"That's not what I hear," Amy said without thinking, then immediately bit her lip. God! Why had she said that out loud?

But Ellen laughed again, and her eyes warmed. "Only when I know someone is trying to put one over on me. And believe me, I've been in this business long enough I can smell a lie a mile away."

Amy gave a mental shudder. She hoped that wasn't true. Because if it was, she was in deep, stinky shit.

Ellen gave her a wink. "But I have a feeling, Ms. Robin Mulcahey, you and I are going to get along just fine. So, if it's okay with you, I'd like to go ahead and get started." At Amy's nod, Ellen pushed a button on a miniature tape recorder. "Okay. Just a little background information first. You've been playing the role of Carly August on *South Riding* for the last two years. How did you get your start in the soaps?"

Amy took a deep breath. "Well, I came to New York after graduating from William & Mary. I knew I wanted to get into acting, but, of course, that didn't happen overnight. The first year I worked as a model for Leonsis & Godbold Publications."

"Oh?" A black eyebrow arched. "The confession magazines?"

"Yeah, I did photo shoots for the stories."

"I've seen some of those magazines." Ellen grinned and waved a manicured hand in front of her face. "Pretty steamy stuff, huh?"

"Some of the stories called for some sexy shots," Amy admitted. "But it was good training for an aspiring actress because we were acting out scenes that revealed a lot of emotion."

Ellen's eyes danced with excitement. "Do you have any photos we can run in *Soap Star*?"

Amy lifted a shoulder in a slight shrug. "You'd have to check with Leonsis & Godbold. They own the rights to the photos. So, anyway, I did that for about a year, all the time going on auditions for various things. I did a few commercials and had a couple of bit parts on the soaps. I was a nurse on *One Life to Live* for about two weeks, and I played a therapist on *Guiding Light* for a month. Then I got a call from my agent about this new soap called *South Riding*. I auditioned for the role of Carly August and got it."

"And now you've been nominated for a Daytime Emmy." Ellen smiled. "Congratulations."

"Thanks. I still can't quite believe it."

"Don't you think it was that nervous breakdown story line that brought the Emmy attention? Up until then, you were just a conniving blond with no heart. Then the writers came up with the story line about the childhood sexual abuse that led to your breakdown, and your character became more vulnerable and sympathetic. You did an outstanding job with what must've been an emotionally wrenching story line. Did you have to draw on real life to make your character believable as a psychologically disturbed woman?"

Amy blinked. *What exactly was the woman getting at?* "Well, if you're asking if I've actually suffered any kind of abuse as my character did, the answer is no. I have a wonderful, supportive family who've been behind me every step of the way. I just imagined what it would be like to have gone through such trauma. And I guess I succeeded."

Ellen glanced down at her notes. "That's right. Your father is former congressman Michael Mulcahey. I guess that helped in the first years you were in New York? Guess you weren't a typical starving actress, were you?"

Amy tried not to show her irritation at Ellen's challenging tone. "Contrary to popular opinion, congressmen are not always millionaires. But yes, I was lucky to have my family's financial support until I was earning a livable salary. But I'm happy to say I didn't need their help for more than a few months. I started working for the confessions, and I shared a small apartment with an artist in the East Village. You may have heard of her. Kerani Rishi? Up and coming Indian-American watercolorist?"

Ellen shook her head. "Can't say that I have. But let's get back to you. What a success story! An apartment on Riverside and West Seventy-seventh. Limo service to work and back. Free clothing from the best designers. Everything a young actress of . . . how old are you?" She scanned her notes. "Twenty-five? Yes? Everything a twenty-five year-old actress could dream of."

Amy knew she sounded defensive, but she had to respond. "I sublet the apartment, the limo service is only during inclement weather, and the only free clothing I've received is the dress I'm wearing to the Emmy Awards."

Ellen gave her a sly wink. "But still, you're a rich young woman in your own right."

"I'm doing well," Amy conceded. "I have a great business manager, and we've been lucky in the investments we've chosen."

The waitress arrived with Ellen's thick pastrami sandwich. Amy's mouth watered, and she regretted not ordering. A turkey sandwich would certainly hit the spot right now. She guessed that meant she was no longer so intimidated by Ellen Aviani.

Ellen noticed Amy staring at her sandwich. "I'll never be able to eat this whole thing. It's huge. Sure you don't want to share half?"

Amy smiled. "Sorry. Didn't mean to stare. It just looks so good."

"Bring us another plate, please," Ellen said to the waitress as she turned to go. She grabbed a knife and began to cut the thick sandwich in half.

"Okay, we're off the record until after we eat." She punched the OFF button of the recorder, then looked up, her gaze skewering Amy. "Now, let's get to the good stuff. Is it true that you married Declan Blair in Las Vegas last week?"

Amy smiled and reached for her iced tea.

Amy had never heard of the Irish actor, Declan Blair. So *what* if he'd been in a half dozen Irish films that never saw daylight west of the Atlantic? True, he'd starred in a Broadway play, garnering reviews that quoted adjectives like "brilliant" and "incandescent," but the play had closed only a month after opening. But this, she'd found out only after walking onto the set one Monday morning and discovering that the good-looking Irish actor had been hired to play her new lover on *South Riding*. She'd read the script the night before with disbelieving eyes and the next morning, dropped it onto the desk of the head writer with a thud that sounded ominously like the gunshot setting off the beginning of a race—or a war.

"You've got to be kidding!" Scowling, Amy took a seat opposite Lana Mitchell. "I can't do this scene."

Lana stared back at her through thick-lensed glasses that gave her the look of a befuddled owl. With an index finger she pushed the red-rimmed frames up her snub nose and sniffed. "What's wrong with it? I think it's dynamite."

"Lana, we all know Carly is a slut, but this . . . *this* sinks her to a new low."

"You think so?" Lana's freckled face brightened. "*Cool!*"

Amy just stared at her, aghast.

Lana sighed and leaned back in her chair, running a slender hand through her cropped auburn hair. "Come on, Robin. Lighten up. You know the name of the game. Carly is a conniving bitch, not to mention an alley cat, and that's just what the viewers want. Sex in the afternoon. And if we're going to keep up with the competition, that's what we've got to give 'em. It was a stroke of genius to get Declan Blair to come on board. Do you have any idea how popular he is in England and Ireland? He broke hearts all over the place when he left that Brit soap to come to America. And you, my dear, are the lucky actress who gets to be the other half of the equation in Operation Sex in the Afternoon."

"But Lana! This script has us *doing it on the desk ten minutes after we meet.*"

Lana's grin widened and she rubbed her hands together gleefully. "I *know*. Isn't it great?"

Amy shook her head and sighed. "The least you can do is let us get to know each other first. It's awkward doing a love scene with a guy I've just met. You should know that."

"Shall I get out my violin?" Lana smirked. "You actresses have such a tough life. Let me tell you, hon, any *one* of my writers would trade places with you in a heartbeat. So, quit yer whining, huh?" Her grin took the sting out of her words, but Amy heard the unmistakable tone of seriousness beneath, and knew she'd lost this battle.

She leaned forward and turned the black-and-white headshot on Lana's desk toward her. "Well . . . he *is* gorgeous, no doubt about that."

In an Oxford University–educated kind of way. Although the accompanying bio stated that he was thirty, he looked much younger, with his tousled blond hair and china blue eyes. The dark blond stubble on his face gave him a rakish sort of charm, intensified by the brilliant white smile that hinted at an irresistibly sweet disposition. Of course, a professional photographer could do wonders in portraying his subject in any way that suited him. Amy had been in the acting business long enough to know that image, whether true or false, was everything. Declan Blair, Irish pretty boy, might look so sweet that butter wouldn't melt in his mouth, but could still turn out to be the Ego from Hell.

"He's pretty, all right," Amy said. "But can he *act?*"

"Can he act?" Lana released an explosive sigh, sending a whiff of garlic-laced breath washing over Amy who tried not to cringe. *My God! What had the woman had for breakfast?* "Go out to the video store tonight and look in the foreign film section for a movie called *The Volunteer's Wife*, and you tell me if he can act." Then she smiled, her hazel eyes dancing with amusement. "Yes, he's easy on the eyes, but he's also one hell of an actor. In fact, just between you and me, I give him six months max to stay on the soap. Hollywood is going to come knocking for this guy, and he's going to be history. Wait and see. But let's get back to you. What you *should* be asking yourself is can he *kiss?* Because that's what they're paying him the big bucks to do. Remember Luke and Laura in the seventies?"

Amy nodded. "Yeah, so . . . ?"

Lana sighed and shook her head. "Yeah, so, in case you don't remember, they were the hottest couple on daytime TV. And that's our goal for you and Declan. We're going to turn Carly and Quinn into the biggest soap opera couple of the decade. And that means we've got to see a lot of heat between the two of you. Understand?"

Amy tried once more even though she knew it was a lost cause. "Hey, I don't have anything against doing love scenes. God knows I've done enough of them. But can't you have the writers do a little revision and *ease* us into a relationship instead of having us jump right into bed?"

Lana glanced at her watch impatiently. "Not into bed. Onto the desk. Forget it, Robin, the script is perfect the way it is." She gave Amy a saucy smile. "See you bright and early tomorrow morning."

Amy stood. She knew a dismissal when she heard one.

Declan Blair was even more gorgeous in person than he was in his promo shots. Not male-model gorgeous, but real-man gorgeous. He was somewhat willowy, standing five-foot-nine, only four inches taller than Amy. Under his Armani suit, his body appeared to be well-toned, but not exactly athletic. He looked more like he'd enjoy a civilized set of tennis rather than a rough-and-tumble afternoon on the soccer field. Forgoing his publicity-photo stubble for the role of the clean-shaven Lord Seabrooke, he looked exactly like the kind of character he was about to play—a haughty, slightly devious British art curator from the tony society of London's elite. In the scene they were about to do, Amy's character, Carly, had just arrived at his London office to entice him to join her in a plan to ruin one of *South Riding*'s most influential citizens. And she would do that by engaging him in a quickie on top of his desk. Amy grimaced. Writers! She could cheerfully strangle every one of them at the moment.

When Amy approached the set, the director, Nancy Logan, introduced her to the man who, within the hour, would be on top of her on the desk, thoroughly performing an oral exam with his tongue. "Declan, this is Robin Mulcahey, who plays Carly."

Declan took her hand, giving her a sweet smile. "Lovely to meet you, Robin," he said in his lyrical Irish accent. "I've been watching the show since I got the news I'd be coming on board. And I have to say, you're quite good at being wicked."

Amy smiled. "Well, thank you. I think." Was it her imagination, or had she felt his hand tremble as it shook hers? True, those beautiful blue eyes did seem a bit apprehensive. Poor guy was probably nervous, just as she was. *Damn* those writers! But God! He smelled good. A combination of heather and something indefinable. Irish soap, maybe?

His eyes met hers again and veered away. She felt her cheeks grow hot. Strange. The effect he was having on her. When he'd smiled at her, she'd felt her heart flip over and her head grow light in a way that hadn't happened for her since Paul.

It didn't make any sense, really. After all, she'd been kissed by countless sexy actors in her three-year stint on *South Riding*, and many more male models in the year she'd done the photo layouts for the confession magazines. But none of them had affected her in a way that was even close to what she was feeling right now. Just at Declan's smile.

Nancy clapped her hands. "Okay, if everybody's ready, let's get going. Take your places, please."

"Damn writers," Amy muttered under her breath as she took her position outside Quinn's office door.

"Action!"

Declan's blue eyes locked upon hers as she approached him. Stopping inches away, she flattened her hand against the raw silk fabric covering his chest and tilted her head back to smile at him seductively. With a groan, he threaded the fingers of both hands through her hair. Amy's breath left her body. Her heart hammered as his eyes swept over her face, pausing on her mouth, lingering. She licked her bottom lip, nervously trying to remind herself she was acting. That look in his eyes—that hungry longing—was fake. He was a stranger, a man she'd just met not a half hour before.

His head lowered and finally—*finally*—his mouth covered hers in a soul-stirring kiss. She moaned, her hands threading through his soft, wavy blond hair, her lips parting for his seeking tongue. Forgotten was the set, the director, the camera. There was only the blood pounding through her veins, the crazy spinning of her brain, and Declan's mouth plundering hers.

He eased her back onto the desk.

"And . . . *cut!*" the director called out. "Okay. That's a print. Let's take fifteen."

Declan released his grip on her and slowly, Amy opened her eyes, struggling to reorient herself. He stepped away, eyes cloudy. With lust, she wondered? Like *her*. She felt the heat rush to her face as she realized how carried away she'd become during the scene. Glancing around at the crew, she wondered if they'd noticed. But everyone seemed to be going about their business as usual. Maybe it was all her imagination.

"Are you all right?" Declan asked, extending a hand to help her to a sitting position. He appeared flustered.

Such a fluid voice—like rich, melted chocolate. Perfectly elegant, like the rest of him. She wanted to dislike him for being so perfect, for causing this turmoil inside her. She'd earned the nickname, *Miss Ice*, on the set because no one had ever seen her unsettled or anything less than professional. Now, because of Declan, she was in danger of melting.

She nodded, not meeting his hypnotic gaze.

His eyes moved over her face, and reaching out, he brushed his thumb across her bottom lip. Amy trembled at his touch, newly horrified by the explosion of desire that coursed through her.

"I've mussed your lipstick," he said.

"No problem." She scrambled off the desk and made her way through a clump of technicians, heading for her dressing room.

In the corridor, she ran into Lisa Muldoon and Stephanie Johansen, two of the young actresses on the soap. Lisa, a dark-haired beauty, grinned at Amy and gave her a thumbs-up. "So, how does the Irish Adonis kiss, Robin?"

Amy smiled and shrugged, feeling her face grow hot again. "Not bad."

"I'll bet," gushed Stephanie, a vivacious girl with long golden brown hair. "That man is so hot! You'd better enjoy him while you've got him, Robin. Word on the street says that he won't be on the soap for long. He's got big-screen ambitions."

Lisa rolled her brown eyes. "Whatever! I just wish I could play a bad girl. You have all the fun . . . getting to make out with the hottest actors. And I get stuck with . . ." She lowered her voice and grimaced. ". . . stinky-breathed Jason Toomey."

Amy just grinned, knowing Lisa was referring to her romantic interest in the May-December story line she was in the middle of taping. "Excuse me, girls, but I've got to take a bathroom break." Amy hurried on down the hall and stepped into her dressing room, locking the door behind her.

She took a seat at her dressing table and stared, wide-eyed, into the mirror.

Robin's face stared back at her, no longer the face of six years ago, but an older, more mature version of the teenager she'd loved in another lifetime. It was the face of a twenty-five-year-old Robin, one that Amy had finally accepted as her own. Because what other choice did she have? Most of the time she could look in the mirror and not even think of Robin. That, thanks to thousands of dollars spent in therapy. Not that she'd ever admitted the truth to her therapist. Rhoda just thought she suffered from an extraordinary case of survivor's guilt. Somehow—through weekly therapy and the passage of time—she'd come to terms with living a lie.

It had taken a long time, but now, she answered to Robin's name without hesitation. When she signed anything, whether it was an autograph or a business document, she automatically signed Robin Mulcahey. Living in New York, without anyone from Robin's past watching her, she'd become a third personality, an odd hybrid of Amy Shiley and Robin Mulcahey. She'd managed to get through what she called "the dangerous years" with a combination of luck and cunning. But even after moving to New York, she continued to be careful, afraid that a mistake would expose her for the fraud she was. It wasn't until she'd passed the two-year mark in New York that she began drinking coffee again, and eating the foods she liked. It was heaven to be able to eat chocolate without guilt. But in all other ways, she'd become her own fictionalized version of Robin.

Only Paul reminded her that, in her heart, she was still Amy Shiley. But thankfully, she never saw him much—just when they got together for the holidays—a time that never ceased to be anything but racking torture for her. It was the ultimate irony, of course. Before the accident, she'd yearned for a family like the Mulcaheys. Now that they were her family, every minute she spent with them, she felt like she was chained to a dentist's chair, being drilled on without anesthesia. And that was when Paul wasn't there.

He'd been with the Denver Broncos for almost six years now, but had sat out the entire last season with a serious knee injury. They communicated frequently by phone and e-mail, and although it nearly killed Amy to hear his voice, it was better than not having him in her life at all. At least, that's what she told herself. To think otherwise would be to admit that this lie she was living had been for nothing. And dear God, if she admitted that, what would be the point of living?

Paul had been depressed during his last phone call, sure that the Broncos' management planned to cut him from the team. Six years in the NFL was approaching the maximum career span for a wide receiver, but he wasn't ready for retirement, feeling he had another year, maybe two, left in him. And although he wore a Super Bowl ring, he didn't feel like he deserved it because he'd been a lowly rookie who'd caught only a couple of passes in the waning seconds.

He'd never married, although he was often seen in public with various beautiful women on his arm, many of them models or actresses. Amy didn't know whether to be happy or sad at this. It would hurt to see the man she loved pledge himself to another woman, but at least she could close the door with finality on the secret hope that someday, somehow, they would find a way to be together.

There had been other men in Amy's life since the torrid nights she'd spent with Jason during her last two years of college. Only two men. She'd fallen into a short-lived affair with a young Jack Nicholson–like model she'd met during a photo shoot for the confession magazines. It had been purely sexual, and she'd ended it, feeling soiled. At least, with Jason, she'd known he'd loved Robin in his way. With this guy, they hadn't even really liked each other. And then, in her second year on the soap, she'd dated a perfectly nice, quite good-looking actor for a period of six months until his character had been killed off and he'd taken a job at one of the West Coast soaps. They'd parted amicably, and remained good friends, staying in touch by e-mail.

Both relationships had lacked the emotional intensity she'd felt with Paul during those two short days before the accident. And she supposed, naive as it probably was, that intensity was what she was looking for in a romantic partner.

Gazing into the mirror, she touched her lips, still feeling the heat of Declan's kiss. Her blood felt like hot chili pepper as it pumped through her arteries.

Had it finally happened? Had she finally found a man who could make her forget Paul?

19

Amy, clad in a fuchsia tankini, lounged on a striped beach chair, feeling the hot Mexican sun grilling her sunblock-slathered body. Her eyes were fastened on the sea green Gulf of Mexico, its gentle waves breaking on the long stretch of sugar-textured white sand beach. A seagull wheeled through the azure sky, squawking noisily as it swooped down to a swell in search of something edible. Slowly, Amy's gaze traveled to the cheap gold band on her left hand, winking in the sunlight. A spasm of gut-aching horror clutched her insides.

My God! What have I done?

Reality was sinking in, and she wasn't sure she was ready for it. Like a drunk awakening with a hangover, she turned her head to the right and saw Declan lying on another lounger, eyes closed, a light sheen of perspiration glazing his golden body. His blond hair curled damply around his ears, giving him a sweetly boyish look. But there wasn't anything boyish about that glistening muscled chest covered in a light carpet of golden brown hair. Or those long, lean thighs and flat sexy stomach. Even his hands and feet were perfectly shaped and exquisitely beautiful. And who knew an Irishman could tan like that? There had to be some Mediterranean blood running through his veins. God, he was gorgeous! He was her . . . *husband.*

Another spasm of horror ripped through her. *Oh, Jesus! What have I done?*

But she knew exactly what she'd done. Yesterday, in Las Vegas, she'd married Declan, and even as the fat minister spoke the words binding them together as man and wife, her gut had been screaming out the wrongness of it all. *You don't love him!* Not enough, anyway. But she'd ignored that shrieking voice inside her, and listened, a stiff smile on her lips, as Declan murmured "I do." A moment later, it was her turn. She spoke the two simple words, all the time hearing her brain screaming, *No! I don't!*

Had she really believed she could live a normal life like a normal person? *Why?* She wasn't normal. Never had been. Especially since she'd thrown away a former life to live out this masquerade. How could she have believed that marrying Declan Blair would save her? And how could she have believed, even for one moment, that marrying him would stop her from loving Paul?

But she would never have done it if it hadn't been for Paul's phone call. It came on a rainy Saturday morning in March, just three months after she'd met Declan. As usual, when she heard Paul's voice, her heartbeat faltered, then sped up. But it was his next words that caused her head to swim drunkenly.

"I've been traded to the New York Giants."

The enormity of that one sentence hit her.

Paul, living here in New York? Oh, God! How could she deal with that?

"It was a disappointment at first," he went on without waiting for her response. "I'd hoped to spend my entire career here in Denver, but I'm starting to get used to the idea of New York. Hey, you're there, and we've got a lot of catching up to do, right? That is, if you're not too big a star to hang out with a nobody like me," he joked.

Amy, still reeling from the shock, couldn't find her voice.

Oblivious, Paul went on, "So, I'll be coming to town in late May for minicamp. Hey, you think you could put me up while I look for an apartment?"

Feeling herself blanch, she just barely managed to control the tremor in her voice. "No problem, Paul. You can stay here as long as you like."

But she knew something had to be done. The thought of staying here alone in her apartment with Paul made her feel as fragile as delicate crystal. One look into his piercing blue eyes, one inadvertent touch between them, and she would shatter into a million pieces.

Her only hope was Declan. For three months, they'd been lovers on-screen; she would simply have to make it a reality in real life. She didn't think it would be difficult. The chemistry they shared was so volatile that the soap's ratings had gone through the roof in the first weeks after Declan's debut. Their story line had generated huge volumes of fan mail that showed no sign of slowing down. In the last three weeks, they'd been on the cover of all four major soap magazines.

Amy knew the sexual heat generated between them was very real. At least, for her, it was, and she thought Declan felt the same way. But off the set, neither of them had acknowledged it. Not that they were unfriendly off-camera. Quite the contrary. Amy found that she liked his quiet professionalism, and she enjoyed the droll humor he began to reveal after he got to know everyone better. She also discovered they shared similar interests in music, literature, and films. Every time they got into a discussion, she found herself disappointed when it was over, even when they disagreed.

One evening after they'd made a promotional appearance at a mall in New Jersey, at Amy's suggestion, the studio's car dropped them off at an Indian restaurant in the West Village, one that had been highly recommended by Amy's former roommate, Kerani.

They dined on curried lamb and tandoori fish, chatting comfortably as the haunting strains of a sitar played in the background. Suddenly, Declan peered at her, intensity blazing in his eyes. "Why are you wasting your talent in the soaps?"

Startled by the abrupt question, she lashed out, "News flash! Sorry to break it to you, but *you're* working on the soaps, too."

His expression remained neutral. "But not for long. My six-month contract expires in May, and I've no intention of renewing it. My agent is already queuing up auditions on the West Coast."

She swallowed the forkful of basmati rice she'd just slipped into her mouth. "I'd heard that, but I didn't believe it. Declan, you're the hottest guy on the soaps right now, and you're going to give that up?"

"Aye. Because I want more than that. And so should you."

Amy shook her head. "I'm doing something I love, and I'm getting paid for it. Quite well, I might add. And you think I should give that up to try and make the jump to the big screen? Do you know how many other soap actors have tried and failed?"

Declan smiled. "Of course. But look at the other side of the coin. Demi Moore. Meg Ryan. Julianne Moore. And those are just three names off the top of my head."

"Well, my last name isn't Moore," Amy said dryly. "Besides, that's a very small percentage of the ones who try it."

Declan's smile faded. He reached across the table and took her hand. "You're an exquisite actress, Robin. You can do anything you set your mind to."

Amy's pulse quickened at his touch. "Yes, I'm a good actress." *You have no idea how good.* "But I'm perfectly happy staying right here on *South Riding.* I know my character. I love her, warts and all. And as long as they want me, I'm staying where I am."

Declan's eyes held hers for a long moment. Amy felt as if a band of iron had tightened around her chest, cutting off her air supply. *Did he realize the magnetic power of those eyes? Was it a conscious thing, a flick of the switch that released this flow of charisma?* No, she didn't think so. And that made him all the more attractive. Amy withdrew her hand from beneath his and picked up her wineglass. The spell was broken.

She knew in that moment that Declan wanted her as much as she wanted him. Why, then, was he so reluctant to carry their romantic relationship off the set? Twice, now, she'd hinted strongly that she was interested. But too much of

Amy Shiley remained in her psyche for her to be anything more than subtle. It didn't matter how beautiful she was or that she was always being hit on by the opposite sex. There was still a part of her that was, and probably always would be, afraid of rejection.

But by the time coffee arrived, she realized she had to try once more. "Want to go back to my apartment for a drink?" she asked, stirring cream into her coffee, purposely summoning a light tone. She didn't look at him directly, instead glancing casually over his shoulder, feigning nonchalance. When he didn't answer, she looked back at him and caught an expression on his face that could only be described as apprehension. Her stomach plunged, and she felt her face flood with color. God, had she misread his signals? A moment ago, she'd been so sure he was interested.

Then the quelling thought hit her, and she looked him directly in the eyes. "Declan, are you married?"

His wary look was gone, replaced by his customary warm composure. He reached for her hand. "No, Robin, I'm not wed. And truth to tell, I find I'm quite mad for you." He massaged her palm with his thumb, sending exquisite shivers rippling through her. "But love, I just told you, not more than a half hour ago, that I'm not going to be here in New York long." His eyes held hers. "And I'm a wee bit afraid that if you and I start up something, I'll be over the moon for you in no time. Where would that leave us? You in New York and me in California. Christ knows those long-distance relationships never work. Perhaps we should save ourselves the heartache and not start something that can only end badly."

He was so sincere that Amy fully intended to respect his wishes. After all, what he said made perfect sense. But that was before Las Vegas.

Word came down from the producer that Carly and Quinn's story line would take them to Las Vegas for a five-day location shoot. That's when Amy decided, subconsciously—at least that's what she told herself—that in Las Vegas, she would pursue Declan, and one way or another, get him into her bed.

It turned out to be even easier than she'd expected it to be. On the Monday shoot after their arrival the day before, Amy and Declan taped an especially steamy scene in a hot tub. After they wrapped for the day, she met him for dinner, then they hit the casino. Neither of them knew much about gambling, so they stuck to the slot machines, drawing a crowd everywhere they went because, inevitably, someone recognized them as Carly and Quinn. They dutifully signed autographs, then turned back to the slot machines until the next soap fan approached. An attentive Grecian-garbed barmaid kept them well supplied with free drinks, Amy with lemon-spiked glasses of Perrier and Declan with Killian's Irish Red ale.

By midnight, Declan was well on his way to being plastered—a state Amy had never seen him in. To her amazement, he'd never looked sexier. The more he drank, the less shy he became. Flirting, caressing her bare shoulder with his long sensitive fingers, planting a soft kiss on her neck, much to the appreciation of their audience, who was used to seeing their favorite soap couple playing at love. Whenever his blue eyes caught hers, glowing with warmth and unmistakable desire, Amy felt herself melting.

She knew she couldn't stand it any longer. For almost four months, they'd been making love on-screen, and she could no longer deny her desire for making it in reality. She didn't care that it wouldn't last. She didn't care if it was based on nothing more than physical attraction. She only knew she wanted him; she had to have him. And she had to have him here, right now, tonight.

He leaned against her heavily as she helped him to his room. *Déjà vu* thoughts of Robin darted through her mind. Was it to be her lot in life to be the ministering angel to drunken souls?

In his room, as she helped him out of his white Dockers and soft silk shirt, and got him into bed, it occurred to her that maybe she'd waited too long, that they should've left the casino a couple of Killian's earlier. She half expected him to pass out as soon as he hit the bed, and was mildly surprised when he pulled her down on top of him, melding his mouth to hers in a plundering kiss. Beneath her stomach, she felt his erection, unhindered by the alcohol.

Their lovemaking was like the eruption of a volcano, tumultuous and fiery, the volatile result of seismic pressure that had been building for months. Afterward, breathless and soaked with sweat, they lay entwined, no words spoken, until finally they drifted into an exhausted sleep. Early the next morning, before the desert sun cast its glaring light through the slats of the blinds they'd forgotten to close, Amy awoke to feel his slender hands stroking her breasts. And again, silently, they made love, slow and sensuously this time with Declan's eyes holding hers, speaking more eloquently than his voice ever could. For the first time ever, Amy didn't think of Paul as she climaxed.

Declan held her in his arms, his gaze sweeping her face with an expression of tender amazement. "I didn't know it could be like this," he whispered, his fingers brushing her tremulous lips. "Thank you."

It sounded so incongruous—being thanked for sex, but coming from Declan, it was the perfect thing to say.

"No, thank *you*," she murmured, stroking a hand up his muscled bicep. "No matter what happens, I'll never forget last night. Or this morning."

They ended up spending the next three nights together. Declan didn't drink anything, and the sex was still good. Better than good; it was incredible! Amy found him to be an adventurous lover. Coming from an Irish Catholic family, and growing up in the remote Aran Islands, his sexual prowess came as a pleasant surprise. She'd expected him to be a fairly ordinary lover, sticking to the typical missionary position as they had that first night. Oh, sure, he'd been fantastic in the love scenes they'd filmed for the soap, but often times, that didn't carry over into real life—according to the many actresses who'd spoken candidly about their affairs with actors. But Declan certainly didn't fall into that category. The sex got better with every session. Each time, after it was over, Declan would murmur in a voice soft with awe, "Good Christ, I never knew it could be so good" or something similar. He'd smile his boyish grin that never ceased to make Amy want to kiss him all over. It was after one of these moments that the thought hit her with the impact of a brick thrown through glass.

My God! Am I falling in love with this man?

They were due to fly back to New York on Sunday. Only two nights left in Las Vegas. God knew what would happen after they returned to New York. Everything could change. On Friday afternoon, after the final wrap, Amy was about to suggest they go to her room, order from room service, and spend the night making love.

But before she could speak, Declan pulled her off into a corner of the set, placed his hands on her shoulders and gazed deeply into her eyes. "Don't speak, Robin, until I've had my say. I've been spending a lot of time thinking about us, and my mind is set."

Amy felt fear clog her throat. She wasn't ready for it to end. Not yet.

His hands tightened on her shoulders. "Marry me, Robin Mulcahey. Right here in Vegas. Tonight."

Amy glanced over at Declan, her eyes traveling the line of golden brown hair that funneled over his lean, hard chest and flat stomach to disappear under the waistband of his floral surfer-style swim trunks. The bright red cotton fabric did little to hide the power of his male sex, bulging even now in its flaccid state. Amy felt the familiar heat between her legs as she remembered their erotic night before with the full moon glinting off the swaying palm trees and the crash of breakers on the beach outside their open balcony doors.

The sex had been unbelievable, rivaling all the times with Jason and even the two nights she'd spent with Paul. But it was unfair of her to even compare Declan with Paul. She'd been a girl with Paul, unschooled in the art of lovemaking. Paul had been the teacher, she the student, following trustingly wherever he led. And it had been beautiful—everything a young woman dreamed of when it came to a first sexual experience. But with Declan, they were equals, both giving and taking, leading and following, pleasing and being pleasured.

But why, then, if they were so compatible sexually, did she have this growing feeling of wrongness? Why did her stomach ache with dread? Why were the voices inside her head taunting her?

You've made another mistake, Amy. You've dug yourself into a deeper hole.

As if feeling her gaze, Declan opened one blue eye, and a slow smile crossed his lean, handsome face. As always, faced with that exquisitely sweet smile, Amy felt her heart melt.

"You're staring, love," he murmured.

Amy grinned. "Just admiring the merchandise."

He cocked an eyebrow, eyes gleaming with mischief. "Is that so? You'd better inspect it closer before you buy, lady. You never know what kind of defects you'll find."

"Oh, I intend to." Amy's lips twitched. "I'm going to give the merchandise a thorough inspection as soon as you've had enough sun."

He reached over and trailed a hand down her suntan-lotioned thigh, sending goose bumps erupting along his path. His bare foot stretched out to brush against the ladybug tattoo on her inner ankle. God, she loved his feet. *How could feet be so sexy?* Winking, he gave her a roguish smile. "I was just thinking I've had quite enough sun for the afternoon. What about you?"

Heart pumping in anticipation, Amy reached for her beach bag. "Race you back to the room."

Amy lay naked in the king-size bed, drowsily watching the paddles of the spinning ceiling fan. The scent of bougainvillea wafted in with the evening sea breeze through the opened balcony doors along with the faint strains of a mariachi band playing at a nearby outdoor restaurant. A sheen of sweat coated her body, evidence of the past three hours they'd spent making love. They'd finally drifted off to sleep as the shadows grew longer, and when Amy awakened, she was alone in bed. The sound of the shower running told her the whereabouts of Declan, and in those moments alone, she thought about what had brought her here to this place in her life.

Maybe it wasn't a mistake to have married Declan. After all, should she have doomed herself to a life alone just because she loved a man she could never have? Better to go on, right? Make a normal life for herself. Well, as normal as possible.

The phone at her bedside rang—two staccato buzzes. Amy, startled from her pensive thoughts, reached for it, noticing as she did the lighted flashing button. Upon arriving in the room earlier, she'd seen they had messages waiting, but Declan hadn't allowed her to retrieve them. His hands on her body and his mouth hungrily devouring hers had convinced her that the messages could wait. After all, they were on their honeymoon, and only their agents knew they were here. Business could wait until Monday.

"Hello," Amy said, expecting to hear one of the two agents' voices on the other end. Instead, it was a soft feminine voice that carried a hint of a British accent. A smile spread over her face. "Oh, Kerani! Hi! I'd forgotten I called you."

After their arrival in Mexico, Amy had left a message on Kerani's answering machine, announcing the news of their impromptu wedding. She'd grown close to the Indian-American artist with whom she'd shared an East Village apartment that first year in New York. And even now that they lived apart, Amy still considered Kerani her best friend.

"I'm so happy for you, Robin," Kerani said, a smile in her voice. "And I understand you have two things to celebrate now."

"Two things?"

Behind the bathroom door, the shower stopped, and Kerani's voice came over the line as clear as if she were in the room. "Of course. Your wedding and the Emmy nomination."

Amy's heart gave a painful kick. For a moment, she couldn't draw in a breath. Finally, she managed to gasp, "*What did you say?*"

The bathroom door opened, and Declan stepped out, a towel wrapped around his waist. His hair, dark blond in its damp state, curled in wiry tendrils over his head. His eyes were incredibly blue in his tanned face. His fresh soap scent reached her before he did. Amy kept her eyes pinned on him as Kerani answered her question.

"Don't tell me you don't know. Robin, you've been nominated for a Daytime Emmy! Outstanding Actress in a Drama Series. They announced it on the E Channel this morning."

"*Oh, my God! You're kidding!*"

Declan, who'd taken the towel from his middle and was rubbing it through his hair, paused and looked at her, concern crossing his face. "What is it, love? What's happened?"

"Just a minute, Kerani." She covered the receiver with her hand and grinned at him. "You aren't going to believe this, Dec, but Kerani just told me I've been nominated for an Emmy!"

Declan dropped the towel, a huge grin washing over his face. Before Amy could take a breath and turn back to the phone, he was all over her, kissing her breathlessly. Finally, laughing and struggling, she managed to extricate herself from him. She grabbed the phone that had fallen to the floor during his attack.

"Kerani, you still there? Oh, sorry. Declan got a little carried away."

Amy felt his eyes upon her. He was sitting next to her on the bed, naked and grinning from ear to ear. Very distracting. "I can't believe it! You're not putting me on, are you?"

"I'm certainly not," Kerani said solemnly. "I'm too well-bred to do that. Hey, listen, I hear Sergey at the door. He's back with Chinese. I'll see you when you're back in town, yes?"

"You betcha. As soon as Declan moves in, and we're settled, I'm having you and Sergey over for dinner, okay? Thanks for calling and giving me the great news, sweetie. See you soon. Bye-bye."

She hung up the phone and turned to Declan. Sometime in the last fifteen seconds, he'd donned a pair of silk boxer shorts. He grinned at her, pride showing on his handsome face. "I'm over the moon about this, love. No one deserves it more." He drew her against him, holding her close. "This calls for a celebration, don't you think? We're going to find the best restaurant Cancún has to offer, and we're going to order the best bottle of champagne in the house. We'll drink a toast to the next Emmy winner of daytime television. Mrs. Declan Blair."

"Robin Mulcahey Blair," Amy corrected, smiling up at her new husband. And for the first time since she'd become Robin Mulcahey, she felt truly happy—and optimistic about her future.

The Daytime Emmy Awards were being held at Radio City Music Hall on Friday night, May 21. A week before, Paul arrived to start his search for an apartment in the city.

Amy had been nervous about sharing her apartment with him, but now that Declan had moved in, it wasn't quite as nerve-racking as she'd expected. Relief washed over her when the two men seemed to hit it off immediately. She wished Declan's reception in Williamsburg had been as friendly. Tammy and Michael hadn't taken the news about her elopement well at all. Their reaction had been a shock. Somehow, Amy hadn't expected it to be such a big deal.

When they flew to Virginia for a weekend so she could introduce them to her new husband, Michael had been downright cold to Declan. Tammy had made it clear how disappointed she was that her only daughter had chosen to run off and get married. Hadn't she realized how much Tammy had looked forward to organizing her wedding? But Declan's Irish charm eventually won her over, and by Sunday evening when they left for the airport, he had Tammy purring like a well-fed mama cat.

But to Amy's astonishment, Michael was as aloof as he'd been during the introductions. She couldn't get over the change in his personality. She'd known Michael Mulcahey for nine years, and she'd never seen him act like this. It was almost as if he were a jealous guard dog protecting his territory. But the territory, in this case, was her—his "daughter." He was as loving as ever with her, although he hadn't tried to hide his disappointment in her decision to get married on the sly. But there was not the least bit of warmth in his attitude toward Declan. In fact, he made every effort to put him down. Not rudely, of course. Mulcaheys were never rude. But he found sly little ways to dig in the knife, making gibes at the rural Irish, even though his own heritage came from the turfcutters of Galway, and at Declan's chosen profession of acting, likening the entertainment business to a glamorized version of a traveling medicine show. It apparently didn't occur to him, or if it did, he chose to disregard the fact, that his own daughter was also a member of that profession.

Declan remained calm and gracious throughout, and Amy felt herself falling for him even more. Not only was her husband talented, charismatic, and loving, he was a class act. And for the first time since she'd met Michael, Amy felt a twinge of dislike. Was this churlish attitude part of the reason why Robin had so often spoken of him in less-than-flattering terms?

Paul, in direct contrast with his father, was warm and accepting of his new brother-in-law. As Amy watched them size each other up, then shake hands, apparently finding mutual approval, she breathed easier, not really understanding why she'd been so nervous about their meeting.

It had been almost five months since she'd last seen Paul. He'd turned twenty-nine in March, and was no longer the young college student who'd taken her virginity. Professional football had carved a stronger, tougher version of the young man he'd been then. His hair was still glossy black, but cropped shorter than it had been in college. His face had lost its youthful sweetness, had grown leaner, cheekbones more prominent. But his eyes hadn't changed. They were still the color of the ocean under a lapis lazuli sky.

Still, even with Declan at her side, Amy's heart plunged upon sight of him—her first love. But as the evening passed, and Paul and Declan became more comfortable with each other, she found herself relaxing. With Declan as her buffer, she didn't feel quite so uneasy around Paul. She didn't kid herself that her feelings for him were dead and buried; she knew she'd never stop loving him. But now that she was happily married, she should be able to keep those feelings locked away in a remote compartment of her heart where she'd be content to leave them undisturbed.

That didn't mean, however, that there weren't some awkward moments. On the Saturday morning after his arrival, Amy and Declan were sitting at the breakfast nook, nibbling on croissants and drinking coffee, when Paul walked in, wearing sweats and a T-shirt, hair rumpled, eyes still cloudy from sleep. But his daze cleared away when he zeroed in on the coffee cup poised at Amy's lips.

"I don't believe it," he said. "When did *you* start drinking coffee?"

Amy felt the blood drain from her face. *Caught!* Her brain scrambled for a plausible answer. *It's tea, not coffee.* But then, she'd never seen Robin drinking tea, either. Not hot, anyway. And Declan, who'd poured her coffee himself, would wonder why she'd lied about something so trivial.

Bless him! He inadvertently came to her rescue. "Christ! The woman is addicted to the bloody stuff! Even got me to give up my morning tea for it."

Paul scratched his head, his gaze roving from Amy to Declan. "That's a switch. She never touched coffee when we lived at home." He moved over to the counter, took a mug from the cabinet, and poured himself a cup. "Things change, huh?"

"It's the job," Amy finally found her voice. Her heartbeat had resumed a rate close to normal. "I started drinking it when I first started working in television. The early-morning cast calls and all. It was the only way I could get my brain to work."

Paul took a seat at the table and reached for a croissant. Ruby Two-Shoes padded into the room and jumped into his lap. He grinned, dropping his croissant onto a plate and scratching her behind her orange ears. She began to purr like a piston engine. "How does Ruby like her new home in the city?"

"Well, it's not exactly new." Amy grinned. "She's been here for what? Three years now."

"I'm glad you took her," Paul said. "Poor thing was probably ignored by Mom and Dad. And I wouldn't trust Jeff alone with her, that's for sure."

Amy snorted. "Got *that* right. He thinks cats are one step away from rodents. I'm glad I have her here, too. She's good company. Right, Dec?"

"Ruby's okay," he said with a shrug. "For a cat. But I'm a dog person myself. Used to have a gorgeous Irish wolfhound back home. Skelly. She was a beauty. Died of old age when I was sixteen, and it was almost the death of me."

Amy looked at Paul. "He wants to get a dog. Can you believe it? I said no way. Not as long as we live in New York."

"We'll get one after we move to California," Declan said. He finished the last of his coffee and stood. "I'm going to jump into the shower."

"Where are you off to on a Saturday morning?" Paul asked, buttering his croissant.

"I'm meeting my agent for an early lunch. We're going to discuss career options."

At Declan's mention of California, Amy's stomach had tightened. Now, at the thought of those "career options," it began to churn. She knew none of them included opportunities in New York. Their sudden marriage had changed nothing in regard to Declan's ambitions. He'd made it clear he had no intention of renewing his contract on *South Riding*. It would be up the end of next month, and if he had his way, he would be working in Los Angeles in July. What that would mean to their marriage, she had no idea.

Declan bent down and planted a kiss on her lips. "Later, love."

Amy smiled up at him, stroking a hand across the soft blond hairs bristling his jaw. "Don't forget, Dec. Kerani and Sergey are coming over for dinner tonight. Eight o'clock."

He gave her a wink and grinned. "Is that your not so subtle way of telling me 'don't be late'?"

"Well, I know how time flies when you're with Jack," Amy said, arching an eyebrow. "Lunch has a way of turning into dinner."

He kissed her again. "Not to worry. I'll be here."

As Declan left the room, Paul smiled at her over his coffee cup. "You did good, Rob. I like Declan. He's cool. Not exactly what I expected, though, when I found out you'd eloped with a soap opera actor."

Amy gave him a mock glare. "Let's not go there. You start bad-mouthing the soaps, and I just might get insulted. But I'm glad you approve of him. He likes you, too. I think he was expecting the worst after he met Dad."

"Good old Dad." Paul grinned. "He didn't like his little Cupcake's choice of husbands?"

Amy felt herself bristling anew. "Oh, he was just being a jerk. I don't know if it's because of the way we eloped or if he just doesn't like Dec." Amy spooned some strawberry jam onto her buttered croissant. "But who could *not* like Dec?"

Paul eyed her. "It's not him. Dad would probably hate *any* guy you married. You've always been his little sweetheart." For a moment, he looked as if he wanted to say more, but instead, he took another sip of coffee.

"Yeah, I guess you're right. I'm sure he'll come around eventually. So, what are your plans today?" She lifted a strand of hair and began examining it for split ends. Anything to keep from looking into those disconcerting blue eyes. It felt so strange sitting here chatting with Paul, just the two of them. It was a situation she'd been dreading. But now that it was happening, it wasn't as bad as she'd expected. Not that she was unaffected by the sweep of his eyes or the attractiveness of his unshaven jaw. Even the subtle male scent of him reminded her of feelings that should never be associated with a brother. She forced herself to push those thoughts away.

Paul reached out and grabbed her hand, pulling it away from her hair. "Stop that! What's *with* you women playing with your hair? Amy used to drive me crazy doing that."

Amy swallowed hard. Oh, God! That habit of hers would be her downfall. She forced herself to grin at him. "Yeah, I know. Where do you think I got it from? So, what did you say you're doing today?" Her right hand automatically headed back toward her hair, but when she saw the warning light in Paul's eyes, she dropped it to the table, imprisoning it with her left one.

He rubbed a hand over his jaw and stifled a yawn. "I'm going to look at a couple of apartments this morning, and I have to check in at minicamp at three."

"But you will be here for dinner tonight, won't you? Kerani is so excited to meet you."

"Sorry, Rob," Paul said. "I have a date."

Amy swallowed the bite of croissant she'd been chewing and stared at him. "A date? Paul! You just got into town yesterday. How can you possibly have a date already?"

He grinned. "What can I say? I'm a fast worker." His blue eyes danced. "Seriously, though, it's somebody from my past. Remember Monica?"

Amy felt her stomach curl. Monica. Oh, how she wished she didn't remember her. In fact, she wished she'd never *met* her. "Monica is in New York?"

He nodded and took a sip of coffee. "Yep. She's been here for over a year now. Plays in a chamber orchestra at the Metropolitan."

Amy fought to keep her expression impassive. But Monica's aloof beautiful face swam in front of her eyes, and she could barely hold back a shudder. She summoned a false note of nonchalance. "Hmmm. I'm surprised she's still available. As beautiful as she was, and with a body to match. You'd think she would've snagged some rich guy and be off jet-setting around the world."

Paul didn't reply, and when she looked at him, she saw his face had flooded crimson. Her eyes widened. "Oh, no! Paul, don't tell me you're planning to screw around with a married woman."

"She hates him," Paul said bluntly. "He's another violinist, and he's twice her age. A doddering old fool who cares about nothing but music. She's bored. Lonely. And so am I. Hey, the sex was always good with us, so what's wrong with giving each other a little joy?"

Amy tried not to let her disappointment show, but it was impossible. "Paul, surely you have more respect for yourself than that. Screwing another man's wife? It's not you!"

He stared at her, eyes fierce. "Look who's calling the kettle black. The same girl I had to forcibly remove from a tabletop before she stripped naked in front of a bunch of frat guys."

How could she respond to that? She remembered the incident well. Robin had been so bombed, she hadn't a clue what she was doing. Paul had been horrified and furious at her behavior. And later that night . . . Amy shook her head. *Don't think about what happened later that night.* She forced the memory back into that remote corner of her heart and willed it to stay there. "That was a lifetime ago."

Paul finished his coffee and stood up. "Look, Rob, I'm happy for you and Dec. Really, I am. But just because you've managed to find your fairy-tale happy ending doesn't give you the right to preach to the rest of us. Most of us aren't that lucky." He left the kitchen.

Amy sat there a moment, staring out the window at the glittering Hudson River under the brilliant May sunlight. Lucky? Is that what he thought? That she was lucky? She choked back a harsh laugh. If he only knew . . .

"Your brother is quite the hunk. Why did you never tell me that?"

Amy looked over at Kerani and grinned. "You never asked. Besides, ever since I've known you, you've been madly in love with Sergey."

"True. But that doesn't mean I can't enjoy the view."

They were walking along a path that meandered along the river in Riverside Park. Kerani had ridden her motorbike over, and was dressed appropriately in denim overalls and a white T-shirt. She wore a brimmed canvas hat pulled low on her forehead over her plaited waist-length black hair. Not for the first time, Amy was amazed at how gorgeous she looked even in the most ordinary clothing. Her beauty was definitely in the genes, because Amy had met her parents, first-generation Indian-Americans from New Delhi who'd met at Harvard. Both successful lawyers in Manhattan, they'd raised three extraordinarily gifted, beautiful children. Asad was a neurosurgeon at Johns Hopkins, Sanjiv, a criminal lawyer in Los Angeles, and Kerani, their youngest, and only daughter, after attaining a degree in art history at Oxford, had chosen to be an artist in the Village.

When Amy had shared an apartment with Kerani that first year in New York, the young artist had taken her under her wing, showing her the ropes of living in the big city. On three separate occasions when they'd been out and about, Kerani had been approached by scouts for various modeling agencies. She had been polite—because she'd been raised to be polite—but as soon as the scouts had walked away, she'd tossed the business card into her purse without a second glance. When questioned about it, she'd shrugged, and said, "Oh, this happens to me all the time."

She didn't have the slightest desire to be a model, she explained. From the age of seven, she'd known she wanted to be an artist, and nothing would sway her from that course. She worked in a small gallery in the West Village, and had already had several showings of her work. Many of her watercolors had sold for generous amounts, and she was beginning to make a name for herself. Amy had no doubt that one day a Kerani Rishi would sell for millions. She owned one herself—a small watercolor of the Manhattan skyline at night; it had been a birthday present that first year they'd lived together.

"So, is Paul joining us for dinner tonight?" Kerani asked.

They'd stopped at a park bench and sat down to enjoy the warm spring afternoon. Amy frowned, thinking of Monica. "No. He has plans. I'm glad you got to meet him, though."

Paul had been leaving for minicamp just as Kerani arrived at the apartment. When her former roommate caught her first glimpse of him, her chocolate brown eyes widened in appreciation. And no wonder! He'd looked incredible in his snug sweatpants and the New York Giants muscle shirt that revealed his defined biceps and shoulders. Just moments before Kerani's buzz from downstairs, he'd approached Amy, blue eyes sober, and apologized for his caustic remarks earlier.

"I guess Dad isn't the only jerk in the family," he said. "Can you forgive me for being so mean, Robby?"

"Hey, it's already forgotten. Besides, you didn't say a thing that wasn't true."

"But it wasn't called for." He wrapped his arms around her in a hug, and Amy's heart did a slow somersault. She closed her eyes and leaned against him, breathing in his familiar sandalwood fragrance. "You're a different person now, Rob," he said quietly. "You've grown up a lot since the accident, and it was unfair of me to dredge up the past like that. You're not the same person who was dancing on that table that night."

Slowly, she drew away from his embrace. "No one stays the same." *Not even you.*

The intercom buzzed, and it was with relief that Amy went to answer it. Paul left shortly after meeting Kerani, and then the two of them decided to go for a walk in the park. Sergey, Kerani's live-in boyfriend and an airline pilot, wouldn't be arriving until after seven, and who knew when Declan would get home?

But when the two women arrived back at the apartment at four, Amy was surprised to see Declan there, sprawled on the sofa, a bottle of Killian's in hand, and watching European soccer on TV. When she walked into the living room, his eyes lit up, and he grinned broadly, but when he saw that Kerani was with her, an unmistakable look of disappointment crossed his face.

Amy's stomach tightened. He had news. Good news, judging from the excitement in his eyes. But it was obvious he didn't want to share it in front of Kerani. Which meant . . . it wasn't going to be welcome news to Amy. And there was no doubt in her mind what that news would be. He was leaving. From the time they'd first met, he'd talked about going to Hollywood. Getting his big break on the silver screen. Had his agent finally come through?

By the time Sergey arrived at seven-thirty, Declan was near bursting point. He'd been drinking Killian's steadily since four o'clock, and with each bottle of ale, he grew more talkative and brash, keeping both Amy and Kerani in gales of laughter with his stories and quips. But despite the fun they were hav-ing, Amy felt a gnawing tension growing inside her. It reminded her of that oppressive silence right before a violent storm. Sooner or later, it would have to break.

And it did, right after Amy served the lasagna. Everyone was digging into their meal, oohing and aahing over how delicious it tasted, when suddenly Declan put down his fork, looked across the table at her, and said, "My agent got me a screen test for this movie in development called *Borderland.*"

Everyone stopped eating and stared at him. Amy tried to force a smile. "Oh, Dec! That's wonderful! When is it?"

Rosy color flushed his cheeks, and he glanced down at his plate of lasagna. "Well, that's the bad part, love. I have to fly out there on Friday. The test is scheduled for that afternoon around four."

It took a few seconds before it sank in. When it did, her eyes flashed to his, and he shifted uncomfortably in his chair. "So sorry, love. It can't be helped."

Amy realized that Sergey and Kerani were staring, but she didn't care. Her eyes were locked on her husband's. "Friday night is the Emmys. You're telling me you're not going to be here? You're not going with me?"

His face was still red, but his eyes met hers, defiance glowing in their blue depths. "If I could change it, I would, Robin, but I can't. This is a once-in-a-lifetime opportunity, and I have to go on Friday. As a fellow actor, you'll under-stand that."

Oh, she understood it, all right. She understood exactly where his priori-ties lay.

Not with her.

20

The impossibly beautiful raven-haired actress strode onto the stage in a slinky sea green evening gown studded with sequins that winked like snow crystals under bright sunlight. Amy pressed a trembling hand against the satin bodice of her black Vera Wang gown and tried to draw in a breath of air, which suddenly seemed to be in limited supply. Her heart pounded against her fingertips like a drum machine gone out of control, and butterflies choreographed a vaudeville dance inside her stomach.

It was the moment she'd been waiting for.

On her left, Paul reached over and took her hand. Their eyes met. He smiled, giving her a wink. "Good luck, Rob," he mouthed.

Amy swallowed hard, managed a sick smile, and looked back at the stage. The actress, last year's Emmy winner, gave a brilliant toothpaste-commercial smile and began reading off the teleprompter, "The nominees for Outstanding Actress in a Drama Series are . . ."

Amy watched the video clips of each actress, barely hearing the dialogue over the drumbeat of her heart. After each clip, her brain shrieked in dismay. *No way can I beat this! She's too good!* All four of them were formidable actresses, three of whom were grandes dames of the soaps and former Emmy winners. The fourth—a relative neophyte like her—had been a darkhorse nominee, having done an amazing job of playing a mute woman living half-wild in the Amazonian jungle after a plane crash. Amy watched the clip, and knew, without a doubt, that this talented young actress deserved the win. If only one of them had been a year younger—twenty-four—they wouldn't be competing against each other, but in the Young Actress Category. The applause for her was deafening. Paul's hand tightened on hers.

"And our final nominee . . . Robin Mulcahey from *South Riding*."

As her clip began, Amy was still thinking about the other actress. How on earth could Amy's portrayal of a sexual abuse victim compare with a role like that? She knew she had virtually no chance. Yet, she wanted it. Badly. She wanted it for Robin, who would've loved the idea of bounding onto the stage and accepting her Emmy with an off-the-wall Robin-like acceptance speech.

Applause filled the auditorium, and Amy realized her clip had ended. She didn't even remember seeing it. Paul squeezed her hand harder as the actress onstage began to open the envelope.

"And the Emmy goes to . . ."

Amy hadn't thought it possible that her heart could pound any harder, but as the actress struggled to open a stubborn envelope that apparently didn't want to share its secret, her pulse careened into overdrive. The edges of her vision blurred, grew spotty, and, for a panicked moment, she thought she might faint.

The presenter finally pulled the card from the envelope, smiled triumphantly, and shouted, "*Robin Mulcahey!*"

Amy sat stock-still, wondering if her mind was playing tricks on her. Had they really announced her name? Applause surrounded her, and blinking, she saw Paul beaming at her.

"Is it me?" she asked, her throat dry. "Did they really say me?"

He nodded, grinning. "Go get your award, Rob."

It finally sank in. With a yelp of delight, she reached for him. He enveloped her in a warm hug, whispering, "I knew you could do it, Rob. I *knew* it. I'm so proud of you."

She clung to him, pressing her face against his black tux, wanting to treasure this moment. Wrap it up in expensive tissue paper and tuck it away in her heart to savor later when life wasn't so good.

Finally, though, he gently pushed her away. "Go get your award, Rob."

Her limbs had turned to jelly, but somehow, she managed to make her way up to the stage, and the beautiful raven-haired actress handed her the Emmy. Amy was surprised at the statue's weight; she'd never held one before. Or even seen one up close. Trembling, she turned to the podium, realizing only then that she'd left her purse at her seat; the acceptance speech she'd written, never believing she'd actually have any use for it, was safely tucked inside. Panic swept over her. She'd have to wing it!

The applause was dying down. Amy stared out at the first few rows of the audience made up of equal portions of familiar faces and strangers. Tuxedos and sequins. The beautifully molded faces of the Talent and the more ordinary ones of the technicians, writers, and executives. All of them with their eyes upon her. For a moment, Amy felt paralyzed with fear. No matter that for the last four years, she'd been acting in front of a camera crew and technicians and other actors. Suddenly, here in Radio City Music Hall, in front of all these television people, she felt exposed. She felt . . . like Amy Shiley.

Hey, bitch! You screw this up for me, and your friggin' ass is mine. You're not Amy Fucking Shiley, anymore. You're THE Robin Mulcahey, Emmy Award winner. So, stand up there and show some goddamn spunk, will ya?

Amy took a deep breath and smiled. She looked at the Emmy in her hands, then turned to the mike. "I *really* wanted this!" Laughter rippled through the audience. Encouraged, she went on, "And I'm thrilled the Academy saw fit to give it to me on my first nomination, because I have to be honest with you . . . I don't think I could follow Susan Lucci's example and be such a gracious loser." More laughter. Amy's eyes found the popular actress, smiling in the front row, and added, "Susan, you are my heroine. It's because of you I'm standing up here today. I wanted to *be* Erica Kane, and now I am . . . but on my own show. I have so many people to thank. My producer, Eleanor Stafford, my director, Nancy Logan, the writers—who constantly surprise me—Lana Mitchell, Veronica Eggleston, Kathy Miller . . . oh, God . . . I'm going blank . . . but the writers are truly the lifeblood of daytime drama, and we, the actors, are only as good as the scripts. I'd also like to thank my family, my brother, Paul, who is in the audience tonight." Amy smiled and blew him a kiss. "My parents, who couldn't be here tonight, but I know they're watching. I love you, Mom and Dad. And finally, my husband, Declan Blair." Teenaged shrieks filled the auditorium, Declan's growing fan base. "He is in California tonight, and couldn't get back for the awards ceremony, but he's probably watching. I love you, Dec. Hurry home! Thank you all so much!" Amy waved the Emmy In the air, smiling. "Thank you!"

She exited the stage to tumultuous applause. As she reached the wings, she clasped the Emmy to her breast and kissed the top of her golden head. "Thank you, Robin," she whispered.

And for a moment, she could almost feel Robin's presence beaming down on her, and hear her delighted voice.

"You *go,* girlfriend!"

". . . my parents, who couldn't be here tonight, but I know they're watching. I love you, Mom and Dad. And finally, my husband, Declan Blair." Robin's voice was almost drowned out by the shrieks of teenagers in the crowd, and Declan felt the blood rush to his face. Out of the corner of his eye, he saw Cedric grinning at him, and his skin grew hotter. He could almost read his friend's thoughts. *Ah, Dec, you're the idol of teenyboppers; what more could a guy want?* "He is in California tonight," Robin went on, ". . . and couldn't get back for the awards ceremony, but he's probably watching. I love you, Dec. Hurry home! Thank you all so much!" Smiling, Robin waved the Emmy in the air, and left the podium.

"Well, at least she didn't forget to thank her good husband," Cedric said, as the camera followed Robin to the wings of the stage.

Declan grinned. They sat in Cedric's home theater, watching the Emmy Awards on a cinema-size screen. "Too right. Bloody good thing she *didn't* forget me. I'd never let her hear the end of it."

Cedric took a sip of merlot from a delicate Waterford goblet. "Yeh, remember that actress who won the Oscar a few years ago? How she thanked everybody in the world except her loving husband. And the poor man was sitting there in the audience with tears running down his face."

Declan shook his head. "Before my time. I was still in Ireland then, making two-bit movies for a pittance. Not a big shot in Hollywood like you."

Cedric cocked an eyebrow at him and gave a rakish grin. "And now, who's the big shot in Hollywood? And me, just a lowly screenwriter and hack novelist."

"Ah, fuck," Declan muttered. "I'm not even the flavor-of-the-month, much less a big shot."

"Yet," Cedric added.

Declan smiled. "Yet." He reached for his goblet. Five years in Hollywood, and Cedric hadn't lost a bit of his Irish brogue. But good Christ. Everything else had changed for him. Taking a sip of wine, Dec glanced around the home theater, impressed all over again. Now, *this* was success. They sat in first-class-inspired black leather chairs facing a cinema-size screen equipped with Surround Sound and assorted cutting-edge technology. And this was just one room in the elaborate "little cottage" Cedric owned on prime ocean frontage in Malibu.

The last time Declan had seen Cedric Shaughnessey had been eight years ago in Dublin. Cedric's first novel had just won the Booker, and was being made into a movie by up-and-coming Irish director, Thomas Fitzpatrick. A small part in Jim Sheridan's *The Boxer* had brought Declan to Fitzpatrick's attention, and that's how he'd ended up with his first starring role as Cedric's protagonist in his award-winning book, *The Volunteer's Wife*. But as amazing as all this was, the truly amazing thing was that Cedric had come back into his life, ever so briefly. It had been the first time they'd met as adults.

The hometown papers had made a big deal of it, of course. Two childhood friends reunited on a movie set. Reporters interviewing both of them, asking daft questions like what was in the water on Inishmore to bring out such artistic talent. Oh, the press had loved them at the beginning. Until word leaked out about Cedric's sex life, effectively hammering the nails in the coffin on the box office take in Ireland. The movie had done well in Europe, though, so it hadn't been a total loss. After that, Cedric packed up and moved to Los Angeles, turning his back on his homeland once and for all.

Now, here they were, together again. Not young men in their twenties anymore. Cedric had turned thirty-three a month ago, and was one of the biggest names in screenwriting and fiction, Ireland's answer to John Grisham. Even that country, famous for their begrudgers, had had to admit his genius, and his last four books had hit all the best-seller lists there, as in the rest of the world. He'd come a long way from the sheep pastures of the Aran Islands.

As had Declan. He was three years younger, just having turned thirty in January. *He* had come a long way from Inishmore, as well.

Cedric nudged his dark brown head toward the screen. "You want to keep watching?"

It was plain that Cedric was bored with the Daytime Emmys. He'd only turned it on because of Declan's insistence. "No, not really," Dec said, shaking his head. "I saw what I wanted to see."

"Good." At the touch of a button, the screen went dark. Cedric stood and stretched his six-foot length. "Shall we go out on the deck?"

Deciding he could use a bit of fresh air, Declan nodded.

Cottage, indeed, he thought as they stepped out onto the five-hundred-square-foot white Italian marble deck overlooking the Pacific. The sun, a reddish orange orb in the evening sky, was making its descent, washing the breakers the shade of burnt sienna. Declan took a deep, cleansing breath of saltwater air and smiled.

California. Why had it taken him so long to come here?

He took a seat on the chintz-cushioned white wicker sofa and raised his goblet to Cedric for a top-off. After refreshing his own wine, Cedric sprawled into a chair adjacent to the sofa and sent Declan a mocking grin. "So . . . do you think she'll forgive you?"

Declan savored the fine merlot on his tongue and swallowed. "Rob? Oh, Christ. Sure, she will. She knows how important this screen test was to me. And God knows, if it weren't for the scheduling conflict, I would've been there."

Cedric eyed him over his wineglass, a gleam in his light brown eyes.

Declan had always been envious of Cedric's unusual eyes. They were changeable, sometimes brown as mud, sometimes brandy amber. His own blue eyes were boring, like everybody else's in his family. When he'd been a wee boy, playing among the monastic ruins on Inishmore, Declan had almost believed Cedric was fairy-born—the offspring of magical creatures so tiny they could only be seen under a magnifying glass. That had been Cedric's tale, anyway. Even then, he'd been the consummate storyteller.

"So, this is it, Dec?" Cedric asked, his generous lips quirking in an amused smile. "True love?"

Declan felt something quake inside him, and forced himself to draw his gaze from those lips, back to Cedric's mystical eyes. "Don't be such a cynic, man. It *is* true love." He felt his face growing hot. "Robin is special. And I'm over the moon for her."

A sober look crossed Cedric's lean face. "I'm happy for you, Dec. You know that." He released a deep sigh and smiled again. "You're lucky, you know. It's not easy finding love. Especially here in Hollywood. Christ! If they're not looking over your shoulder to see if there's someone better-looking and more powerful and richer to replace you, they're looking in a mirror to make sure the skin's not sagging and the crow's-feet aren't showing and the caps on their teeth are still holding their own. So, perhaps it's not such a surprise to find me a wee bit cynical these days."

Declan's heartbeat picked up a notch; he tried to cover it by taking another sip of wine. Summoning a note of casualness, he said, "So, you're not seeing anyone special?"

Cedric grinned and ran a slender hand through his close-cropped brown hair. "Afraid not. In between lovers these days."

Declan decided not to analyze the feeling of relief that swept through him at Cedric's declaration. He'd come to terms with that whole thing years ago. Live and let live. Wasn't that the philosophy? Besides, it wasn't relief he felt. It was just . . . excitement. About being here in California. About the success of his screen test this afternoon. The certainty that his career was about to really take off. That was all it was.

A uniformed maid appeared at the French doors. "Dinner is ready to be served, Mr. Shaughnessey."

"Thank you, Mariah." Cedric turned to Declan and smiled. "Shall we?"

Declan placed his emptied goblet on the glass-topped wicker table next to the sofa, stood, and followed Cedric inside.

Paul unlocked the door to Amy's apartment and waited for her to enter. She smiled at him, wondering why he refused to stand still. And why was he staring at her with that concerned look in his eyes? Gorgeous eyes, she mentally corrected. It should be against the law to have eyes that gorgeous.

"Such a gentleman," she said, stepping unsteadily into the foyer. "A gentleman with killer blue eyes. They should be registered as Mel Gibsons . . . I mean, lethal weapons."

Paul grabbed her elbow to steady her. "Robin Mulcahey Blair, you're just a bit drunk."

"And why not?" Amy clutched her Emmy in one hand and kissed the top of its burnished gold head. "It's not every day you win an Emmy. So *what* if I had a few too many glasses of champagne? Is that a crime?"

"Of course not." Paul guided her into the living room and sat her down on the plush floral sofa facing a love seat across the oval glass coffee table. The arched leaded-glass windows overlooked the river, and beyond it, the lights of the Jersey cities of Fairview and Cliffside Park still glowed even though it was almost three in the morning. "Let's just say, though, your condition has brought the ghosts of the past a little too close for comfort. I haven't seen you this drunk since before the accident." He stared at her a moment, then turned toward the kitchen. "I'll put on some coffee."

Amy sat on the sofa, holding her Emmy on her lap, running her hand over its cool, gleaming wings. Paul was right. She *had* overdone it tonight. The post-Emmy parties, the attention, the congratulatory toasts of champagne—all had combined to make her drop her usual caution, and just, for once, have fun.

She still couldn't believe it had happened. She'd won! It was just too, too perfect! Except, of course, for Declan not being here. She frowned. What was he doing right now out in sunny California? Had he even taken the time to watch the Emmys on TV? Immediately she felt ashamed of her thoughts. He'd been truly upset about having to miss her big night. He'd even tried talking his agent into rescheduling the screen test, but it couldn't be done. So, it was wrong of her to be even the teeniest bit mad at him. Wasn't it?

Paul stepped into the room with two mugs of hot coffee. She smiled up at him. He'd been here for her, at least. Big brother Paul. Coming to the rescue. She giggled, taking the mug he handed her. If only he knew she wasn't his little sister at all.

"What's so funny?" he asked, settling into the chair near the sofa.

"You," Amy said, taking a sip of the coffee. "You're such a mother hen."

He grinned. "Maybe you bring it out in me." His eyes settled on the Emmy, which she'd placed on the coffee table. "I'm really proud of you, Rob. You've become one hell of an actress."

Amy practically choked on the coffee she'd just swallowed as the laughter exploded out of her. *Oh, Paul! You have no idea how true that is!*

He shook his head, a puzzled grin on his face. "What? What's so funny about that?"

"I was just thinking about 'Gambols,' and my role as a horny tavern wench. Yes, I guess I have come a long way."

"Damn right. And you've done it all by yourself, too. Who would've thought you'd be so good at it?"

"Yeah. Who would've?" Amy heard the irony in her voice, and wondered if Paul noticed it. The coffee was already working to dissipate the nice buzz she'd achieved, and she found herself wanting to return to the carefree haze of a few moments ago. She was starting to think again. About things better kept in the past. And that was one place she didn't want to go with Paul here.

Thank God he'd be moving into his apartment in the Village next week. She only had to get through tomorrow, and then on Sunday, Declan would be home. On Tuesday, Paul would move into his apartment, and then she wouldn't have to see him so much. Life would be much easier then.

The caffeine running through her bloodstream was not only taking the edge off her tipsy state, it was making her heart pump faster, injecting a surge of energy that was probably not the best thing to have at three in the morning.

"I'll never get to sleep now," she murmured. "You should've just put me to bed and let me pass out."

"And then you'd wake up puking all over yourself," Paul said. He placed his mug on a coaster on the coffee table and stood. "I have an idea." He left the room, heading down the hall toward the bedrooms. A moment passed, and he walked back into the room carrying an ancient-looking square blue box. "I saw this in the closet of my room. I can't believe you have it. We could never get you to play Trivial Pursuit back home."

"Oh, you've got to be kidding! It's three in the morning, Paul. And I'm still half-drunk. You expect me to actually *think*?"

He smiled and placed the box on the coffee table. "We'll play for a little while. Just until we're sleepy."

She watched him take out the two rectangular boxes of cards and place them beside the game board. She'd found the game at a rummage sale in SoHo with Kerani one Saturday morning and had bought it on impulse. Kerani's Sergey and Amy's date from the soap, John, were coming over for dinner that night, and they'd thought it might be fun to play Trivial Pursuit afterward. That had been the one and only time they'd ever played it, and Amy had won.

"What color piece do you want?" Paul asked.

"Oh . . . green, I guess." She watched his square hands setting up the game board. That was one thing Paul and Declan had in common. Beautiful hands. Hands that made her shiver with longing when they stroked her.

She tried to remember what Paul's feet looked like, but couldn't. He'd kicked off his shoes sometime earlier, and was now wearing only his black socks. Declan's feet were even more beautiful than his hands. Long and slender with perfect nails that he swore had never been pedicured. So perfect, her husband. From the top of his flaxen head to his lovely unpedicured feet. Suddenly she missed him with a longing so intense she wanted to cry, and a lightning bolt of fear jagged through her. *What if he didn't come home?* It could happen. He could be offered a part in a movie, and end up staying in California. That's what he wanted, after all. Oh, God! What would she do? Without him to be her barrier against Paul . . .

"Brown," Paul said, reading the card. " 'What came first, the book or the phrase *Catch-22*?' "

Amy realized he was staring at her, waiting for an answer. She was still thinking about Declan and wondering what she'd do if he didn't come home.

"Come on, Rob. You've gotta know this. We learned it in high school."

Amy rolled her eyes. "And that was . . . what? Ten years ago? Okay, I'll take a stab at it . . . the book."

"Right."

Amy tossed the dice again and moved six spots.

" 'What baseball position are you playing if you're in the corn?' "

"Outfield," Amy said without hesitation.

Paul looked surprised. "Yeah! I would never have guessed you'd get that one."

Amy smiled and rolled the dice. "Hey, I'm a lot smarter than you give me credit for."

"I've always known you were smart. You hid it well. Okay, next question. Literature. 'Who was the first novelist to present a typed manuscript to his publisher?'"

"Hmmm . . . that's a tough one." Amy wrapped a strand of hair around her index finger, scrunching her brow in concentration. How long had the type-writer been around? Definitely before Hemingway. Maybe Tolstoy? She frowned. Her brain wasn't cooperating.

"God," Paul said softly.

She looked at him. "What?" He was staring at her with a strange expression on his face. A look that seemed shocked, scared, and mesmerized all at once. "What's wrong?" she asked again when he remained silent.

He shook his head slightly and glanced away. "Oh, nothing. It's just that . . . you're doing it again, playing with your hair like that. Reminds me of . . ." His eyes returned to hers. "It just reminds me so much of Amy. She used to do that all the time, remember? I used to tease her about it."

Amy stared at him. A siren wailed somewhere in the city. Someone in trouble.

In trouble, like she was. She looked into Paul's sad eyes, and knew he was thinking about her, wondering, perhaps, what his life would've been like if she hadn't "died." And she knew she was in trouble.

Because she wanted to tell him the truth. It welled inside of her—this urgent need to come clean—like lava threatening to spill over the lip of the volcano, unstoppable, overpowering.

She could make him understand why she'd done what she had. Yes, she'd *make* him understand. No doubt, he'd hate her at first. As he dealt with the shock of Robin's death and Amy's deception, it would be only natural that he'd react with anger and bitterness. But after he really thought about it, after she confessed her desperate reasons for doing it, he'd come around. And then, the two of them could face the future together. They could finally make a life with each other.

The phone rang. Amy stiffened, unable to move. *Oh, God!* What had she almost done? Was she *insane*?

Paul had picked up the phone on the coffee table. "Hey, Declan! Good to hear from you, man. Yeah, our little Emmy Award winner is sitting right here. Hold on." Grinning, he passed the phone over to her.

"Hi, Dec," she said, still feeling close to panic at what she'd almost done.

"Congratulations, love. Did you get my message? I've been calling you every hour since nine o'clock. I guess you've been out celebrating?"

"Yeah, we went to a few parties. Can you believe it, Dec? I *won*!"

"That, you did. No surprise to me, love. Those other ladies couldn't hold a candle to you. I'm so proud of you, Rob."

Amy's hand tightened on the phone. "So, how did your audition go?" She almost held her breath, waiting for his answer.

"Not bad. Quite good, actually. But of course, I probably won't hear anything for a few weeks."

"So, you're coming home Sunday?"

There was a slight hesitation, and Amy felt her stomach muscles tighten.

"Well, actually, love, that's another reason I called." Declan's voice sounded strange, almost timid. "You see, I've run into an old friend here. From Inishmore, would you believe? And . . . uh . . . he's invited me to stick around for a couple of days. It's been years since we've seen each other, and you know, we're just sitting around the pool, getting reacquainted. So . . . if you don't mind too much, I thought I'd catch the red-eye back on Monday night. I'll go to the set straight from the airport."

"But . . ."

"Would you be a love, and pick up my breakdowns on Monday?"

"Aren't you taping on Monday?" Amy asked. The next week's breakdown scenes were distributed to the actors every Monday. That way, they knew in advance which days and what times they were supposed to report to the set.

"I've already worked it out with Nancy," Declan said. "They're shooting around me, and I'll stay longer on Tuesday to catch up."

"It sounds like you've already made up your mind," Amy tried, but couldn't keep the bitterness from her voice. "Why did you even bother to call and ask me?"

"Ah, love. Don't be that way. He's an old friend, for Chrissake!"

Amy knew she was being unreasonable. But Declan was determined to move to California. Couldn't he wait until then to reacquaint himself with his old friend? Didn't he understand that their time together was limited?

"Whatever," she said. "Look, it's almost four in the morning. I'm tired. I'll see you on Tuesday."

"I love you, Robin. You know that, don't you?"

She bit her bottom lip, trying to hold back threatening tears. "Yeah. I love you, too. Bye."

She placed the phone in its cradle and looked up to see Paul gazing at her with concern. "Okay. Where were we? Oh. The first novelist to use a typewriter." She shook her head. "I don't know . . . um . . . Shirley Jackson?"

Paul glanced at the card in his hands and shook his head. "No. Mark Twain."

Amy pushed the dice over to Paul, but he didn't move to roll them.

"Robby, you okay?"

She looked up at him. "He's not coming home until Tuesday," she said softly. Then she burst into tears.

Without a word, Paul got up, came around to where she sat on the sofa, and took her into his arms. She closed her eyes and cried against his ruffled white shirt. For herself, for Paul, for Declan.

For the terrible mess that was her life.

21

The dream woke Paul as effectively as if he'd been dunked in the icy waters of a mountain stream. He bolted up in bed, heart pounding, sweat coating his heated skin. Beneath the cool sateen sheet, his penis reared, rock-hard. He took a deep, shuddering breath and raked his trembling hands through his hair, shaken to the core.

It had been so pleasant at first. The dream. He'd felt Amy's lips on his, seeking, insistent. Felt the warmth of her velvet peaches-and-cream skin against his. She'd slid down the length of his naked body, kissing and nuzzling. His chest, his stomach. And then she'd taken him into her mouth, just as he'd taught her to do. He'd groaned with pleasure, threading his fingers through her silken blond hair. Long, exquisite waves of pleasure rocked through him until he knew he could take no more. He gently pushed her away, rolled her over, and slid down to pin her beneath him. He kissed her mouth longingly, tasting himself on her succulent lips. He drew away. Whispered, "I love you, Amy."

And saw her face dissolve into Robin's.

Now, his stomach churned. But thankfully, his hard-on had dissipated. *What kind of sicko am I, anyway?* To have an erotic dream about his own sister?

He threw back the sheet, got out of bed, and stumbled toward the guest room bathroom. Inside, he leaned over the sink, cupping his shaking hand under the stream of water from the faucet. He took a long swallow of water. *Better, but not great. Not even close.*

He stared into the mirror. Saw haggard eyes, black stubble, and unruly, sweat-soaked black hair sticking up where his hands had furrowed through.

"You need to get laid, guy," he whispered. "It's been too long."

He'd call Monica tomorrow, he decided. The other day, she'd practically begged him to take her to bed. He hadn't acted on the invitation because of Robin's disapproving words that morning. That, and because something inside him screamed it *would* be wrong to get involved with Monica. That soulless coupling wasn't the answer. But maybe that had been a mistake. Maybe that was exactly what he needed.

Christ! She wanted it. He needed it. And screw what Robin thought. She was in no position to be his moral judge, after all. She was his sister, for Chrissake, not his priest.

You'd do well to remember that, bro. She's your sister.

And normal guys don't have sex dreams about their sisters.

Declan listened to the roar of the surf outside his bedroom windows in Cedric's Malibu cottage. Wearily, he closed his eyes and allowed his mind to drift away to the edges of sleep.

It had been an awesome day. The night before, he and Cedric had been up until almost sunrise, talking about old times in Ireland, then segueing to Hollywood gossip and the latest inside information on which players were doing what. They'd finally gone off to bed as dawn washed the dark Pacific silver, and had slept until early afternoon. By the time Declan joined Cedric poolside for a catered lunch of caviar, smoked salmon, and *foie gras,* accompanied by a bottle of Vintage Reserve 1995 Veuve Clicquot Ponsardin, he found that Cedric had invited "a few" friends over for "a little thing."

The "few" friends turned out to be about fifty people including well-known faces like Ashley Judd and George Clooney, and "the little thing" became a full-fledged party which had lasted until about an hour ago—four-thirty on Sunday morning.

Declan had thoroughly enjoyed himself. It fit his fantasy of what life in LA would be like once he became a big star. But it, of course, would be different when that happened. *He* would be playing Cedric's part of the charming, popular host. The one they'd all be fawning over, the hottest box office draw since Tom Cruise. He'd be the one the young starlets would be seeking out, hoping he'd suggest them as his romantic lead in his next movie. The one the struggling screenwriters would be hitting up, hoping to slip their scripts past the agencies and right into the hands of the Talent—Declan Blair. The one the directors would be soliciting, hoping to get his commitment to the package deal they were trying to sell to investors. It was all about hope—Hollywood.

Yes, and all this would be his someday soon. But meanwhile, he would enjoy it as it was. And be glad he had a powerful friend like Cedric in Tinseltown.

Tomorrow . . . later today . . . they were going hiking in the canyon, just the two of them. It would be like old times on Inishmore, backpacking over the crumbled stones to the cliffs overlooking the Atlantic and trekking to the monastic ruins.

He smiled, and his spirit began to slip away into a dream.

He was in Cancún with Robin. But the beach that had been so packed with sunbathers was empty except for the two of them. Robin sat astride him, her golden skin glistening with suntan oil. She smelled of coconut and pineapple. A delicious female piña colada. The sea green ocean spanned the horizon behind her. He could hear the surf crashing on the sugar white sand. Robin gave him a lazy smile and reached behind her to untie the strings of her bikini top. It fell to the blanket, and his suntanned hands covered her perfectly shaped breasts, caressing their creamy texture. She leaned down, and her mouth covered his, her tongue silken, insistent. Beneath the warmth of her lush bottom, he found himself hardening, his blood heating. He placed his hands on her trim waist, holding her down as he ground against her. She dragged her mouth away from his and began to slide down his body, planting a trail of kisses down his chest and stomach. He closed his eyes and groaned.

When she reached the waist of his surfer shorts, she untied the drawstring with maddening slowness and began to tug them down. He lifted his hips to help her, and felt the cool ocean breeze on his erection. A moment later, her warm hands encircled him, and he felt himself grow harder, bigger. Lazily, he opened his lust-glazed eyes, and saw through an opening of stone, not the azure blue sky of Cancún, but roiling clouds of gray, and the peculiar light that can only be Ireland. Directly above his head, a stone ceiling loomed, giving shelter against the rain he now heard falling outside.

An intoxicating warm mouth encircled him, and he forgot about where he was. It didn't matter. There was only the feeling. This earthquake that was building inside him, rocking him with pleasure. Sending him to heights he'd never glimpsed before.

It didn't take long. His fingers threaded through her hair, tightening as the climax shuddered through him, destroying him with its intensity. For a long moment, they lay quietly, his hand still enmeshed in her hair, her warm cheek lying against his thigh. As his heartbeat slowed to a thunder, he began to stroke her hair. It felt different. Shorter, more wiry. He felt her move under his hand, sensed her inching up to him. He smiled and opened his eyes.

Saw the brandy amber eyes holding his. The full lips smiling so tenderly, lovingly. Cedric's face. "Remember how it was with us, Dec? That's as good as it gets."

Gasping for air, Declan bolted up, fully awake now, his stomach roiling. *Oh, God! What have I done?*

He touched his stomach; it was sticky with come. The satin sheets beneath him were wet, too. *Oh, Christ Almighty!*

Nausea choked his throat, and he barely made it to the bathroom in time. Moments after expelling the contents of his stomach, he sat on the white marble floor, his arms wrapped around his knees, rocking back and forth, his body trembling.

I've got to go home. Today. Now. I've got to get back to Robin.
She's the only thing that can save me.

The din from the street below seemed miles away. It was quieter than usual because it was Sunday afternoon, and even Manhattan slowed down on Sunday afternoons. Unless there was some ethnic parade or a street fair going on. But not today. It had been raining when Amy awoke that morning. Not a half-hearted spring drizzle that, although it was a nuisance, didn't prevent people from scurrying around, doing last-minute Sunday errands that had been put off all weekend. But a gray curtain of rain that sluiced down out of gunmetal skies, drenching the green areas of Central Park, turning the city into a grim, waterlogged island of misery. It was the kind of day that if you had to be out, a vacant taxi was nowhere to be seen. Amy knew this from experience, and even though she had errands that needed to be done—dry-cleaning to be picked up, groceries to be bought, a planned visit to Barnes & Noble to buy the new book by Amy Tan—when she looked out her window to Riverside Drive and saw the relentless rain, she burrowed back into bed and slept another two hours.

When she finally got up, it was almost noon, and still raining. A perfect Sunday to laze around. She'd made coffee, filled a ceramic bowl with Cinna-Crunch Pebbles and fat-free milk, and shuffled to the sofa, nestling into the cushions and covering herself with a soft cotton throw. With the cereal bowl in one hand and the television remote in the other, she channel-surfed until she found something halfway interesting—*Dirty Dancing*—which, apparently, could be found on at least one cable station at any time of the day somewhere in the world at any given moment. And there she'd stayed throughout the whole day, only getting up to use the bathroom or get something else to munch on from the kitchen. It was her kind of Sunday.

She just wished Declan was here to share it with her.

But she was alone. Paul had left on Saturday afternoon, mumbling something about a date with Monica. The very mention of her name had brought a scowl to Amy's face, but before she could muster a comment, Paul had glared at her and growled, "Don't start with me, Robin." So she hadn't said a thing. He'd been in an unusually bad mood all day. Moody and morose as she'd ever seen him. No, *like* she'd never seen him. Instinct had told her not to pursue it. He'd either get over it, or would eventually sit down and talk about whatever was bothering him.

He'd left, and hadn't come back. Amy's eyes were fixed upon the television where Baby's big sister was onstage wearing her Hawaiian-print bra and sarong, singing in an off-key voice, but her mind was picturing Paul and Monica. Tucked beneath satin sheets in a king-size bed in her Upper East Side apartment—not that she knew for sure that's where the haughty Monica lived, but it fit her fantasy—spending the rainy Sunday afternoon making love and sleeping in each other's arms. Where the cranky old husband was stowed away, she had no idea, but it was a sure bet he was in a place where he wouldn't be a nuisance to the lovers.

Amy ground her teeth and lurched up from the sofa. Still wearing the red plaid flannel shorts and white tank top she'd slept in, she shuffled into the kitchen, took the half-empty pint of Ben & Jerry's Cherry Garcia out of the freezer, fished a large spoon out of the utensil drawer, and returned to the living room just as Patrick Swayze entered the resort and walked over to Jennifer Grey's table.

Transfixed by her favorite scene, Amy finished off the pint of Cherry Garcia, and by the time Johnny looked into Baby's eyes, and mouthed, "and I owe it all to you . . ." she was crying tears that rolled down her cheeks in a stream to match the rain falling outside. When the credits began rolling, she buried her face in a cushion and sobbed.

And the hell of it was she didn't even know why. Two days ago, she'd won an Emmy. She had a wonderful career, a fantastic apartment, and a drop-dead gorgeous husband who loved her. No, he wasn't here at the moment, but she knew he loved her. And she loved him. She *did* love him. So . . . why was she bawling her eyes out?

PMS. That must be it. Her period was due any day now. So, why *not* cry? A good cry was essential to good mental health, so why not indulge herself? When she finally sat up and wiped her wet face with the corner of the cotton throw, she felt as if a burden had been lifted. Another movie had started sometime during her crying jag. *Beetlejuice.* She'd hated it the first time she saw it, but after doing a round of channel-surfing without finding anything better, she kept it on. Even idiocy was better than the quiet of an empty apartment.

The voices on the TV grew faint, and somewhere deep within her consciousness, she knew she was dreaming. No longer was she wearing her plaid shorts and tank top; instead, she was in Jennifer Grey's pink chiffon dress and dancing with Patrick Swayze. He was singing to her, "I've had the time of my life . . ." his blue eyes gazing deeply into hers. She smiled up at him, swishing her skirt about her legs. He twirled her around and wrenched her body close to his. She moved with his rhythm, her face tilted upward, her body aligned with his. He smiled down at her, and a tiny shock zipped through her as she realized it was no longer Patrick Swayze she was dancing with, but Paul. A light sheen of sweat coated his stubbled face, and his blue-black hair gleamed damply under the bright lights. His eyes were locked on hers, a searing sapphire that held her transfixed. As the music ended, he drew her against his body, anchored her there by a hand at the small of her back. Her palm rested against his chest where she could feel the deep, even thud of his heart. She tilted her head to look up at him. Saw him gazing at her with a somber expression on his lean, handsome face.

"I love you," he whispered.

He bent his head, and his mouth covered hers, softly, tentatively. She gave into his kiss, sliding her hands up the back of his neck, threading into his silky black hair. The kiss deepened, became more hungry, more animal. She moaned, thrusting her body against him, wanting more, wanting everything.

"I love you, Robin. Christ, I love you so much it hurts."

Something was wrong. The voice wasn't right. This wasn't Paul's homespun, almost southern Virginia accent. No, those words had been spoken with the lilt of an Irish accent. His mouth covered hers again, and she felt the length of his body settling on hers. His scent was different, too, not the spicy sandalwood fragrance of Paul, but the fresh, green hint of Irish fields and smoky turf fires. She opened her eyes and struggled to focus on his face. But it was only when he broke the kiss and drew away to gaze down at her that she saw the blue eyes—not Paul's—the bold, sweet lips, and the soft shadow of a blond beard on his patrician face.

"Declan," she whispered, recovering from the first jolt of surprise. "You're home."

He smiled down at her, sliding a hand beneath her tank top to caress the flat of her stomach. "I missed you, love. I woke up last night wanting you so desperately, it hurt. And I knew I had to come home."

Amy bit down on her bottom lip as guilt washed through her. Why was she still having fantasies about Paul when this wonderful man loved her? Then, his words resonated in her brain. *I knew I had to come home.*

"Is this home, Declan?" she asked quietly.

A shadow flickered in his eyes, but it was gone so quickly, Amy thought she must've imagined it. His smile gentled. "*You* are my home," he whispered.

He kissed her again, this time more urgently. After a long moment of mounting excitement, Amy pushed him away. "Paul could come in any minute. Let's go to the bedroom."

Grumbling good-naturedly, Declan rose from the sofa and helped her up. Holding hands, she led him to the bedroom and closed and locked the door behind them. Before she could catch her breath, Declan had her naked and writhing beneath him on their king-size bed as the rain outside played a stamping tattoo on the windows.

The sex was mind-blowing. Better than it had ever been before. It was almost enough to make her forget about the *Dirty Dancing* dream of Paul.

Almost.

The intercom crackled in Amy's dressing room. Curled up on the twin-size bed, still wearing the jeans and T-shirt she'd worn on her ride into the studio, she looked up from next week's breakdown script.

"Robin Mulcahey and Lisa Muldoon," blared the disembodied female voice. "Please report for camera-blocking in ten minutes."

Lisa played Carly's latest nemesis in a long line of enemies, and today, they had a knock-down-drag-out to tape for a scene that would reach the TV screens in approximately three weeks. It would be a carefully choreographed fight sequence that would come across to the viewers as rather slapstick. But according to what she was reading for next week's scenes, it would turn deadly serious.

On Friday, Carly had caught Lisa's character, Daniella, in bed with Carly's former lover, and she'd had a hissy fit. In today's taping, her hissy fit would spill over into mayhem after Carly grabbed a handful of Daniella's glossy black hair, initiating a fight that would, hopefully, transcend the famous Linda Evans–Joan Collins fountain fisticuffs in *Dynasty*. Up until today, Amy had been looking forward to it. Lisa was a likable actress, professional beyond the tender age of twenty-three, and Amy always enjoyed working with her.

But now that she'd read next week's breakdown, her stomach churned. Because she couldn't believe what she was reading. But there it was. In black-and-white.

> *Quinn steps into his office, and reaches for the light. Nothing happens when he flicks it. Suddenly he stiffens, expression wary.*
> Quinn—"Who's there?"
> *A gloved hand comes out of the darkness, holding a gun. With a click, the safety is released. The gun fires. Three rapid shots. Quinn clutches his chest and sinks to the floor, a shocked, horrified expression on his face.*

"They've killed him off," Amy whispered, her hand shaking as she turned the page of the script.

She didn't know why she was so stunned. Everyone knew that Declan had no plans to renew his contract at the end of the month. But as long as his character was alive, she supposed she'd hoped he'd change his mind. Especially after yesterday afternoon when they'd celebrated his homecoming from California so enthusiastically in the bedroom. "*You* are my home," he'd said. And she'd believed him. Believed that he'd meant it. That California could wait at least another year until she could join him.

Of course, death meant nothing in a soap opera, she reminded herself. Soap characters came back from the dead with the same frequency as hurricanes hitting the East Coast in the fall. But the least—the very least—Declan could've done was negotiate an open-ended contract that would allow him to go on hiatus and come back at a later date. Todd Manning did it on *One Life to Live*. Luke and Laura had come back to *General Hospital* at least two or three times. Why not Quinn Connelly on *South Riding*?

She scrambled off the bed, grabbed the script, and left the dressing room she shared with Stephanie Johansen. Snaking her way through the honey-combed halls of the ABC building, she passed Wardrobe on her right and then Hair & Makeup on the left before reaching the tiny lobby, where the security guard, a black man in his fifties, sat across from a long table holding a coffee urn and a tray of pastries. To a guest, it would appear that it was the food he was guarding, but the truth was he was there just in case any rabid fans got past security in the lobby upstairs.

"Hi, Johnny," Amy called out. "How's it going?"

He smiled, lowering his newspaper. "Not bad, Rockin' Robin."

Usually, Johnny's affectionate nickname for her produced a smile. But not today. Her mood was way too foul.

A black bug skittered up the wall beyond his right shoulder. Without missing a beat, Amy slipped off her left loafer and slammed it against the cockroach, leaving a sickening smear of bug innards on the already dingy wall. The mayhem gave her a grim sense of satisfaction. Johnny scratched his head and smiled weakly. "Guess it's time to call the exterminators again."

"Guess so." Amy slipped her loafer back on, skirted his desk, and headed for the stairs. "Right now, I have another cockroach to crush." She knew she was being unreasonably bitchy, but she felt so betrayed. Why hadn't Declan told her they were writing him out of the soap?

At the top of the stairs, she went through a steel gray door onto the cavern-like set. Stepping over lengths of cable, she followed the noise of the technical crew until she reached the outer edges of the Red Fox Tavern set, stopping behind camera number three. On the set, Declan sat on one of the barstools, a tall glass of imitation Guinness between his hands. The barkeep, a fatherly actor named Teddy O'Reilly, recited a line, more or less in character, as the director, Nancy Logan, barked out instructions to the cameramen to block the afternoon's scenes.

Amy chewed her bottom lip, her eyes skewered to the back of Declan's head. His blond hair was in need of a cut. It curled around the bottom of his Canali collar, hardly fitting for his character, an Oxford-bred British art curator who'd arrived in the hoity-toity horse community of South Riding for a bit of underhanded business. But then again, he was due to be axed soon, so what did it matter? Fresh anger swept through her. How long had he known about this?

"Okay, that's it," Nancy Logan said, leafing through her notebook. "Next scene, Carly's apartment. Five minutes, folks."

The overhead lights blinked out, and Amy stepped past the camera, heading for the set. Declan ran his hands through his rumpled hair and swiveled around on his barstool. Their eyes met, and a sweet smile crossed his lips.

"Hey, love . . ."

"Don't 'love' me, Declan Blair." Amy slapped the breakdown script onto the bar between them. "When were you going to tell me, huh? Were you going to wait until I woke you up one morning to go to work, and say, 'Oh, sorry, love, but they killed me off. Have a jolly good day at work.'"

Declan's smile froze. He glanced past her shoulder at the technicians puttering around behind them, face pinkening. "Perhaps this isn't the time or place, Robin . . ."

"Oh, why not? Apparently, I'm one of the last to know. So, it's official, then? You're really not renewing your contract?" She tried desperately to blink back the angry tears filling her eyes, but was completely unsuccessful.

His eyes gentled. "Oh, love . . . I've never been anything but honest with you. From the very beginning, I told you I wouldn't be staying with the show." He reached out a hand and covered hers that rested on the padded bar. "You've known that. So, why has it come as such a shock to you? You knew my contract was up at the end of the month."

"I thought . . . after last night . . ."

"Oh, darlin'," he murmured, his Irish accent thickening. He brushed a strand of hair away from her face, his touch gentle and loving. "I got the part, love."

"What?"

"The part. In Cedric's new movie." His eyes held hers, imploring. "He told me at the airport that the part was mine if I wanted it. And I do, Robin. I'd be daft to turn it down. Surely you can see that, can you not?"

She drew her hand from beneath his, her body going ice-cold. "So . . . you're leaving."

He nodded slowly. "Shooting starts the beginning of July. I'm going out a month early to find a place to live."

"In a week," Amy said softly. "You're leaving in a week? Just *when* were you planning on telling me this?"

"Ah, don't be like this, love." He placed his hands on her shoulders, turning her to face him. "Nine months, Robin. That's all we've got to get through. Your contract will be up in March. By that time, the movie will be in the can, and I'll have my choice of scripts. I'll find us a nice place to live. Maybe a bungalow on the beach. Or a house in the Canyon. Whatever suits your fancy. Love, it'll be the life we've always wanted. The life we deserve."

Amy stared at him stonily. "The life *you* want. Not me. I'm happy here in New York. I love my job. I love my life here. What makes you think that California is the answer to *my* dreams?"

He gazed at her for a long moment, and Amy saw the determination in his eyes. She knew she'd lost the battle. Ambition was a tough opponent, one that she stood no chance of conquering. "I've got to do this, Robin," he whispered. "I've *got* to."

She backed away, and his hands slipped off her shoulders. Turning, she saw several of the technicians staring at them, but as soon as they saw her notice them, they began to busy themselves with whatever they'd been doing before she'd caused the scene. It would be all over the studio by lunchtime. Robin's spat with her heart-throb husband. The rumor mill would no doubt have them filing for divorce by the day's end. It would then, of course, reach the ears of the soap magazine gossipmongers, and probably be plastered on the cover page of next week's *Soap Star* magazine. She could just see the cover line. *"SR's Carly brawls with sexy costar hubby on the set; two cameramen injured in melee."*

"Robin." Declan scooted off the barstool and reached out a hand to stop her. "Tell me you'll join me in California in March. I don't know how I can leave unless I know that."

Then don't leave. That's what she wanted to say. But who was *she* to demand that he give up his dream for her? *Yes, but isn't that exactly what's he's asking you to do?* It wasn't the same, though. Not really. With her three years of experience on *South Riding,* and the added validation of the Emmy, she would have no problem at all getting a part on one of the West Coast soaps. In fact, she'd probably be such a hot property that she could have her choice of any of the daytime dramas. And who said she'd have to stick to daytime drama, anyway? Maybe she could even get a role on one of the popular prime-time shows? A legal or medical drama that would really allow her to spread her acting wings. Gain some real respect in the business. Not that respect was so important to her. But still . . . it was something to think about.

She turned and met Declan's gaze. "You're my husband," she said. "And I love you. Of course I'll come to California next March. I just wish you'd told me last night."

"I'm sorry. I should have. But I didn't want to ruin our reunion." He gave her a heartbreaking smile, cradling her face in his long, slender hands. "You don't know what it means to me to hear you say you'll join me in California." His thumbs brushed away the tears that had managed to escape from her eyes despite her best efforts, no doubt ruining the makeup Sonia had so expertly applied just a half hour ago. "Because the truth is . . . I need you, Robin. You're my lifeline, and if I didn't know you'd be joining me next year, I'm not sure I could get through the next months."

The intercom gave a squawk, and then Nancy Logan's voice rang out, "Robin and Lisa, I need you on the set of Carly's apartment, *pronto!*"

"I've got to go," Amy said.

"Indeed." Declan bent his head, brushing his lips across hers. "Let's go to dinner tonight. Somewhere special, okay?"

Amy nodded and stepped away from him. "Sure." She turned and headed for the set of her character's apartment.

"Well, I guess this is it," Amy said, gazing up at Declan's somber face.

They stood at a crowded gate at JFK, arms wrapped around each other. A sign above the head of a ticket agent showed that Flight 671 to Los Angeles was now boarding. They'd already boarded the first-class ticket holders, and although that was where Declan would be sitting, he'd lingered, reluctant to say good-bye. Amy realized it was up to her.

She forced a brave smile and gave him a gentle push. "Go on. Get on that plane, Mr. Big Movie Star. I'll be fine."

His hands tightened on her shoulders as his eyes searched hers. "I know you will. It's me I'm worried about. Christ! I'm going to miss you so much."

"You'll be back for Thanksgiving," Amy said. "That's only . . . what? Five months?"

He closed his eyes. "Sounds like a bloody eternity."

"And I'll be coming out for Christmas, don't forget." *Whoop de whoo! Christmas in Hollywood. Now, that sounded like fun.*

"Maybe you can get a few days off and come out over Labor Day?" Declan suggested. "That's only a couple of months away."

"I doubt it. I'll be in the middle of a really intense story line, remember?" Amy smiled. "I'm on trial for your murder."

Declan groaned. "Oh, yeh. Forgot."

Amy reached up, enclosed his head in her hands, and kissed him firmly on the lips. Then she gave him another gentle push. "Now, *go!*"

A strange look crossed Declan's face. Almost like panic. "Maybe this is all wrong," he said. "What if I go out there and fall flat on my face?"

"You won't." Amy held his gaze. "Declan, you are an extraordinary actor. Oscar material. We both know it. Now, go out there and prove it."

Amy knew what she was doing. His moment of uncertainty could've been her ticket to keeping her life safe and secure, just the way she wanted it. But how could she kill his dream for her own selfish reasons?

"I don't know if I can do it without you," Declan said quietly. "Don't you know, Robin, you're my lifeline?"

He kept saying that. And she wanted to believe it. But if it were true, why was he leaving her?

She squeezed his hands between hers. "You won't be without me. Next year at this time, we'll be together for good. Only you'll be a big movie star, and we won't be able to go anywhere without hordes of your fans descending on us."

"Excuse me. Mr. Blair?" A flight attendant called out from the gate. "You'll have to board now. We're getting ready to close the doors."

A shrill scream erupted from somewhere behind them. "*It is Quinn! I told you!*"

Amy glanced back to see a young redheaded woman hurtling toward them. Declan grabbed Amy's shoulders and gave her one more quick, hard kiss. He turned and strode to the gate, glancing back once to flash her a smile. Then he was gone. The young woman stopped abruptly at Amy's side, her freckled face dropping in disappointment.

"Oh, damn." The redhead stared at the door that had closed behind

Declan, then turned and looked at Amy. Her brown eyes widened in recognition, and she gave a soft gasp. "Oh! You're Carly!"

Amy nodded and forced a smile. She waited for the woman to dig into her purse for a slip of paper for an autograph. Instead, she sidled closer and arched an eyebrow. "So, tell me, Carly. Is Quinn as hot in bed as he looks?"

Amy's jaw dropped. She'd heard fans say some outrageous things, but this took the cake. And it rendered her totally speechless. She stepped past the woman and walked away.

"Hey!" the woman shouted, in a shrill Bronx accent. "You should know. You're married to him, aren't ya? Is his dong as big as they say?"

Amy began to run. She reached the taxi stand, breathless and on the verge of tears. A few minutes later, she collapsed into the backseat of a thankfully air-conditioned cab. By the time the taxi reached the Queensboro Bridge, she was crying slow, silent tears. It was only when the cab turned onto Seventy-seventh Street that Amy dug a tissue out of purse and began to dab at her eyes. She didn't want the doorman to see her like this. Not that she didn't trust him, but it paid to be careful. She didn't want next week's soap magazines boasting cover lines like *SR's Robin Mulcahey's Heart Broken by Hubby's Desertion to Hollywood.*

"Good evening, Miss Mulcahey." The doorman tipped his cap.

"Hi, Jack." Robin managed a smile and walked through the door he held open for her.

She took the elevator up to the seventh floor. As soon as she stepped into the corridor, she saw a bouquet of multicolored balloons attached to a basket outside the door of her apartment. She smiled. Declan. It was so like him to think of something like this to help her get through the first lonely night without him.

She unlocked the door, grabbed the basket, and brought it inside. Through the clear aqua cellophane, she could see a video case, a box of microwave popcorn, and a supersize box of Hot Tamales. Odd choice, she thought. Declan knew she couldn't watch a movie without munching on Junior Mints. She placed the basket on the dining room table and pulled the card out of the envelope.

Rob:

I know you're feeling down tonight with Declan gone, so I thought this would cheer you up. It always did when we were kids. Don't start the movie without me. I'll be over at 7:30. Love, Paul.

She dropped the card to the table, her heart racing. Paul! Of course, Paul. The wonderful big brother looking out for his little sister. With clumsy fingers, she untied the ribbon that fastened the balloons to the basket and allowed them to float to the ceiling. Reaching inside the cellophane, she drew out the video.

Ferris Bueller's Day Off.

She smiled, remembering the evening Robin had put this movie into the VCR. It had been during one of those sad weeknights following the death of Princess Di. Amazingly enough, Amy had never seen the classic teen movie before, and they'd both laughed their butts off at Matthew Broderick's savvy portrayal of a popular teen who had cutting school down to a science.

The intercom buzzed. Heart thumping, Amy walked to the door and punched the button. "Yes, Jack?"

"Your brother is here. The football star."

Amy smiled. Jack was a huge Giants fan, and he'd been thrilled to learn that one of his building's occupants was the sister of a brand-new Giant. "Send him on up. Thanks."

Amy hurried into the powder room to check her makeup. The crying jag in the taxi had surely left its mark on her. But the expensive waterproof mascara she used had held up remarkably well. She grabbed the extra tube of lipstick she kept in the medicine cabinet and quickly applied some. By the time she stepped out of the bathroom, Paul was knocking at the door.

"Hi, Rob."

Amy caught her breath. *Damn! He looks good.* He'd apparently just come from minicamp. His black hair was still damp from a shower. He wore khaki cargo shorts and a navy muscle shirt emblazoned with NEW YORK GIANTS. His toned biceps gleamed with a golden tan that made his blue eyes deepen to the shade of indigo.

He scrutinized her. "How you doing, kid?"

Amy tried to answer, but out of nowhere a lump had formed in her throat, and she felt perilously close to tears again. Paul stepped into her apartment and, without hesitation, took her into his arms and held her close.

"I know it's tough, Rob," he murmured. "But you'll get through this."

Amy surrendered to the warmth of him, nestling her face against his chest, inhaling his crisp, Irish Spring scent, feeling the comforting thud of his heartbeat beneath her ear. It was wrong; she knew that. To allow him to comfort her under false pretenses like this. He thought he was giving brotherly support. And she was taking what he gave, knowing what she felt wasn't sisterly at all. She leaned into his embrace, and the blood that coursed through her veins recognized him as a man—as the one man in the world who could make her feel so gloriously alive, so heady with desire, so crazy in love. No, not even Declan could make her feel like this. No matter how much she tried to convince herself it wasn't true, she knew the love she felt for her husband couldn't come close to what she felt for Paul.

And it was wrong. So very wrong.

But at the moment, God help her, she just didn't care.

Amy took the bundle of mail from her box in the foyer, pocketed her key, and turned to the elevator. Most likely there would be a letter from Declan in this pile. He'd turned out to be quite the letter writer, which was rather surprising in this age of e-mail and cell phones. But Dec was endearingly old-fashioned that way. He wrote long, engaging letters describing the day-to-day activities on the *Borderland* set, and after she'd read them, it felt like she'd been there. For the last six weeks, he'd been shooting on location in Ireland, and his joy at being back in his homeland bled through every line.

And just because he was an avid letter writer didn't mean he never phoned. He called at least once a week, sometimes more often. Just last week, he'd telephoned from Galway, begging her to try to get away for a couple of days and come to Ireland.

"You'll love it, Robin. I swear, you won't want to leave."

And of course, for that very reason, she couldn't risk going. On *South Riding,* they were in the thick of the trial, and she was working twelve to fifteen hours, five days a week. It would be insane to fly to Ireland on a Friday night and have to return on Sunday.

When she'd said so, Declan's voice had been soft with disappointment. "Oh, Christ, Robin, I miss you so dreadfully."

"Thanksgiving is only two months away," she'd reminded him, trying to summon a cheerful note.

A soft meow, that always sounded like a question mark to Amy, announced Ruby Two-Shoe's presence. The orange cat padded into the foyer from the direction of the bedrooms, her amber eyes gleaming in what Amy swore was happiness at her arrival home. She dropped the mail on the foyer table and knelt to scoop the cat into her arms. "Hi, baby!" As if a switch had been turned on, Ruby began to purr as she snuggled her orange face in the crook of Amy's arm. "You're such a sweetheart."

Amy stood, still holding the cat. She adjusted her slightly, reached for the mail with her free hand, and headed for the sofa. With Ruby on her lap, she began sorting through the pile of letters. And there it was. The familiar light blue airmail envelope with the Irish postage stamp. A thick envelope, bulging with two, maybe three days' worth of news about the shoot. Amy glanced through the rest of the mail. She'd read Declan's later after she'd changed into comfortable shorts and poured herself a tall glass of iced tea. Although it was late September, New York City was suffering through an unseasonable heat wave, which added to the fatigue and discomfort of the long hours at the studio.

What was this? She paused, staring at a business-size envelope with the return address of the New York Giants office. Her heart began to thud. She slipped an index finger beneath a loose section of the flap and ripped it open, drawing out a slip of paper and three tickets for Sunday's game against the Seattle Seahawks. Opening the note, she read Paul's neatly printed letters.

> *Robby, here are some tickets for Sunday's game. I thought you might want to ask Kerani and Sergey to come along. Maybe we can all go out to dinner afterward? Love, Paul.*

A quirky twist of fate had the Giants playing their first three games away this season, and the one coming up this Sunday would be the first home game at Giants Stadium. The thought of seeing Paul play in the flesh was exhilarating. It was really quite surprising it hadn't happened before. But then again, she supposed it had never occurred to him to invite her to come to Denver for a game. After all, she wasn't even supposed to *like* football. The year he'd gone to the Super Bowl with the Broncos, he'd been a rookie, thereby entitled to only two tickets, and, of course, Tammy and Michael had taken them.

The phone rang, and a startled Ruby jumped off her lap and skittered out of the room. Amy picked up the extension in the kitchen, still gazing down at the tickets in her hand. "Hey, Rob," Paul's cheerful voice rang in her ear. "You get the tickets?"

"Yeah. Just now."

"So, you going to come and see your big brother get walloped by my old pal, Dexter Moganis?"

Amy smiled. "Well, if you're going to let that happen, I'm not sure I want to."

"Hey, what do you expect? The guy is as big as a Mack truck."

Amy wrapped the phone cord around an index finger and grinned. "I expect you to catch a couple of touchdown passes, that's what."

"Will you come if I promise you one touchdown?"

She heard the grin in his voice and her own widened. "I'll accept two, and nothing less."

"Okay. It's a promise. So, do you think Sergey and Kerani will be interested?"

Amy rolled her eyes. "Are you kidding? Kerani has been dropping hints since the season began."

"Okay. I'll send a car to collect all three of you at your apartment at . . . say, noon. How does that sound?"

"Super. Oh, and Paul?"

"Yeah?"

"What do I get if you don't make those touchdowns?"

A slight pause, then a brief laugh. "Tell you what. I don't make at least two TDs, I pick up the tab for all of us at dinner. Sound fair?"

"That depends." Amy paced the small area in the kitchen that the phone cord allowed, enjoying the banter. "Where are we going for dinner?"

"Well, there's that Sbarros down near Times Square."

"In your dreams," Amy retorted. "I was thinking something more like Balthazar in SoHo."

Paul groaned. "Little sister has become rather highfalutin, hasn't she? Must be that Hollywood husband of yours. How's Dec doing, by the way?"

Amy felt her smile stiffen. "He's having the time of his life in Ireland. Last night he asked me to come over for a weekend, but of course I can't. Not with this trial story line I'm in the middle of."

"You should do it," Paul said. "Try to work it out so you can take some time off." His voice softened, "Remember how Amy used to always talk about wanting to go to Ireland? You should do it for her."

Her heart panged. Only once had she and Paul had a brief conversation about Ireland, and yet, even after all this time, he remembered how passionately she'd wanted to go. "Well, I'd like to, but the timing is wrong." She swallowed against the lump in her throat. "Maybe someday."

"Well, just remember, Amy didn't have a 'someday.'" His voice sounded wistful. "Listen, I've got a call on the other line. I'll see you on Sunday, okay? Later, Rob."

Amy pushed down on the receiver and dialed Kerani. Her friend answered on the third ring. "Hey, Rani," Amy said. "You and Sergey doing anything on Sunday afternoon?"

Not only did Paul live up to his promise of catching two touchdown passes, but on the second one he made a near miraculous one-handed catch on the thirty yard line, evaded a cornerback and a safety intent on sandwiching him, and ran the ball into the end zone untouched.

Amy jumped to her feet and cheered, hugging first Kerani, then Sergey in her delirium. This was so much better than watching football on television. The noise of the crowd, the smell of hot dogs and beer, the camaraderie of the fans rooting for the home team—it was almost an assault on her senses, but a good one. Watching jersey #22—Paul—jump into the air to grab a high-sailing pass, even though he knew he'd be hit by a two-hundred-pound cornerback as soon as he came down with the ball, nearly stopped her breathing. Of course, it had always been scary on TV, but here, overlooking the fifty yard line, it was magnified many times over. She lost count of how many times she followed the same routine: the Giants quarterback, Mike Dallas, dropping back into the pocket, letting go of a beautiful spiraling pass. Amy would bolt to her feet, clutching handfuls of her hair as Paul reached for the ball. More often than not, he caught it, and only once had he been hit so hard that it looked like he'd been injured. But, thankfully, he'd just had the wind knocked out of him.

Now, as he celebrated his touchdown in the end zone, Amy high-fived Kerani one more time and sat back down, taking a long draw of her Budweiser. Since the Emmys, she'd stopped being so cautious about drinking. After all, Robin had loved beer. And in the years since she'd moved to New York, Amy had to admit she'd mellowed. An occasional beer wasn't going to turn her into an alcoholic like her parents. Still, she rarely had more than one, even when she was in a place like this, where it flowed copiously. But as she glanced over to her left and down two rows, she saw something that made her want to down another beer. Very quickly.

Monica. The petite beauty sat with perfect posture just a few feet away, her glossy blue-black hair falling like a shining curtain to her bare shoulders. Perfectly straight, perfectly styled. Amy saw only the profile of her patrician face, but she knew it was her. She could never mistake Monica Ashton for someone else.

Her pleasure somewhat spoiled, Amy turned her attention back to the football field. New York kicked off to the Seahawks, and the ball soared high. The Seattle player caught the ball, saw the rush was on, and tried to dodge it by running backward. Big mistake. He was downed, but not before he lost the ball.

"Collins, you pussy!" screamed an outraged Seahawks fan somewhere above Amy. *"Next time pretend it's your boyfriend's ass cheeks and keep a grip on it!"*

Laughter followed his insult, and Amy grinned. Her gaze fell on Monica again who, at that precise moment, looked back to glare at the drunken fan. Her blue eyes connected with Amy's. For a second, she stared coolly as if trying to place the familiar face. Finally, her lips stretched in a tight smile and she lifted a slim hand in a tepid wave.

Don't knock yourself out, bitch. Amy waved back, returning her frosty smile with one of her own. She couldn't remember ever disliking someone as much as she did Monica. But was it just because of Paul? Had her jealousy for the too-good-to-be-true violinist clouded her judgment? Or was she really the arrogant ice princess Amy suspected she was? As the Seahawks took a time-out, her thoughts drifted back to Monica's insensitive comments when she, Amy, lay broken and bandaged in a hospital bed, and decided that yes, indeed, Monica was a piece of work. Only one question remained: What on earth did Paul see in her?

Stupid question. She let her gaze drift over to Monica. Saw her slim, pale shoulders, her shining black hair. A slinky red bandeau hugging her firm, full breasts like a lover. It didn't take a rocket scientist to figure out it had a lot—if not everything—to do with what happened between the sheets. Somehow, she didn't think they sat around her Upper East Side apartment discussing world politics or the latest in medical advances.

Why was Monica here, anyway? She'd never shown an interest in football. Did she even understand what was happening on the field? Amy rolled her eyes. Monica probably thought a tight end was a new body slimmer marketed by Victoria's Secret.

Amy had a horrible thought. Surely Paul hadn't invited her to dinner. No! He wouldn't. He knew how Amy felt about his dirty little affair with the married woman.

But after the game, when their limo pulled up to the entrance nearest the locker rooms, the first thing Amy saw was Monica waiting outside the gate. She was dressed in skintight black knit Capri pants, platform shoes, and that sinful-looking red bandeau.

"Shit," Amy muttered.

Kerani looked at her. "What's wrong?"

"It seems Paul's girlfriend is joining us."

"Oh, the married chick?" Kerani leaned toward the window to stare out.

Sergey did, too. His brown eyes widened in appreciation. "That's a violinist?" he murmured in a thick Russian accent. "Good God! I chose the wrong profession."

Glaring, Kerani dug her elbow into his side. "In your dreams, Sergey." She looked at Amy. "Implants?"

Amy's lips twitched. She nodded. "I'd bet my life on it."

"No *way!*" Sergey said, leaning closer to get a better look, and was rewarded with another elbow in the ribs from Kerani.

Just then Paul walked through the gate and approached Monica. Amy grimaced as they embraced. He was too damn tall for her. He had to hunker down in order for their mouths to meet. The two of them looked like Lurch and . . . *Tinkerbell*, for God's sake!

"Have they no shame?" Kerani muttered. "Where's her husband, anyway?"

"Probably locked away in a nursing home. She's just waiting for him to die so she can collect his life insurance and move on to the next victim. Oh, here they come. I guess I'd better be good." Not wanting to be caught spying, Amy settled back in the limo and folded—clenched—her hands in her lap.

Kerani's eyes danced. "I have a feeling this is going to be one interesting evening."

"Me too," Sergey agreed, his eyes fastened on Monica as she and Paul approached the limo.

Kerani scowled at him. "Hey, just remember who you're going home with tonight, darling."

Amy speared a piece of chicken breast onto her fork and popped it into her mouth. The delectable aroma of their food warred with the overpowering scent of the Estée Lauder perfume Monica wore. Amy glanced across the table at Monica's plate. Paul's girlfriend had ordered an entree of roasted vegetables in a tomato tortilla wrap. It looked yummy—*not!*

"How's your tortilla, Monica?" Amy said, making an attempt at being friendly.

"Wonderful!" Monica arched a black eyebrow at her. "I see *you're* still eating dead animals."

Paul hastily reached for his beer. "How about a toast?" Lifting his glass of Heineken, he grinned. "To . . . to . . ." His grin had frozen. He glanced at the others. "Any ideas?"

Sergey came to the rescue. "To the Giants' decisive win over the Seahawks."

"And to Paul's three touchdowns," chimed in Kerani.

They all drank to him. Afterward, Monica placed her goblet of white wine onto the linen-draped table and dabbed at her glistening red lips with her napkin. "So, Robin . . ." Her lips curled in a Mona Lisa smile, but her eyes remained arctic cold. "Are you still working on that little soap opera of yours?"

Amy's fork paused in midair. She met Monica's appraising gaze. "Why, yes, Monica. I'm still working on my little soap opera."

"How nice. Paul tells me you won some kind of award this year?"

"Yes." Amy gave her a chilly smile. "It's called an Emmy. Maybe you've heard of it." She tried but didn't succeed at keeping the biting edge from her voice.

"I need another beer," Paul said, even though his glass was still half-full. "Where's our waiter?"

"And more breadsticks would be good," Kerani suggested. "Where *is* that waiter?"

Sergey gazed between Monica and Amy as if he had front-row seats at a tennis match. Amy was glad to see *someone* was enjoying himself tonight.

Monica smiled and speared a strip of green pepper. "Yes, I think I may have heard of the Emmys. Not that I ever have time to watch TV. But what I don't understand is why are you wasting yourself on television? Don't the *really* talented actors go on to movies?"

Amy stared at her, then glanced at the others to see if they'd picked up on her unbelievable insult. Paul's face had gone noticeably pink, and Kerani wore an expression that screamed out "Oh, shit." Sergey's brown eyes danced, and Amy could almost read his mind. *"Hot damn! Catfight!"*

Well, she wasn't about to get into a screaming match with Miss High-and-Mighty, even though it would do her heart good to grab her by her glossy black hair and push her smirking face into her plate of vegetables.

Instead, she smiled sweetly. "An interesting opinion, Monica."

Her beautiful face expressionless, Monica shrugged. "I could've stayed where I was comfortable with the Nob Hill Chamber Orchestra, but there was no challenge in doing that. So, I went for the big time and here I am doing what I love in the most important city in the world. It seems to me that you should want more out of your career than playing the same shallow character year after year on a cheesy soap opera. Doesn't it bother you that your viewers are mainly bored housewives and ditsy teenage girls?"

Amazing, thought Amy. The woman had absolutely no clue what an arrogant bitch she was.

Paul was looking around frantically, and when he saw their waiter heading toward them, he practically tackled him. "Could we have another round of drinks, please? So, Sergey . . . Mike's arm is looking pretty good, wouldn't you say? Did you see that last TD I caught in the end zone? Man, it practically tore a hole through my stomach."

Amy sat absorbing Monica's catty insult. She felt the blood heating her face. Her hand had tightened convulsively on her fork. A thousand retorts swept through her mind, but they all began with four-letter words, and she'd be damned if she let this witch force her into a scene in one of Manhattan's trendiest restaurants. She had been recognized by at least a couple of women when they'd entered the establishment, and situations like this always managed to find their way to the gossip columns.

Mustering her self-control, Amy just smiled and continued with her meal.

But Monica wasn't done with her. "Apparently, your husband knows where the money and fame is, doesn't he? He certainly didn't stay on your little soap for long."

Paul laid down his fork and glared at Monica. "That's enough." His face looked like it had been carved from stone. Except for the telltale muscle twitching in his right jaw.

Monica glanced at him in surprise, opened her luscious mouth as if to protest, then, seeing his expression, remained silent.

Amy threw her napkin to the table and stood. "Excuse me." Heart thudding, she stalked into the ladies' room. Just seconds later, Kerani followed her in. "You okay, Robin?"

Eyes closed, Amy stood at the sink, clutching the edge of the counter.

Slowly, she opened them, turned to her friend, and managed a smile. "Of course," she said woodenly. "I'm sure these homicidal feelings will pass. Thanks for asking, though."

Kerani grinned and headed for a stall. "Just remember. She might act like a queen, but I could've sworn I heard her fart earlier."

"If she did, it probably came out smelling like Estée Lauder. At least, I'm sure that's what *she* thinks," Amy muttered. "And maybe it does. I don't think she's human."

"You're probably right," Kerani said through the stall, her rich, velvet voice laced with humor. "Maybe we should ask Paul if she sleeps in a coffin during the day."

Amy burst out laughing. Oh, how she loved Kerani and the way she could lighten her mood with one simple statement. "See you back at the table," she said, heading for the door.

She stepped out of the ladies' room feeling calmer, determined to ignore the Nob Hill Princess for the rest of the evening. But when she saw Paul standing there, apparently waiting for her, anger swept over her again.

"Thanks so much for defending me," she snarled.

He eyed her, a puzzled look on his face. "I figured you could take care of yourself. What's up with you, anyway? You just sat there and let her lambaste you."

Amy swallowed hard. He was right. The real Robin would've chewed Monica up in tiny pieces and then spit her out for the dogs. "Yeah, well . . ." she finally sputtered. "She took me by surprise. She's a . . . a . . ." What would Robin have called her? ". . . a tight-assed bitch who acts like she has an icicle stuck up her twat. I'm surprised your dick hasn't frozen off from screwing her!"

He blinked in surprise, and they stared at each other for a long moment. *Did I really say that?* Amy wondered. Paul grinned. "Now, *that's* the Robin I know and love."

Amy sighed and shook her head. "Why did you invite her to join us tonight, Paul? You know how I feel about her."

His face sobered. He sighed, running a restless hand through his hair. "Because, Rob, I want you to get to know her. Look, I don't expect you to understand this or approve of it, but we're going to get married."

Amy's mouth dropped open in dismay. She felt as if she'd been kicked in the chest by a mule. The door to the ladies' room opened, and Kerani stepped out. Her eyes lit up when she saw them. "Hey, did you move the party out here in the hall . . ." Her voice drained away as her eyes swept from Paul to Amy. "Sooooo . . . catch you back at the table." And she hurried away.

Amy looked back at Paul. "Excuse me for bringing this up, but won't marrying a bigamist wreak havoc on your squeaky-clean athlete's image?"

He shook his head. "Her husband is dying with some kind of liver disease. It's just a matter of time. Obviously, Monica can't leave him now, but as soon as he's . . . uh . . . passed on, and the proper amount of time is past, we're getting married. Hey, don't look so horrified. We were engaged years ago, and I broke it off. We have a second chance now, and I'm not going to screw it up."

"Screw it up?" Amy glared up at him. "Paul Mulcahey, if you think that marrying that bitch isn't going to screw up your life more than you can ever imagine, you're out of your fucking mind!" She turned and strode back to their table.

Kerani, Sergey, and Monica looked up as she approached. Amy grabbed the denim shirt she'd brought along to ward off the evening chill. Her eyes fastened on Kerani. "I'll catch a taxi home." She studiously avoided Monica's gaze. "Call me later, Rani. You aren't going to believe what I have to tell you."

Kerani's dark eyes lit up. "Yeah? Can you give me a hint?"

Amy glanced at Monica. "Yeah, manipulation and morons."

"Oh . . . God! Dec!"

Amy arched, her legs tightening around Declan's waist as he thrust into her. An agonized moan escaped her lips, a call for release that she didn't really want. Not yet. Hot water from the shower head sprayed down upon them, streaming down their naked bodies and producing clouds of steam billowing in the sea green tiled stall. Her nails dug into his California-tanned shoulders as she rode him closer to the pinnacle. His sapphire eyes held hers, his lips slightly parted as he took in light, shallow breaths. His hands held her waist, directing her movements, dictating their rhythm. Slow . . . maddeningly slow . . . then a subtle quickening of the tempo . . . a deepening of the pressure. Declan bit down on his bottom lip, eyes darkening to almost black. And just as Amy teetered on the edge, he grimaced, his hands clutching her to him, strengthening the core of their connection, intensifying it. With a sharp cry—*Declan!*—she plunged over the edge.

Afterward, she clutched him, waiting for their mutual shuddering to ease, then finally collapsed against his chest, closing her eyes and breathing in the sweet smells of soap, Declan, and satisfying sex. The hot water cascaded over them, so soothing, so deliciously warm. Enclosing them in a world of heat and wet and magic.

It was at moments like this—these all too few moments of perfection—that she really believed everything would be all right. That *they* would be all right.

Declan gazed down at the familiar sci-fi sphere of Los Angeles International Airport's terminal as the 747 banked for its landing approach. Lights were just beginning to come on as twilight descended on the San Fernando Valley. A melancholy time, he thought. Especially when it's the Sunday night after Thanksgiving. Three days of overeating and good sex and too much American football did nothing to prepare one for the routine of Monday morning.

But oh, what a weekend it had been. He smiled, closed his eyes, and leaned back against the soft leather of his first-class seat, remembering the lazy hours of sweet lovemaking he'd shared with Robin. Five months apart had made them ravenous for each other. He'd taken the red-eye from LA on Wednesday night, arriving at LaGuardia at nine-thirty in the morning. He'd instructed Robin not to pick him up, telling her how he'd been fantasizing about coming into their bedroom and kissing her awake. And he'd done just that. She'd been like a sweet, silken kitten, awakening slowly beneath his caresses and lingering, hot kisses. But as he continued to explore her body, slipping his hands under her white satin chemise to cup her lush breasts, she became a tigress, much like she'd been during those steamy days and nights in Cancún. They'd made love for hours until it was time to get up, shower, and make their way downtown for Thanksgiving dinner at Kerani and Sergey's.

He'd been glad Robin had decided not to go to Williamsburg this year. Declan knew Mike Mulcahey disliked him intensely, and he'd just as soon not have to deal with the man. But the real reason Robin had turned down their standing invitation wasn't because of her father. Apparently, Paul had planned to bring his girlfriend down, and for some reason, Robin detested her. Declan hadn't met the woman, so he didn't quite understand Robin's animosity toward her. Odd, though. That was one thing he'd always admired about his beautiful wife. She was easygoing and seemed to get along with almost everyone.

"Ladies and gentlemen, please make sure your seats and trays are in the upright position as we prepare for landing."

Declan straightened and adjusted his seat, still smiling as he thought about Robin. They had hardly been able to contain themselves at Kerani and Sergey's, so anxious they were to return to their apartment to make love again. And that's pretty much all they'd done throughout Thursday night, Friday, Saturday, and this morning. That last time, in the shower, Christ . . . it didn't get any better than that. The intensity of their lovemaking had made it even harder to say good-bye at the airport. There, they'd clung to each other as if he were a soldier going off to war.

"A month," he'd told her, grasping her slim shoulders and gazing down into her amazing blue eyes. Christ, she'd been so beautiful, her fine-boned face flushed from love, her silky blond hair tousled from his hands.

In less than a month, she'd be coming to California for Christmas. Just for a week, but it was better than nothing. Then in March, she could get out of her contract with *South Riding* and come to LA for good. Everything would be perfect then.

His career was on the rise, and the buzz on *Borderland* was better than good. The all important O word—Oscar—had even been mentioned in *Variety*. The film had wrapped in early October, but before Declan could even draw in a breath, his agent had sent over a pile of scripts offering roles written especially for him by some of Hollywood's best screenwriters. All because of the buzz.

He'd finally decided on *French Quarter*, a psychological thriller set in New Orleans written by a relatively new scribe riding the waves of a surprise summer box office hit. It was a story about a man and two women, and involved sexual obsession leading to murder. Not exactly a nice family movie. But the money was more than he'd ever been offered before, and when he heard that the producer was in talks with Charlize Theron and Catherine Zeta-Jones for the female leads, he'd signed on the dotted line. Shortly afterward, the two actresses committed, and the project was green-lighted. Initial shooting would start in April.

He hoped Robin would understand why he couldn't stay in New York with her until then. He'd tried to explain that he couldn't leave Tinseltown as long as his star was on the rise—that it was important to be seen at all the right parties, with the right people. And thanks to Cedric, he knew who those people were, and how to get the right invitations, when and how to be available for paparazzi. Because of Cedric, Declan's photo had appeared in the last eight issues of *People*. *Borderland* was slated for a June 30 release, still over six months away, but already his new Hollywood agent had been fielding calls from *People, Premiere,* and *Entertainment Weekly* wanting interviews. No *way* could he leave LA with all this going on.

And another thing. Robin would be moving out in March, and he hoped to find the perfect house for them, maybe something similar to Cedric's cottage in Malibu, but on a smaller scale. Or would Robin want to live in the secluded canyon? Cedric had put him in touch with the real-estate agent he'd used, and he'd already looked at a few places in Pacific Palisades and Santa Monica. But so far, nothing had come up that felt right. No big hurry, though. Cedric had assured him he could stay with him until he found exactly what he was looking for.

It was grand hanging out with Cedric. Being with his childhood friend was like having a small part of Ireland here with him in this crazy fucked-up town called Hollywood. Poor lad. What had he done over Thanksgiving? He'd had no specific plans when Declan left for New York, and Dec felt bad about that. It seemed wrong, somehow, to leave his friend on his own. He'd even suggested that Cedric come to New York with him, and was ashamed at the relief he felt when the offer was refused. He wasn't sure he was ready to introduce Cedric to Robin. For the time being, at least, it seemed easier to keep his California life separated from his New York one.

As he stepped through the arrival gate at LAX, the first face he saw was Cedric's darkly handsome one, his chameleon eyes glowing. They embraced.

"Welcome home, Dec," Cedric grinned. "Christ, this place was a fucking cemetery all weekend. I'm that glad you're back, man."

"You didn't have to come fetch me, Ced. I could've hailed a cab."

"I told you, I've been bloody bored out of my skull. Come on. Let's go home."

Declan threw his bag into the space behind the bucket seat of Cedric's silver blue BMW Z8 convertible and climbed into the passenger seat. He leaned back and closed his eyes as Cedric started the ignition and the engine revved. The evening air was warm and dry with the Santa Ana winds carrying the hint of orange blossoms. They ruffled through Declan's hair as Cedric maneuvered the car onto the freeway. He smiled. Despite his sadness at leaving Robin, it felt grand to be back in California.

Traffic was unusually light on the freeway, and before he knew it, the security gates to Cedric's cottage were opening to allow the BMW entry. Cedric sped up the drive and parked the car in the underground garage next to his hunter green Tahoe.

"Hungry?" he asked.

Declan thought about it and realized that he was. He and Robin had gone back to bed after having only bagels and coffee that morning, and he hadn't eaten on the plane. "I could probably eat a bite."

Cedric grinned. "Well, don't get your hopes high because Mariah has the weekend off." He grabbed Declan's bag from the back and headed up the stairs that led to the interior. "But I make one hell of a turkey-and-cheese sandwich."

Barely suppressing a groan, Declan followed him. "Turkey? Maybe we should call out for a pizza?"

"We can do that. Tell you what, why don't you go jump in the hot tub, and I'll call for the pizza. You look wiped, lad."

"Yeah, that I am." Declan headed up the curving wrought-iron banistered stairs toward the guest wing. "The hot tub sounds grand. A dip in the pool even better. Just remember, though, no friggin' anchovies."

Cedric grinned up at him, his mystical eyes glowing in the light of the Waterford chandelier. "Wimp."

"Fuck you," Declan said sweetly. "Meet you out at the hot tub in five."

But when he stepped out on the terrace in his swim trunks a few moments later, the hot tub was empty, and so was the pool. Complete darkness had fallen, and the only light that illuminated the deck was from a few strands of tiny crystal lights strung on the pool house and the eerie blue-green glow of submerged lights in the pool's depths. The water looked inviting, and doing several laps in the pool would be just the antidote to his weekend of sloth. But his muscles ached from the six-hour flight, so he decided to sit in the hot tub for a few minutes first.

He hit the switch on the wall of the pool house and the water in the hot tub began to churn. Lowering himself into the steaming bubbles, he sighed as the heat enclosed him. Good God, this felt good! He stretched his legs, leaned back, and gazed up at the star-studded sky, unusually clear for Southern California. A bat fluttered past, emitting high-pitched squeaks, and disappeared behind the pool house. From somewhere down the beach, soft jazz floated on the evening air. Oh, Christ . . . this was the life. What more could a man want? Besides his woman next to him to enjoy it, of course. What was Robin doing right now? His flight had arrived about six-thirty. It must be almost eight by now. That meant it was eleven in New York. She was probably in bed. Her morning on the set would begin early. *Oh, Robin, girl, I miss you already . . .*

Footsteps padded on the pool deck, and Declan sensed Cedric getting into the hot tub. He couldn't bring himself to open his eyes, but managed to murmur, "You order the pizza?"

Cedric didn't answer. Slowly, Declan opened his eyes and glanced to his left. His friend was a mere shadow just a couple of feet away.

"Ced? You order the pizza?"

"Not yet," Cedric said. "I thought maybe we'd like to unwind a bit first. I brought you a glass of wine, though." He extended a goblet. "Here."

"Lovely, thanks." Declan took it from him and sipped the crisp chardonnay. "Mmm . . . good." He closed his eyes again. "Christ, I'm tired."

"So, how was Robin?" Cedric asked.

Declan smiled. "Oh, she was grand. Grand, indeed."

Cedric stretched out his legs, accidently brushing a foot against Declan's. "Sorry. Was she, now? Grand, huh?"

"Ahhh, yeh. It was that great having a few days with her." Declan shifted slightly to give Cedric more room.

They fell silent, and in the interval, there was just the sound of the churning water and the low hum of the hot tub accompanied by the muted roar of the ocean in the distance. Declan allowed his mind to drift, thinking over his good fortune, a dynamite up-and-coming career, a gorgeous wife, good friends. It was just too good to be true.

"Don't fall asleep now," Cedric said, bringing him back to the present. "I wouldn't want you drowning on me."

Declan grinned and opened his eyes. "Death is the very last thing on my mind." Had it grown lighter out here, or was Cedric closer than he'd been a minute before? He could certainly see him better. His friend was gazing at him with his odd eyes, which seemed even more unusual than ever in the starlight. They seemed to be glowing, reflecting the light back to the sky.

Suddenly Declan felt the hairs rise on the back of his neck, and he was overcome with a sudden urgency to get out of the hot tub—away from Cedric. But that was bloody stupid. Cedric was his friend. Had been his friend since he was a wee lad. Except for that one summer. But that was best left in the past.

Still, Declan couldn't shake this oppressive feeling that had come over him. He couldn't even figure out what it was made up of. Part fear, definitely. Part foreboding. But something else, too. Something he couldn't identify. Or didn't *want* to identify.

Declan stood abruptly and climbed out of the hot tub.

"Where are you going?" Cedric asked.

"Into the pool. Hey, why don't you go order that pizza?" Declan didn't wait for an answer, but strode across the deck and dived into the deep end of the pool.

He swam furiously the length of the Olympic-size pool, dived into a somersault, and swam back. After six laps, he stood up in the shallow end and slicked his hair back from his face, his heart hammering with exertion.

He heard movement behind him, the soft splash of water. Not movement made by someone swimming, but by someone wading toward him. His gut tightened and his heart lurched. He couldn't bring himself to turn, even when he felt the warmth of another human body radiating toward him.

He tried to speak, but his vocal cords were paralyzed. The warm body stopped just behind him, only inches away. Declan's heart had tripped into overdrive. Still, he couldn't turn. Couldn't make himself move even though he knew—somehow, he knew—he stood at a crossroads. He could turn one way, toward Robin and what the world would refer to as normality; he could do that by moving now. Heading toward the side of the pool, climbing out and going into that house and getting his things and leave this place forever. Or he could stand still, like he was doing, and wait for the inevitable. Take the other road and follow it . . . to hell, if may be.

Agonizing seconds passed before two incredibly warm hands snaked around him, fingertips touching his abdomen. Soft, feathery caresses, skimming against his flesh, sending goose pimples prickling his arms, legs, stomach. Declan drew in a sharp breath, and his respiration became staggered, ragged. The hands flattened on his chest, pressing. Almost against his will, Declan leaned back. He felt Cedric's body fit against him, and he realized his friend was nude. He felt Cedric's hot breath near his right ear. Staggered like his own. Cedric's hands began to move again, caressing his chest and stomach in slow, sensuous circles, moving lower. Against his buttocks, Declan felt Cedric's rigid member, pressing gently. And to his horror, he felt his own penis stir and harden.

And still, he couldn't move, couldn't speak. Couldn't protest. Cedric's hands moved down past the waistband of Declan's swim trunks, his right one moving unerringly to his cock, rock-hard now, straining against the cotton fabric.

Declan's breath exploded from him and he closed his eyes as cascading waves of pleasure rocked through him. He groaned, and when he finally found his voice, it came out hoarse. "Oh, Christ, Cedric! What are you doing to me, man?"

Cedric's voice was smooth as silk, and his Irish accent thicker than ever when he answered, "*You* know."

Isn't that Nicolas Cage chatting with Robert Duvall over by the steamed shrimp buffet?

Amy took a sip of wine and tried not to stare. Yeah, that's who it was, all right. *Jeez, Cedric must know every celebrity in Hollywood.* Everywhere she turned at this party, she saw famous faces. A few minutes earlier, she'd been chatting with Tom Hanks and Halle Berry. Of course, they'd hadn't a clue who she was. Not until Cedric came to the rescue and introduced her as "Dec's gorgeous wife, Robin." Apparently, the guests who'd come to Cedric's annual Christmas Eve party weren't big daytime television fans. The first three times someone asked what she did for a living, she'd replied with the truth. "I'm an actress on the daytime drama, *South Riding.*" And in each case, a strange phenomenon had occurred. Smiles became forced, and eyes began to dart around the room, presumably in search of more interesting prey. The fourth time someone asked what she "did," Amy decided to experiment.

"I'm Declan Blair's wife, Robin," she replied with a bright—hopefully not *too* manufactured—smile.

And lo and behold, she was actually able to hold on to someone's attention for more than two minutes. Apparently, that old Hollywood stereotype about superficial people with plastic smiles and no heart was based on truth. *Why on earth is Declan so enamored of this place?* It seemed completely alien to his warm, down-to-earth personality.

She'd had about all she could take of Hollywood—and its stars—tonight. It was after midnight, and a headache was starting to throb at her temples. Where *was* Dec, anyway? Would it be terribly rude if the two of them slipped away to their room? After all, Cedric was the host, not Declan. They were guests in his home, but did that mean they had to stay up until everyone had left? God *knew* when that would be. Last night—or rather, this morning— they'd stayed at a Beverly Hills party hosted by the president of Columbia Pictures until almost three. In fact, in the two days she'd been in California, she'd barely had more than five minutes alone with her husband. For God's sake, they hadn't even had a chance to make love!

She placed her wine goblet down on the tray of a passing waiter and began to thread her way through the clumps of glamorous guests. If an extraterrestrial dropped in on this party, it would believe the entire human race was made up of supermodels—or else, it had dropped onto the set of the average soap opera. Her gaze scanned the room. Where *was* that man of hers?

As she started past a circle of tuxedo-clad men, a hand reached out and encircled her bare arm.

"Excuse me, gentlemen." Cedric smiled at his friends. "I must have a moment with this beautiful young woman." Stepping away from them, he took Amy's other hand, enclosing them both in his warm grasp. His unusual gray-brown eyes glowed as he smiled down at her. "Robin, love, have I told you how *brilliant* you look in that gold dress?"

Amy smiled up at her handsome host. "Actually, I think you *have* mentioned it, Cedric, but thank you."

She'd just met Cedric the day before, but he had such a charismatic personality that she felt like she'd known him for years. And God! Was he ever good-looking! Hard to believe he was a screenwriter and not an actor. With his tall, lean Clint Eastwood–like body and those killer eyes, he'd be a cinematographer's wet dream. And to think, Declan had said he was not only single, but didn't even have a girlfriend. Too bad she didn't know anyone to fix him up with.

Cedric scanned her, his eyes moving lazily down the length of her body. Amy felt herself blushing. *Was he flirting with her?*

"Not many blonds can carry off that color, but I must say, it looks grand on you."

"Well, thanks." She shifted uneasily, wishing she had the nerve to pull her hands out of his. His eyes really *were* disconcerting. It was almost as if he were analyzing her, peeling her psyche apart, layer by layer. And that made her *very* uncomfortable.

Still, she was glad he approved of her appearance. She'd ordered the strapless gold satin gown from Valentino, and it had cost her nearly a month's paycheck. Horribly extravagant, she knew, but Declan had warned her that they would be attending some "top-line schmoozefests," and he wanted to make sure she wore something spectacular. Not that everybody here was dressed to the nines. One young producer whom Declan had assured her had a lot of "heat" going for him was wearing baggy shorts slung down to his butt crack, Birkenstocks with red socks, and a poinsettia-decked Tommy Bahama shirt over an ancient Rusted Root T-shirt. Over by the largely ignored dessert buffet stood a prepubescent pop tart who had no earthly right to be out this late on Christmas Eve, wearing a black leather jumpsuit zipped down just enough to reveal an obviously manufactured cleavage. And Amy had seen several women scantily clad in red bikinis trimmed with white fur, high heels, and Santa hats—supposedly Hollywood's nod to the holidays.

A chamber orchestra at one end of the massive reception hall took their seats and began to play Celtic Christmas music. Cedric moved closer, lifting his voice over it to ask, "So, Robin? Are you enjoying yourself here in La-La Land?"

Amy nodded, still unnerved by his intense scrutiny. She took a step backward, drawing her hands out of his. He wasn't flirting at all, she realized. He was dissecting her with those odd flintlike eyes.

"Oh, sure." *Liar, liar, pants on fire.* "But I feel like I'm getting a bit of a headache. I think I'm going to call it a night soon. Have you seen Declan?"

Although the smile remained on his face, there was a subtle change to his expression. Had his eyes gone a degree cooler? "Ah, Robin, lass, go on to bed if you're not feeling well. But don't be dragging Dec along with you."

"You're not serious, are you?" Amy said, unsure if he was teasing her. "You know, we're still pretty much newlyweds, and well . . . we haven't been . . . you know . . . together since Thanksgiving." She felt her face growing hot. Dear God, what had possessed her to admit something so personal to a near stranger? "So, it would be nice to have some time alone with him."

Cedric shrugged and took a sip of his whiskey. "Understandable, of course. It's just that there's some real players at this party, and Dec needs to make himself available to anyone who wants to meet him. This is much more than a social event, love. It's business for people like me and Dec. You understand that, don't you? And you wouldn't want to do anything to interfere with his career, would you, now?"

She felt the first twinge of anger rippling through her but tried to hide it with a cool smile. "Of course not, Cedric. But if it's all the same to you, I think I'll find my husband and excuse myself. Whether he wants to come with me or not is up to him."

Like his chameleon eyes, Cedric's personality underwent a sudden change. His handsome face lit up in a beguiling smile that washed over her like liquid sunshine. He pulled her close in a warm hug. "Ah, love, forgive me. I get so wrapped up in the business of schmoozing, I forget what's important. You're absolutely right. Go find your man and get out of here. I'll have one of my staff send up a bottle of my best wine from the cellar."

Amy hugged him back and murmured her thanks. She turned and maneuvered through the crowd, eyes searching for Declan's blond head. A tuxedo-clad waiter materialized in front of her, offering a tray of stuffed mushroom caps. She declined with a smile and moved on.

She found Declan with Wolfgang Petersen in a corner near the sparkling eighteen-foot Christmas tree. He smiled as she joined them and, interrupting their conversation, introduced her to the director of *Das Boot* and *The Perfect Storm*. After a cordial greeting, Petersen turned back to Declan, and they resumed talking about the director's latest film. Amy smiled and tried not to look too bored as she waited for the right moment to draw Dec away. It finally came when Drew Barrymore sidled up to the director and attracted his attention. He turned from Declan and gave her a warm hug.

Amy placed a hand on Declan's arm, and whispered, "Honey, I'm getting a headache, so I'm going upstairs."

A concerned look crossed his face. "Oh, love, I'm sorry." He brushed his lips against her forehead. "Poor girl. I've run you ragged, haven't I?"

Amy smiled, relishing the warmth she found in his embrace. "It's okay. We'll take it easy tomorrow." She reached up and touched a finger to his lips. "I'll take some Tylenol and wait up for you, okay?"

He kissed the pads of her fingers. "Only if you want to."

"I do."

He squeezed her hand. "I'll try not to be too long."

Amy did as promised. She took two Tylenol and soaked in the jetted tub for a half hour, and thankfully, the headache went away. The wine Cedric had sent up cooled in an ice bucket on a side table. She lit candles around the bed and on the dresser. Finally, propping herself on two plump pillows, she opened the new Nora Roberts novel. Thank God Robin had turned her on to this genre. She would never have discovered romance if not for her. But in this novel, the love scenes were so steamy, she found herself growing increasingly frustrated at Declan's absence. At two-thirty, she closed the book. *Where is Declan?*

Sighing, she blew out the candles, turned off the light, and fell into an exhausted, jet-lagged sleep.

Even in her sleep, she felt the weight on the king-size bed shift, and deep in her subconscious, she knew Declan had finally joined her. She smiled, reaching out instinctively for him. He was way over on the other side of the bed, so far that even stretching out a leg, she couldn't touch him. Gradually, she began to fight her way up through the levels of consciousness.

"Declan . . . honey?" she murmured, scooting across the baby-soft Egyptian cotton sheets to find him.

No response. He lay on his side, his back facing her. Surely he couldn't be asleep already.

"Babe?" She tucked her body up against his, curling around him like an affectionate cat. "I stayed awake as long as I could."

His heat enveloped her. God, she was horny! He wore only a pair of white briefs. His back was broad and delightfully warm. She pressed against his firm buttocks, breathing in his musky male fragrance. Her lips traveled up his shoulder to his neck. With her left hand, she brushed away strands of silky blond hair from his nape, nibbling at her favorite spot. He wore his hair longer these days. And the longer it got, the more it curled naturally. She liked it this way. Made him even sexier.

He gave a soft groan as she continued kissing his neck, slipping her hands around him to caress his hair-roughened chest.

"Sweetie, you too tired?"

He didn't answer, but Amy felt his bottom push subtly against her pelvis, so she took that as a "no." She smiled, cupping herself around him and allowing the palms of her hands to slide down his muscled chest to his flat stomach.

"Oh, baby, I've missed you so much," she whispered. "I want to make love to you so bad."

Her hands slipped down to his crotch. He was erect, ready for her. She smiled, stroking him through the cotton of his briefs. A soft moan escaped him. Fully awake now, she got to her knees and nudged him over onto his back. Deftly, she slid his briefs off his hips, down his smooth muscled thighs, and tossed them over the side of the bed.

"Mmmm . . . Dec, darling," she murmured. "I can't wait to taste you."

She took him into her mouth. He groaned softly, arching his back. Taking her time with him, she tasted and teased. Taunted and tormented. And when she knew he was within seconds from exploding, she climbed astride him, taking the length of him inside her. She rode him slowly. Sensuously. God, he felt so good. So big and deliciously full inside her. Their tempo quickened, and she was close, so close.

"*Oh, God, Declan!*" she cried out, teetering at the edge.

His hands were clasped around her waist, holding her, guiding her. At the sound of her excited cry, his eyes opened, and in the light of daybreak, she saw his dark pupils, glazed with arousal. She held his gaze as she rode him, watched as the misty look faded from his eyes, and saw something flicker on his face. Something she couldn't identify. But whatever it was, it didn't fit with the moment. No matter. She was almost there, almost . . .

Something changed. At first, she wasn't sure what it was. But something was wrong. And she . . . oh, God . . . she was so . . . *so* close. She grinded against him, hoping she was imagining it. But no. She wasn't. He was no longer filling her. Like a balloon losing its air, he was slipping away.

She slumped against him, breathless and frustrated. For a long moment, she lay still, heart thudding. The burning at her core raged fiercely, unrelieved, making her chew her bottom lip in agony. Beneath her palm, she felt Declan's heart pounding. *What happened?*

Finally, she managed the strength to roll off him. She dropped onto her back and stared up at the vaulted ceiling, visible now in the light of dawn. Beside her, Declan lay in the position in which she'd left him. Except for the sound of his labored breathing, he was silent. Questions flashed through Amy's mind, all beginning with "what happened?" But she knew she couldn't ask. She knew what happened. The real question was "why?"

Finally, Declan spoke, "I'm sorry, love."

Only three words, but they came out so forlorn that Amy could only turn on her side, place a gentle palm on his chest, and kiss his damp neck. "It's okay," she whispered. "It happens."

She realized it *was* okay. The fire inside her had dissipated to a mere ember. She could live without an orgasm. This happened to couples all the time, didn't it? Just because it had never happened before didn't mean anything. Probably Declan had had too much to drink at the party. Everybody knew too much alcohol could cause impotence. Of course, it had never stopped him before, but there was a first time for everything. And another thing, he hadn't had much sleep in the two days she'd been here. Maybe that was the problem.

But why had he become aroused in the first place? She hadn't imagined that erection. She hadn't imagined how good he'd felt inside her until he'd lost it. *Why?* Had she done something to turn him off? And if so, what had it been?

As if he read her mind, he spoke, "It's not you." His voice was rough with emotion. "I don't want you to think that. It's all me. I'm not feeling myself these days."

Amy propped her chin on her hand, her elbow resting on the mattress. "Want to talk about it, Dec? What's bothering you?"

Dawn washed the bedroom in muted tones of gray, but she could see his face clearly as he stared up at the ceiling. Not only did he look fatigued, he wore an expression Amy thought looked almost haunted. *God, what is going on with him?*

"Honey, is it your career? Has something gone wrong?"

He finally looked at her, and the sadness in his eyes alarmed her.

"Tell me, Declan. What's wrong?"

He shook his head. "It's not my career. It's just that I'm trying to work through some personal things. I can't really talk about it right now."

Amy caught her breath as a cold feeling of dread curled in her stomach. "Is it another woman, Dec?" she asked softly, heart accelerating. "Have you met someone else?"

He groaned and drew her close, cradling her head against his shoulder. "*No!* Don't say that, Robin. You're the only woman in the world for me. You've *got* to know that, love."

Amy's heartbeat resumed its normal rhythm. She placed a gentle kiss against his neck. "Then whatever it is, we'll work through it. When you're ready to talk, I'll be ready to listen."

"I know you will."

He fell silent, and neither of them spoke for a long time. Outside the high-transomed windows, the first birds began to chirp their morning songs. It was Christmas Day. Amy's eyelids closed, and she began to drift away. Suddenly Declan turned on his side, his hand sliding under her satin chemise to cup her breast. Immediately the unquenched furnace inside her roared back to life. She drew in a sharp breath as his hand slid down her belly, questing between her parted legs, fingers exploring.

"You're still wet," Declan whispered. "My cock might not be working, but there are other things I can do."

Amy released a long, shuddering breath, giving herself up to his caresses. "Oh, yes, Dec. *Yes!*"

"I'm sorry I can't go to Williamsburg with you," Declan said.

Amy shrugged and glanced out at the traffic whizzing by on both sides of them on the freeway. Declan was still getting used to driving in America, and he was overly cautious in his shiny new gold BMW Z8 convertible—a car identical to Cedric's except for the color. Amy couldn't help but be amused by the competition between the two Irishmen. She was surprised Declan hadn't gone ahead and bought a beach house at Malibu so he could have a little "cottage" like Cedric's. It was a good-natured rivalry—two boyhood friends making it big in Hollywood. But of course, Declan would never admit there was any such thing as competition between them. In some ways, Dec was so sweetly innocent about life. That was one of the reasons she loved him.

Up ahead, a green directional sign showed they were approaching the airport exit. Amy's stomach tightened. It was a gray, smoggy day in Los Angeles—the kind that made, or *should* make, one question the sanity of living here. Amy wasn't sad to be leaving the cold-hearted City of Angels, but leaving Declan was another story. When they were together, she never—or rarely—thought of Paul. And she was convinced that if they could just have a normal married life, she could get beyond this mad, crazy *thing* she had for Paul. He could go ahead and marry his witch of a girlfriend, and although she could never approve of it, at least, she could live with it. If only she and Declan could be together all the time.

Soon, though. That would happen soon. In less than three months. Amy sighed as Declan pulled onto the exit ramp. Of course, that meant she'd be moving out here permanently. She already hated this place. Hated it with a vengeance. Could she ever be happy here? Even with Declan? Maybe. If they didn't have to live in the immediate Los Angeles area.

On Christmas Day, they'd driven up to Big Sur, staying in a quaint bed-and-breakfast decorated with turn-of-the-century antiques. It had been the ultimate romantic getaway with a stone fireplace in their room and a queen-size lace-canopied bed. And in that bed, there had been no problem with impotence. Just that one rather odd moment that Amy had decided to push from her thoughts whenever it threatened to intrude. Declan had insisted on using a condom even though he knew she was on the pill. When she'd asked why, he'd murmured something about being extracautious, that now would be a horrible time to bring a child into the world. And she'd allowed her suspicions to be pushed to the recesses of her brain as Declan made love to her like he had in the past.

As they neared the terminal, he reached over and grasped her hand. "You sure you're not mad about Williamsburg, love? It's just that I've got that *Premiere* interview scheduled. And it really wouldn't look good if I didn't make Sheridan's New Year's Eve party."

"I said I understood, Dec. Forget it. No big deal."

"Besides, your da hates my guts. Why cause trouble?"

"Yeah, no point in that. I'm just wishing I hadn't said I would be there for New Year's. But it's been months since I've seen Mom and Dad, and you know how they get when they think I'm ignoring them. I'm just glad Paul and the Dragon Lady won't be there."

Declan chuckled. "Do you know that your face looks like a little thunder-cloud when you mention her?"

"Yeah, well . . . I don't like her."

Declan gave a mock gasp. "Really? I would never have guessed." Signaling, he moved into the lane for short-term parking.

"You can just drop me off," Amy said. "My flight will be boarding soon."

He glanced at her. "You're sure?" Without waiting for her response, he moved back into the terminal drop-off lane.

Amy tried to hide her surprise. She hadn't really expected him to take her up on the offer. Was he in *that* much of a hurry to get rid of her? "No, sure. It's fine."

Declan shrugged. "I did mention I might join Cedric and some of the lads at the Marmont for drinks later."

"Well, we wouldn't want to disappoint Cedric, would we?" Too late, she realized how sarcastic she'd sounded.

He looked at her, eyes troubled. "I honestly don't mind coming in and waiting with you."

Don't mind? Hardly the romantic response she'd hope to get from a husband who wouldn't be seeing her again for three months. *What is Hollywood doing to Declan?* It wasn't just his hairstyle and wardrobe that had changed. He didn't even talk like Dec anymore, lacing his vocabulary with words like "heat" and "schmoozefest" and "B.O." which he'd had to explain was *not* body odor but box office.

"No, it's okay. We're already in the drop-off lane. And like I said, I'll be boarding soon."

Declan double-parked next to a Lexus at the TWA curbside, and got out of the car. By the time Amy joined him, her luggage was already on the curb.

He *was* anxious to get rid of her!

But when he took her into his arms and gave her a lingering kiss, she realized she was imagining things. It was the holidays, and the airport was crazy. He was simply anxious to get her on her way so he could get out of the traffic.

He drew away and gazed at her, smiling. "The next time I pick you up here, you'll be coming to stay."

"Yes." Amy smiled. "Just do me a favor, sweetie. Stay with Cedric until I get here. I want to help pick out our house." Somewhere as far as possible from LA but within a reasonable commute. Maybe Encino or Studio City.

His face sobered. "You can count on it, love." He kissed her again and she turned to go. "Robin!" His hands tightened on her shoulders.

"Yes?" She stared at him. He wore an odd look, a mixture of desperation and something else. Pain? Guilt, maybe? Again, she felt a flicker of disquiet settling inside her. Their conversation after his failed lovemaking attempt came back to her. He swore there was no other woman, so what was eating at him? And what about the condoms? Despite his denials, was he cheating on her? "Dec, what *is* it?"

"I love you," he said, his voice roughening. "You know that, don't you? I *do* love you."

She forced a smile, even though a cold dread was working its way through her soul. "You sound like you're trying to convince yourself of that."

He groaned and crushed her against him, his mouth finding hers. He kissed her frantically, and even in that, she sensed desperation. Finally, he released her. "I love you," he said earnestly, eyes holding hers. "Don't ever forget that."

"I love you, too, Dec," she said, biting her trembling bottom lip to hold back tears. "I'll see you in March, okay?"

He nodded soberly. "In March."

She kissed him again, grabbed the pull handle of her luggage, and walked toward the automatic doors. When she looked back a moment later, Declan was already gone.

24

God, this party was as dull as all the ones in Hollywood. Or was it *her*? Unlike Robin, Amy had never been a party person. And that hadn't changed with the donning of Robin's identity. She hated . . . no, *detested* . . . the small talk, the drunken laughter, the bullshit. And it wasn't that she was antisocial, nor any longer shy as she'd been in her teens and through college. As long as she was one-on-one with another person, she was fine. But put more than a few people in the room, and she became the introverted Amy Shiley again. Only problem was, it was Amy Shiley *inside* the svelte body of an attractive, well-known actress. Well-known by soap standards, she amended. That made it doubly hard to play the part of the social butterfly.

A tuxedo-clad waiter passed with a tray of champagne, and Amy reached out for a glass. She was going past her usual limit, but tonight, she didn't care. If alcohol was what it was going to take to get her through this endless New Year's Eve, then so be it.

Sipping her champagne, she made her way through the ocean of guests. Would it be possible to slip away completely? What she wouldn't give to be able to go up to her room and sink into the jetted tub for a long soak. But Tammy and Michael would freak. She wasn't a teenager any longer who could get away with stuff like that. Even Robin would've thought twice before ducking out of a party hosted by her parents that was, after all, part New Year's Eve celebration and partly in honor of their daughter's homecoming. They'd made it perfectly clear that her presence at the party would be the star attraction. Oh, how they both loved having a celebrity daughter, even if she was only known by daytime TV standards.

It was only two hours into the party, and Amy was already exhausted from playing the part of soap star, answering endless questions from curious socialites and fending off flirtatious advances by aging politicians and businessmen. She sighed. Still almost two hours until midnight. How was she ever going to make it?

Was Declan enjoying his party at the other end of the country? No. She'd forgotten it was still early in California. He was probably just now getting ready for it. Some marriage they had! Separated by three thousand miles, living separate lives. God, it sucked. Big-time. But not for much longer, thank God. She wasn't anxious to move to the West Coast, but if it meant having a normal marriage, she was all for it.

Amy passed by a group of women gathered around Tammy. Robin's mother looked stunning in a floor-length cranberry dress with a front side slit to the knee. Her hair had been freshly blonded the day before and gleamed like spun honey under the lights. To Amy, she looked even more beautiful than she had when they'd first met seven years ago. Robin had certainly inherited some great genes. Tammy had to be pretty close to fifty, yet her face was as unlined as that of a twenty-year-old. And her body was trim and athletic, thanks to the daily tennis she played at the country club. Of course, having plenty of money also helped. It might not buy you the fountain of youth, but it sure the hell allowed you to rent it for a while.

"Robin!" Tammy called out, her face lighting up in a brilliant smile. "Come here, dear. I have someone I want you to meet."

There was no escape. Plastering a smile on her face, Amy joined the group of women, and for the next twenty minutes, she was forced to hold court and "tell all" about the exciting life of a soap opera queen. They simply refused to believe that her life was not all that exciting, so she finally resorted to fictionalizing some of the gossip she'd heard from Betty, the makeup lady, who had a habit of embellishing facts. Finally, though, she ran out of stories and was just about to excuse herself when Tammy grabbed her arm.

"Did I tell you that Robin is moving to Los Angeles in March? To join her husband. You know she's married to that darling Irish actor, Declan Blair, don't you?"

A chorus of excited squeals erupted from Tammy's friends.

"Oh, my Lord!" gushed an overweight brunette, fanning herself with a pudgy diamond ring-decked hand. "He is simply *gorgeous*! I saw him in *People* magazine last week, and I almost died. *He's* your husband, Robin?"

"What I want to know is . . . what are you doing *here*?" a thin redhead asked, her crimson lips pursed. "If *I* were married to Declan Blair, I wouldn't let him out of my sight! With looks like that, he's probably got to beat women off with a stick!"

Amy started to respond with a joke, but a slurred voice behind her interrupted. "Declan Blair? *Women* aren't his problem."

Amy turned to see Mike standing behind her, a half-empty glass of scotch in his hand. He was grinning, his face flushed, eyes bloodshot. A chill seeped through her along with a eerie feeling of *déjà vu*. For a moment, it wasn't Mike she saw, but her own father, staggering around the trailer, a drink in hand.

She'd never seen Mike drunk before, and it made her feel ill. This was supposed to be the perfect family. It had seemed that way back when Robin was alive. Could she have been wrong? She'd given up everything to be a part of this wholesome American family. Traded her soul for it. But now, looking at Mike, she saw he was no better than her own father. Only richer, wearing a white collar instead of blue.

Revolted by the stench of liquor wafting toward her, Amy turned away. Screw New Year's! She was going to her room. But Mike clamped a sweaty hand on her shoulder and turned her around to peer blearily into her eyes.

He gave a drunken laugh. "You know what I mean, don't you, Cupcake? Why don't you admit the truth to all these lovely ladies, huh? Your marriage to that mick is a sham. Everybody knows Declan Blair is as fairy as they come."

Amy felt the blood drain from her face. Beside her, she heard one of the women gasp. Amy stared at her father. "*What did you say?*"

His upper lip curled. "You heard me. He's queer. A closet queen. A nancy boy. Whatever you want to call it, Cupcake. Your *husband* is queerer than a two-dollar bill." He stared at her, a challenging light in his blue eyes.

The edges of her vision blurred as the room seemed to close in around her. The noise intensified—conversation of those not in their immediate circle rose in a blaring cacophony, grating on her brain. The overpowering stench of expensive perfume emanating from Tammy's society friends seemed like an assault. But through it all, a thought of pure, crystal clarity bloomed in Amy's mind. *Mike isn't drunk at all*. He was faking it to give himself an excuse for making such an outrageous comment. But then, that would mean he was either crazy or just downright evil.

Tammy stepped between them, eyes sparkling with anger. "Michael, that will be enough! I think you'd better go upstairs and sleep it off."

Amy was still reeling from Michael's outlandish remark, but when Tammy spoke, something even more incredible happened. Mike's eyes filled with tears. He reached out a quivering hand toward Amy.

"I'm sorry," he blubbered as Tammy determinedly drew him away, her face cold as a mask carved from ice. "I'm sorry, Cupcake! You've got to believe that. I'm sorry . . . so sorry . . ."

Amy felt the pitying eyes of Tammy's friends upon her. Flushing, she murmured her excuses and walked away from them. She kept walking until she reached the swinging kitchen door, and then left the house through the mudroom. Stepping out onto the stone walkway that led to the covered pool, she stood under a clear starlit December sky, shivering in her black taffeta gown. But at least, out here in the cold, she could breathe.

Wind chimes tinkled in a gust of icy wind, reminding Amy of the summers spent out here. Especially that first summer with Robin. They'd both been so young and carefree then. Jeff, who'd already returned to Harvard after the Christmas break, had taught her to swim that summer. It seemed like several lifetimes ago.

Amy bit down on her bottom lip as a shaft of pain speared through her midsection. Michael *had* been drunk. There was no other explanation for the outrageous, horrible, completely untrue things he'd said about Declan. She knew Mike didn't like him. He'd made that obvious from the start. But the intensity of that dislike ran much deeper than she'd ever expected.

Declan, gay! Absolutely ludicrous. He was the most virile, red-blooded, enthusiastically heterosexual man she'd ever met. What in the world had put such an idiotic idea in Mike Mulcahey's brain?

Amy waited until the FASTEN SEAT BELT light went off before reaching for her carry-on, tucked under the seat in front of her. She pulled out the diary covered in pink Victorian-flowered fabric and, opening the first page, read the feminine scrawl in black ink.

> *To my darling daughter, Robin. I'm so sorry I had to cancel our lunch date. Please forgive me. I promise I'll make it up to you. Happy 13th Birthday, Darling. Love, Mom.*

After she'd gone to Robin's room on New Year's Eve, a strange compulsion—maybe the result of bringing in the New Year with a bunch of strangers—had made Amy seek out the cedar box that held Robin's journals. It was locked as it had been when she'd first found it the day she'd unpacked it in the dorm. But this time, she was determined to find the key. It was time for Robin to give up her secrets. Countless times, Amy remembered finding her scribbling frantically in her notebook, her expressive face lost in thought. More often than not, Amy's appearance had caused her to stop writing and lock the notebook away in the cedar box. Amy remembered how hurt she'd felt when that happened. They were best friends, closer than sisters. Why did she act so furtive about the notebooks? Was she afraid that Amy was going to read over her shoulder? Hadn't she trusted her enough to know that she'd never do something like that?

But now, the notebooks were hers. She'd found the key in Robin's jewelry box. And she knew in her heart that Robin wanted her to read them. Wanted her to know who the real Robin Mulcahey had been. Numerous times throughout the last few years, Amy had started to read them, but in the words, she could hear Robin's engaging voice, and the pain had been so bad, she hadn't been able to keep reading. Now, she knew she had to force herself to do it. It was almost as if Robin's spirit was urging her to do so.

As the 727 flew toward New York City, she opened the diary to the first page and began to read Robin's looping handwriting in peacock blue ink.

March 19, 1991—Mommy bought this diary for me for my 13th birthday. Big stinking deal! She thinks buying me a present will make up for her changing her mind about lunch. She'd promised it would be just the two of us. She'd even made reservations at the Trellis, and then we were going to spend the afternoon shopping on Duke of Gloucester Street. But no!!! She gets a phone call from this so-called client who wants to see a house down on the James Fucking River, and all her plans with me go right out the window! Typical. She's never had time for me. Why should things change now that I'm thirteen? But at least I have Daddy. He took me shopping at the Gap outlet, and bought me the coolest denim miniskirt. It's so rad! I also got a white T-shirt to wear with it, and the coolest little anklets that go perfectly with my funky Mary Janes with the chunky heels. Daddy says I look so hot in my new outfit. Well, he didn't say that, exactly. More like, 'You're turning into quite a beautiful young woman, Robin.' Oh, yeah. I forgot. He also got me a new nightie. It is soooo rad. And you'll never believe where we found it. Victoria's Secret. Oh, it was priceless, seeing Daddy in that store. His face was all red as I picked up panties and bras just to psych him out. Well, I'm finally starting to get boobs now, so I'll have to wear a bra soon. Anyway, he bought me a white knit chemise with tiny red hearts all over it. It was on the clearance rack, a leftover from Valentine's Day, but that's okay. Mommy was still gone when we got home. There was a note saying she had some evening showings and wouldn't be home until late. Really pissed me off because I thought we could at least all go out for dinner as a family. But it was just me, Daddy, Paul, and Jeff. We went out to The Library for gyros. Some birthday dinner, huh? Oh. Gotta go. Daddy is coming in to say good night. At least I have one parent who cares about me.

Amy closed the diary. She couldn't read more just now. It was the second time she'd read this entry, and like last night in Robin's room, it had brought her to tears. She'd so clearly heard Robin's voice. It may have been her thirteen-year-old voice, but it was her. And God, she missed her. Poor thing, she'd sounded so unhappy. Amy was finally beginning to understand some of her animosity toward Tammy. It sounded like Robin had felt terribly neglected by her mother.

A flight attendant made her way down the aisle, gathering empty glasses and trash. She smiled in recognition when her eyes met Amy's. "I'm a big fan of *South Riding*," she said, pausing at her side. "I even tape it when I'm flying."

Amy smiled, but before she could respond, the flight attendant murmured a Happy New Year, and moved on. Relief washed through her. She didn't really feel like chatting right now. Not when her thoughts and heart were so full of Robin. She reached under the seat in front of her and drew out her purse. A moment later, she was holding a photograph in her hands—one taken just after she and Robin had moved into the sorority house the beginning of their sophomore year. Two blond girls smiled into the camera, arms wrapped around each other. Everyone had said they looked like sisters, and she could see why. They'd been so happy on that late-summer day. So young and alive, with their whole lives in front of them. And yet, just five months later, Robin was gone.

Amy focused on her own face—her *former* face. She saw a pretty girl, maybe not as pretty as Robin, but special in her own right. Her heart twinged. That face was gone forever. What would she look like now if she hadn't decided to become her best friend? What would that face look like at twenty-seven?

She was still mulling over it when the plane landed at JFK. And that's when the idea hit her.

She knew someone who could answer that question.

A disturbing dream woke Amy in the pewter winter light of dawn. She lay stiffly, staring up at the ornate gold etchings on the ceiling fan as it emerged from the darkness. The dream was still fresh in her mind. It had been vivid, so real that she could almost smell the lingering scent of Robin's favorite citrus cologne.

In the dream, they were sitting side by side in front of a long makeup counter. The mirror facing them was circled by Hollywood-style lights. It was almost as if the two of them were backstage at a beauty pageant. Robin gazed into the mirror, dabbing on mascara and talking a mile a minute. She had a date with Jason, she was saying, but first she had to complete the talent competition. Although she was due onstage in two minutes, she had no idea what she was going to do for her talent. "Do Lady Macbeth," Amy suggested, turning to the mirror to apply her lipstick. She froze, staring at the mirror as icy fear shot through her.

She had no reflection.

She woke with a start, heart thundering, breathing shallow. In her dream, Robin hadn't looked the way she had before she died. She was older, the age Amy was now. In fact, she'd looked exactly like Amy. They could've been twins. The only difference was that Robin had a reflection, and Amy didn't. Even an amateur shrink could figure that one out.

Amy reached for the phone on her bedside table, her hand trembling. She punched out the number from memory, and after five rings, the phone was picked up. "Hello," a sleepy voice murmured.

With horror, Amy realized what time it was. Not even five o'clock. Too late, though. She'd already awakened Kerani. "I'm sorry, Rani. I know it's early, but . . . well . . . I'm having kind of a crisis. Can I come over sometime today? I really need to talk."

Kerani didn't hesitate. "Give me an hour," she said, already sounding alert. "And bring breakfast."

Amy hung up the phone, trembling. She needed to tell Kerani everything. She couldn't live with this lie another day. But could she do it? Did she dare confess?

"Oh, my God! Paul!"

Heart in her throat, Amy stared at Sergey's wide-screen TV, where Paul was jumping up for a long, sailing pass from the New York Giants quarterback. With a miraculous one-handed catch, he came down with the ball on the five yard line, but not before a two-hundred-plus-pound Atlanta cornerback slammed into him in a collision so violent, the thud of their pads rang from the field. Amy's heart froze as she leaned toward the TV, her eyes locked on Paul writhing on the Astroturf.

"Oh, shit. He's not getting up."

"Give him a moment," Kerani's calm voice soothed. "He probably just had the wind knocked out of him."

She was right. A couple of minutes later, Paul was on his feet, cocking his head from side to side to reorient himself. The Giants fans who'd made the trip to Atlanta for the first playoff game were roaring. It was first and goal for New York on the Falcons five yard line.

Amy was glad she'd decided to stay at Kerani's for the game. She'd come over with the intention of confessing everything about the lie she was living. But now that she was here, she was having second thoughts. She'd already asked Kerani to do the sketch, and she hadn't seemed particularly shocked about why she wanted her to age the face of a dead girl. Besides, why ruin such a perfect winter afternoon with the ugly truth?

It was so cozy here in Kerani's East Village apartment—the one they'd shared a lifetime ago. Outside, snow was coming down hard, but here, in the small living room, a fire burned cheerily in the brick fireplace, and the aroma of fresh-baked chocolate chip cookies—Kerani's specialty—filled the air. All that, and New York was ahead by ten points—soon to be seventeen points, if everything went according to plan in the next three plays.

The camera focused on the Giants team huddle. Amy caught her breath as they showed Paul in a close-up. Just the back of his head, but she knew it was him by the way his black hair curled slightly under his helmet. God, she loved his neck, especially right where the hairline met it. It had been one of her favorite places to kiss . . .

She shook her head. Bad thoughts. *I have to stop doing this!*

The commentators were discussing Paul, commenting about how he was going to his first Pro Bowl in February. His stats flashed on the screen, followed by a head-and-shoulders shot and his vital statistics. Six-foot-four, 220 pounds. He didn't look that big on-screen, next to the others in the offensive line. But in person, Amy always felt dwarfed by him, but in a good way. He felt so solid and protective. Especially when he'd made love to her. He'd been slighter then, his muscles not so built up from years of football, but even then, he'd made her feel so petite, so womanly.

Stop it!

The Giants broke their huddle and trotted into position at the five yard line. Paul was wide right, poised to run. The center snapped the ball, and Mike Dallas, the Giants quarterback, dropped back for the pass. Paul sprinted to the end zone, and, for a few seconds, he was wide-open. Amy held her breath, fingers crossed. The ball sailed into the end zone, and even though, at the last second, Paul was covered by an Atlanta cornerback, he caught the ball for the touchdown.

Amy and Kerani screamed with delight, high-fiving each other from where they sat on the sofa.

"We're going to the Super Bowl," Kerani chimed in song. "We're going to the Super Bowl."

Amy grinned at her. "You're jumping the gun a little, aren't you? We still have two more games."

"We'll win," she said confidently, then grinned. "Or I'll paddle your brother's very attractive bum."

Amy laughed. Her eyes returned to the screen, where Paul held the football in the air in one brawny bare-skinned arm, grinning from ear to ear. Her heart panged at the sight of his bicep flexing as he moved. In another lifetime, she'd touched that arm, caressed it, kissed it. Why, oh, why, couldn't she get past this . . . this *obsession*?

The phone rang, and Kerani got up to answer it in the kitchen. Amy watched the field goal kicker kick the extra point. There were three minutes left in the game. Not much chance Atlanta would come back now. The station went to commercial, and yawning, Amy tossed off the soft fleece blanket she'd curled up in. She glanced over at the windows and saw it was still snowing. Padding over to the window in her thick socks, she gazed down at the snow-clogged street four stories below.

New York was getting its first major snowstorm of the season. Good thing it had started on a lazy Sunday morning. Only a few brave souls were venturing out—just the usual taxis and city buses—and of course, the typical insane few who refused to let Mother Nature's fury interfere with their normal lives. It had started snowing just as Amy arrived at Kerani's brownstone that morning. Now, it was—Amy glanced at her watch—after four, and still coming down in huge, feathery flakes.

"That was Sergey," Kerani said, stepping into the living room. She looked gorgeous in a silk Indian tunic and pants, her long, black hair secured in a thick braid down her back. "JFK and LaGuardia are shut down, so he's stuck in Orlando for the night. Poor guy."

"Yeah, that sucks." Amy turned from the window. "I should go after the game, Rani. The studio will probably send a car for me in the morning, and I should read over next week's script again."

Kerani shook her head, frowning. "No way. I've got a pot of chili simmering on the stove, and I don't intend to eat it by myself. Call up the studio and tell them to pick you up here in the morning. There's no point in you going out in this mess when you can sleep in your old bedroom."

"I don't know . . ."

Kerani glared at her. "I finished the sketch during halftime. If you want to see it, you'll shut your mouth, sit down at the kitchen table in front of a hot bowl of chili, and give me no further trouble. All right?"

"Okay," Amy said meekly. "Can I see the sketch first?"

"Absolutely not." Kerani whirled and glided out of the room. "Perhaps with coffee and cheesecake."

And she meant it. It wasn't until after they'd cleared the table and deposited the chili bowls in the dishwasher that Kerani mentioned the sketch again. She'd ground coffee beans and brought a chocolate-swirled cheesecake from the refrigerator. Besides being a talented artist, her friend also happened to be a fantastic cook. How she stayed so slender after making so many scrumptious desserts, Amy would never understand.

Kerani placed a silver pie server next to the cheesecake. "You go ahead and slice this. I'll get the sketch."

The brewing coffee permeated the room, filling it with a sense of tranquility Amy remembered from her days of sharing the apartment with Kerani. Her hands quivered as she drew out Kerani's Pottery Barn dessert plates. It was silly, this excitement she felt at the prospect of seeing her old face again. Well, the face that would've been hers if she'd kept it.

That morning when she'd slid the photo of her and Robin across the breakfast table to Kerani, she'd asked if there was any way the artist could imagine what she—Amy—would look like in seven years, and do a sketch accordingly. Kerani had gone one step better. She'd scanned the photo into her computer, blown it up, and then, using a special program, had "aged" Amy, turning the adolescent face into one of a twenty-six-year-old woman. Working from the computer, she'd sketched it in pencil. But she hadn't allowed Amy to see the computer-generated image. Now, in just a few minutes, she'd be looking at her old face—the way she'd look like now if she hadn't tampered with nature.

Kerani returned to the kitchen and placed a folder on the table next to the slices of cheesecake Amy had served, then turned to pour the coffee. Amy's fingers itched to open the folder. But Kerani's love of drama forbade it. Reading Amy's mind, she spoke, "Wait until I've poured the coffee. I want to see what you think."

Amy tried to stem her impatience. Finally, Kerani set two mugs of steaming coffee on the table, sat down, and placed an elegant brown hand on the folder. Her chocolate eyes held Amy's. "Just remember . . . this is an educated guess. We can't possibly know how your friend would've really looked if she'd lived. You understand that, don't you?"

"Of course," Amy said, trying to summon a light tone to her voice. "I'm just curious."

Still, Kerani didn't move her hand. She scanned Amy's face, a look of concern in her eyes. "This will probably be quite painful. Seeing her as she would've looked as an adult. Are you sure you're ready for that?"

Amy thought of the dream. The way she'd sat there staring into a mirror that held no reflection. A shudder ran through her. She nodded. "I'm ready," she whispered.

Kerani opened the folder and slid it over to her. Amy stared at the sketch a long moment, feeling a knot forming inside her throat. The penciled sketch of the woman gazed back at her, oddly familiar, yet, alien. It was like she was gazing at someone she'd known in a past life. Someone tantalizingly familiar. Someone she should know intimately, but who still remained a stranger.

The woman in the sketch looked nothing like Robin Mulcahey. Except for the blond hair and blue eyes. Where Robin's face was fuller with higher cheekbones, this face—Amy's—was more narrow, the nose just a bit sharper. Her lips weren't so full and sensuous as Robin's. Still, she wasn't lacking in beauty. Not at all. Her beauty was quieter, less flamboyant. Something else. There was a certain vulnerability in that face. A sadness, perhaps loneliness, even though the face wore a soft smile. It made Amy's heart ache. Grief surged inside her like a rogue wave, coming out of nowhere, threatening to swamp her.

She'd never grieved for this face. Not really. Her grief had been for her best friend. But now she realized that she—Amy—had died just as surely as had Robin. Only her body had lived on. But everything else, her personality, her hopes and dreams, her very *soul* had died on the day she'd decided to take on Robin's identity. And there was no one to blame but herself. Now, this face gazed up at her with forlorn eyes—eyes that held accusation and contempt, or so it seemed. Kerani was right. She hadn't been ready for this. She probably would never have been ready for it.

"Robin?" Kerani reached across the table and touched her hand. "I was afraid of this. It's made you cry."

Amy brushed a hand across her cheek, surprised to find it wet. She hadn't even known she was crying. But her heart felt as if it wanted to burst out of her chest. She pushed the sketch away and dropped her head onto her folded arms, giving in to the sobs engulfing her.

Kerani allowed her to cry for a few minutes, then she began stroking her head, murmuring in a soothing voice, "I know you miss her, Robin. And I know you feel guilty because you lived through the accident, and she didn't. But it was karma. Her time to go. Remember, though, she is always with you in spirit."

Amy sobbed harder.

"We have to be philosophical about these things," Kerani went on. "Who's to say that death is a bad thing? Perhaps *Amy* is the lucky one. Perhaps she really *has* gone to a better world, and we're the unfortunate ones. That's the only thing that makes sense, really. So many senseless tragedies in the world . . ."

Amy lifted her head and gazed at her friend through tear-blurred eyes. Again, her early-morning compulsion to confess everything welled inside her like a volcanic eruption. *Oh, God, it's too heavy a burden to keep carrying alone.* She took a deep breath, expelled it, then met Kerani's gaze.

"You don't understand," she said quietly. "Amy *didn't* die in that crash. *Robin* did. I'm the only one in the world who knows that, and I know it because . . . I'm *not* Robin. *I am Amy.*"

25

Tweny minutes later, Kerani leaned back in her chair and released a deep, astonished breath. "Jesus H. Christ," she whispered in her prim British-tinged accent.

Amy stared down at her Christmas red acrylic nails. "So, now you know the whole sordid story."

Kerani had listened to her confession without comment, her expression composed. Amy hadn't known what she'd expected. Shock, of course, and Kerani hadn't disappointed her on that. Her velvet brown eyes *had* revealed shock. But she'd also expected disgust, condemnation. There had been none of that. Just a nonjudgmental silence.

"I did it because I just wanted to belong to a real family," Amy said, feeling the need to explain further. "Robin was gone, and with her was gone my chance to have that family. But when I realized they thought I *was* her, it seemed like the answer to everything. They would have their daughter, and I'd have the family I'd always wanted."

Kerani reached across the table and clasped Amy's hand. Still, she didn't speak. The hum of the refrigerator's motor powered on, inordinately loud in the silence.

Amy shook her head and gave an ironic laugh. "Despicable, isn't it? I've done something more vile than anything Carly August would ever *dream* of doing."

"Desperation makes people do strange things," Kerani said quietly. "For a little while, you had everything you ever wanted. A best friend. A family who welcomed you with open arms, and then, in the blink of an eye, it was gone. Your survival instinct kicked in. Look at the way you grew up. Neglected by your real parents. Finding your father after he shot himself. Christ, Robin! It's understandable you'd want to hold on to the stability you found with your friend's parents."

Amy shook her head. "Understandable? I don't know. It sounds so insane now." She buried her face in her trembling hands. "Oh, God! Kerani, maybe I'm as messed up as my mother was. Maybe I belong in an institution. Would a stable person do something like this?"

"Don't beat yourself up, Robin. I mean . . ." Her voice trailed away uncertainly.

Amy looked up, her mouth twisting in a bitter grin. "Awkward, isn't it? Go ahead. Keep calling me Robin. I've lived this charade too long to give it up now."

Poor Kerani. Amy almost wished she'd remained silent. In her rush to share her shocking story, she hadn't given a thought to what it would be like for her friend. To find that everything about the woman she thought she knew was a big lie. The truth was, she was a stranger sitting in Kerani's kitchen. Kerani had never *known* her. Not the real person. Even so, she was trying to console her.

"You poor girl." Kerani gazed at her solemnly. "How have you managed to do it all these years?"

Amy shrugged. "No choice." She bit her bottom lip. Might as well go for it and tell her everything. Maybe Kerani had missed her calling. There was something so priestlike in her expression. It encouraged confession.

"That's not all, though."

Kerani's eyes widened. "There's more?"

"Yeah." Amy took a sip of coffee, lukewarm now.

"Wait." Kerani grabbed their mugs and stood up. She dumped the contents into the sink and refilled the mugs with fresh coffee. "Okay. Go ahead." She sat back down at the kitchen table and reached for the hazelnut-flavored creamer.

"This is really weird," Amy began, breathing in the rich aroma of Kerani's Arabian coffee. "I don't know how you're going to take it."

Kerani rolled her eyes. "Hey, I've just listened to a story that Hollywood would've passed on because it's too implausible. I think I'm ready for anything." But the tremble of her hand on her coffee cup belied her words.

Amy hesitated, unsure of how to begin. At the beginning? Tell her how she'd fallen for Paul at first sight? About those wonderful days they'd spent in the first hours of 1998? Or just blurt it out?

"I'm in love with Paul."

There. She'd said it. Directly, with no added frills. She'd stepped up to the plate and hit the home run. Thrown the Hail Mary pass and now waited to see if it was a touchdown.

Kerani was silent for a long moment, eyes wide. Finally, she digested the information and said, "Your . . . I mean . . . Robin's brother?"

Amy nodded. "I've loved him since that first Thanksgiving we met. At first he thought of me as Robin's teenybopper friend, but that changed on New Year's Day 1998." Seven years ago. And still, she hadn't forgotten the magic of it.

"What happened?" Kerani asked quietly, her slender brown hands clasped around her mug.

"He was my first lover."

Kerani expelled a shocked breath. "Oh, wow. So, why . . . how come you . . . I mean, when Robin . . ."

"He'd dumped me . . . and went back to his girlfriend, Monica."

Kerani's mouth dropped open. "You mean, *that* Monica? Monica the Bitch?"

"Yeah, the same." Amy's lips twisted in a bitter smile. "They go way back. He sent me a Dear Jane e-mail on the day of the accident, and I was convinced it was over. I didn't think I had anything to lose, and at least if I 'became' Robin, it was a way to stay close to him. It was better than having him out of my life completely, you know."

For the first time since Amy had shared her story, Kerani became clearly agitated. She slid the plate of untouched cheesecake toward her and with a vicious slice of her fork, scooped up a huge wedge. "God, you're a masochist." She shoved the cheesecake into her mouth and went for more.

"I know." Amy nodded miserably. "But that's not the worst of it."

Kerani swallowed her cheesecake and stared. "Go on, then."

Amy's eyes dropped. Her fingers traced the outline of a blossom on the blue damask place mat. "I found out . . . afterward . . . that he *does* love me. He did, anyway." And she told her about finding Paul's message on the answering machine.

Kerani released a tremulous breath, and whispered, "Jesus." Her eyes dropped to Amy's untouched slice of cheesecake. "Hey, if you're not going to eat that, pass it over."

She devoured the cheesecake, a distracted look on her classically beautiful face. Amazing she could eat like that and stay so supermodel thin, Amy thought, not for the first time. Kerani ate like a three-hundred-pound nose tackle, and never gained an ounce.

From the living room, the mantel clock chimed eight times. A snowplow rumbled past on the street below. Kerani didn't speak until she'd finished every crumb of Amy's cheesecake. She dropped the fork to the plate and pushed it away. Folding her arms on the table, she met Amy's expectant gaze. "I'll say one thing for you. You sure as hell know how to screw up your life."

Something about the matter-of-fact way she said it struck Amy as funny. Laughter bubbled up in her throat, and once she started, she couldn't stop. For a moment, Kerani peered at her cautiously, wondering, no doubt, if she was finally cracking up. But realizing that Amy's laughter stemmed from genuine humor and not hysteria, she grinned, then began to laugh, too.

"You're right," Amy giggled. "And I thought my mom had screwed up *her* life. But at least she had the good sense to shut herself off from reality. I, on the other hand, decided to *change* my reality. How sick is that? I didn't like the person I was, so what the hell? I'd just become somebody else!"

Kerani grinned. "Hey, maybe you could pitch the idea to the story editors at *South Riding*." Then she shook her head. "No! They'll never go for it. Sounds too much like the story line on *Days of Our Lives*. It's not even close to being original enough for a soap. They were doing the identity switch story line back in the sixties."

"Yeah, I can't even screw up my life right!"

They burst into renewed laughter.

"Wait, wait! How about this?" Amy grabbed Kerani's arm, still giggling. "We could turn it into a Broadway show. Make millions on it. We could call it *The Amy Shiley Story* . . . better known as *Invasion of the Body Snatchers II*."

They howled. Finally, Amy managed to get her laughter under control. She smiled across the table at Kerani, who was wiping her streaming eyes with a napkin. "Oh, God, Rani. What would I do without you?" Just like that, she was blinking back sudden tears. "You always know just the right way to make me feel better."

Kerani sobered and reached across the table to clasp her hand. "That's what friends are for."

Amy nodded. "I've been very lucky, you know, despite the way I've managed to screw up my life. I haven't had a lot of friends, but I've had three really good ones. You're the third."

Kerani blinked quickly and pushed away from the table. "Enough sentimentality. You're going to make me cry, and I *so* don't do that in front of anyone. More coffee?"

Amy shook her head. "Better not, or I'll be up all night."

"So, what are you going to do?" Kerani poured herself another cup, grabbed the creamer, and added a generous amount.

"What do you mean?" Amy stared at her, brow furrowed.

She cradled the mug in her hands, leaning back against the counter. "Paul. You *are* going to tell him, aren't you?"

Amy's jaw dropped. "Are you crazy? I can't tell him."

"But you love him, and he loves you. How can you *not* tell him?"

"Oh, right! I'll just call him up and say, 'Hey, Paul, what's happening, dude? By the way, remember Amy? Well, good news. She's alive, and I'm her. Sorry about Robin, though, but what the hell? Lose a sister, gain a girlfriend."

The corner of Kerani's mouth twitched. "Well, that's one way of doing it, but I'd suggest trying it with a *bit* more tact."

Amy pushed away from the table and stood. "I can't believe you'd even suggest telling him. *How?* How could I do that to him? Not to mention one other little detail. Have you forgotten I'm married?"

Kerani sobered. "Oh, God. Declan."

"Yeah, Declan."

She moved back to the table and sat down. "Jesus," she whispered. "But I thought you were crazy about him."

"I am. I love him, I do." Amy rested her forehead in the heel of her hand, gazing down at the table. "God, it sounds so crazy, doesn't it? I don't understand it myself. I love Dec with all my heart, but . . . I'm *in* love with Paul. Does that make any sense at all? Or am I just totally screwed up? Don't answer that." She looked up at Kerani. "So, you see . . . I have no choice. I just have to get over Paul. And maybe I will once he marries that witch. Because if he goes through with that, I'll lose all respect for him."

"Well, it's obvious you're not the only one screwed up. Think about it. Paul lost the woman he loves in a car accident. After a tragedy like that, a lot of men would turn to drugs, sex, or alcohol. Perhaps Monica is Paul's crutch. He uses her to blot out the pain. I think you should tell him the truth, Robin."

Amy shook her head. "I can't. It's way too late for that. Besides, I could never hurt Declan. He loves me."

"Okay, but imagine this. Suppose this . . . identity switch had never happened. You're Amy, and both Declan and Paul are in love with you. Which one would you choose?"

Amy caught her breath. Her eyes dropped. "There's no contest," she whispered. "It would have to be Paul."

Kerani didn't speak for a long moment, just gazed at her. Then, gently, she said, "I think you should tell him."

★ ★ ★

April 20, 1991

I just got home from the spring dance with Jason. It was soooo rad! I wore that glittery black dress I found at The Limited last week, and did I ever look hot! I'm so psyched that Daddy talked Mom into letting me keep it. She got all bent out of shape when I showed it to her. Said that thirteen was too young to wear a strapless dress with black sequins. Well, DUH!!! What does she know? Daddy said I'd look great in it and that I should be able to wear it if I wanted to. Mom just gave in to him. Typical. Like she really cares what I wear. As long as she's closing another million-dollar sale, it's all good. Anyway, Jason looked really studly in his tux. We double-dated with his older brother, Chris, and his date—this snobbish chick named Briana. Barely said two words to me the whole night. Not that I care. Stuck-up bitch. Anyway, the dance was fun. We didn't stay that long, though. Just a little after ten, Chris hauled us out of there, and drove us to this park near the river. Then the jerk made me and Jason get out of the car so he could get it on with Briana in the backseat of his father's Pontiac. Told Jason to go for a walk and not come back until 11:30. So, that's what we did. Jason is cool, though. So laid-back about everything. And I think he really likes me. Well, I thought he did. I might be wrong. Anyway, everything was great for a while. Jason is really easy to talk to when you can get him away from all those other lame guys at school. He's such a clown in class, but when it's just the two of us, he's really pretty rad. He talked about how he's going to be this big rock star someday. He taught himself to play the guitar, and he says he can play that Guns 'N Roses riff from "Sweet Child O Mine." Cool!!! I told him I wanted to hear it sometime. I adorrrrre Guns 'N Roses. Axl Rose is soooo yummy! Anyway, we were talking down by the river, and then all of a sudden, Jason leans over and kisses me. I didn't know what to do. I mean, it really blew me away. So I just sat there and let him kiss me. But it was weird, you know, because our braces clanked against each others', and man, it was just kind of . . . I don't know . . . awkward. I don't think I did it right because Jason got this really funny look on his face, and it seemed like he was blushing. But it was hard to tell because it was pretty dark. And then he said that we had to go back to the car, and he barely spoke to me the rest of the night. He didn't even kiss me good night at the door, so I guess that means he doesn't like kissing me. Jeez, what did I do wrong? I wish Mom was the kind of mother who could talk to me about stuff like that. But I've seen that impatient look on her face when I interrupt her at work. She just never has time for me. Oh, I suppose I could ask her to pencil in an appointment for me, but who needs her, anyway? She'd rather be out showing one of her two-million-dollar river estates than talking about sex with her only daughter. I guess I'll just have to ask Daddy. He probably knows more, anyway, about stuff like that. I can talk about anything with Daddy, and it's cool. Oh! Here he comes. More, later.

Amy turned to the next page in the journal and found it blank. She flipped through the next few pages. Odd. No more entries after that one. Why? She threw back the down comforter and crawled out of bed. From the street below, a snowplow rumbled past, its flashing light casting a yellow glow upon her walls. In her thick, warm socks, she padded across the wood floor to her closet and took the cedar box from the ledge. Placing it on the bed, she opened it and gazed down at the stack of steno pads, each one dated in Robin's looping handwriting. It had taken Amy hours of practice to get her handwriting to match Robin's. Her own had been smaller and more precise, whereas Robin's reflected her personality—vibrant, confident, and outgoing, full of loops and curlicues. And instead of dotting an *i*, she drew little circles. Now, with years of practice, Amy's handwriting was almost identical to Robin's. Only an expert would be able to tell the difference.

There were twelve steno pads in all. Amy sat on the edge of the bed and looked through each one, searching for a date in 1991 when the Victorian diary had ended. There was none. The earliest notebook started in December 1994. Apparently, Robin had stopped keeping a journal for three years. Why? Had her life become too busy? She'd always been on the go in college, but Amy remembered her always writing in her journal every night before bed, no matter how late it was. Except when she was drunk, of course.

Amy went back to the 1994 journal, opening it to the first page.

Okay, I've decided to start writing again. Life has really sucked for the last few years, but it's all good now. This is the new Robin Mulcahey. I'm not taking any crap anymore. Not from anybody. I've just got to get through the next three years, then I'm leaving this fucking place. I'm going to New York to become an actress! Oh, I know I'm expected to go to college first, but fuck that! Once I graduate from high school NOBODY is going to tell me what to do. Anyway, I'm still dating Jason, but not exclusively. I'm too young to be tied down to one guy, and since I made varsity cheerleader last year, my popularity has soared. Of course, I'm not so naive as to believe that's the only reason. Word has gotten around—thanks to Jason, I'm sure—that I'll do pretty much anything with a guy, except have intercourse. I'm good at what I do, especially now that the braces are off. So, yeah, I date lots of guys. But Jason is still my favorite. He's sweet, and you know, I think he really cares about me. I just wish he'd quit pressuring me to fuck him. I've told him from the beginning it'll never happen. It just won't. What's the big deal, anyway? Why should he care HOW I make him come? God, men are scum. But then, so am I.

Amy closed the notebook, frowning. Something had happened between those two journals. It had been a sweet innocent girl who'd written that last entry in April of 1991, a girl who wasn't even sure how to kiss a guy. After that, a three-year silence. The beginning entry in 1994 had been written by a promiscuous, cynical, and yes—angry—girl of sixteen. A girl who seemed proud of her erotic prowess with, apparently, a variety of high school boys. A girl who seemed to hate everyone around her, including herself.

What had happened to Robin during those three years of silence?

Amy put the notebook down and reached out to turn off the lamp on the bedside table. She could only hope that reading the rest of Robin's journals would give her the answer to that question. For some reason—she didn't know why—it suddenly seemed urgent that she unlock the secret of those missing years.

26

"Time to go, Carly." The grim-faced prison guard stood at the door of the cell.

Wearing an orange prison jumpsuit that clung to her curves far too sensuously for it to be real life, Amy sat up on the narrow bunk and slowly got to her feet, sending the irons encircling her wrists and ankles jangling. The extra playing the prison guard grabbed her arm and led her out of the cell. The camera zeroed in on Amy's face as she moved down the narrow corridor. She concentrated on keeping her expression stoic, but allowed her bottom lip to tremble just a bit. They reached a door at the end of the corridor, and her escort opened it. Amy stepped in, eyes widening as she focused on the electric chair. She could feel the blood draining from her face. Counting to ten, she held the expression, using a tactic taught in Soap 101 to end a scene just before the cut to commercial.

"*Cut!*" called out Nancy Logan. "Okay! Good job, Robin. You can go. See you tomorrow morning bright and early, okay, dear?"

"Sure thing." Amy released a sigh of relief and stepped away from the execution room set. Nancy had been in a great mood today, and it was always a pleasure working for her when that was the case. Unfortunately, though, in her years at *South Riding*, Nancy Logan had earned the nickname of Mommie Dearest because of the days when she *wasn't* in such a good mood. There was no in between with her; she was either super nice and motherly . . . or a holy terror. And no one ever knew which one would show up on the set on any given day—June Cleaver or Joan Crawford.

All this week, Nancy had been a treasure to work with, but sooner or later, all hell would break loose. That was a given. Thank God, it hadn't been today because Amy wasn't sure if she could've handled it. They were going to be drawing out this execution scene over the next week. Amazing how the writers could stretch out a story line. No wonder viewers could take a week off and come back and pick right up as if they hadn't been gone. But that was the beauty of daytime drama.

Amy left the set and headed downstairs. Just thinking about another week playing a condemned woman exhausted her. She was already suffering from the emotional drain. When had this stopped being fun, anyway? She almost wished the writers had gone ahead and killed her off instead of letting her be rescued by the last-minute confession of the real killer. Dying in an electric chair would certainly be a challenging way to go for any actress. But the suits apparently were holding on to the hope that she'd renew her contract at the last minute.

That wasn't going to happen. The end of March was just a little over six weeks away, and she was counting the days until she could get out of her contract and head for California. Once she could have a real marriage with Dec, everything would be okay. Maybe she'd even get up the nerve to audition for some prime-time roles out there. Yes, California could be the best thing for her right now. And best of all, she'd be far away from Paul and the temptation to do exactly what Kerani encouraged her to do. Tell him the truth.

When she stepped through the stairwell door, Johnny looked up from his guard desk and gave her a big grin. "Hey, there, Rockin' Robin. How's it going?"

"Well, they didn't kill me yet, so I guess I'm okay."

He laughed and started to respond, but the phone on his desk rang. Amy hurried on down the hall toward her dressing room. She adored Johnny, but had found from experience that once you got him chatting, he'd keep you there all night. And right now, she just wanted to go home, make herself a big pot of Kraft macaroni and cheese, and plop herself down in front of the TV to watch mindless drivel until bedtime. In fact, she might just spend the whole weekend doing that. It sounded like heaven.

As she approached her dressing room door, she saw it was ajar. Stephanie must've come in, after all. Odd, though. She hadn't seen her roommate all day.

"Hey, I thought you were off today," Amy said, stepping into the room.

"I am," said a familiar male voice. "We were good boys, so Coach gave us the afternoon off. Says if we're not ready for the playoff game against Minnesota on Sunday by now, we'll never be."

Amy's heart immediately kicked into overdrive. Paul sat at her desk, looking casually gorgeous in dark blue jeans and a gray tweed turtleneck sweater. She tried to recover her composure with what she hoped was a relaxed smile.

"Oh, Paul! How did you get in here?"

His grin widened. "Well, Antonio upstairs is a Giants fan, and he had me escorted down to Johnny, who, would you believe, *also* is a Giants fan, and naturally, he knew I was your brother, so he told me I could wait for you in here." His eyes flicked down her body. "Nice outfit."

Amy glanced down at her orange jumpsuit and grimaced. "Well, it's not really my color."

In the corridor outside, a raucous laugh broke out, followed by a feminine Bronx accent heckling her companion. The hairdresser and makeup artist in one of their frequent, but good-natured, spats. Their voices trailed away as they turned the corner.

Amy strode to the closet and grabbed her street clothes, the white Aran sweater Declan had given her for Christmas and a pair of black woolen slacks. "So, what brings you to the studio, Paul?" She tossed the clothes on the bed.

"I've got a surprise for you."

Amy looked at him. His words shook her. She hadn't seen or talked to him in a couple of weeks. Had Monica's elderly husband died? Oh, God! Surely, Paul hadn't already married that horrible woman!

"Well?" she said cautiously.

He grinned. "How would you and Dec like to come see me play in the Pro Bowl?"

Amy drew in a sharp breath. "Oh, my God! In *Hawaii*?" When she'd left for work this morning, there had been drifts of snow four feet high in some places, the remainder of last weekend's storm. And that had frozen solid from Wednesday night's ice storm. The forecast for Sunday was calling for more snowy/icy/whatever precipitation. They weren't sure yet which it would be. Anyone's guess. Hawaii sounded really, really good.

"Aloha Stadium," Paul said, stifling a yawn. "Four o'clock. February 6." He reached for his sheepskin-lined bomber jacket, which lay across the desk, and drew out an envelope. "Got you two seats on the forty-six yard line."

Amy beamed him a huge smile. "Oh, wow! February 5 is Declan's birthday. Wouldn't that be a wonderful way to celebrate it? We could fly to Honolulu on Saturday, spend the night in a romantic hotel room in Waikiki. Maybe I can even finagle a week off. What's that beautiful old hotel there? The pink one?"

"The Royal Hawaiian," Paul said, grinning at her excited chatter. "That's where I'm staying. But I'm flying in on Thursday to get in a few rounds of golf before the game. So . . . may I take your enthusiastic response as a yes?"

"You *betcha*! Do I look stupid? A chance to go to Hawaii in the dead of a New York winter?"

Paul feigned hurt. "And here I thought it was the chance to see me play in my first Pro Bowl that had you so excited."

"Oh, silly! Of course I'm excited to see you play. But *Hawaii*! I've never been there before. How cool is that?" A thought occurred to her, and she frowned. "Wait. Is Monica going? Please don't tell me you've got her sitting next to us."

A guarded look crossed Paul's face. "No. Monica won't be there." He hesitated, then added, "I've broken if off with her, Rob. Something happened during the holidays that convinced me you've been right about her all along."

Amy stared at him, at a complete loss for words. But it was impossible for her to hold back the surge of relief his admission sent through her. She tried hard not to smile when she finally managed to speak. "What happened? Want to talk about it?" *God, do I sound as cheerful as I think I sound?*

He glanced at his watch and got to his feet. "Not now. I've gotta go." He grabbed his jacket and slung it over his shoulder. "I'm meeting some of the guys down at the Sports Break." He crossed the tiny room, took hold of her shoulder, and gave her a brief kiss on the cheek. "Get some rest, sis. You look like you've been through the wringer this week."

"Well, thanks," she said sarcastically. "I love you, too."

He grinned and gave her a wink. "Don't get your knickers in a twist. You look gorgeous as always, but tired. So . . . call me when you check into the hotel, okay? I'll take you and Dec out for drinks."

"Okay. When do you leave for Minneapolis?"

"Tomorrow morning."

"Well, good luck on Sunday." She crossed her fingers. "And catch a couple of TDs for me. I'll be watching on TV."

He grinned, gave her a brief salute—then he was gone.

The drone of the 747 roared through Amy's head as she gazed out the window at the dark sky thirty-eight thousand feet up. Occasionally, the glimmer of the moon silvered the passing clouds, rendering a breathtaking view to those passengers not reading or sleeping. Amy was one of them, but she found something melancholy about the moon's luminous glow. But then, maybe that was just her state of mind. Although she knew they were flying at an incredible rate of speed toward the West Coast, it seemed to her like they were going at a slow crawl. Her nerves were screaming with impatience to get to California and to Dec. It had been five weeks since she'd seen him. Five long, lonely weeks.

Her flight was due to arrive at LAX at 10:30 P.M., but for her, still on New York time, it would be one-thirty in the morning. A very long day. She'd had an early call at the studio this morning, and had put in twelve grueling hours. Not that it had been especially strenuous work. All she'd done was lie in a hospital bed during her scenes, but considering the circumstances, even that had been exhausting. Nancy had donned her Mommie Dearest persona, making Amy pay in advance for her requested week off. The trip to Hawaii had, apparently, *really* pissed the director off, because she'd been hell on wheels all day long. A scene that would usually take a half hour to film ended up taking two hours—and no one, from Nancy's assistants down to the lowliest technician, escaped the wrath of the director when she was operating in what was known on the set as PPMS—Perfectionist Premenstrual Syndrome—mode.

Amy sighed, glad to be on a plane heading away from New York. A week off was exactly what she needed. It had taken some fast talking, but she'd managed to get the entire week off from the soap after writers obligingly sent Carly into a coma. *Who said you couldn't have flexibility working on a soap?* There was always the coma plot to fall back on.

Amy smiled. She couldn't wait to get to California, and into Dec's arms. *Please dear God, let Cedric be off somewhere so I won't have to spend valuable time making small talk with him.* She just wanted to be alone with Declan. She had an early birthday present she wanted to give him, and for that, they certainly didn't need a third wheel.

The real birthday present, of course, would be the trip to Hawaii. They'd be flying out tomorrow morning around eleven, arriving in Waikiki in the early afternoon. There would be plenty of time to frolic in the warm surf and perhaps even have a romantic interlude in their hotel room before meeting Paul for drinks in the evening.

She'd thought about making the trip to Hawaii and the Pro Bowl game a birthday surprise for Dec, but the logistics of it were just too complicated. It was kind of hard to take someone on a surprise trip without alerting him to it. *Hi, Dec, guess what? I'm coming into LA . . . coincidentally on your birthday, and oh, by the way, could you have a bag packed with something you'd wear in the tropics and . . . oh, yeah, clear your calendar for the next week.*

After thinking about it for a while and not being able to come up with any way to do it, she'd given up on the surprise part of it and simply called and told him about it. His response had been a bit bewildering. In fact, he hadn't seemed all that enthusiastic. Well, she hadn't expected him to be excited about the football game. No matter how hard he tried, Declan just couldn't seem to drum up any interest in American football. After all, it wasn't hurling. But still, she *had* expected him to be thrilled at the getaway to Hawaii, especially since he'd be spending it with the woman he loved. But he'd sounded distracted on the phone, maybe even a little depressed. He'd brushed it off when she'd asked him what was wrong, murmuring something about being tired and keeping too many late nights with Cedric and his friends.

Amy took a sip of the bottled water the flight attendant had brought her and smiled. This trip to Hawaii was exactly what Declan needed. Some time away from Hollywood's social scene and the obligatory *schmoozefests.* In fact, once she moved there, she intended to see that they both shunned that lifestyle as much as possible. It was a proven fact that Hollywood couples who kept to themselves had much more stable marriages than the ones who were constantly in the limelight. No *way* were they going to fall into that trap.

"Excuse me, Miss Mulcahey?"

Amy looked up to see a freckled-faced teenaged girl smiling down at her, revealing a mouthful of gleaming silver. Immediately, Amy thought of Robin and the journal entry about her braces and the awkwardness of kissing Jason. The girl looked nothing like Robin, but still, Amy felt a flood of warmth for her. She smiled back. "Hi."

The girl's smile broadened. "I'm a huge fan. Can I have your autograph?"

Amy nodded and took the slip of notebook paper the girl held out to her. "Of course. What's your name?"

"Debby. Are you going out to California to see your husband?" she gushed. When Amy nodded, she giggled. "I think Declan Blair is *so* hot!" A tide of crimson flooded her face. "No offense. I mean . . . I know you're married to him and all, but I just love him. As an actor, I mean. When will his movie be out, do you know?"

Amy handed the paper back to her. "I think he said it'll be released in June."

The girl practically jumped up and down. "Oh, I can't wait! I'll be first in line to see it. Well, thank you for the autograph."

"You're welcome. And I'll tell Declan you're a big fan." The girl blushed bright red and grinned. Thanking her again, she hurried down the aisle back to her seat, clutching her sheet of paper like it was the Holy Grail.

Amy pushed the button to release her seat back into a reclining position and closed her eyes. June. In June, she'd be living in California with Declan. They'd go to the premiere of *Borderland* together, and who knew? By this time next year, she could be living with an Oscar winner.

And Paul would be very far away.

"You're leaving now?" Cedric asked, looking up from his lounge chair beside the pool.

Declan nodded. The knot in his throat prevented him from speaking. Cedric swung his legs over the side of his chair and stood. Moonlight washed over his muscled body, bare except for red Speedo swim trunks. He walked toward Declan, a grave look on his craggy face. Dec felt his heart do a slow somersault. It was always like this with Cedric, and he'd given up trying to understand it. He only knew this was how it had to be.

"This *is* the right thing, you know," Cedric said quietly.

Declan nodded again, and this time, he managed a hoarse response. "I know."

Cedric stopped in front of him, his eyes searching. The moon slipped behind a cloud, leaving his face partly in shadow. But Declan thought he saw sadness in his expression—a genuine sorrow. Cedric lifted a hand and touched Dec's jaw.

"Be gentle," he said.

Declan's heart twisted in agony. Gentle? No matter how gentle he was, it was going to rip Robin apart. But he knew Cedric was right. He had to do it. But first, he had to make Cedric understand.

"I *do* love her," he said urgently. "You know that, don't you? I *do!*"

The moon drifted out from behind the cloud, and Declan saw Cedric nod. And he also saw he hadn't been mistaken. Cedric's face was somber, his emotion genuine.

"I know that," Cedric said. He reached toward him, his thumb tracing the line of Declan's lower lip. "But you love *me* more."

Amy saw Declan before he saw her. He was dressed entirely in black—black turtleneck, black slacks, and black jacket. Even his sunglasses were black. But his hair was blonder than ever. Compliments of the California sun or of Antoine, Cedric's hairdresser on Rodeo Drive? Why was he wearing those sunglasses at ten o'clock at night, anyway? If it was to appear incognito, it wasn't working. A couple of middle-aged women stood at his side, and he was signing autographs. Soap fans, obviously.

He looked up and saw her. For a second, he stiffened, his lips freezing in midsmile as he handed a sheet of paper back to one of the women. Something about the expression on his face sent a wave of uneasiness through her. She didn't know why. For God's sake, she couldn't even see his eyes, and she'd learned long ago that Declan's eyes were the barometer to his moods. So, there was absolutely no reason to think he wasn't happy to see her.

"Robin, love!" His rich, Irish voice enveloped her. Welcoming, so obviously thrilled she was here.

There. That proved she was being silly. His smile was warm as he approached her. A moment later, she was in his arms, inhaling the woodsy scent of Ralph Lauren Romance for Men—the cologne she'd bought him for Christmas. *Oh, God,* it felt good to be in his arms. After a long moment, he released her and drew back to gaze down at her. Amy realized that strobes were flashing all around them. Paparazzio. It didn't matter. She was with Dec, and she didn't care if the whole world knew it.

She beamed up at him. "I missed you so much, Dec."

"Me too, love."

Her smile became a mock frown. "Why are you wearing those awful sunglasses? Don't tell me you're going Bono on me. May I?" She reached for his glasses, and when he didn't object, took them off. "There. That's better. I've missed your gorgeous blue eyes."

But it wasn't better, really. Something *was* wrong. Some emotion swam in those cobalt eyes of his, and she wasn't sure what it was. But instinct told her it wasn't good.

"What's wrong?" she asked.

He shook his head. "Nothing. Let's just get out of here."

Amy tried to pretend it was nothing, that her instincts were wrong. That the alarms screaming inside her brain were the result of a long week at work and jet lag. "Okay," she said. "Let's get out of here. But first . . ." She reached up and curled a hand around the blond curls at the back of his neck, drawing his head down for a kiss. It was anything but a hello kiss. It was a kiss of hunger, of naked sensuousness, maybe even of desperation. For a brief heart-stopping moment, he didn't respond. He held her stiffly, allowing her mouth to devour his. But then, just as Amy was about to pull away in disappointment, he moved his lips against hers, deepening the kiss. Relief washed over her as his tongue slipped between her teeth, dancing with hers.

It's all right, she thought, as she returned his kiss with abandon. *Everything is going to be fine.*

"Where are we going?" Amy asked when Declan took the exit for 405 instead of getting on Highway 1 toward Malibu. It was going on eleven, really too late for dinner. She just wanted to go home with him and spend the rest of the night in his arms.

"Beverly Hills," he said. "I've booked a room at the Beverly Hills Hotel for the night. A bungalow, actually."

Amy felt her spirits rise a notch. This was exactly what she was hoping for— a romantic night alone with Declan. And a bungalow at one of the most prestigious hotels in the world certainly fit the bill. But why did Declan seem so far away? So remote? Could it possibly be her imagination?

"That's a great idea," she said brightly.

He glanced over his shoulder and veered into the next lane to pass an SUV poking along at seventy miles per hour. *Impressive*, thought Amy. His driving confidence had certainly increased since her last visit. She waited until he was back in the right lane before speaking again.

"So, how's Cedric?"

A muscle flexed in his jaw. "He's grand. He says to tell you hello."

Amy watched him closely. "You two aren't fighting, are you?"

He gave her an appraising glance. "Not at all. Why do you think so?"

"Oh, I don't know. A certain edge in your voice, I guess."

He shrugged, his hands tightening on the steering wheel. "Sorry, love. You're imagining things."

Am I? Am I imagining this distance that I feel between us? What's happened to you, Declan? What's happened to us?

But, of course, she couldn't say these thoughts aloud. It would make them too real. Instead, she reached over and turned up the radio. Karen Carpenter's rich, melted chocolate voice flowed out of the stereo's speakers singing "Masquerade."

By the time Declan pulled up in front of the famous pink complex with the hunter green awnings on Sunset Boulevard, Amy felt perilously close to tears.

But the sight of the sprawling Mission Revival–designed hotel chased the melancholy mood away, for the moment, anyway. It really was magnificent—the Beverly Hills Hotel. The immaculate green lawns, the profusion of fragrant flower gardens of azaleas, roses, bougainvillea, and hibiscus carpeting the grounds. And so much history. In the famed Polo Lounge, Marlene Dietrich had been thrown out for the shameless sin of wearing—gasp!—slacks. And Elizabeth Taylor had honeymooned here with who *knew* how many husbands—perhaps in the very bungalow they'd be staying in tonight.

As the valet driver slid into the BMW, Amy went to Declan and threw her arms around him. "Thank you," she murmured, burying her face into his black sweater. "This is so perfect."

For a brief moment, his hands tightened on her shoulders, and she felt the brush of his lips against the top of her head. Then, abruptly, he drew away from her. She caught a glimpse of his face before he turned to the doorman who waited patiently beside a cart stacked with their luggage. Her heart twisted at Declan's expression. Haunted, sorrowful. As if he had news of a loved one's death.

Heart hammering, she followed her husband into the Beverly Hills Hotel.

27

"*Wow!*" Amy breathed, gazing around the suite with astonished eyes. "I'm impressed. I hate to think what you paid for this."

After tipping the bellboy, Declan closed the door and turned to her. His lips were smiling, but his eyes still wore a grave look that sent the alarm bells ringing again. "You don't want to know," he said.

Amy ran a finger across the silk damask settee in the living room. Absolutely gorgeous! Even the walls were covered in mint green silk. The bungalow was decorated in a French country theme with burnished mahogany end tables arranged around the settee and a couple of lush chairs. A baby grand piano in the corner immediately brought to mind a Liberace or Dudley Moore sitting there, pounding out a new composition.

And oh, my God—the bedroom! She supposed she should try to act more jaded about the luxury. After all, Robin Mulcahey had been surrounded by elegant surroundings all her life. But it was Amy Shiley who was reacting now, and there was no way in the world she could not show her delight. The bedroom was almost as large as her entire apartment in New York. An elegant king-size canopy bed with burgundy silk drapes flowing in a river at each corner dominated the room. Amy could barely suppress a giggle of excitement. She couldn't wait to get in it with Declan.

But first . . .

She headed for the bathroom and her grin widened when she saw the sunken Jacuzzi tub, more than big enough for both of them. The bed could wait. *This, first, then . . .*

She felt her skin grow warm as she anticipated what they would do in the tub . . . and in the bed. Turning, she saw Declan standing at the door of the bedroom, staring at her. There it was again. That haunted look in his eyes. But *no!* She refused to give in to it. Whatever was wrong, she'd fix it. She had to!

"Come on, Dec." She moved across the room to him and draped her arms around his neck, her lips nibbling leisurely at his throat. "Let's take a bath together. I want you naked . . . right *now!*" She pressed her body into his, snaking her hands inside his jacket to encircle his waist.

He relaxed against her, and she felt a sudden triumph. *That's it, Dec, let me take care of whatever is wrong with you.* His arms tightened around her, his chin anchored on her head. She kissed the hollow of his throat, felt him swallow convulsively. Beneath her palm, his heart pounded. Rapid and hard. Still kissing him, she slid her hand down to his belt buckle, then moved lower to his crotch. Touched him intimately.

But something was wrong. She drew away from him and peered up at him, confused. "Dec?"

He wasn't aroused. Not at all.

"Robin, we've got to talk." His voice came out strangled with emotion.

She stepped back and looked at him. Saw that his eyes were filled with tears. Her heart plunged. Oh, God! It was worse than she'd expected. *Had someone died?*

"Should I sit down?" she asked, trying to put a jocular note in her voice. It failed miserably.

He held out his hand in a silent plea. She took it and followed him back into the living room, her heart racing.

"This is really serious, isn't it, Dec?"

He nodded. "Aye, love. It is."

Dropping her hand when they reached the settee, he sat down and gestured for her to join him. She did so, her brain whirling with scenarios. A death in his family? Or . . . *oh, God* . . . maybe it was *him* who was dying. Or something almost as hard to take—another woman? She'd asked him about that during her last visit to California, and he'd denied it. Had he lied?

He sat stiffly, his hands flat on his thighs. She fastened her gaze on them. Such beautiful hands. She'd always loved his hands. But where was his wedding ring? Her heart thudded. He wore a ring, but it wasn't the one she'd placed on his finger during their wedding. This one was more than a simple gold band. It was a brilliant diamond glittering in a burnished gold setting. A half carat at least.

Declan took a deep breath and ran a trembling hand through his wheat blond hair. At least, Robin thought she saw a tremor. His eyes were still shimmering with unshed tears.

"Okay. Tell me," she said. "Get it over with."

"I'm not sure how to begin," he whispered. "I don't want to hurt you."

"Nothing you say could possibly be worse than what I'm thinking." *Oh, please, God, don't let that be a lie.* "Just tell me."

His somber eyes met hers. "I love you, Robin. Christ knows I do, but . . ."

"But?" Amy felt as if her heart had stopped beating. Nothing could follow that "but" except devastating news. She closed her eyes and waited. An unearthly quiet seemed to settle inside the bungalow. No breath of sound broke the silence. There was only the dreadful drumming of her heart.

"I'm in love with someone else." His voice was quiet, but to Amy's ears, it sounded like the detonation of a bomb. The words drilled into her brain, followed immediately by the roaring of blood through her temples.

She stood on legs that felt sticklike, almost as if they were no longer a part of her at all, and walked over to the window overlooking manicured lawns and tropical palm trees. *Déjà vu.* She'd been here before, heard these words before. Felt this aching emptiness in her soul. And then she remembered. No, not *déjà vu.* Just her own words echoing back to her. Words she'd uttered barely a month ago during her confession to Kerani.

I love Dec. But I'm in love with Paul.

Karma. It had caught up with her. She'd lived a lie for seven years, and now, it was time to pay for that lie. Everything was falling apart.

"Who is she?" Amy asked quietly, still gazing out the window. Amazing how calm she felt now that she knew. She'd been right; not knowing had been the worst of it.

He took a deep breath and expelled it. She heard him get to his feet and approach her. Please don't touch me, she thought. Right now, she was handling this bad news just fine. But if he touched her, she'd lose it. She knew she would. But he stopped a few feet away. She could feel his gaze impaling her.

"It's not a *she,*" he said quietly. "It's Cedric."

She stiffened, her brain scrambling to make sense of this gibberish that had come out of Declan's mouth. *Cedric?* But Cedric was his friend. How could he . . . ? Then a visceral pain slammed through her midsection, and she doubled over, clutching her stomach. *Oh, God!* She had been wrong, so wrong! This was much, *much* worse than not knowing. Oh, God . . . oh, *God*! She couldn't have heard him correctly. It made no sense! Cedric? Declan and *Cedric*? *Oh, Jesus!*

Michael had known! Oh, dear God, Michael had tried to warn her, and she hadn't listened. Hadn't entertained for a moment the thought that he might be right. All this time apart, all those gushing letters from Ireland, the phone calls where he'd whispered how much he missed her. All lies. Because during all that time, he was getting it on with Cedric. How long? Had it started right after he left New York? All those months . . .

The Christmas party! Cedric had tried to keep her from luring Declan to their room. Of course. He'd been jealous. He hadn't wanted to share his lover with his wife. And later that night when she'd tried to get Declan to make love to her, he hadn't been able to perform. Because she didn't have the right equipment? Because she wasn't Cedric?

She moaned, feeling the bile rising in her throat. Another memory. Later that week at the quaint little inn in Carmel, Declan *had* made love to her, but only after insisting on using a condom. Now, she understood why. He'd been screwing Cedric, and honorable man that he was, he'd practiced safe sex to protect her.

Ironic laughter warred with nausea, and the nausea won the battle. Clutching her mouth, she bolted for the bathroom.

"*Robin!*" Declan called after her, his voice edged with panic.

She reached the bathroom just in time and, gagging, collapsed to her knees in front of the toilet. Everything she'd eaten on the flight came up. After the first wave of nausea subsided, she clung to the bowl, trembling. Out of the corner of her eye, she saw Declan at the door. She fumbled at the roll of toilet paper and finally managed to tear off a length to wipe her mouth.

"Get out of here," she whispered when she was finally able to summon the strength.

"Robin, please, you've got to let me explain."

Amy took a deep breath, expelled it, then wearily turned to look at him. "*Get the fuck out of here.*" It wasn't a scream. She was too weak to scream. But he understood she meant it. She watched him go. Saw the tears streaking his white face, and felt nothing. Another spasm of nausea shook her body. She retched until there was nothing more to bring up. Then she collapsed to the bathroom floor, too weak to cry, too devastated to do more than curl into the fetal position and allow the waves of shock to consume her.

Amy didn't know how long she sat on the cold marble floor of the bathroom, hugging her arms around her knees for warmth. It was quiet outside the door. Had Declan left?

She hoped so. She didn't know if she could look at him right now. Maybe not ever again. Because she knew what she'd see if she looked into his tear-stained eyes. Him and Cedric . . . touching . . . kissing . . . and everything else.

She shuddered and clutched her knees to her chest, rocking back and forth. How could it happen like this? An hour ago . . . *fifteen minutes ago* . . . her marriage was intact. Solid, or so she'd believed. Now, it was over. Just like that. But it had been a mockery from the very beginning. Just like Mike had said it was.

But was Declan the only deceiver here? A harsh laugh escaped her. No, not by a long shot. She had married him, knowing she was in love with someone else. And when it came down to deception, Dec had a long way to go before he'd reach her level. Maybe the least she could do was to go back out there and let him explain. That is, if he was still here. Maybe he'd taken her at her word and got the fuck out.

She slowly got to her feet, her limbs trembling. At least the wrenching nausea had subsided. But it had left a sour taste in her mouth and an empty feel-

ing in her gut. She felt calmer now, though, ready to listen to what Declan had
to say. Not that it really mattered. What could he possibly say to make it easier
to take?

He hadn't gone. When Amy stepped out of the bathroom, he was sitting on
the settee, staring blankly into space. A half-empty glass of bourbon stood on
the mahogany end table next to him. It looked inviting.

"I think I'll have one of those," she said, heading toward the bar. A stiff
drink. That was the ticket. So *what* if she ended up an alcoholic like her parents? Who the fuck cared? And besides, maybe they had the right idea, after
all. Drink until you don't give a shit about what happens.

Declan's gaze followed her. He wore a haggard look on his lean face. Like
he'd just survived a plane crash and still couldn't quite believe he'd come
through it intact. "Are you going to let me explain?"

Amy shrugged, pouring herself a generous measure of scotch. She tossed it
back like a pro, barely grimacing. Then poured herself another. "So, explain."

Declan waited until she'd taken her drink to the chair opposite the settee.
She sat, crossed her legs, and took a sip. It burned down her throat and hit her
stomach with a satisfying explosion.

"I want you to know I didn't plan this."

Amy nodded. "Okay." The effects of the scotch were already kicking in. She
felt calm. Totally under control. Even the funereal scent of an elaborate bouquet of fresh flowers on the nearby coffee table didn't seem as potent as it had
a moment before.

Declan spoke in a soft, ragged voice. "I've known Cedric for years. We
grew up together in Inishmore. He was . . . oh, Christ! There's only one way to
put this. He was my first lover. But I've been in denial about that for years.
Telling myself we were just fooling around. That it was no more than normal
curiosity." He paused, waiting for her to respond, but she remained silent. "He
went away to college, and I didn't see him again until I got the part in his first
film. By that time, I was in my twenties, and he was out of the closet, living
openly with his male lover. It sickened me, knowing what he was. I'd had a
couple of relationships with women, and I'd told myself that what had happened with Cedric had been the folly of hormone-charged adolescence. We
wouldn't have turned to each other if there'd been a willing female around.
But I know now that I was lying to myself. The truth is, I was sickened, not
because Cedric was gay, but because I was jealous."

He stood and crossed the room to the bar. Amy watched him, and somewhere deep inside the numbness, she felt a flicker of sympathy for him. He
was so obviously distraught.

He poured himself another glass of bourbon and turned to her. "I've been
lying to myself all these years," he said. "And I didn't know it until a few
months ago. Until the night I returned from Thanksgiving." His face reddened.

"I see," Amy said softly. So. The night after he'd returned from a weekend of leisurely sex with her, Cedric had "convinced" him that girls weren't his cup of tea, after all. The sympathy she'd felt a moment before disappeared.

He twisted the bourbon glass in his hands, his eyes dropping from hers. "It's unforgivable. I know that. I was unfaithful to you. Not just that night, but over and over. God help me, but I simply have no willpower where Cedric is concerned. And I can't tell you how much I hate myself for that."

Amy finished her drink and placed the glass on the end table. "Why now?" she asked. "Why the sudden attack of conscience? Is Cedric forcing you to make a choice? Him or me? Is that it, Declan?"

The flush on his cheekbones deepened, and Amy knew she'd hit a bull's-eye. Ah! So, Cedric was suffering from an attack of the Green-Eyed Monster. Apparently, seducing her husband wasn't enough; he wanted the whole nine yards.

"I can't go on like this," Declan said softly. "Living this lie. It's killing me, Robin, and it's not fair to you."

Amy bit back an ironic laugh. Living a lie? Little did he know he was dealing with the Queen of Lies. She took a deep breath. "So, what now, Declan? You want to take a trip across the border for a quickie divorce?"

His eyes met hers, and the pain she saw in their depths seared her heart.

"I think we both need to get on with our lives," he said quietly. "You deserve someone who can love you without reservation."

She shrugged and gave a grim smile. "Okay. Do it. The sooner, the better, I guess."

Surprise flickered across his face. Had he expected her to protest? To cling to him, crying and begging him not to leave her? What kind of woman would want to hold on to a man who was in love with someone else? That was something she'd never understood in the soap opera story lines. The scheming women—her character included—who tried to hold on to men who didn't love them. Well, she wasn't about to play that role in real life.

"I'm so sorry, Robin," Declan murmured.

Amy stood, grabbed her glass, and headed back to the bar. "I think you should go now, Dec."

His eyes followed her. "Are you sure you're okay?"

Amy's laugh came out in a harsh bark as she reached for the scotch bottle. "I *will* be. Just as soon as the booze kicks in. Good-bye, Declan. You can send the divorce papers to my lawyer."

For a moment, she heard nothing but silence, then, finally, his footsteps as he headed for the door. But there, he stopped. She turned to look at him. He stood at the door, his hand on the knob, head bowed.

Amy's throat tightened, and she knew she couldn't let him go without asking the question whispering through her brain. "Did you ever love me, Dec?"

He turned. His eyes, shining with tears, met hers. "I *do* love you," he said softly.

Amy nodded, her hand trembling on the bottle of scotch. "I love you, too," she whispered.

He swallowed hard, took a deep, shuddering breath and opened the door. "Good-bye, Robin."

I'm not Robin, she wanted to shout. For some reason, it seemed especially cruel that he would walk out of her life, never having known her. *My name is Amy Shiley, the woman you love . . . the woman you're leaving for a man.* But there was no point in confessing now. It would only complicate a situation that was already way too complicated.

After the door closed behind him, Amy poured herself another tumbler of scotch and lifted it to her lips. Blinking back tears, she raised the glass in a mocking toast and swallowed the contents.

And there, in the posh bungalow of the Beverly Hills Hotel, Robin Mulcahey Blair aka Amy Shiley, proceeded to get dead-dog drunk.

After all, it was in her genes.

28

"Where to, pretty lady?" asked the swarthy Samoan wearing a bright turquoise Hawaiian shirt and a heavily perfumed *lei* of plumeria around his thick, brown neck.

"Aloha Stadium, please." Amy slid into the backseat of the taxi.

The driver got into the front seat and peered at her in the rearview mirror. "No problem, pretty lady, but you're getting there late, yah? It's fourth quarter already, and the AFC is leading by a touchdown." He turned up the volume of the radio so she could hear the commentator's play-by-play.

". . . Thomas Jeffereys is wide-open. He comes down with the pass and . . . oh, my God . . . I thought Taupin had him down, but he wrestles away and is gone. He's at the ten . . . the five . . . *touchdown . . . AFC!*"

"Correction." The driver smirked. "The AFC is leading by *two* touchdowns."

Amy adjusted her sunglasses against the glare of the Hawaiian sun. She'd never been in Hawaii before, and hadn't known what to expect as she stepped out of the airport terminal into the bright February afternoon. Heat, surely, but that wasn't the case at all. It had been balmy and pleasantly warm, with gentle tradewinds teasing her hair and gently caressing her winter-dry face. Tall coconut trees swayed against a pristine blue sky, and somewhere not far away waited the turquoise Pacific and its sugar white beaches. As the plane descended over the island of Oahu, she'd peered out the window at the lush, mountainous green island surrounded by the ocean, its depths measured by graduating shades of deep blue to sea foam green. Like a brilliant emerald floating on a sea of aquamarine.

She was glad she'd decided to come, after all. Even if her head did feel like it might as well be the football being kicked around right now on the field at Aloha Stadium. *That's what happens when you indulge in a two-day drinking binge without giving a thought to the consequences.* As a result, instead of boarding a plane for Honolulu on Saturday afternoon as she'd planned, she'd hibernated in the bungalow at the Beverly Hills Hotel, drinking, puking, and sleeping it off before starting the whole cycle over again. It was a good thing for her that the hotel hadn't thrown her out. Who knows where she would've ended up before finally coming to her senses?

That happened this morning when she'd opened her eyes and found herself on the floor of the bungalow, the light streaming in the window, blinding her with its brilliance. Maybe it was the pain that shot through her head when she sat up, making her feel as if some samurai warrior had lopped her with his sword right down the middle of her brain. Whatever, she knew it was time to get her act together. Trembling, with every muscle in her body aching, she managed to get to the phone and call the front desk.

"What day is this?" Her voice was raspy with disuse.

"It's Sunday, Mrs. Blair," said a bemused female voice. "February 6."

Amy licked her dry, chapped lips. "Do you know what time it is in Hawaii?"

A moment of silence, then, "I believe it's about 8:00 A.M, ma'am."

Okay. It was still possible. Maybe.

"Mrs. Blair? Is there anything else?"

"Yes. I need to get to Honolulu as soon as possible. Can you call the airlines and see if there are any seats available? Anything will do. As long as I can get there today."

"I'll see what I can do, Mrs. Blair."

The Beverly Hills Hotel staff was reputed to be one of the best in the business, and now, Amy believed it. Because the girl had done it. By four o'clock, Amy had been on a United flight, in first class, no less, heading for Honolulu. It had cost a fortune, but she really didn't care. After all, Declan was paying for it. She'd put it on his credit card. As guilty as he was feeling, she didn't think he'd mind. Besides, he and Cedric, happy couple that they were, were rolling in money. Or *would* be once Dec had his Oscar nomination. She didn't think a few grand less was going to bother him.

The Samoan taxi driver beeped his horn at a car that cut him off, then swerved into the far left lane to pass him. Apparently, taxi drivers were the same the world over. As the car sped down the freeway, Amy looked out her left window, catching a glimpse of a white structure on a deep blue body of water. "What's that over there?" she asked the driver.

He glanced over. "Oh, that's Pearl Harbor, pretty lady. The *Arizona* Memorial. This your first visit to the islands, yah?"

"Yes."

His dark eyes scrutinized her. "And no one met you with a *lei*. Such a shame."

"Oh, well. I didn't expect anyone to meet me." *I expected to come here for a romantic week with my husband.*

"Here we are, pretty lady. Aloha Stadium."

She could tell he was curious. Why would a woman who'd obviously just flown into the islands be going straight to a football game instead of a hotel? Amy was glad she'd had the forethought to have her luggage sent on to the Royal Hawaiian. It would've looked really strange to go into the stadium with two suitcases.

She handed the driver a twenty and told him to keep the change. He thanked her with a broad smile, a silver-filled tooth gleaming in the sunlight. She opened the door to get out.

"Wait, pretty lady, wait."

She paused and looked at him. He lifted the plumeria *lei* over his head and passed it over the seat to her.

"Take it," he said. "Everyone should get a *lei* when they arrive in the islands. Especially a pretty lady like you. Please. I want you to have it."

His unexpected kindness brought a lump to her throat, and she was glad her dark sunglasses hid her eyes. "Thank you," she said quietly. "It's beautiful." Still smiling, she got out of the car and waved.

"*Aloha.*" He grinned, moving his hand in an odd little gesture, thumb and pinkie extended, and pulled away.

The perfume of the flowers floated in the air as she settled the lei around her neck. Its petals felt cool and velvety against her skin. What a lovely custom. The taxi driver's unexpected kindness lifted her spirits, and now, more than ever, she was glad she'd decided to come to Hawaii, after all. Not that she knew what she was going to do as far as Paul was concerned.

She kept hearing that conversation with Kerani in her mind. *Tell him the truth. Tell him you're Amy.* Her argument against it had been Declan. He was her husband. She couldn't—wouldn't—hurt him. Better to leave things as they were.

But now? Everything had changed. Of course, there were still reasons to remain silent. Her revelation would destroy lives. Michael and Tammy would never forgive her for her duplicity. And what about Paul? What made her think Paul would forgive her? After all, she'd done a horrible—some might call it *monstrous*—thing. So, how could she possibly be toying with the idea of coming clean?

I'm not going to think about this now. She'd come to Hawaii to lick her wounds, to find solace with the one person in the world she loved beyond reason. Even if it didn't make sense. Even if spending time alone with him would, in the end, cause those wounds to deepen and leave scars that would never heal. For once, she would go with her instincts and do what felt right. And if that meant confession, well, if it happened, it happened. She wouldn't think about that now.

The crowd was counting down the seconds as she walked up the ramp to the stadium. Talk about bad timing. There was no way she would find Paul now. She should've just gone straight to the hotel.

The players were still on the field, shaking hands with each other and chatting with old friends from other teams. Some were heading into the locker room tunnel almost directly below where Amy stood. She scanned the numbers on the navy blue jerseys, searching for Paul, and there he was, walking straight toward the tunnel. He took off his helmet and ran a hand through sweat-dampened black hair.

"*Paul! Up here!*"

He looked up and saw her. At first, his eyes lit up and a smile creased his weary face. But it disappeared quickly, and his brows lowered. "Robin, where the hell have you been?" He shouted over the noise of the crowd. "I've been worried sick!"

"It's a long story," Amy yelled back. "Where do you want me to meet you?"

"Wait right there. *Don't move!*" Paul trotted over to a young blond guy in a New York Giants T-shirt and pointed up at Amy. The kid grinned and gave him a thumbs-up. Paul glanced up at her, frowned, and mouthed the words "Stay right there." Then with a wave, he turned and strode into the tunnel.

A few minutes later, the blond kid in the Giants T-shirt appeared at Amy's side. "Hi. I'm Steve. Come on. I'll take you to Paul."

"Okay. By the way, I'm Robin." Amy smiled.

He grinned and led the way down the ramp and around the stadium. He glanced back once, giving her a curious appraisal. "So . . . are you Paul's girlfriend?"

Amy's heart skipped a beat, but she managed to keep a smile on her face. "No. I'm just his sister."

"Cool," the young man grinned, his blue eyes lighting up with interest. "So . . . you doing anything tonight?"

A scantily clad waitress with waist-length black hair—apparently a prerequisite for the job—placed two elaborate drinks in front of Paul and Amy—a piña colada for him, a strawberry daiquiri for her. Amy stared, horrified, at the pineapple spear swimming in the crushed ice. She'd forgotten about the problem of fresh pineapple, and how it would be in such abundance in Hawaii. Now, what was she going to do? She couldn't tell the waitress she was allergic to it in front of Paul.

"What's wrong, Rob?"

They were sitting on the *lanai* of the Royal Hawaiian Hotel facing the beach. Somewhere to their right, the sound of drums throbbed—a Tahitian dance in progress. They'd chosen not to watch the show because they hadn't had a chance to talk since she'd met him after the game. Instead, they'd found a relatively secluded spot at a wrought-iron table nestled amidst palm fronds and fragrant plumeria trees. Flaming torches flickered around them, casting dancing shadows, but still allowing enough light to see each other clearly.

And she saw he was watching her closely. She bit her lip, her brain spinning. His eyes moved to the pineapple. "Excuse me," he called to the waitress who'd already turned away. "Could you please bring the lady another daiquiri without the pineapple, please? She's allergic."

Amy's stomach plunged; she could feel the blood draining from her face.

"Of course, sir." The waitress took her drink, giving Paul a flirtatious smile. "I'll be right back with another one."

Paul grinned at Amy. "Okay, so I exaggerated the truth a bit. Mom wrote me once and told me how you couldn't eat pineapple since the accident. Said you somehow associate it with that night."

Amy nodded, suddenly able to breathe again. "Yeah, it's weird, isn't it?"

Paul studied her, blue eyes solemn. "It's been seven years. I guess something like that really sticks with you, huh?"

"Yeah." Amy gazed at the tall silhouettes of the coconut palms swaying in the tradewinds. A three-quarter moon hung in the cloudless sky, beaming its silver wash onto the waves breaking on the beach. The drums of the Tahitian dance had stopped, replaced by the strumming of a ukelele, and although Amy couldn't see the stage, she imagined raven-haired hula dancers moving gracefully to the music. A perfect Hawaiian night. "I guess you don't ever really get over something like that."

Paul was quiet for a moment. Then, "I still miss her, you know. You'd think after seven years . . ." His voice trailed away as the waitress approached with her drink.

After she'd gone, Paul took a deep breath, crossed his arms on the table, and leaned toward her. "Okay, what's up with you? Where's Declan, and why didn't he come with you? And where the hell have you been? I called New York. I called Dec. I called the Beverly Hills Hotel."

Amy looked at him. "What did Dec say?"

"Not much. He's the one who told me I might find you at the Beverly Hills Hotel. That was this morning right before I left for the stadium. You'd already checked out."

"Weren't you curious that Dec was still home? That he wasn't with me?" Amy lifted the daiquiri and took a sip. It was icy, tart, and delicious.

Paul shrugged. "Yeah, sure. But he wouldn't tell me anything. Just said I should talk to you."

Amy shook her head, her lips twisting in an ironic smile. "Poor Dec. He's probably terrified that the big, brawny football player brother will come gunning for him."

A look of concern crossed Paul's face. "Why? What has he done?"

"Something he couldn't help," Amy said quietly. "We're getting a divorce, Paul. He's in love with someone else."

Paul almost choked on his drink. He swallowed hard, his blue eyes sparking. "That *bastard*! He was screwing around on you?"

Amy reached out and placed her hand on his forearm. At the touch of his warm skin, the silky dark hairs carpeting his arm, her stomach dipped, and a warm flush enveloped her. She moved her hand back to her side of the table. Touching him was too dangerous.

"Paul, I don't want you to freak out about this. Dec and I have talked about it, and I understand what he's going through. He didn't mean to hurt me. He's heartsick about it. But sometimes you just can't help how you feel. Sometimes, you love someone for the wrong reasons . . . or you love them for the right reasons even though your situation makes it forbidden. I can't blame him for that. And I don't want you to, either."

He stared at her a long moment without speaking. A muscle flexed in his jaw, and his eyes glittered. His hand, resting on the table, was clenched in a tight fist. But finally, it relaxed, and he took a deep breath and nodded.

"Okay. If that's the way you want it. But I hate like hell knowing Dad was right about him all along. I liked Dec. I really did."

Her heartbeat faltered. "Dad told you?"

Paul took a sip of his piña colada. "He didn't have to tell me anything. Everybody knew Dad couldn't stand him."

"Oh." Amy realized they were talking about two different things. "Well, you shouldn't stop liking him. Dec is a good person, and Dad *is* wrong about him. He doesn't know him like I do." She took a deep breath and met Paul's gaze. "Paul, Dec and I married for the wrong reasons. We were both lonely, and circumstances threw us together. But we were in love with other people. He didn't realize it, though, until recently."

"Who is she? Don't tell me some Hollywood bimbo?"

Amy took another sip of her daiquiri. "It wasn't a woman, Paul." No point in hiding the truth. He'd find out sooner or later. As soon as the tabloids got wind of the story. "It turns out that Declan is gay. He fell in love with the screenwriter of the movie he just filmed." Amazing how calm and matter-of-fact she sounded. Amazing that she *felt* so calm and matter-of-fact about the end of her marriage.

But she could feel Paul's shock in his silence. Finally, he found his voice. "Christ! *Dec?* I can't believe it."

She shrugged, smiling grimly. "Yeah, it's a tough one to swallow, isn't it? But the thing is, Paul, it wasn't just a quick roll in the hay. Apparently, it all started back in their teens when they lived in the Aran Islands. And Dec spent twenty years denying his feelings. I can't blame him now that's he's finally found his happy ending. We should all be so lucky, huh?"

"Yeah, I guess so." His voice betrayed his uncertainty. "But Christ, Robin, I don't know how you can be so understanding."

"Because I saw the look on his face. I saw the anguish. He didn't make this decision lightly, and in the end, it's the best thing, isn't it? I don't want to live with a man who doesn't love me wholeheartedly. What kind of woman would I be if I accepted less than that?"

"You're right." He reached across the table and squeezed her hand, sending a tremor through her. "You deserve much more than that."

Amy took a deep breath, and tried to calm the excitement she felt at his touch. "So, what happened with you and Monica, anyhow? You never told me."

He drew his hand away. "Let's just say I finally realized she's a selfish bitch," he said quietly. "Guess you were always right about her."

"What made you finally see the light?" She glanced back at him and saw him shrug.

"Oh, she took me to her apartment one afternoon during the holidays, and her husband was there, wheelchair and all. She introduced us like he was the help or something, and I took one look into his eyes and saw that he knew exactly what was going on. She thinks because he's old and frail he's oblivious to her playing around. I saw he wasn't oblivious at all, and for the first time, I saw myself through his eyes. And it made me sick to my stomach. I broke things off with her that night, and I haven't seen her since."

"Good for you."

Silence fell for a moment, then Paul said quietly, "You said you were in love with someone else, too, Robin?"

She couldn't look at him. Instead, she turned her gaze to the graceful palms near the beach. "Yes." And before he could ask, she went on, "With someone you don't know."

"And that someone . . . is there any chance for the two of you now? I mean, after the divorce?"

Amy shook her head, and to her horror, felt tears erupting in her eyes. "No. There's no chance for us. It's impossible."

Paul reached across the table and covered her hand with his. "I don't believe that," he said softly. "As long as he's here . . . as long as he's alive, nothing is impossible."

Amy wrenched her hand away and stood. "Excuse me. I'll be right back." Heart thumping, she hurried down the path that led to the hotel.

It took her fifteen minutes to compose herself enough to return to the table. She went back with the full intention of pleading a headache and going up to her room. But Paul had already ordered another round of drinks. He looked up when she approached and gave her a smile that crinkled around his blue eyes in the most attractive way.

"Hey, I've just had the greatest idea. You have the whole week off, right? How about if we go check out the Big Island?"

★ ★ ★

"It's like going from one world into another!" Amy gazed in wonder out the window of the rented Cavalier as the skeletal remains of scorched trees disappeared into the mist behind them and they reentered the world of sunshine and warmth. They'd just descended the volcano, Kilauea, where they'd left their luggage in the cottage they'd checked into just a half hour before. They were on their way down to sea level to visit the famed black sand beaches of the Big Island, where the temperatures hovered in the mideighties. Quite a difference from the midfifties on the top of the volcano, not to mention the mist and drizzle that had prevented them from viewing the crater. That's why they'd decided to visit the beaches first, and maybe later in the afternoon, the weather on the higher elevations would have improved.

"We're back in the real Hawaii." Paul grinned. "Shall we put the top down?"

"Yes, let's," Amy agreed. Maybe it was her trailer park roots showing, but she couldn't restrain her excitement at riding in a convertible. "I'm glad I put this sweater and jeans on over my shorts. I'm going to have to strip down."

Paul found a place to pull off the road, then pushed the button to lower the top. They each got out of the car and peeled off their cotton sweaters and jeans.

"I'm glad the tourist board warned us about the cold here," Amy said. "It didn't occur to me to bring sweaters to Hawaii."

Paul shrugged, smiling. Amy couldn't help admiring his biceps in the snug red muscle shirt he wore over navy swim trunks. "Well, they've got to do their part for the economy, you know."

"Well, good. That puts my mind at ease. I've helped out the Hawaiian economy, and damn well, I might add. This sweater cost almost two hundred bucks."

"That's what you get for shopping in Waikiki. We should've taken that girl's suggestion and gone to Ala Moana Mall."

"Like we had time." Amy tossed the sweater into the backseat. "You were the one who booked us on a god-awful early-morning flight!"

"We only have a week. Why waste time?" Paul climbed back into the driver's seat. "Ready?"

Amy scooted into the passenger seat and closed the door. "Let's go."

They drove off down the road, the sun on their upturned faces and the tradewinds blowing through their hair. For the moment, fleeting though it may be, Amy realized she was, indeed, in paradise.

"Can you believe how gorgeous this is?" Amy gazed off the Volcano House deck into the massive crater of *Halemaumau* at the summit of Kilauea. "I'm so glad the weather cleared up."

"Me too." Paul took a sip of his beer. "After lunch, let's head over to the rain forest and check out the lava tube."

"Okay, but I think we're doing this in the wrong order. What's going to top the lava flow?"

"Yeah, well . . ." Paul shrugged. "We can't control the weather."

After checking out the black sand beaches, they'd climbed back into the Cavalier and taken the Chain of Craters Road through Kilauea's East Rift Zone toward the coast. The highway had ended in a black ocean of hardened lava posted with warning signs. DANGER! STEEP CLIFFS. ROUGH SURFACE. There, they'd parked the car along the road and hiked the two miles across blackened rock patterned with cracks and crevices toward a spume of white smoke marring the azure sky. As they grew closer to the actual lava flow, the air became sulfurous, and Amy found herself trying not to breathe in too deeply. This couldn't be healthy! And then came the sound, the sizzling and crackling of the lava as it greedily burned its path to the ocean. Finally, they were close enough to actually see the flow, and it was a sight that was truly wondrous. It streamed, bloodred, from a crevice in the hardened lava, thickening as it cooled into a viscous pool, silver-gray on its surface, but glimmering red beneath as it moved toward its union with the ocean. And the heat! It was staggering—so hot it felt like the hair on her forearms was about to erupt into flame. Almost frightened by the intensity, Amy moved back from the cliff's edge where it was somewhat cooler. How awesome and moving, the power of Mother Nature.

On the drive back to the summit, they'd stopped off at a barren spot overlooking the ocean where a tidal wave had wiped out a small fishing village in the 1800s. Nothing was left of the village. Now, there was just blackened lava and the constant wind blowing across the desolate landscape in what seemed like a mournful lament. It was a haunting place, and neither of them wanted to linger. Paul had suggested they drive to the Volcano House and have lunch, and she'd quickly agreed.

A waitress placed their orders in front of them and hurried away. Amy's stomach growled as she reached for her club sandwich. That hike across the lava had really given her an appetite. Paul, too, apparently. Amy grinned. He was already devouring his cheeseburger as if he hadn't eaten a decent meal in months. She took a bite of her club sandwich and gave a soft moan of appreciation. It was just how she liked it—the smoked turkey thinly sliced, the bacon crisp.

"That good, huh?" Paul asked, one black eyebrow arched in amusement.

"Oh, yeah. Delicious. How's your burger?"

He didn't answer. In fact, he'd stopped chewing, and his eyes were fastened on the sandwich in her hand.

"What's wrong?" Amy stiffened. "Oh, God. You don't see a bug, do you?" That was the one thing she didn't like about Hawaii—the bug population. They were everywhere, and most of them were big and exotically hideous. Much, much worse than those wimpy little creatures she routinely murdered in the studio.

He cocked his head and gave her an odd look. "When did you start eating turkey, Rob?"

Amy's stomach plunged, and her heartbeat skipped. She could practically feel the blood drain from her face. Her mind whirled. She saw Kerani's sympathetic brown eyes. Heard her voice in her brain.

Tell him the truth. What have you got to lose?

Trying to calm herself, she placed her sandwich back on the plate and reached for her glass of iced tea. She took a long swallow, wishing she'd ordered a mai tai. Better yet, a straight shot of tequila. She put down the glass. Her eyes met Paul's, and although her pulse was racing, she spoke without a tremor in her voice.

"Paul, I have a confession to make."

Paul placed his half-eaten cheeseburger on his plate and looked at her.
"Okay," he said slowly, eyes wary. "I'm listening."

Amy's heart hammered. She had no idea how to begin. There was no easy
way to say it. Perhaps the best thing to do was just blurt it out like she had with
Kerani. Was it her imagination or had the clatter of silverware ceased at the
other diners' tables? Why did it suddenly seem so quiet out here?
She took a deep breath. "Paul, I . . ."

Fate, God . . . maybe the Hawaiian fire goddess, *Pele*, intervened. The table
began to tremble, then shudder, as if an invisible hand was juggling it up and
down. Plates and glasses clattered and slid as the deck beneath their feet
shook violently. Paul's eyes locked on Amy's as his face drained of color.

The earthquake—at least, that's what she thought it was—intensified, and
plates and glasses tumbled to the wood deck, shattering. Amy's nails dug into
the tablecloth as her stomach roiled in terror. She imagined the deck giving
way beneath them, flinging them out onto the gritty black earth, perhaps to be
swallowed up by an incoming tsunami.

In the distance, there was a belch, and then a low, guttural boom. Immediately the violent shaking eased, then stopped. Amy stared at Paul, almost
afraid to breathe.

"What the hell was that?" she whispered.

A cell phone rang at the next table, breaking the ominous silence that had
fallen, and a bearded young man answered it. All the diners on the deck were
quiet, probably from shock. The bearded man's voice rose in excitement. "Oh,
Jesus! You're sure? For Chrissake, don't let them leave without me. I'm on my
way." He jumped up from his table and began to stride past them.

Paul stopped him. "Do you know what happened?"

The man's brown eyes danced with excitement. "A new vent has opened up along the East Rift Zone. It's producing lava fountains over four hundred meters high!"

"Oh, my God," Amy breathed, unable to even imagine such a thing. "We were just in that area this morning."

"Jesus," Paul whispered, awestruck. "That would be about as high as four football fields end to end. Are you a seismologist?"

The bearded man laughed. "Hell, no! I'm a helicopter pilot. Jack Stevenson is the name." He dug out a business card from his shirt pocket. "Pele Helicopter Tours. You want to go see this fountain of fire, I'm your man. I'll take you up as soon as it gets dark, and I guarantee you'll see one hell of a good show. Gotta go now, though. Call me if you're interested." He hurried off like a kid who'd just seen the ice-cream truck pull into the neighborhood.

Amy looked at Paul and saw the excitement glittering in his eyes. "Are we interested?" she asked.

He grinned, and years seemed to vanish from his face. "Does a bear shit in the friggin' woods?"

It was the most magnificent sight Amy had ever laid eyes on. The fountain of fire spewing up from the rift glowed in shades of bright orange, deep claret, and rich crimson. Hard to believe such an awesome force of nature could be so beautiful, yet, so deadly.

Jack Stevenson's helicopter hovered near the spectacle, but not so close that Amy felt they were in any danger. Thank God Stevenson appeared to be the cautious type. She couldn't think of a worse death than being flung into a fountain of lava to be roasted alive. Come to think of it, wasn't that an ancient ritual in some cultures? To fling a virgin off the ledge of a rumbling volcano? Not that she qualified, of course. Thanks to the man sitting beside her, she'd lost that status seven years ago.

"Jesus!" Paul leaned toward her, gazing out the window in astonishment. "Have you ever seen anything so incredible in your life?"

Amy glanced at him, and her heart spasmed. The light from the lava fountain cast an orange glow upon his face, but it was the joy from within that showed so clearly in his boyish grin, the excitement dancing in his eyes. It took away the years from his face, and for a moment, Amy imagined it was a younger Paul who sat next to her—the same young man who'd sat with her in a car parked at Cohoke Crossing in West Point, Virginia. So many years had passed since that night, but still, she couldn't deny the feeling that swept through her now. An encompassing sense of desire for the one special man she'd fallen in love with so long ago. That night had ended with him in her arms. She wanted it again, even more than she had that first time.

"Yes, it's incredible." Amy turned back to the spectacle, blinking hard to hold back tears that were suddenly threatening.

"Amy would've loved it," Paul said. "Did she ever tell you this was one of her dreams? To see an active volcano?"

She shook her head. Had she? She remembered telling Paul that, but she didn't think it had ever come up in conversation with Robin. Amazing, how good his memory was of the things they'd discussed in their all-too-brief relationship.

"Two things she'd wanted to do," Paul went on, his voice edged with bitterness. "See a volcano and go to Ireland. And she didn't get a chance to do either one."

Tell him, Amy. Now's your chance. He just gave you a perfect opening.

But no, she couldn't do it. Not with the helicopter pilot within hearing. This was something that had to be said in private . . . or not said at all. *Later,* she told herself. *Maybe tonight after we return to the cabin.* But even as she thought this, she wasn't sure she could actually do it. Telling Paul the truth was a monumental task. Maybe it would be easier for everyone if she just kept living this lie. She'd done it for seven years; why not keep it up for the rest of her life? Wouldn't that be the easiest solution for everyone?

"Well, folks, we've got to get back to base." Jack Stevenson barked out. "I've got five more trips scheduled tonight."

The helicopter banked hard to the right and headed toward Hilo. Amy craned her neck for a last glimpse of the lava fountain until it was nothing more than a crimson glow in the dark night. The farther away they flew from it, the more the sadness in her heart deepened.

Paul yawned and pointed the remote control at the TV set in the corner of the small living room, and began to channel-surf. From the bathroom down the hall, the roar of the shower competed with the noisy clang of the ancient plumbing. He sighed and glanced at his wristwatch. One o'clock. *Women.* He shook his head. *Why is she showering, anyway? We're going to the beach, for God's sake.*

They'd slept in this morning, neither of them budging from their bedrooms until after eleven. Then they'd lingered over coffee and cinnamon rolls from a Hilo bakery, discussing their plans for the day. Or rather, for the afternoon, because the day was half-over. He gave another exasperated sigh. And if Robin didn't get her butt out of the shower, the whole day would be gone.

Last night, Jack Stevenson had told them about a great beach on the Kona side of the island called Captain Cook's Landing. According to Stevenson, it offered some of the best snorkeling in the Hawaiian Islands, and since they only had a few more days here, that was something he really wanted to do. *If his slowpoke sister would ever get her act together so they could leave.*

He glared down the hallway and shouted, "Hey, Rob! You're not meeting the queen of England, for God's sake! Let's *go!*"

No response. Of course, she couldn't hear him over the beat of the water. He groaned and hit the channel button. Saw the opening credits of *South Riding,* and began to grin. Well, hell. *Might as well watch and see what Rob is up to on her soap.* He'd never dare admit it to her, but he hadn't watched it in ages, not since the novelty of having a sister on TV had worn off. There she was now.

In fact, he remembered the day she'd filmed these scenes. How could he forget that ugly orange prison jumpsuit that somehow managed to make her look slim and sexy despite the grotesque color? Typical show business. Only on TV or the movies could a woman on Death Row look like a Victoria's Secret model.

On the screen, Robin was lying on her back on a bunk in a prison cell, staring up at the ceiling. A single glistening tear trailed prettily down her face. Was it manufactured or had she really produced it? That was something he kept meaning to ask Rob, but he kept forgetting. Do actors really manage to cry on command, or are the tears created by the makeup department?

The scene did that weird, wavy thing that meant "flashback," and dissolved into Robin and Declan in bed together, apparently indulging in some after-sex pillow talk. The camera was shooting behind Declan's shoulder, and Robin was gazing at him, her face propped on her hand. Paul felt a flush creep up from his neck. Jesus, the one time he turns on his sister's soap, he has to see her practically naked doing a love scene. *Look at that!* The sheet barely covered her breasts.

The camera switched to Declan as he gazed soulfully into Robin's eyes and whispered that he loved her.

Bastard! Paul still couldn't get over Rob's revelation about his sexuality. Like most heterosexuals, he believed he'd had expert radar for sorting out gays from straight guys, but in Declan's case, it had failed him utterly. There hadn't been the slightest hint—not a flicker of a question—about his leanings. Poor Rob. She was putting up a good front, but he knew she had to be devastated. Still . . . hadn't she mentioned being in love with someone else when she married Dec? He had no idea who. Unless it was that drug-hazed Jason idiot from high school. Christ, he hoped not. What a loser.

On the screen, Robin suddenly sat up to lean closer to Declan, and the sheet slipped lower. That's when Paul saw it. The small crescent-shaped mark on the slope of her breast peeping above the sheet. His heart lurched, and he leaned forward, trying to get a better look. But it was too late. Robin drew the sheet higher, covering it, just before her lips met Declan's for a passionate kiss.

Paul sat frozen, his hands flattened on his thighs. His eyes were locked on the TV, but he wasn't really seeing it anymore. Jumbled thoughts careened through his brain as his heart began to pound. It was like he was watching a movie backward, trying to make sense of the scenes. Or solving a puzzle created by Mensa masterminds, an impossibility for normal intellects. Pieces didn't fit. Didn't compute.

But something jarred. Something beyond his reach, but close, tantalizing. Like the misty images of a dream that linger through the day, but dissolve into nothingness when trying to capture.

From the bathroom down the hall, there was a wrenching groan from the pipes, and the shower stopped. Paul refocused his gaze on the television and saw that the soap had moved on to another story line.

By the time Robin stepped into the room, he'd recovered his composure. At least, outwardly. He turned to look at her. She wore a navy floor-length velour robe, tied at the waist, her bare feet peeping out below it. Her hair was wrapped in a towel.

She gave him a bright smile. "Almost ready. I just need to get into my swimsuit and put some foundation on my face. And before you ask why I need to put on makeup, I'll tell you. It has sunscreen in it, and I can't afford to get burned."

Sunscreen. Robin had never used it as a teenager. He remembered how she used to brag about how she could slather on the coconut oil and tan golden brown instead of burn. But that was before she became an actress and realized how fragile young skin was, and how devastating the sun could be on it.

"And don't think I didn't hear you yelling at me to hurry up," Robin said saucily. "Hey, I thought this was a vacation, not boot camp."

His gaze swept over her face, lingering on the nearly invisible scars at the hairline above her ears. So many surgeries. All to bring back her predamaged face. Now, here she was, as beautiful as ever. Better than ever. But different. No one had ever said it, but they all knew, even Robin had to know, that the accident had put her life back on track, changed it for the better.

But . . .

His eyes focused on the shawl opening of her robe, revealing the creamy slope of her neck, a curve of her breast. That mark he'd seen on the TV Robin. Had it been manufactured by the makeup department in the same way he suspected tears were? Was her character some kind of tough broad who tattooed her breast? Was it just a product of his imagination that he felt like he'd seen that mark before? It hadn't taken more than a few seconds to realize exactly where he'd seen it.

He remembered it all too well. Remembered brushing his lips across it. Telling Amy it looked like a crescent moon.

Impossible. He knew that. Still . . . what had he seen? Or what had he *imagined* he'd seen?

"What are you staring at?" Robin asked.

He looked away from her, but not before he saw a flicker of . . . wariness? . . . in her eyes. "Nothing." He made a show of glancing at his wristwatch. "But hey, if we want to rent that catamaran to go to Cook's Landing, we've got to get going."

"Okay. I won't be more than a couple of minutes." She turned and disappeared down the hall.

Paul looked back at the TV where a raven-haired Hispanic beauty argued with a male-model-type actor.

He had to know. There had to be a way to find out what that mark was on Robin's breast.

He'd figured out how to do it. Now, he was just waiting to summon up the nerve to go through with it. Paul reached for his can of Coke and took a sip, squinting out at the sea green lagoon where he'd caught a glimpse of a giant sea turtle swimming lazily in the warm, clear water. He'd seen the same one—at least, he thought it was the same one—up close and personal only a half hour ago as he and Robin snorkeled inside the reef. Everything Stevenson had said about this place was true. Hundreds of varieties of exotic fish, and pure, clear water in which to view them. Plus, because the beach was off the beaten track, it wasn't overrun by tourists. Which was all well and good considering what he was about to do.

Robin lay on her stomach next to him, dozing. Two hours of nonstop snorkeling had tuckered her out. Him, too. And no wonder. The current had been strong, and the constant pressure to fight against it, even wearing fins, had taken its toll of them. His calves and thighs ached like he'd been skiing black diamonds in fresh powder. And he was a conditioned athlete. He could only imagine how wasted Robin was feeling.

He glanced from her to the sun making its descent over the ocean, turning the waves garnet as they crashed on the reef offshore. Glancing at his wristwatch, Paul felt his stomach muscles tighten with apprehension. The catamaran and gear had to be back at the Kona snorkeling outfitter by six-thirty. Forty-five minutes away.

It was now or never.

And he had to know. With a grunt, he hoisted himself off the blanket and tossed the remainder of his Coke into the sand. He walked down the beach to the water, knelt, and filled the soda can. Slowly, his jaw set, he returned to the blanket. Stared down at Robin's perfect back, bare except for the tiny strings of her bikini. He'd slathered sunblock on her back earlier at her request, and again, he'd marveled about her fear of sunburn. It was so out of character from the sister he'd grown up with.

He glanced around the beach. It was nearly deserted. Only a couple of late sunbathers about a football field's length away. His eyes returned to Robin.

She appeared to be sleeping soundly, her face turned to the left, lips slightly parted.

She'll kill me for this. Childhood pranks were one thing, but they were no longer children. But how else would he be able to find out?

He knelt beside her, watching her face carefully to make sure she didn't awaken. His hand hovered over her back, trembling slightly.

What the fuck is wrong with you? Just do it. You're not going to see anything, anyway. It was probably all just a figment your imagination. But do it. Get it over with, and prove it was your imagination.

He grabbed the end of the string tied around her neck and tugged. It came undone easily. He held his breath, waiting to see if she'd felt anything. She didn't move. Her breathing was rhythmical, steady. Paul released his breath and reached for the Coke can. He closed his eyes briefly, sucked in another deep breath and poured the water on her back.

With a sharp gasp, she bolted up from the blanket. *"What the . . . ?"* Her eyes blazed, furious, and then widened in horror as she realized her bikini top was hanging by the bottom strings. She grabbed the two triangles and slapped them against her breasts. "My God, Paul! Are you freakin' *nuts?"*

He stared at her, his brain spinning. He couldn't speak, couldn't form his mouth to say a single word.

Because he'd seen it. There was no mistaking it this time. It was exactly what he'd thought he'd seen on the TV a few hours earlier.

A brown mark on her left breast. A mark shaped just like a crescent moon.

Paul sat at the pine dining table and stared across the room at the fire he'd just built in the stone hearth. From the kitchen, he could hear Robin moving around, apparently preparing a pot of coffee.

Coffee. She'd hated the stuff as a teenager. Wouldn't touch it. It was only after she'd moved to New York and become an actress that he'd first noticed her drinking it. Just another piece to add to the puzzle.

A splatter of rain pelted against the front window, and Paul shivered, cold despite the fleece sweatshirt he wore. By the time they'd returned to Hilo, and grabbed a bite to eat at a hole-in-the-wall Mexican restaurant, darkness had fallen, and with it had come a cold, drenching rain. The weather had been even worse on Kilauea. Rain, swirls of fog, and bone-chilling air—for Hawaii—had enclosed the summit. As soon as they'd arrived at the cottage, Robin had headed for the bathroom and a hot shower, and he'd built the fire.

A few minutes ago when she stepped into the room and announced the shower was free, he hadn't moved, even though the grit of sand itched on his scalp, and the ripe smell of his dried sweat mingled with that of the suntan lotion he'd used. He just couldn't summon the energy. With a shrug, Robin had gone into the kitchen to make coffee.

She was still pissed at him, he supposed, even though she hadn't mentioned his prank since it happened. God knows she had every right to be indignant about the stunt he'd pulled. Even now, he could see her stormy blue eyes filled with anger and confusion as she retied her bikini strings behind her neck. Hear her furious voice, "Grow up, will you?"

They'd both been quiet during dinner at the Mexican restaurant. He'd eaten mechanically, and even now, couldn't remember what the hell he'd ordered. His brain was spinning with the implication of what he'd seen. And what it meant. How was it possible that Robin would have the same birthmark on her breast that Amy had had? He'd heard of freaks of nature, but this . . . this was too much. Coincidences like that just didn't happen.

Besides, he'd played that prank before when they were kids. He'd seen Robin's flat, boyish chest. Many times. Surely he would've noticed a birthmark back then. Birthmarks didn't just appear years later, did they? And even if that were true, it was just too *Twilight Zone* that a crescent-shaped birthmark would appear in the very same spot. *So, what the hell is going on?*

His mind felt like it was racing the Indy 500. Going in circles. How could this be? How *could* this be? And then, out of nowhere, the thoughts formed. All the little things. The little differences. So many differences since the accident.

Robin's sudden love for Ruby the cat. She'd been indifferent to her from the time Paul had first found her in the bushes and brought her home. And Ruby had appeared to dislike her. Yet, today, the cat lived with Robin in New York. The last time he'd visited her in her apartment, Ruby had curled up in Robin's lap for an hour, dozing contentedly.

Then, there was Robin's interest in football. She'd never been able to watch two minutes of a game as a teenager. When she'd been a cheerleader in high school, she hadn't known the difference between offense or defense, and had to take her cues from the other cheerleaders. Now, she could discuss football intelligently. And really seemed to enjoy watching it.

And there was the drinking. Before the accident, Robin had been on her way to becoming an alcoholic. Now, she barely touched the stuff, usually choosing a soda over a beer. And the only time he'd seen her close to intoxicated was after the Emmys that time.

What about the other day in Honolulu? He remembered the horror in her eyes when the waitress had placed that daiquiri in front of her, a spear of fresh pineapple sticking out of the crushed ice. Mom had said it was because she associated pineapple with the night of the accident. But . . . did that account for the fear he'd seen on her face at the sight of the drink?

Another thing. Her scent. That heady scent of coconut and peach that he would always, *always* associate with Amy.

And finally . . .

He swallowed hard, his clasped hands tightening. There was the turkey. The club sandwich she'd been eating at the Volcano House yesterday. He'd been shocked when he'd realized she was eating turkey—a meat she'd always detested at home. It was a running joke in the Mulcahey family—how Robin would rather have a bologna sandwich on Thanksgiving Day instead of the succulent roast turkey the rest of the family adored. He'd brought it to her attention, hadn't he? And she'd said . . . what? He glared into the fire, think-

ing. She hadn't answered, he remembered, because of the earthquake. But . . .
no. She *had* said something just before the building started to shake. What had
it been?

Think. He closed his eyes, massaging his temples with his fingertips. He
saw her eyes widen with dismay after he mentioned the turkey. And then, her
face had become resigned.

Paul, I have a confession to make.

His heart began to pound. He heard a footstep and looked up to see Robin
step into the dining area, two mugs of steaming coffee in her hands. Her hair,
still wet from the shower, was combed back from her face, giving her the
appearance of a woman much younger than twenty-six. She wore snug jeans
and a long-sleeved pink top that hooked down the front and hugged her
shapely curves. His eyes centered on her left breast.

"Piping hot coffee. Doesn't it smell great?" Her brow furrowed. "Ooooh,
listen to that rain out there. It's really coming down." She placed the mug down
in front of him, leaning so close he could inhale her shower-fresh fragrance.

His hands tightened. It was all he could do to restrain himself from reaching up and pushing back the vee opening of her top to see the birthmark again.
To reassure himself he hadn't gone off the deep end. Because what he was
thinking was just too "out there." What he was thinking could get him committed to the loony bin.

Robin started to take a seat to the left of him, then hesitated, glancing over
into the living room. "Where is that guest book I was glancing through? I
wanted to write about our helicopter ride to the eruption."

Paul opened his mouth to tell her to leave that for later. That they had to
talk. But nothing came out, and she headed into the living room. He watched
her. She moved gracefully, in the way her actor's training had taught her. Her
blond hair had grown almost to her shoulders, and because it was so fine, had
already started to dry. Her shoulders and waist were slim, but not anorexically
so, like some actresses. Her hips in those snug jeans were perfectly shaped,
beautifully proportioned. From the back, she could've passed for Amy. *Insane
thought.* But there it was.

She returned to the dining table, carrying a thick green guest book. Plopping it down, she smiled at him. "Have you had a chance to look at this? It's so
cool." She took a seat to his left and began to turn the pages. "Oh, this is the
one I wanted to read you. Listen to this. It's so sweet. 'We're newlyweds
spending our honeymoon here on Kilauea. Tonight we hiked across the hardened lava to where the flow empties into the ocean. It was so romantic! I told
Frank I want to come back here on our 50th anniversary.' " Robin looked up at
him, eyes shining. "Oh, Paul. I hope they do get to come back. I hope they
have a long, happy marriage."

Paul stared at her, and suddenly, his heart was thudding so hard it drowned
out the sound of the rain beating against the roof. "Why were you eating

turkey yesterday, Robin? You hate turkey. For as long as I can remember, you've hated turkey."

Silence. For a long moment, the only sound Paul heard was the blood rushing through his brain. He watched the color ebb from Robin's face. Saw the frightened-doe-in-the-headlights look in her eyes.

Feeling like he'd just boarded a runaway train, and there was nothing to stop it but a stone wall or a crumbled bridge at the end of the line, he waited for her answer.

Amy felt the room grow dark around her. Suddenly she couldn't draw enough air into her lungs to breathe. She fought back the panic that threatened to engulf her as she stared at Paul's white face. A myriad of emotions fought for position in his blue eyes. Confusion. Anger. Accusation. Hurt. Fear. And yes, horror. Like he knew the truth already. Maybe not consciously. But somewhere, deep inside, he knew the truth.

She began to tremble. "Paul . . . I . . ."

His hands were clasped in front of him, resting on the pine table. Her gaze dropped to his white knuckles. She couldn't bear to watch his eyes. Not while she told him.

The gig is finally over, Amy. You always knew this day would come, didn't you? Well, girlfriend, it's here.

She released a tremulous breath, and said, "You're right. Robin never liked turkey, but I did. I am *Amy*, Paul. Robin is dead."

Stark silence filled the room. There was just the crackle of the fire and the batter of rain against the windows. For a long moment, Amy stared down at the table, waiting for his response. When it didn't come, she finally got the nerve to look at him.

His face was white as parchment, his eyes stricken as if he'd just seen someone he loved mowed down right in front of him.

Amy felt as if a knife were sawing through her heart and was forced to look away from the pain and confusion in his eyes. *Oh, God. How can I make him understand?* She took a deep breath and went on, "Robin died in that accident seven years ago, and I took over her identity because I didn't think I had a life worth living as Amy Shiley. I had lost you, and I'd lost my best friend. I didn't want to lose my makeshift family as well, so when I came to, and your parents were calling me by Robin's name, and I realized she'd died, I decided to *become* her. That way, I could at least be close to them . . . to you. I thought it would be the best thing for everybody. Your parents wouldn't lose their daughter. You and Jeff wouldn't lose a sister. No one would care if Amy Shiley died."

Paul was suddenly shaking his head, blue fire in his eyes. "What the *fuck* are you talking about?" He stared at her, a nerve twitching in his jaw. "You're insane."

"Why did you ask me about the turkey, then?" Amy's eyes locked on his.

"You had to have suspected something. And if you mean I'm insane because of what I did, well, yes, maybe I was when I decided to let everyone believe I was Robin, but Paul, you've got to believe me, I've been paying for my insanity for the *last . . . seven . . . years.* It's been hell . . . living this lie. Being close to you and not being able to . . ." Her voice broke as she realized she wasn't getting through to him. "Oh, God. You *do* think I'm crazy, don't you?" Well, why not? Who wouldn't think she was crazy?

"You can't be Amy," Paul said, his voice raspy with emotion, eyes haunted. "Amy is dead."

She shook her head in frustration. "Paul, how can I convince you I'm not lying? *I'm not Robin!* I'm Amy Jessica Shiley. I was born on October 12, 1978, in Daytona Beach, Florida. My parents were Ray and Vicky Shiley. Dad shot himself in the bathroom of our trailer in Newport News, and Mom died in a nursing home in Richmond in 1999." She sucked in a deep breath, waiting to see any change in his expression. There was none. Only pity and disbelief. She reached out a hand and covered his. He shrank away from her, shoving both hands under the table. A wrenching pain shot through her at his rejection. Her voice lowered with urgency, "Paul, I gave you my virginity on January 1, 1998. It was after we went to Cohoke Crossing. We listened to *Secret Garden* on the CD player in Robin's Camaro. You told me that I was beautiful, that any guy would be lucky to have me for a girlfriend. But I wanted you."

Something flickered in his eyes, and Amy felt hope rise inside her. Maybe she was starting to get through to him.

"I practically offered myself to you right there in the car, but you played the noble gentleman. Do you remember how you stopped at the 7-Eleven and bought condoms? How could Robin know that? We went back to Windsong, and you came to my room, remember? Remember how wonderful it was, Paul? You made my first time so special, so perfect. I loved you with all my heart and soul. And I know now that you felt the same way, even though maybe you didn't realize it at the time. You broke my heart with that e-mail. When you told me you'd gone back to Monica. That's why I let Robin talk me into going out to that bar in Richmond that night. And that's why I let those guys buy us drinks. You see, I didn't care anymore whether I became a drunk like my parents. For the first time in my life, I understood why they needed to drink. Life is so much easier when you're not seeing it through clear eyes. But I was inexperienced at drinking. That's why I only had two beers. Robin got blitzed, of course. So, I got behind the wheel of her Camaro. I remember skidding on the ice and seeing the headlights of the semi coming at us. The next thing I knew, I was waking up in the hospital, and your parents were calling me Robin." Her voice died away. She stared at him, waiting for a response.

Confusion warred with disbelief in his eyes. It was plain that some of what she'd said had sunk in, making him doubt what seemed impossible. But she saw he was fighting that doubt, clinging to the reality of what he saw. And why not? She was still speaking through Robin's lips. Everything she said, every expression crossing her face, belonged to Robin. If only he could look into her eyes—*Amy's eyes*—and see the truth.

But he shook his head, running a trembling hand through his rumpled hair. "You knew all that. Amy must've told you everything. You were best friends. She probably gave you a blow-by-blow account of everything that happened between us."

Amy gazed at him sadly. "Do you believe that of me? Much as I loved Robin, I would never have shared intimate details of our relationship with her. What happened between us was sacred to me, Paul. Surely you know that." She could see now that he wanted to believe her. It was evident in the haunting sadness in his eyes. Her pulse raced. He sat stiffly, staring at her with that wounded expression. She reached out a trembling hand and cupped the side of his bristled jaw. "You have to believe me, Paul. It's me. Amy. I think something inside of you recognizes that. Please let yourself listen to the part of you that knows me." She held her breath, waiting, her eyes locked with his.

He wrenched away from her and shoved his chair back. "Oh, you're good, Robin! Now, I know why you deserved that Emmy. You could probably sell tickets to an ice-skating competition in hell." He stood and strode into the living room, then whirled and stared at her with wild eyes. "What do you take me for, anyway? An idiot? *Christ!* You'd better make yourself an appointment with your shrink as soon as you get home, little sister, or somebody is going to lock you up."

Amy's shoulders slumped in defeat. How on earth could she convince him she was telling the truth? Abruptly she jumped up and headed for the bedroom. "Wait here. I have something to show you."

He was sitting on the sofa, staring broodingly into the fire when she returned.

"Here. Look at this." She handed him the sketch Kerani had drawn from the age-enhanced photo of herself taken just before the accident. "This is what I should look like now. If I hadn't done what I did. I had Kerani sketch it for me. She knows the truth. We can call her. It's the middle of the night in New York, but if you don't want to wait, wake her up. She'll tell you I'm not lying."

He gazed at the sketch, his brow furrowed. "This doesn't mean anything." He handed the sketch back to her. "And why should I believe Kerani? For all I know, you've got her convinced it's the truth. Like I said, Rob, you're one hell of an actress."

Amy shook her head, exasperated. "Oh, God. How can I convince you I'm telling you the truth?"

"You can't." Paul gazed at her, pity on his face. "Rob, I think maybe you should go back to New York tomorrow. You need some kind of counseling. Maybe I do, too. I've been thinking some crazy thoughts." His hands raked through his hair. "Christ! Our family is more fucked up than I ever believed we were."

Amy watched him, at a complete loss for words. Then the lightning bolt struck. "Oh, my God! That's why you did that this afternoon. Threw the water on me. You saw . . ." She walked toward him. "Paul, you must've suspected something, or you would never have done such a juvenile thing. You saw my birthmark. That proves I'm telling you the truth!"

He lifted his head and gazed at her with dull eyes. "I've racked my brain trying to think of an explanation for that. The only thing I can come up with is that for whatever reason . . . you want to be just like Amy. It doesn't make sense, but why else would you try to duplicate her birthmark?"

"I didn't try to duplicate it, Paul," Amy said quietly. "You're grasping at straws now."

Her hands went to the hook-and-eye closures of her knit top. She stared at him as she undid the first three. "Look at me, Paul." She took a step closer to him and waited for him to do as she requested. When he did, she pushed aside the fabric to expose the slope of her left breast. "You can't manufacture this. It's not a tattoo or a sticker or a paint job. It's my skin."

His gaze centered on the crescent-shaped birthmark, and his face went a shade paler.

"The skin I was born with," Amy whispered, watching his face. "It's who I am. Do you remember kissing this, Paul? You said it was like a crescent moon. Remember? I *am* Amy. I am the woman who has loved you since I saw you in the airport that first Thanksgiving. I've never stopped loving you."

His eyes seemed to be transfixed by the birthmark, and Amy watched the change in his expression. From confusion and fear to acceptance. Relief rushed through her. Finally! He believed her. He got to his feet and reached out to her, his fingers trembling as he touched the birthmark. Her heart skipped a beat, and a rush of tenderness swept through her, weakening her knees. For a long moment, he stared at the birthmark, then his eyes moved to hers. She saw his amazed expression through a veil of tears.

"It *is* me, Paul," she whispered. Her hand covered his, pressing it against her breast. "I never left you."

"Oh, my God," he said softly. He drew his hand away from hers and stepped backward, shaking his head as if trying to reorient himself. He sank down on the sofa and buried his face in his hands.

Amy's heart almost stopped beating. She didn't know what to do, what to say. It was up to him now. Was she being foolishly naive to think he could accept what she'd done, be able to forgive her and start all over again? The silence seemed to go on forever as Amy stood there watching him sit like a statue on the sofa. Finally, he lifted his head and stared at her, his face naked with pain. Amy drew in a sharp breath, tried to speak, but couldn't.

"How could you do that?" he asked quietly. "How could you do that to my family? My sister is dead, and none of us had a chance to mourn her."

Amy's heart ached as tears pooled in her eyes. "I told you. I did it because I was scared. I was all alone in the world, and for the first time in my life, I had a family who made me feel loved and wanted. I didn't want to give that up." Tears streaked down her face as she took a step toward him. "They were calling me Robin, Paul. They told me Amy was dead, but I knew it was Robin they were talking about. I knew I'd lost my best friend, my only link to your family. I thought if I pretended to *be* Robin, it would save everyone a lot of grief. No one would miss me. No one would care if I died. I know it was crazy and horrible and unforgivable, but at the time, it made perfect sense. Try and understand where I was, Paul. You had just dumped me. I was heartbroken, thinking I'd lost you forever. And then, I lost Robin. Can't you see? Amy Shiley had no reason to live. Her world had crumbled around her. At least, if I *became* Robin, I'd have a family, and I'd get to see you from time to time. That was my reasoning then." She shook her head, her hands clenched in front of her. "It didn't take me long to realize what a mistake it had been. But by that time, I was in too deep."

Paul stood slowly. He looked past her as if unable to meet her eyes. "You should have kept lying," he said softly, his voice dead of emotion. He turned and, like an old man, walked out of the room.

Amy sank to the sofa and stared into the dying flames. Barely more than embers now. A blessed numbness had settled over her. Even her tears had stopped flowing. So, this was what it felt like to totally and irrevocably screw up your life. Was this rock bottom? Or could things get any worse? Well, yes, she supposed they could. If Paul went back to Williamsburg and told his parents the truth. What then? Charges? For the first time—unbelievably—the thought of criminal charges swept through her mind. What laws had she broken? Impersonation? Fraud? God knows what else. Oh, the tabloids would have a field day with this.

EMMY AWARD WINNING SOAP STAR
SENTENCED TO THIRTY YEARS IMPRISONMENT

Paul stepped back into the living room, his suitcase in hand. "I'm going over to the Volcano House to see if they have a room for the night." He spoke in the neutral tone of a stranger. "I'll get a flight out of Hilo tomorrow, then get back to New York as soon as possible. This place is paid up for the week. I'll leave the rental car for you." Without waiting for her response, he turned to the door.

"Paul?" She had to ask. She had to know what to expect. "What are you going to say to Tammy and Michael?"

He turned and looked at her. She'd never seen him look grimmer.

"Nothing," he said curtly. "Knowing the truth would kill them. I can't do that to them."

He opened the door and stepped out into the cold rain. It closed behind him, but an icy gust of air lingered in the room. Shivering, Amy ran her hands up and down her arms and stared into the darkened fire. Nothing left now but blackened logs glinting with dying embers. She felt cold all the way through to her bones.

PART THREE

"So, do you have big plans for your birthday, Cupcake?" Michael's jovial voice boomed in Amy's ear.

She closed her eyes and took a deep breath before speaking in what she hoped was a natural tone. "No, I'm just staying at home tonight. They had a cake for me on the set today though."

"That's great, honey. Mom and I would come up if we could get away, but . . . you know how that goes."

Amy didn't respond, but she was thanking God for small favors. After a slight hesitation, Michael went on, "Hard to believe my baby girl is twenty-seven today, isn't it?"

Hard to believe you're such a despicable bastard, Amy thought grimly.

"You okay, Cupcake?"

Her hand clenched on the receiver as she fought to keep her voice neutral. "I'm fine, Dad. Just tired. It was a long day at work."

"Okay, then. Hold on. Your mom wants to say hi."

"Robin?" Tammy chirped. "Happy birthday, sweetie. Did you get the gift I sent?"

Amy glanced at the rectangular box she'd picked up at the post office on her way home. "Yeah, but I haven't had a chance to open it. I just walked in when the phone rang."

"Oh, it's just a little something I found at Lladró. It reminded me of you. Would you be a darling and open it now while I have you on the phone?"

Amy managed not to sigh, but she couldn't help gritting her teeth. "Okay. Hold on."

It was a figurine of a mother on her knees hugging a little girl dressed in pink. Amy tried not to feel bitter. She really tried. After all, maybe Robin was wrong. Maybe Tammy hadn't known.

"It's beautiful, Mom. Thank you." *But how could she not have known?*

Tammy laughed. "I knew you'd love it! Well, sweetie, I've got to run. We're having a little dinner party tonight, and the guests will be arriving any minute. I just wanted to wish my little girl happy birthday."

"Thanks, Mom." Amy moved closer to the phone unit, glad that the conversation was winding down.

"Oh, Robin?" Tammy's voice rose as if she'd just remembered something. "Have you seen Paul lately? I haven't heard from him in ages."

Amy's heart spasmed. Like it did every time she thought of Paul. "Not recently," she said slowly. "But I'm sure he's all right."

"Well, if you talk to him, tell him to call home sometime. It would be nice to hear his voice."

Yes, it would, Amy thought. It would be nice hearing his voice saying, "I forgive you, Amy." But that wasn't going to happen. It had been over a month since he'd left her in the cabin on Kilauea. And she hadn't seen or heard from him since. But what had she expected after dropping such a bombshell on him? *Hey, no problem, honey . . . so, you stole my sister's identity and you've been living her life the past seven years. Everybody is entitled to a mistake.*

"Well, thanks for calling, Mom," Amy said briskly. "Hope your dinner party goes well." And before Tammy could say more, "Talk to you soon. Bye-bye." She hung up the phone.

Cradling the creamy porcelain figurine, she dropped onto the sofa, gazing at it through cynical eyes. Oh, how Tammy would like to believe she'd been the perfect mother—always there for her darling little girl, but if what Robin wrote was true—and why on earth would she lie about something so monstrous—Tammy wouldn't have won any Mother of the Year awards.

Amy still couldn't believe what she'd read last night. Not only had it caused her to lose sleep, it had haunted her thoughts all through the long day on the set. She'd read it over and over, thinking that perhaps she'd somehow misconstrued it, but no, it was there in teal ink, every word an indictment against Michael. For months now, Amy had been working her way through Robin's journals. And last night she'd found the sealed envelope stuck in the pages of Robin's last journal. There was no writing on it, just a blank envelope. She'd opened it with trembling fingers, knowing instinctively it had something to do with those missing years in her journals.

Amy placed the figurine on the coffee table, stood, and went into her bedroom. She opened the drawer of her nightstand and reached for the envelope. One more time. She'd read it once more and then decide what to do. Paul, at least, should know about it. And what he chose to do with the information, then . . . well . . . she'd leave that up to him.

She unfolded the letter.

March 20, 1994
It's over. I'm not taking this bullshit anymore. Yesterday was my 16th birthday, and my father raped me for the final time. Tonight I was ready for him. I didn't think he'd come again so soon, but I was prepared just in case. I'd hidden a butcher knife under my mattress this afternoon, because after last night . . . after that last rape . . . I decided I couldn't take it anymore. I'd either have to kill myself or kill him. And then I decided he was the one who should die, not me. So, when I heard him step into my room in the middle of the night—I'd quit locking my door a long time ago because he'd managed to get in, anyway—I grabbed the knife, turned on my lamp, and told him flat out that if he ever touched me again, I'd cut his balls off. I don't know if I really could've made good on my threat. Probably not. But I would've killed him. I just couldn't . . . can't . . . go on like this any longer. And now, for the first time, I'm going to try to put it down in words.

It started . . . I think . . . three years ago on my thirteenth birthday. Although, now I'm not so sure that was the beginning. I have dreams of when I was younger, before I even started school. It's hard to describe them, but they're about Daddy, and they are bad dreams, so who knows? Maybe he was sexually abusing me when I was a preschooler. Naive as it seems, I didn't realize that's what he was doing in the beginning. Stupid me . . . I thought he was just giving me the love I never got from Mom. Making up for her coldness. It started innocently enough, I suppose. On my thirteenth birthday, he just held me in his arms, caressing and kissing me. I was upset because Mom had bailed out on me again, and he was there to make me feel loved and wanted. What an idiot I was. I actually enjoyed it. He made me feel loved, and I guess I needed that. But those caresses turned into something else. I can't, even now, go into detail about the things he did . . . the things he asked me to do for him. It's just too disgusting, and I'm ashamed of it. Because I did the things he asked, knowing it was wrong, knowing it was unnatural. It was "our secret lessons." That's what he called it. He was teaching me how to be the kind of woman men couldn't resist. I remember exactly when this started. It was after I told him about Jason and the problems we had kissing with our braces on. That's when he suggested the lessons. I was only thirteen, but I knew, deep in my heart, that the things we were doing were wrong, but at first, I just allowed it to happen. I loved my father. I didn't want to push him away, so it went on for months, and he gradually grew bolder. Once, I protested when he began to touch my breasts, but he just whispered that he was showing me how much he loved me. I knew that it was wrong, and here's

*the part I don't want to write, but I have to because . . . well . . . if
I'm going to be honest, I've got to be completely honest. I liked the
way it made me feel when he touched me like that. So, I just allowed
it to keep happening. He taught me how to please a guy, and after
my "lessons," I practiced on Jason and some of the other guys in
school, and before I knew it, they were all drooling after me. I liked
that, too. It made me feel powerful and in control. But technically, I
was still a virgin. I had no intention of giving up my virginity until I
was ready. I'll never know when that would've been because on the
night of my fifteenth birthday, my father raped me. It was awful. It felt
like he was tearing me apart. I fought him, but he was too strong.
And that's when I finally put a name to what he'd been doing to me.
Sexual abuse. I didn't know what to do. I couldn't go to my mother
because then I'd have to admit how long it had been going on.
Besides, how could my mother not know about it? And if I did go to
her and tell her the truth, her first thoughts would be for the reputation of the family. If a scandal like this got out, they would be ruined.
So, I knew there was no point in going to her. I also thought about
talking to someone at school—the school nurse . . . or maybe I could
call Family Services in the Yellow Pages. Or go to a priest. But I did
none of those things. I was too afraid—afraid of being sent away
somewhere. To a foster home or a girls' school. So, for a full year, my
father came to my room once or twice a week, and raped me. The
first few times I fought him, but finally, I became resigned. I just let
him do what he had to do, hating every second of it, and finally, hating him. It was disgusting and vile. Thinking about it makes me want
to throw up. I don't know if I'll ever be able to have sex with any
man. Intercourse, I mean. I don't mind doing everything else. Oral
sex is my specialty. But just the thought of a man—even Jason—putting his dick inside me . . . Oh, God! I guess I'll always see my father
looking down at me, grunting and heaving . . .*

At this point, there were violent slashes of teal ink as if Robin was screaming aloud and using her pen as a weapon on the paper.

*But it's over now. I think I scared him tonight. I'm sure he believed
me when I told him I'd kill him. Oh, he started blubbering and crying. "But I love you, Cupcake. I'd never do anything to hurt you." Oh,
God, how I wanted to kill him at that moment. What the fuck did he
think he'd been doing these last three years? Using me as a sex toy, a
substitute wife—his own flesh and blood? How I wish I had the nerve
to go to the newspaper and tell them everything. Ruin his ass. His
political career. Oh, wouldn't the Democrats have a field day with*

that? Right-wing Virginia Congressman Arrested for Sexual Abuse of Daughter. Ha! Wouldn't that be a friggin' hoot? But again, by doing this, I'd be destroying everything I have. My home, my way of life, my brothers . . . not to mention how it would be to have to deal with all the talk . . . everybody at school. No, I can't do it. I just have to stay silent and keep the knife with me in case I need to threaten him again. And try to get through two more years here at home, and then I'll go off to New York and make a new life for myself.

I've just reread what I wrote, and I feel sick to my stomach. But I'm glad I wrote it all down. I'm going to put it away now in a sealed envelope and never, ever look at it again. My new life begins tomorrow. I am Robin Renee Mulcahey, and I will never, ever let anyone hurt me again.

Amy folded the letter and slipped it back into the envelope. Tears streaked her face just as they had last night when she'd read it the first time. And again, she felt the horror Robin's confession had evoked.

Oh, God. At first, she'd tried to believe it was all a sick fantasy that Robin had made up. Maybe no one had realized how sick she was. That the poor girl had been mentally ill. But it just didn't wash. Amy knew, as sure as her heart was beating, that every word Robin had written had been the truth. It all made sense now. Jason's astonishment when she'd had sex with him the evening her mother died. He'd blurted out something about how she'd finally let him fuck her. She hadn't understood it then, but now, it was all clear. Promiscuous Robin—the girl who'd bragged that she was the Queen of Fellatio—had refused to have intercourse with all those guys she'd dated. And right there, in that desk drawer, was the reason why.

Amy wiped the tears away from her cheeks and gave a harsh laugh. To think, she'd "become" Robin so she could be a part of the television family she'd always longed for. But instead of the Cosbys, she'd joined *Melrose Place.* She was trapped in her own personal soap opera.

The limo hired by ABC pulled up to the front of her apartment building, and the driver jumped out and opened Amy's door, holding an umbrella to protect her from the cold spring rain.

He smiled as she stepped out of the car. "Congratulations again on winning another Emmy, Miss Mulcahey. You sure you don't want me to come back a little later and take you to some of the post-Emmy parties?"

"No, I don't think so," Amy said, summoning a smile. "I have a feeling this headache is here to stay. The best thing for me to do is take a couple of Tylenol PMs and go to bed."

He walked her to the door holding the umbrella over her head. "Hope you feel better soon."

The doorman opened the door for her. Cradling her second Emmy award, Amy stepped into the building. "Congratulations, Miss Robin," the doorman said, giving her a wink. She smiled her thanks and headed for the elevators.

As she stuck the key into the lock of her apartment, she heard a rustle down the corridor.

"Hello, Amy."

She stiffened and turned, heart hammering. Paul stood there in a tan rain-splattered trench coat, his black hair glistening wetly. He looked like he'd aged since she'd last seen him three months ago.

"The doorman recognized me and let me wait inside," he said. "Can we talk?"

Amy shrugged and turned back to the door. "Come on in."

He followed her inside. She closed the door behind him, then shrugged out of her velvet evening coat. His eyes scanned her. Her dress was a San Carlin design, a black satin strapless gown with a dramatic red underskirt that fanned out in the back. Her hair, which had grown out past her shoulders, was done up in a French twist reminiscent of Grace Kelly. She could see the reluctant admiration in his eyes, but she could also see that he wasn't thinking of her, but of his sister. It would be that way forever, she supposed. How could it not?

His eyes moved to the statuette in her hands. "Two for two, huh? Congratulations."

"Did you see the show?" Amy moved to the coffee table and put down the award.

"Some of it. I saw you win . . . and I heard you thank Robin in your acceptance speech."

She looked at him. "I thanked Amy." She walked across the room to the coat closet. "Can I take your coat?"

"I know. But you meant Robin." He took off his coat and handed it to her. "It was a nice acceptance speech."

Amy hung his coat in the closet next to hers. "I meant every word of it. I wouldn't have been able to get where I am today if it weren't for her. You know that better than anyone."

Paul walked around the room, his brow furrowed. He picked up a crystal turtle, the one made out of lava she'd bought on the Big Island. He examined it and put it down again, then moved on to the Lladró figurine. Instead of picking it up, he touched the mother's smooth brown head with a forefinger. Then he began to walk again. He reached the huge windows overlooking the city, stopped and gazed out at the lights, his hands clasped behind his back. "So, I hear you've extended your contract at *South Riding*."

"Just another six months. I'm not sure what I'll do after that." Amy tried to relax, but it felt like her heart was trying out for the Olympics. She was more nervous now than she'd been tonight just before they called her name at the Emmys.

"Mom tells me your divorce came through." He continued to stare out the window.

"Two weeks ago," she replied. "It was easier than getting married in Vegas. I guess that's how it is when you part as friends."

He glanced at her, a quizzical expression on his face. "Not many women would be so forgiving."

"Dec isn't a monster. I can't hate him because he loves someone else." *Because I understand too well how he feels.*

Paul turned back to the window, and another awkward silence fell. Amy glanced toward the kitchen. "You want some coffee?"

"Yeah, sure."

Relieved at having something to do, she went into the kitchen and began to ladle coffee grounds into the basket. He stepped in behind her. Startled, she looked up and coffee grounds went flying over the counter. Her hand trembled as she reached for a sponge to clean it up.

"I guess that was hard for you, huh?" he said. "To give up your coffee?"

She shrugged, her heartbeat steadying. So, this was how it was going to be. Polite and civilized. "It was tough. I gave up a lot. Trouble was, I didn't realize the extent of how much until it was too late." She poured water into the coffeemaker and glanced at him. "So, does this mean you've decided to start speaking to me again?"

He picked up an apple-shaped kitchen timer and turned it over in his hands. "I've been going in circles the last few months. Hating you one minute, feeling sorry for you the next. Almost understanding you at times."

Amy leaned back against the counter, staring at him. Weird. She felt calm now. In control. "And . . . you've come to some kind of resolution? A decision?"

He looked at her. "I don't want to hate you any longer. I just . . ." He shook his head. "I don't know how we can resolve this."

Amy took a deep breath. "Maybe it would be best if we just stay out of each other's way."

He gazed at her, a sober look in his eyes. "What if I told you I don't want to do that?"

Flustered, she turned away and reached for the mugs in the cabinet. Coffee began to drip into the carafe, its rich aroma permeating the room. She wanted to ask him exactly what he meant, but she was afraid. Afraid that his response wouldn't be what she wanted to hear?

"I told you I watched you on TV tonight," Paul said. "When you went up to accept the award, they showed you from behind and . . . I saw that it *was* you. I mean, for the first time since you told me the truth, I really looked at you and saw Amy, not Robin."

She reached for the sugar, trying desperately to keep her face composed.

"And when you got up to the podium and looked into the camera, it was still you. Crazy as that sounds. I saw you and not Robin."

She looked at him then, and his expression took her breath away. His face was solemn, his eyes penetrating. Her heartbeat faltered.

"And I realized something tonight, Amy . . ." Her name on his lips sounded like a caress. "We don't fall in love with the face or even the body. We fall in love with the soul, that mystical something beneath the skin. And I've never had the chance to tell you. Not really. But I love you, Amy. I love *you*."

She held the sugar bowl between her hands, and watched as he took a step toward her. Her brain was reeling. Had she really heard that? Or was this some cruel trick of the mind? Was she so far gone that she was hallucinating now? Imagining words that he could never say?

He took the sugar bowl out of her hands and placed it on the counter. Then cupping her head in the cradle of his hands, he kissed her forehead, softly, sweetly—a butterfly of a caress—and drew away from her, eyes tender.

"Oh, Paul . . ." Her voice was ragged, thick with emotion. She still couldn't quite believe this was happening. *He loved her!* Did that mean he could forgive her? But then she remembered, and her smile vanished.

"What?" he asked.

She tenderly brushed a hand over his jaw, and then moved away from him. "You've got to know something. I've been wrestling with it for two months, trying to decide whether to tell you or not, but . . ." She shook her head. "I think she would want you to know."

"What is it?" He stared at her, puzzled.

She glanced over at the coffeemaker. "Why don't you pour the coffee? I've got to go get something."

In her bedroom, she opened the nightstand drawer and stared at Robin's envelope.

When she returned to the kitchen, Paul was sitting at the table, stirring milk into his coffee. Another mug steamed on the table. Amy hesitated in the doorway, the envelope in her hand. Maybe it would be better if he didn't know. But then, if she didn't tell him, their new relationship—if there was to be one— would begin with another secret between them. And that, she couldn't bear. No more secrets. It had to be this way.

Amy walked over to the table and placed the envelope down in front of him. "I found this in Robin's journal. I think you'd better read it."

She sat down at the table as he unfolded the letter and began to read. The blood immediately ebbed from his face, and his mouth tightened into a grim line. At one point, he closed his eyes, muttered a "dear God," then took a deep, shuddering breath and continued reading. Amy had to look away; she couldn't stand to see the pain on his face. Had she made another mistake? Maybe it *had* been wrong to give him the letter. It would destroy him, destroy the whole family. Yet, she knew . . . she could almost feel Robin's approval. In life, she hadn't had the nerve to make her father pay for his sins, but now, perhaps it was time.

Paul finished reading the letter, folded it, and slipped it back into the envelope. Then he tunneled his hands through his hair and sat motionless, elbows propped on the table, his hands cradling his head. Amy didn't speak. Just waited.

Finally, he looked at her, his blue eyes glimmering with tears. "That fucking bastard," he whispered, barely suppressed rage in his voice. "What kind of animal could do that to his daughter?"

Amy could only shake her head. "I thought *I* had a bad father. I actually *envied* Robin her father."

Paul slammed his fist on the table causing their coffee mugs to tremble. "*Christ!* She tried to tell me. Several times, she tried to tell me, and I just blew her off. I thought she was just exaggerating things. She did that a lot. That morning after you and I . . . got together the first time . . . she said something. Something about being a slut . . . and blaming him for turning her into one. And did I push her for more information? *Hell, no!* I just let her go. *Jesus!* I'm a bad as *he* is."

"No, you're not. Don't ever say that, Paul. You're not at all like your father."

He stared at her, then suddenly pushed away from the table and stood. "I'm going to Williamsburg. I'm going to find that bastard, and I'm going to beat the crap out of him!"

"No." Amy stood and hurried over to him, grabbing his arm. "You're going to calm down first. We're going to figure out what to do. Whatever is best. What *she* would want us to do."

His eyes met hers. "What is that, Amy?"

She'd want us to love each other. Make a life together. But now wasn't the time to say it.

"You have to decide that, Paul. But I just want you to know I'm tired of living this charade. If you want me to come with you to Williamsburg and admit everything to Tammy and Michael, I'll do it. If you want me to hand over this letter to Michael, I'll do that, too. It's up to you. I'll do whatever you want."

Even if it means leaving you, and your family, and never looking back.

32

Paul downshifted to a crawl as his sleek black T-bird approached the silver span of the Delaware Memorial Bridge. Through half-closed eyes, Amy focused on his corded arm as his hand rested on the gearshift, admiring the muscles defined by years of catching footballs thrown by top-caliber quarterbacks, who got most of the glory. She loved his arms. Loved the way the black hair covered his forearm in a light silken carpet. Felt the urge to touch it, running her fingertips up and down its length, feeling the steel of muscle beneath his sinewy skin. But of course, she couldn't act upon that urge.

The other night, even after he'd admitted how he felt about her, nothing had happened between them. She wanted to believe it was the revelation of Robin's sexual abuse that had stopped them from delving further into their feelings for each other. But she knew it wasn't just that. No matter how he felt; no matter how *she* felt, the obstacle now was one thing, and one thing only. Her identity. How could there possibly be a future for them if the world thought she was his sister? And it wasn't just that. How could she expect Paul to make love to her when it was his sister's face he saw every time he looked at her? Oh, he could talk about the soul and what's beneath the skin as much as he wanted, but the reality was quite different. When it came right down to it, Amy knew that nothing had changed, really. There was still no future for them, no matter if they loved each other. Not as long as she continued living this charade.

Paul paid the toll and accelerated into the right-hand lane. They were in Delaware now. Soon, they would reach Maryland, and, finally, Virginia. If everything went according to plan, they'd be in Williamsburg by four o'clock, and Michael should still be at his office on Richmond Road. Amy didn't want to think about it. She dreaded the confrontation, but agreed with Paul it had to be done.

As if reading her mind, he glanced at her. "I'm starting to have second thoughts. I don't like you going in there alone."

Amy looked at him. "But we decided that was the best way. He's not going to admit anything if you're in there with me."

"He doesn't have to admit it," Paul said shortly. "I know the bastard is guilty. I believe every word Robin wrote."

"Me too. But, Paul, he is your father. If there's the slightest chance Robin made this stuff up because of some vindictive plan to ruin him, we need to know that before we start making accusations."

Paul's hands tightened on the steering wheel. His face grew grimmer. "But how can we ever prove it's not true? Even if he denies everything, we can't be sure he's not lying. And my gut feeling tells me he's slime."

"If it's true, I think he will admit it," Amy said. "Just give me ten minutes with him, then come in. If he hasn't admitted it by then, we'll show him the letter. He'll have to be one hell of an actor to not reveal guilt when he reads that."

"Okay." Paul nodded grimly. "But I'll be right outside, and if I hear anything that sounds like you're in trouble, I'm coming in."

Amy touched his arm, unable to stop herself. "It'll be okay, Paul."

His eyes met hers solemnly. "Will it? I'm destroying my family today. How can it be?"

"Not you," Amy said gently. "If the family is destroyed, it's because of Michael, not you."

He nodded and looked back at the road. But Amy saw in the slump of his shoulders that he wasn't convinced it was true.

Michael's navy Lexus was parked in the reserved space in front of his law offices. Paul pulled in next to it and turned off the ignition. For a moment, he sat stiffly, a pensive expression on his face as he gazed at the front of the building.

Finally, he turned to Amy. "You ready to do this?"

She took a deep breath and released it. Somewhere on the road to Williamsburg, she'd lost her nerve. "We don't have to do it, Paul. What does it matter now? Robin is gone. He can't hurt her anymore. We'll be destroying your parents' marriage. Everything you've always known. Maybe we should wait until you talk to Jeff and see what he thinks you should do."

Paul shook his head. "I'm not going to call Jeff in England and tell him about this. He's looked forward to this European trip too long. Besides, no matter what happens . . . if Mom leaves Dad, it's not going to affect his future.

Nothing is going to stop his graduating from Harvard. Besides, I have to do this for Robin. Thinking about her . . . dealing with that . . . that monster . . . night after night." He closed his eyes and bowed his head as if trying to blot out the images. "It makes me want to kill him. No, Amy, the truth has to come out. That son of a bitch has gotten off scot-free for too long."

He'd already convicted and sentenced Michael, Amy realized. And hadn't she done the same thing? Did she really believe Michael would be able to convince her he was innocent?

She reached for the door handle. "Okay. Let's do it."

Paul looked at his watch. "Ten minutes. Then I'm coming in."

Michael's secretary, a pretty brunette in her midtwenties with long red nails to match her crimson lips, looked up as Amy entered the office. It was tastefully decorated with cherry furniture and Oriental rugs in hues of pearl gray and Williamsburg blue, creating an aura of calm sanctuary. But not for long, Amy thought.

The secretary smiled. "May I help you?"

"I'm Robin, Michael's daughter. Is he in?"

The brunette's smile grew warmer. "I *thought* I recognized you! I'm a big fan of *South Riding*. Of course, I have to tape it and watch it at night. I have to tell you, I was really worried when your character was diagnosed with ovarian cancer. And just after getting acquitted for Quinn's murder. But it looks like you're in remission now. Does that mean you're staying on the show? I'd heard you were trying to get out of your contract."

"Well, I'll be on the show at least until the end of September." Amy glanced at Michael's closed door. "He *is* in, right?"

"Oh, yeah." A flustered look crossed her pretty face. "I'm sorry! It's not every day I have a soap star in my office." She picked up the phone and punched a button. "Mike? Guess who's out here? Your daughter!"

His door opened immediately, and Michael stood there, dressed immaculately in a black Canali suit, a quizzical smile on his handsome face. But his blue eyes were wary. Or was that her imagination? She felt like she was really seeing Michael Mulcahey for the first time. That look in his eyes—the one she'd always taken for good humor—seemed lecherous now. Decayed, like a beautiful apple that seemed perfect on the outside, but when it was cut open, was crawling with maggots.

"Robin! What a great surprise! I didn't know you were coming down for the weekend."

Amy forced a smile and shrugged. "A last-minute decision. I wasn't on Friday's schedule, so I thought why not? I haven't been home in a while. I saw your car outside and decided to pop in."

"Well, come on in and sit down for a few minutes. Betty, could you bring us some coffee. Oh, damn!" He hit his forehead with the heel of his hand.

"What am I thinking? You don't drink coffee. How about a soda, Robin? You want a soda?"

"No, thanks." Amy stepped into his office, her pulse racing. "I'm fine."

"You still want coffee, Mike?" Betty's voice followed her.

"No, on second thought, I've had enough today." He closed the door and turned to Amy, shaking his head. "Great girl, that Betty. I didn't think I'd ever be able to replace Paula when she moved to Denver, but Betty has just been fantastic."

Amy watched him move around his desk. He seemed jittery and unsure of himself—something she'd never noticed in Michael before. Did he suspect something was up? But why? He sat down at his desk and reached for a crystal paperweight containing three goldfish frozen in midswim. Amy stared at his hands as he turned the paperweight over and over, and could barely suppress a shudder. Her heart raced. She didn't want to do this. But it had to be done. Didn't it?

"So, Robin . . . what's up?" He stared down at the paperweight.

And that's when Amy realized why he was so uneasy. Robin had always made it a point never to be alone with her father. A rebellion thing, Amy had always assumed, but now, of course, she knew the real reason. Michael, if Robin's allegations were true, was surely wondering why she was here in his office.

She took a deep breath. "I think you know."

He stiffened, his hands freezing on the paperweight. He didn't look at her.

"I'm tired of living this lie," she said quietly. And oh, that was so true. "I'm tired of protecting you. My therapist tells me I'm never going to get better until I confront the person who hurt me. That's you, Dad. You know it, and I know it. And I think it's time that Mom knows it."

He looked up at her then, and she saw the blood had drained from his face. He swallowed hard. His eyes darted around the room as if searching for an escape. Amy felt her stomach dip. Here was their answer. She'd never really believed Robin had made it up, but they had to know for sure. Forcing herself to meet Michael's eyes, she waited for his response.

Finally, it came in a harsh croak. "*Why?* Why, now? After all these years?"

Before she could answer, Michael's intercom beeped. "Mike, you'll never guess what?" Betty's cheerful voice filled the room. "Your son just walked in. Paul. Shall I send him in?"

If possible, Michael's face went even paler as he searched for a reply. "Tell him . . . uh . . . can you tell him . . ."

"He knows," Robin said quietly. "Better let him in."

Something seemed to die in Michael then. Right in front of her eyes, he appeared to shrink in size and substance. "Tell him to come in," he said softly. His eyes met hers. "You told him? You promised me you'd never tell."

"It doesn't matter what I said," Amy answered, feeling something close to nausea churning in her stomach. "You don't make deals with the devil."

Paul stepped into the room, his face set in granite. Amy watched their eyes lock. They stared at each other a long moment. On Richmond Road, traffic roared by. A horn blared, unnaturally loud in the quiet of the office. A nerve twitched in Michael's jaw, and she thought she saw his lower lip tremble. Finally, after what seemed like an eternity, Paul looked at Amy.

"You okay?"

She nodded.

He turned back to his father, studying him a moment before speaking. Then, "Why did you do it, Dad?" His voice was deceptively soft. Almost gentle. But Amy could see by the tension in his posture that he was restraining himself from doing physical violence. She only hoped it wouldn't come to that. Paul outweighed his father by thirty pounds, and was in the best shape of his life. If he wanted to, he could kill him without thinking twice about it. "Wasn't Mom enough for you?" Paul spoke in a neutral tone as if he were commenting on the weather. "You had to pick on your little girl to satisfy your sick urges?"

Michael's face had gone from white to mottled gray. "*Oh, God! Stop it!*" With a moan, he buried his face in his hands. His shoulders shook as harsh, strangled sobs burst from his throat. Amy and Paul watched him. Disgust welled inside her as she thought of the many nights poor Robin had probably sobbed into her pillow after being violated by the slimeball who now cried so piteously into his hands.

Paul waited until Michael had sobbed himself out before speaking again. His voice was colder than Amy had ever heard it. "I want you to go home tonight and tell Mom everything. *Everything.* I think she has a right to know that she's sleeping with a monster. If, after she's heard the truth, she still chooses to stay with you, then as far as I'm concerned, she's no better than you. You deserve each other. But if you don't tell her, I swear to God, I'm going to the newspaper. And you can kiss your law practice good-bye."

"It's my word against hers," Michael spoke frantically. Apparently, Paul's threat had ignited the fight in him. "No one will believe her. I'm an upstanding citizen in this town. Everyone knows what kind of girl Robin was. Wild and screwed up. Hell, she slept with half her graduating class at William & Mary. You think they'll believe her cockeyed stories?"

Paul bolted across the room before Michael got his last sentence out, and had him by the lapels of his expensive Canali suit. "You bastard," he growled, his eyes glinting fire. "You're the reason she was so screwed up, and you know it. I should break your filthy neck right now and be done with it."

"Paul, don't." Amy was at his side, placing a restraining hand on his arm. "Let him go."

After a moment's hesitation, Paul released his father. But his eyes were steely when he spoke again, "You have until tomorrow morning to tell Mom the truth. If you haven't, I *will* go to the newspaper, and tell them everything. And you know what? I think they'll believe her. But if they don't . . ." He shrugged. "It won't really matter, will it? The newspapers will have a field day with the accusations. And that'll be enough to ruin you, you perverted son of a bitch. No one will give a rat's ass about you and your fucking practice. And Mom? You think she'll stay with you when your bad press sullies her precious family name? Think again."

Michael's Adam's apple bobbed as he swallowed hard. His eyes bugged out, darting around in desperation. "Why?" he asked in a choked voice. "Why, now? Do you realize what you'll be doing to our family? It happened so long ago . . ." His eyes shifted to Amy. "I told you I was sorry. I've told you over and over . . ."

"It doesn't matter," Paul said. "Being sorry doesn't change anything, *Dad.* You still don't get it, do you?" He shook his head in disgust. "You really don't understand what you did to your daughter. Because it's all about *you,* isn't it? Well, not this time. This time, it's about Robin, and the damage you did to her." Paul looked from Michael to Amy. "He doesn't realize it, does he, Amy?"

Amy gasped. Did Paul realize he'd called her by her real name? She couldn't tell if Michael had caught it or not. He was still staring at Paul, his eyes tormented and frightened. Paul's cold eyes settled on him, and his upper lip curled in a snarl. "You killed her, you fucking bastard. You killed her a long time ago."

"You think he'll do it?" Amy asked Paul as they sat at an outdoor table in front of the Trellis Restaurant on Duke of Gloucester Street.

Paul lifted a shoulder in a shrug and took a sip of red wine. "He'd better. Or tomorrow he's going to wish he had."

Amy glanced down at her veal medallions smothered in mushroom sauce. Why had she ordered this? She wasn't even hungry, even though it was well past dinnertime. "I hope he does. I don't know if I can bear seeing Tammy's face when you . . . we . . . tell her."

"I know. But she's got to know. Wouldn't you want to know if it were your daughter?"

Amy nodded. "Yes, most definitely, but . . ."

A young boy wearing a New York Giants T-shirt appeared at their table, eyes shining as he held out a pen and napkin to Paul. "Can I have your autograph, Mr. Mulcahey? I'm a big Giants fan."

"Yeah, I can see that." With a glance of apology at Amy, Paul took the napkin, gave the kid a grin, and scribbled his name on it quickly. "Here you go."

Clutching his prize, the boy thanked him and ran back to his table. Paul looked at Amy. "But . . . ?"

She met his eyes. "Robin seemed to think Tammy *did* know. And did nothing."

He took a deep breath and released it. "I don't want to believe that. I *can't* believe it. Mom may not have been the best mother in the world, but I can't believe she'd tolerate his actions. That would make her as bad as him. Maybe even worse."

"You're right. I'm sure she didn't know about it. Robin was probably just lashing out." Amy laid her fork down, giving up on dinner. Her stomach was tied in knots.

"You're not hungry?" he asked.

She shook her head and reached for her cup of decaffeinated coffee. "I just wish this were all over. It's so much worse than I thought it would be." Especially when she thought Paul was about to tell Michael the truth about her. But thank God, he'd stopped himself. One crisis at a time was enough.

Paul glanced at his wristwatch and signaled for the check. "Maybe we should just call it a night. Go back to the hotel and try to get some sleep."

Amy nodded, but she didn't think she'd be able to sleep. It was still early, only eight-thirty. And such a beautiful night, pleasantly warm and carrying the scent of lilac on the breeze. Across from the restaurant, a horse-drawn carriage ambled down Duke of Gloucester Street, a cloaked man in a tricorn at the helm. The sight brought to mind her college years, especially the night she'd walked with Paul down this very street, thinking how impossible a future with him would be. That night had ended with him in her arms, briefly though it was. Now, a future with Paul seemed as far away as ever. And even though he knew the truth, she was still paying for the horrendous mistake she'd made on that early morning she'd awakened to hear Tammy and Michael calling her by Robin's name.

Maybe after this was all over, the best thing to do would be simply to go away. Somewhere away from all the Mulcaheys. For her own sanity, and for Paul's. She could see the torture in his eyes every time he looked at her, and it killed her. Why should he, too, have to pay for her mistake?

"Excuse me, Miss Blair . . . I mean, Miss Mulcahey?" A plump redhead stopped at their table. "I'm a big fan. Would you mind signing this for me?" She held out a map of Colonial Williamsburg. "Here. I have a pen, too."

Amy signed the map, "Best Wishes, Robin Mulcahey," and handed it back to the woman.

"Thank you so much," the woman said gleefully. "I can't wait to tell everyone I met you." And she bustled off.

Paul's eyes met hers, and he gave a halfhearted grin. "The perils of fame," he murmured. "You ready to go?"

"Yeah." She stood, and together, they left the restaurant.

They were silent during the ride to the hotel. They'd rehashed everything since their meeting with Michael, and the things they wanted to say, at least on

Amy's part, were better left unsaid. Outside her door, they parted with a polite good night, and she stepped into her pleasant, but sterile hotel room, her heart heavy, feeling lonelier than she'd ever felt in her life.

Yes, maybe California. Dec was there, but it was a big state. At least there, she could finally put Paul behind her. This time, for good. It would be the best thing for both of them.

33

Amy turned the light off and stepped out of the bathroom. Naked, except for the towel she had wrapped, turban-style, around her head, she walked to the bed and grabbed the bottoms of her mint green cotton pajamas and pulled them on. Grabbing the television remote, she pressed the power button, tossed it on the bed, then slipped on the button-down top. The baby-soft fabric felt comforting against her damp skin. She'd just taken a long, hot shower, and it had made her feel almost human again. It had been a tough, emotionally exhausting day, but now, thankfully, it was over. Of course, there was always tomorrow to get through, but she wouldn't think about that now.

She settled onto the king-size bed and began to channel-surf. A love scene caught her attention. Meg Ryan and Nicolas Cage. She recognized the movie right away because it was one of her favorites. *City of Angels*. She'd first seen it a year after it was released in the theaters, having rented it on one of those lonely Saturday nights while recovering from another reconstructive surgery. The heartbreaking love story between a mortal woman and an angel had been exactly the kind of movie she could get lost in back then. And still, it intrigued her. Maybe because she could identify with such an impossible love.

As always, she found herself getting caught up in the story even though she knew tragedy lurked just around the corner. Tugging the towel from her head, she reached for the comb on the bedside table. By the time she'd combed the tangles out of her wet hair, the TV screen was showing Meg preparing breakfast for Nicolas the next morning after their night of passion together.

No, Meg. Forget the stupid pears. Don't go to town.

Tears were already welling in Amy's eyes when the knock came at the door. She jumped and glanced at the clock on the bedside table. Almost eleven-thirty. It could only be one person this late. Or else, someone had the wrong room. Heart thumping, she slid off the bed and crossed to the door to peer through the peephole. Her nerves jangled at the sight of Paul standing outside, staring off down the hall, a pensive expression on his face. She closed her eyes and took a deep breath, trying to still her suddenly rapid heartbeat. Then she opened the door.

His face was solemn. "Can I come in?" he asked quietly. "I need to talk to you."

She stepped back, opening the door wider, and he walked in. He was still wearing the clothes he'd had on earlier—black Dockers and a gray ribbed-knit top. His gaze swept over her, taking in her mint green pajamas.

"Did I get you up?" he asked.

She shook her head. "I was just watching the end of a movie."

Paul glanced at the TV screen where Nicolas Cage was clasping Meg Ryan to his chest. "You sure I'm not . . . I mean . . . we can talk tomorrow?"

Amy shook her head. "No, I've seen this movie before. It always ends the same. You want a drink? I have ice and sodas."

"Sure. That would be great."

A few minutes later, they sat at the writing desk, sipping colas. Amy watched him. He seemed nervous, drinking his soda too fast, and tapping his fingers on the desk. Her stomach churned. What awful thing had he come to say?

Finally, she broke the silence. "So, what is it, Paul?"

His gaze met hers. "There's only one way we can be together," he said slowly, his eyes holding hers. "We have to tell Mom the truth."

Amy stared at him as panic fluttered in her stomach. "Are you serious?"

He nodded solemnly. "It's the only way. You have to become yourself again."

"But how?" She shook her head, mind racing. "It'll kill your parents when they find out the truth. Paul, they might even press charges against me. Do you have any idea how many laws I've probably broken?"

His jaw tightened. "I won't let that happen. In fact, I think that's the last thing we have to worry about. The only thing Mom finds unforgivable is scandal. Look, Amy, when Dad tells her what he did, or even if we're the ones that have to tell her . . . she's going to be in shock from that. We might as well tell her everything, right?"

"I don't know." Amy hugged her arms, feeling a sudden coldness creep over her skin. On one hand, she was elated that Paul wanted to make a life with her, but the thought of admitting her deception to Tammy filled her with dread. "It seems so cruel. Hitting her with all of this at once."

"Mom is a lot stronger than you give her credit for," Paul said quietly. "Amy, I want us to make a future together. We have to do this. We have to tell Mom and"—his face twisted in revulsion—"my *father* . . . the truth."

She stared into his earnest face. He was right. It was the only way they could be together. But did he realize what it meant? How was she going to be able to look Tammy in the eyes and tell her that her only daughter was dead?

As soon as Paul turned the T-bird into the driveway of Windsong, they saw the James City County Sheriff's car parked in the driveway. Amy's stomach plunged, and from the way Paul's face had paled, she knew he felt the same way.

"What do you think it means?" she asked quietly.

He shook his head, brows furrowed. "I don't know. But I have a bad feeling in my gut."

He pulled up behind the sheriff's car and turned off the ignition. Then he sat still a moment, as if reluctant to move. Amy couldn't bring herself to reach for the door handle. "Maybe Tammy called the police after Michael told her the truth?" Her offer of an explanation sounded tentative and weak, even to her own ears.

"No," Paul said flatly. "Mom would never do that. It wouldn't be 'seemly.'"

The front door opened, and an older, grayer Stella stepped outside onto the portico with a uniformed officer. Paul opened his door and got out of the T-bird, striding toward the house to intercept them. Feeling as if she were moving underwater, Amy followed, heart drumming. Paul was already talking to the sheriff. Behind them, Stella's watery eyes connected with Amy's, and she felt her stomach dip again. The housekeeper's face was bloodless, her mouth quivering. Morning sunshine haloed down upon the woman, revealing every line of her sixty-plus years.

"I'm sorry, son," the sheriff was saying in a soft, sympathetic voice. "It's a terrible shock, I know."

Amy's eyes darted to Paul. His face was the color of gray putty. She hurried over to him. "Paul, what is it?"

The sheriff tipped his hat. "I'm sorry to tell you this, Miss Mulcahey, but . . ."

"I'll tell her," Paul spoke through stiff lips. "Thank you, Sheriff."

With another tip of his hat, the sheriff strode off to his car. Paul stared after him, his body unnaturally still.

"Paul, what's happened?"

He looked at her—or rather, through her. "He killed himself." His voice was flat, emotionless.

Her heart plummeted. "Oh, God!" There was no doubt at all who he was referring to. And there was also no doubt in my mind what Paul was thinking. *We killed him. You and I.* She swallowed hard, feeling the guilt sweep through her. Paul looked away, watching the sheriff pull around the driveway and turn onto the road toward Williamsburg. Seconds ticked by as neither of them moved. Then, like a lightning bolt, Amy saw Robin's face in her mind. Heard her voice.

Don't you dare feel guilty, Amy. He took his own life. Because he's not only a pervert. He's a coward, too. And you can't let Paul think anything else.

Amy put her arms around Paul and buried her face in his chest. After a moment's hesitation, his arms curved around her, holding her. She knew Stella was watching from the portico, but it didn't matter. To the housekeeper's eyes, they were brother and sister, comforting each other in their grief.

Amy eased away from him and peered up into his dazed eyes. "It's not our fault, Paul. Don't even think that. Instead of standing up and facing the music, he chose to take the easy way out. Just like my dad did. And neither one of them cared that he was leaving a mess for someone else to clean up."

She was relieved to see some of that frightening blankness disappear from his eyes. He looked at her as if suddenly realizing she was there, then nodded slowly. His hands skimmed up her arms, tightening briefly before releasing her. "We'd better go see how Mom is doing."

Stella met Paul on the steps and, throwing her arms around him, burst into ragged sobs. "Oh, my poor boy! It's so awful!"

He hugged her for a long moment, consoling her with meaningless phrases. "It's okay, Stella. We're going to get through this." When her sobs finally subsided, he released her. Her plump face mottled and tear-streaked, she turned to Amy, holding out her fleshy arms.

Amy went into them, hugging the housekeeper. Her homey scent of vanilla enveloped Amy, bringing to mind good moments from the past. Dry-eyed, she held Stella in a long embrace, knowing the woman's grief was genuine. She'd loved Michael, of course. What was not to love? He'd been a good employer, and from her perspective, a genuine and warm man. But she hadn't known the real man, had she? Would she wonder why his only daughter wasn't shedding tears at the news of his death? Because there was no way Amy could play the part of the grieving daughter. No matter how good an actress she was, she couldn't . . . *wouldn't* . . . shed tears for a man who'd systematically abused an innocent, young girl—his own child—for years.

Stella finally released her, wiping at her red-rimmed eyes with a tissue she'd dug from her apron pocket. "I just don't understand it," she gurgled. "He had such a good life. He had everything. What could have made him do such a thing?"

"I guess we'll never know that, Stella," Paul said, patting her shoulder. "Where's Mom?"

"She's in the parlor," Stella sniffed. "I couldn't help but hear the sheriff break the news to her. I was going to go to her after I showed him out, but now that you two are here, I'm sure she'd rather have you with her."

When they stepped quietly into the parlor, they found Tammy sitting on the sofa, her perfectly styled blond head bowed. She was dressed in an elegant hunter green suit. Her briefcase was on the Aubusson rug next to her trim feet clad in Cole Haan alligator pumps. The expensive scent of Fifth Avenue per-meated the room. Apparently, the sheriff had caught her just before she left for a business engagement. Paul stepped toward her. "Mom?"

She looked up, and Amy was astonished to see that her makeup was immaculate, her eyes dry. She hadn't known what she'd expected. Tears, per-haps. Hysteria, maybe. But she certainly hadn't expected to see Tammy as calm and collected as ever. True, her color was a bit pale, but that was to be expected, surely. She'd just been told her husband of thirty years was dead.

"The sheriff told you?" she asked, her voice brittle, yet, contained. She stood up abruptly and moved across the room to the bar. "He killed himself. The bastard. Shot himself right there in his office after his secretary went home for the night. A cleaning lady found him this morning." Tammy lifted a carafe of brandy and poured the amber liquid into a glass. Amy watched for a telltale tremor of her hand, but didn't see one. The woman was obviously made of the same ice she was dropping into her drink. She lifted the glass to her lips and swallowed the brandy in one gulp. "You two want a drink?"

Paul shook his head. Amy couldn't bring herself to speak. Tammy poured herself more brandy, and cradling the glass between her slim, manicured fin-gers, turned to them. "I can't believe he'd do such a thing," she murmured, eyes glittering brightly. "What a scandal this is going to be."

At first, Amy thought it was unshed tears making Tammy's eyes shine like that. Now, she realized it was anger. Maybe even fury.

Paul's gaze slid to Amy. *You see? What did I tell you?*

Amy was having trouble reconciling this bloodless creature with the Tammy she'd known all these years. No, her "adopted" mother had never been overly warm, but she'd been human. This woman was a cold stranger.

Tammy finished the brandy and slammed the glass down onto the bar. "Oh, well. We'll just have to muddle through it, won't we? He's left us no choice."

"Was there a note?" Paul asked.

Tammy whirled and began to pace from the window to the fireplace. "No! And that's what worries me. If he got some young girl pregnant, and it gets out . . ."

Amy's heart almost stopped beating. *What had she said?*

Paul's face had gone white. "Mom . . . what do you mean?"

She looked at her son and blinked. It was almost as if she'd forgotten they were in the room. Two bright spots of color bloomed on her cheekbones. And for the first time in memory, Amy saw Tammy's composure crumble. Just a bit.

She sighed and turned away. Pausing in front of an ornately framed oil painting of a mountainous landscape, she reached out a slim hand to straighten it, even though it looked perfectly centered on the wall. "There are some things about your father that you two don't know. I might as well tell you now because whatever made him kill himself must be pretty bad, and if we don't do something, it'll get out to the public, and I can't let that happen. He must've gotten himself in too deep this time, and suicide was the only way he saw to get out." She moved back to the sofa, sat down, and crossed her legs.

Her blue eyes moved from Paul to Amy. "You know your father only served a couple of terms in Congress. Well, I'm sure you don't know the reason why he didn't stay in Washington. He was caught in bed with the sixteen-year-old daughter of his chief of staff. Luckily, my family had the money and the right connections to pay the guy and his little slut daughter off, and keep the lid on everything, but the price Michael had to pay was his congressional career. I knew if he stayed in Washington, sooner or later, someone would dig up the dirt, and I wasn't about to risk that. He came back to Williamsburg and started up his law firm. I made it clear that I would tolerate no more bad behavior. I didn't really care what he did as long as he was discreet. But *damn* him! He got careless!" Her brow furrowed. "That must be it! Something is about to break, and if he brings this family down with him, I hope he roasts in hell!"

She stood and strode toward the door. "I've got to go call the office and cancel my appointments for the day. Oh, and I've arranged for the Staunton Funeral Home to pick up the body. Paul, could you call Jeff? I'll get his number for you."

Paul reached out and grasped his mother's arm. He glared at her, his mouth set in a thin, grim line. "You knew about the young girls?" His voice was deceptively quiet. "Did that include your daughter?"

The blood drained from Tammy's face as she stared at her son. Amy felt her head swimming, and, for a moment, she thought sure she would faint. *Oh, poor Robin. Not only did you have a monster for a father, your mother knew, and she didn't care.*

Tammy recovered quickly. She lifted her chin, gazing at Paul defiantly. "What are you talking about?" Her voice dripped ice.

Paul released his mother's arm. He turned to Amy. "Did you bring in the letter?"

"It's in my purse." With numb fingers, Amy pulled out the letter and handed it to Paul.

"You'd better sit down, Mom. Even if you knew about this . . . and I'm betting you did . . . it's not going to be an easy thing to read. But then again, you might surprise me." He gazed at his mother, a look of disgust on his face.

Oh, God, what have I done, Amy wondered. Because of her, Paul had lost both parents in one horrible day. *Not you, Amy.* It was Robin's adamant voice in her mind again. *Paul never had the parents he thought he did. It just took him longer to find out.*

Tammy returned to the sofa, sat down, and began to read Robin's letter. Paul and Amy watched her silently. His face was white and grim. He looked older and more careworn than he had that morning in the hotel room. As if he'd lost something precious.

Tammy read the letter, her expression stoic. Not even a flicker of an eyelash or the tic of a muscle marred her perfectly made-up face. After she finished reading, she folded the letter in half and dropped it to the sofa cushion beside her. Then she looked up and squarely met Paul's accusing gaze.

"I never knew for sure," she said in a quiet, even voice. Her eyes moved to Amy, flat, emotionless. "I figured if it were serious, you'd come to me. But you didn't. So, I pushed the suspicions away. I figured it was better to leave things alone."

"Better for who, Mom?" Paul snarled. "For the family name? What if she *had* come to you? What would you have done then?"

Tammy blinked and stared back at him silently.

"You can't answer that, can you? Bet I can take a guess though. You would've told her she was imagining things. Or maybe you would've accused her of lying. *To protect the family name!*"

Tammy stood, her brows lowering. "I don't have to take this abuse!" She strode toward the door, but Amy, obeying some urge inside her, blocked her way. She stood in front of "her mother," impaling her with her gaze.

They were almost the same height, Amy being only an inch taller. Although her face remained calm, Tammy's eyes revealed her agitation.

"You're worse than he was," Amy said quietly. "How can you live with yourself?"

Tammy flinched, and Amy knew she'd scored a direct hit. And in that one second, she felt the rage take over, and she wanted nothing more than to have the guts to pull out Tammy's immaculately dyed blond hair by the roots. "How could you do that to her? Your little girl. You knew she was being violated by that . . . that *predator*! And you did nothing. You just let her suffer. You destroyed her life, do you know that? You and Michael. You made her hate herself. She thought she was worth nothing. That's why she became a sexual plaything for every guy on campus. Because of you, Tammy. You and your worthless piece-of-shit husband! And to think . . ." Her voice softened in amazement. "I thought you were the perfect family. That's why I wanted so desperately to be a part of it."

Tammy was staring at her as if she'd lost her mind. "What are you talking about?" Her eyes darted from Amy to Paul standing behind her. "Paul! What's wrong with your sister? Is she having a nervous breakdown?"

"She's not my sister, Mom," Paul said quietly. "Remember Amy Shiley? The girl you supposedly buried in the family plot back in 1998? Well, you buried the right girl, but you had the name wrong. This is not Robin, *this* is Amy Shiley. My sister . . . your daughter . . . the one that you allowed your husband to rape repeatedly . . . is dead."

"That is the most outlandish thing I've ever heard!" Tammy stared from Paul to Amy. "Do you seriously expect me to believe this wild story?"

"It's the truth," Amy said wearily. She'd just told her everything, and she really didn't feel like begging her to believe it. Tammy was right. It *was* outlandish. But that didn't make it less true.

Tammy turned to her son. "You believe her? You believe this . . . ridiculous story?"

"I know it's true," Paul said.

Tammy gave a harsh laugh, and turned back to Amy. "My God! I've always known you were high-strung . . . maybe even a bit unbalanced, but . . ." Her gaze fastened on Paul. "Paul, you've always been the levelheaded one. How did she brainwash you into believing this . . . *insanity*?"

Paul stared at Tammy, his face as expressionless as a stone carving. "Mother, listen to me carefully. Amy and I became lovers during the holidays before the car accident. She has a crescent-shaped birthmark on her left breast. That's how I know this woman sitting here is Amy Shiley, not my sister. Amy, show her."

Amy approached Tammy on trembling legs. Unbuttoning her white blouse, she pushed the lace-trimmed edge of her bra aside far enough to reveal the brown birthmark on her breast. Tammy's eyes widened, and her face went a shade paler.

"Robin didn't have a birthmark on her breast, did she, Tammy?" Amy asked quietly. "Maybe you wouldn't know that, even if she did. But she didn't. I did, though. Paul remembers it. I'm Amy Shiley, Tammy. And Robin *is* dead." As if the accident had happened yesterday, Amy felt a spasm of grief clutching her insides. Oh, God, she still mourned Robin. Especially now that she knew what a traumatic childhood she'd had.

Tammy lifted a trembling hand to her mouth. "I think I'm going to be sick."

"Swallow it," Paul said coldly. "The only thing that's making you sick is the thought of the scandal if this gets out. But I think if we work together, we can come up with a plan that will leave all of us happy."

Tammy dropped her hand to her lap and gazed at her son. Apparently, her nausea had passed. "I'm listening." Her voice was arctic.

Paul looked at Amy and held out his hand. Swallowing a lump in her throat, she turned away from Tammy and went to his side, feeling the warmth of his hand enclosing hers. "I love Amy," Paul said quietly. "There's only one way for us to be together and that's if she can regain her own identity. And that's where you come in, Mother."

Tammy lifted her chin and glared. "What can I do?"

"The only decent thing," Paul said. "You have to give your daughter a proper funeral."

34

A PRIVATELY OWNED ISLAND OFF THE COAST OF MEXICO

Declan stepped out onto the eight-foot marble veranda and took a deep breath of the fresh early-morning air. The breeze carried a hint of the sea, just visible in the distance past the lush green undergrowth carpeting the acreage from the villa down to the sandy white beach below. It was blessedly cool out here this morning, as it usually was this early, and the air was redolent with the perfume of honeysuckle. Declan and Cedric had quickly learned that the grilling Mexican sun wouldn't touch this side of the villa until midafternoon, so each morning the veranda served as their cool sanctuary before the heat drove them inside or down to the pool.

Sensing his presence, Cedric looked up from the table, where he sat reading a newspaper. He smiled and lifted his cup of coffee in greeting. "Good morning, Dec. You slept late this fine morning."

Declan crossed the veranda to Cedric and kissed his lips lightly, sifting a caressing hand through his dark brown hair. "Good morning, love." He sank into the chair opposite Cedric and reached for the coffeepot. "I think it's finally starting to sink in that I'm on a much-needed break. Can you believe it? I have a whole month where I don't have to live my life by a schedule. I can eat when I want, sleep when I want . . . as *much* as I want. No dealing with phone calls, shooting schedules, publicity appearances. Christ, it's sheer heaven!" He poured a generous amount of cream into his coffee and stirred, a smile on his lips. "I don't even have to read a bloody script if I don't want to."

Cedric's dark eyebrow arched. "Well, I wouldn't go that far. You've got a dozen scripts piled up around the place. And only twenty-eight days to make a decision about your next role."

"Don't remind me." Dec sighed. "I'll get to it. But just for a wee while, I want to forget about Hollywood, and just rest. Three films in six months is bloody insane."

Cedric smiled. "Bollocks! You're loving every minute of it. Admit it. You should be happy you didn't win that Oscar. I daresay you wouldn't be enjoying this wee R&R if you had." He picked up a basket and extended it to Declan. "Croissant?"

"No, thanks." Declan grimaced. "It's way too early for food. I'll just stick with coffee for the time being. So . . . has our guest made an appearance this morning?"

Cedric shook his head. "Not yet. But speaking of our guest . . ." He handed Declan the newspaper. "I just now saw this."

Hidden on the back page of the entertainment section of the *Los Angeles Times* was a two-inch column with a glaring headline that would've ordinarily turned his gut to water. But he read it without batting an eyelid.

SOAP ACTRESS DIES IN CAR CRASH IN MEXICO

Emmy-Award-winning Daytime Television Actress Robin Mulcahey was killed in a fiery one-car accident on a coastal highway in Mexico on July 23. The cause of the accident is still under investigation, but unconfirmed reports state that there was evidence at the crash site that the actress had been drinking. Publicists at *South Riding,* the daytime soap in which Ms. Mulcahey was a cast member, state that she was in Mexico on holiday when the accident occurred. Ms. Mulcahey's brother, NFL football star Paul Mulcahey, flew to Mexico to identify the remains, which were subsequently shipped back to her hometown of Williamsburg, Virginia. Funeral services were held for Ms. Mulcahey in Williamsburg on July 27, and droves of fans attended from all over the country. In an ironic twist, it was learned that Ms. Mulcahey, while a student at William & Mary, had survived a serious car accident that took the life of her best friend and sorority sister, 19-year-old Amy Shiley, in 1998.

"Gruesome." Declan took a sip of coffee and shook his head. "Amazing, isn't it? The money those Mulcaheys must've spent to pull off something like this? Think of the people they had to pay off."

"Quite." Cedric nodded. "Then again, didn't Michael Mulcahey leave Paul a whole boatload of money?"

Declan shrugged. "Some kind of trust fund, but according to Amy, he's using that to fund some foundation for child abuse in New York. No, it's his mother's money that's paying for all this." He indicated the newspaper. "She must be one desperate lady to want to hush up this whole thing."

"And why not?" Cedric's eyebrow arched, a wry smile pursing his lips. "You have to admit, Dec, it's a whopper of a story. Girl takes over her dead best friend's identity and lives her life for seven years. And all the time, she's in love with her 'brother.' Christ! I know at least a dozen producers who'd kill for the rights." His amber brown eyes twinkled. "I don't suppose there's any chance at all we can option it? I could write one hell of a screenplay."

Dec gave him a mock glare. "Don't even think about it, Cedric."

"Oh, not now, for God's sake. In a few years, perhaps. After everything has calmed down."

A footfall sounded behind them. Cedric's eyes moved past Declan's shoulder, and his smile widened. "Well, here is the lovely lady now. Good morning, love. Come join us. The coffee is hot, and the croissants freshly baked."

"Yeah, right," said a muffled feminine voice. "Like you can tell that I'm lovely . . . which I'm not."

Declan turned to see Amy step onto the veranda wearing flax cargo shorts and a sleeveless white blouse. Her face was swathed in bandages. He smiled. "Amy! Good morning! How are you feeling this morning, love?"

"Like I'm the ball in that hurling game you made me watch on satellite last night." Even though her voice was muted through her bandages, Declan was pleased to hear she sounded lighthearted enough. "I'd forgotten how bad it feels to recover from surgery." She gingerly sat down at the table next to Declan and sighed. "And this is just the beginning."

Declan reached for her hand and squeezed. "It'll be worth it, darlin'. You'll see."

"I know." Her blue eyes shone through the narrow slit in the bandage. "How can I thank you for all you've done for me . . . and you, Cedric."

Cedric flushed and reached for his napkin. "We're honored to help." He stood and pressed a hand on Declan's shoulder. "Enjoy your breakfast, you two. I'm off to the shower."

After Cedric stepped into the villa, Declan turned to Amy. "Cedric just showed me this." He passed her the newspaper. "It appears that Robin is officially dead."

Amy read the paragraph, then reached for the coffeepot. Her hands were shaking. Declan reached out and took the coffeepot from her. He poured the steaming brew into a china cup. "It's okay, love. It's almost over."

"I can't help thinking about poor Jeff," she said softly. "Paul says he didn't take it at all well when he learned the truth about me. And then . . . mourning Robin for the first time . . ." She shook her head.

"He just needs some time to come to terms with everything. And, at least, Robin had her funeral."

"Yeah, I guess that's some comfort."

They were silent for a long moment, each lost in their own thoughts. Then Declan felt Amy's eyes upon him. "I meant what I said. Thank you. I didn't want Paul to get you involved in this, but now, I'm glad you're here for me. It means a lot."

He reached out and placed a hand on her shoulder. "I'm glad he asked me to help. I really care about you, Robin . . . I mean, *Amy.* Don't you realize that, girl?"

A glimmer of amusement lit her eyes. "Even if you can't get my name right? No, seriously. We've asked a lot of you. Involving you in this cover-up. Putting me up here for God knows how long while I go through all these surgeries. And now, I need to ask you another favor."

"Anything, love. How can I help?"

Her eyes dropped, and although he couldn't see her face, he sensed she was blushing. "Paul is working with some of Tammy's Washington contacts to build me a new identity. A social security card, birth certificate, all that stuff you don't think about until you need it. Obviously, I can't use Amy Shiley because she's dead. I'm keeping Amy, of course. But I need a new last name. And I thought about using Jackson, my mom's maiden name. But she was adopted, and well . . . her parents never spoke to her after she ran off with my dad. It would just feel weird to use their name. So . . . I was wondering if . . . would you mind if I took the name Blair? I mean, it *was* my name at one time, and . . ." She shrugged. "I just feel like if I could call myself Amy Blair, I'd feel more comfortable. Is that all right with you?" Her anxious eyes met his.

Declan smiled and leaned forward to plant a kiss on her bandaged forehead. "I'd be honored if you used my name. Of course"—his grin widened—"it won't be Blair for long, according to Paul." His hand covered hers and squeezed. "I know the two of you are going to be very happy, love."

"Thanks, Dec. I've loved him for . . . well . . . just about forever." Through the tiny opening for her mouth, he could see the flash of her teeth as she smiled. "I *am* glad Paul told you everything. I should've known you'd be understanding about it. You're a great guy, you know. You don't judge people. Even when they deserve it."

He gazed at her a moment, then said, "I understood because we both were doing the same thing, you know. Living a lie. You didn't judge me when I told you how I felt about Cedric. What right would I have to judge you?"

Tears sparkled in her eyes, yet, he knew she was smiling. "Oh, Dec. I've really missed you."

He squeezed her hand again and smiled, feeling close to tears himself. "I've missed you, too, love. And remember this, you've always got a friend in me, Amy Blair. And that, my love, you can count on."

Amy stood on the veranda off her bedroom and stared out at the glimmering turquoise ocean in the distance. She'd been here in Mexico six months now, and today, she would finally see her new face.

A myriad of emotions swirled through her—fear, anxiety, hope, and antici-
pation. She felt each one in turn, and sometimes, all of them at the same time.
For the first time in almost eight years, she would, once again, be Amy Shiley
Blair. And if everything went as planned, in a few months, she would become
Amy Shiley Blair Mulcahey. But who was she, *really*? What had happened to
the soul of Amy Shiley during this seven-year masquerade?

Paul loves me.

She had to keep reminding herself of that, because she was having a tough
time loving herself. *Paul loves me.* Despite the horrible thing she'd done. He'd
made that clear during his frequent visits to Mexico. Not by action. He'd never
touched her in an intimate way, nor had she expected him to. Even with the
bandages covering her face, it was unthinkable that they should step toward
that line. They never spoke about it, but it didn't need to be said aloud. Only
when Amy had her own face back would they be able to move ahead as a
couple.

And today was the day. Paul and Dr. McGraw would be arriving at any
moment.

Amy hugged her churning stomach and took a deep breath, trying to calm
herself. It had been impossible to eat this morning. She'd known she wouldn't
be able to keep anything down. The fear was too strong in her now. What if,
after all these surgeries, she still didn't look anything like her former self? And
worse, what if she still looked like Robin?

Oh, God. If that happened, there would be no hope for her and Paul. No
hope at all. That would be a just punishment, wouldn't it?

You wanted to be Robin? Well, you're stuck with her now. Forever.

She shuddered and turned away from the view. As she stepped inside her
bedroom, there was a tap on the door, and her heart jumped at the sound of
Declan's voice. "Amy, love? Paul is downstairs with Dr. McGraw. Shall I send
them up?"

She closed her eyes and tried to steady her breathing. Finally, she found her
voice. "Yes. Send them up."

His footsteps faded. Amy took a seat at the dressing table and folded her
hands in her lap. She took a deep breath and released it slowly.

I'm ready.

Amy watched Dr. McGraw's brown eyes as he unwound the bandage from her
face. She waited for a flicker of alarm, a dawning of horror or disgust, but his
eyes remained placid. Interested, but placid. Behind his left shoulder, she could
see Paul sitting on the edge of her bed, his body tense, eyes locked on her face.

She felt a flutter of panic. He would see her face before she would. Why
had she thought that would comfort her—having him here for the unveiling.
What if something had gone horribly wrong? What if she was disfigured
beyond repair?

Almost as if sensing the turmoil of her thoughts, Paul stood and approached her, reaching down to enclose her hand in his. He gave her hand a reassuring squeeze, and just like that, the panic disappeared. It would be okay. Paul was here, and whatever happened, they'd face it together.

The doctor removed the last of the bandage, and Amy felt the cool air of the white ceiling fan brush against her skin. Dr. McGraw's gaze swept over her appraisingly, and he smiled. "Ahhh . . ." he murmured. Then he stood and looked at Paul. "I'll leave you two alone."

Amy watched the doctor walk away. He opened the door and stepped out into the hall, closing it behind him. Slowly, she turned and looked up at Paul. And caught her breath at the sight of the tears shimmering in his eyes.

"Is it bad?" she whispered, her throat dry.

Paul took the doctor's vacated seat and leaned forward to grasp her hands. "You're beautiful," he whispered, his gaze holding hers. "You're Amy."

Amy's heart spasmed, then tears welled in her own eyes. "I am? You're sure?"

Paul gave her a tender smile. "See for yourself." He reached for the hand mirror, which lay facedown on the desk.

She took it, her hand shaking so badly she couldn't hold the mirror still. Paul's hand covered hers on the handle, and the mirror steadied. A face swam into view, a slightly swollen, reddish face, but one that looked vaguely familiar. Eight years older than the one she'd last seen in the mirror on a wintry January night in Williamsburg. But hers. Definitely the face of Amy Shiley.

Silent tears rolled down her new face, and still, she couldn't stop staring at it. "It *is* me, isn't it? It's really me?"

Paul took the mirror from her, placed it on the desk and drew her to her feet. Then he took her into his arms. She buried her face against his chest and began to sob.

"It's you, Amy," he whispered, kissing the top of her head. "The woman I love."

A Mexican priest married them on the beach with Declan and Cedric in attendance. Amy wore a white muslin dress that reached her ankles and a circlet of wildflowers on her short cap of blond hair. Robin would've approved.

After the ceremony, Declan and Cedric took off on Cedric's private jet for a film festival in Stockholm, leaving the villa at their disposal for their honeymoon. Amy once again stood on the veranda off her bedroom, gazing at the sunset's burnt sienna rays kissing the ocean. How long ago the morning seemed when she'd stood here fighting her fears. What a difference a few hours made.

She heard the bathroom door open behind her, and turned to see Paul step into the room, his black hair wet from the shower, a towel wrapped around his waist. Droplets of water clung to his tanned shoulders, trailing down the carpet of black hair on his chest. He stared at her, his eyes soft and very blue.

Heart pounding, she stepped into the room. She was trembling. It was almost as if she were that same girl he'd first made love to so long ago at Windsong. But then . . . wasn't she? For the first time, Amy felt like that girl had never really left.

Paul smiled as she came toward him. When she was a few inches away, he reached out and placed his hands on her shoulders. "Smell me," he said, drawing her against him. "What is the scent?"

Amy inhaled, and smiled, feeling the warmth of his skin radiating around her. "You used my shampoo."

He threaded his fingers through her damp hair. "Coconut, right?"

She nodded.

"And peach shower gel?" His gaze scanned her face, lingering on her mouth.

"Yes," she murmured, light-headed from the rapid beating of her heart.

He lifted a strand of her hair and breathed in, eyes still closed. "I'll always love the scent of coconut shampoo."

His eyes opened, and the tenderness she saw in them made her knees go weak. "Remember that Thanksgiving night in your room? Your scent was everywhere. I think I even mentioned how much it reminded me of you."

Amy nodded, her hands clutching his waist. "I wanted to tell you then. So badly. I almost did. But I wasn't brave enough. I didn't want you to hate me."

"I could never hate you, Amy," he whispered. "Even if I wanted to. I know, because I tried. I love you."

She smiled tremulously, her heart feeling like a helium balloon floating up to the ceiling. "I've never stopped loving you in all these years."

"I know that now." Slipping his hands under the damp fall of her hair, he cupped her head. And then, his mouth was on hers, tentative at first, but deepening with urgency. With a soft moan, Amy twined her hands around his neck and kissed him back, nestling against his warmth, knowing that for the first time in eight years, she was exactly where she needed to be.

He stood in front of her, a solid body of sinew and muscle. Her eyes were on the level of his chest. His height made her feel small and delicate. She'd always loved that. With a soft sigh of surrender, she slid her palms up his chest, pausing over his heart, where she could feel it beating. His hand cupped her jaw. He gazed at her, his expression tender and full of love.

He backed up to the bed, his hands on her wrists, drawing her with him. He sat down and guided her between his knees. Eyes fixed on hers, he slowly removed her robe. She was naked beneath it. She caught her breath as his warm fingers slid over her breasts. His gaze moved to the birthmark above her nipple. With his hands on her waist, he drew her closer. He bent his black head, and his lips skimmed her birthmark so gently . . . so tenderly Amy felt like she might shatter into a million pieces. She closed her eyes and drew in a deep, staggered breath, feeling a tear track down her cheek. He slid his hands up her back and pressed his face against the valley of her breasts, clutching her to him.

"Something inside me knew it was you," he said in a whisper, his breath warm against her sternum.

Amy threaded her fingers through his glossy black hair. This was a dream. It had to be one of her crazy impossible dreams. But it felt so real. *He* felt so real.

Paul drew away and lifted his head to look at her. Barely breathing, she met the heat of his blue gaze and felt her limbs go weak. His hands settled on her hips, and his mouth traced a line down from her breasts to her stomach. She stood in the cradle of his legs, quaking at the touch of his warm hands on her skin. Eyes melded with hers, he released her, only to remove the towel from his waist, and then eased her down upon his lap, straddling him. His hands imprisoned her head as his mouth claimed hers in a hungry kiss.

Finally, after several exquisite moments of long, drugging kisses, Amy dragged her mouth from his, heart thumping. She drew in a sharp, ragged breath as she eased herself onto his erect penis, slowly drawing him in, taking all of him inside her, inch by inch. She bit her lip, still holding his gaze, knowing if she moved too quickly, she would be over the edge. Gone. His hands moved slowly up her waist to her shoulders, as if learning the map of her body, memorizing it. He reached her neck, his thumbs meeting at the hollow of her throat, caressing there before traveling upward and cupping the back of her head lovingly. His eyes held hers, and she saw the love shimmering there. Knew it was for her. Only for her.

For a moment that seemed to last into eternity, they were still, joined together, eyes and bodies locked. One entity, one soul. It was a moment of exquisite pain and beauty. A new beginning? Amy didn't want to let it go, wanted to hold on to it forever. But they both knew it couldn't be held.

Paul moved first. Cradling her head, his mouth captured hers, and she opened to him, drinking in his need and answering with her own. Moving to the primal beat of an ancient dance, Amy rose and fell on him. He closed his eyes in ecstacy, hands slipping from her head to encircle her waist, guiding her.

At the moment of climax, Amy's hands clenched into his raven hair, and her eyes met his. Her mouth opened, and, with a sharp gasp, she fell over the edge and into the abyss. Moments later, as she shuddered against him, she heard him cry out her name—"*Amy!*" and felt the explosion of his own climax. Hearts thudding, skin to skin, they held each other tightly as if they would never, ever let go.

Epilogue

★ JUNE 2006 ★

It was a beautiful old cemetery near the James River—an ancient place of peace and sanctuary landscaped with manicured lawns and beds of fragrant flowers. The last time Amy had been here, it was to see her mother put to rest next to the grave of her daughter. A shiver rippled up her spine as she gazed at the name etched into the weathered tombstone.

AMY JESSICA SHILEY—
OCTOBER 12, 1978–JANUARY 23, 1998

So weird, seeing your own name on a tombstone.
No coffin lay in this grave though. Not anymore. The coffin that held Robin's bones had been moved to its own burial site, and now lay under her own tombstone—finally. Amy turned and walked a few paces to her mother's marker. A smaller stone, a little less elaborate.

VICTORIA J. SHILEY—
AUGUST 18, 1960–NOVEMBER 27, 1999

Well, Mom, I've come full circle, haven't I? I'm not Amy Shiley anymore, though. Only in soap operas can people come back from the grave, and even Tammy Mulcahey, with all her money and power, couldn't accomplish that.
Amy gazed down at the gold band on her left ring finger paired with its matching diamond, sparkling in the midafternoon sun. *I have a new name now, Mama. Amy Blair Mulcahey. And it's legal.*
"You would've liked Paul, Mama," she whispered through misted eyes.

She knelt and placed a rose from her bridal bouquet on her mother's grave. Then she stood and looked over to her left, her heart tightening at the handsome figure of her husband kneeling at another grave nearby. She walked toward him. Paul looked up as she neared and gave her a smile tinged with sadness.

Amy reached his side. He stood and wrapped an arm around her, pulling her close. Her gaze moved to the pink-toned tombstone, glittering in the sunlight.

ROBIN RENEE MULCAHEY—
MARCH 19, 1978–JULY 23, 2005

"I wish she could've been here for our wedding," Paul said quietly.

"Me too." Amy murmured. "She would've made a gorgeous maid of honor."

"Would've been the life of the reception, too." His voice rang with humor. His arm dropped from her shoulder, and his hand found hers.

Her smile dimmed as she glanced up at him. "I think she'd be happy for us, Paul. Don't you think so?"

His eyes met hers. Warm, loving. "I'm sure of it."

Silence fell. For a long moment, they gazed at Robin's grave, hands entwined. A light breeze from the river sifted through Amy's short cap of hair, bringing with it the scent of carnations from a bed nearby.

"Do you think she would've ever married?" Amy asked finally. "Would she have found a man she could've finally trusted?"

He shrugged, his hand squeezing hers. "I think she might have. Who knows?"

"Maybe in time, Jason would've won her over. I think he really loved her, you know." Realizing what she'd said, she blushed and glanced up at him "I'm sorry. I guess it makes you uncomfortable, me bringing Jason's name up."

He shook his head. "I don't blame you for turning to him for comfort back then. I'm glad he was there for you. Anyway, it's all in the past." He turned her to face him, hands on her shoulders. "It is, Amy. All of it's in the past now. We're making a new beginning."

She smiled up at him, her heart somersaulting at the love in his eyes. "It's all I ever wanted, you know. You. A family."

"We'll start our own family. And we'll be good parents, Amy. We'll do things differently than our parents did." He gazed down at her. His hands tightened on her shoulders. "Our kids are going to have the kind of family life you and I never had. We're going to be there for them. I promise you that."

She nodded. "I know." Slipping her arms around his waist, she leaned against him, feeling the comforting thud of his heart beneath her ear. For a long moment, they held each other silently.

Finally, Paul drew away and glanced at his watch. "Hey, we'd better get going. This time tomorrow, we'll be honeymooning on Kilauea. But not if we don't make that flight to New York."

Hands linked, they left the Mulcahey plot, neither of them sparing a glance at the other tombstone. Tammy had insisted on burying Michael next to Robin. Amy knew it had galled Paul to give in to her on that, but she'd convinced him that it really didn't matter. Robin's spirit had long ago escaped that coffin. She could, even now, feel it around her.

They walked toward Paul's T-bird. When Amy reached the passenger side of the car, she paused at her reflection in the window, and her heart jumped. It was still too new, this feeling of surprise she felt every time she caught a glimpse of herself. But it wasn't an unpleasant feeling. In fact, it was similar to the way she felt when she had a new hairstyle that really suited her, and each time she saw herself in the mirror, it gave her a little "Is that me? I like that" thrill.

But though she loved looking like herself again—well, like the self she would've been if she'd left nature alone—what she hadn't been prepared for was the totally bewildering sensation of loss she still felt on occasion. The loss of Robin's beloved face. Strange, she knew that. But there it was. She supposed a psychiatrist would have a field day with her if she chose to go down that road. But she didn't think she'd need to do that. Not now that she had Paul. He was her lover, her therapist, and her husband all rolled up in one. And with his love, she knew she could get through anything.

"Amy?"

She realized he was peering at her from the other side of the car, a half smile on his lips. Abruptly, he turned and came around the car, taking her into his arms. His eyes roved tenderly over her newly sculpted face.

"Did I tell you how very beautiful you are today, Amy Blair Mulcahey? I can't believe it's possible but you're even more gorgeous today than you were in your wedding gown yesterday."

She smiled up at him, feeling that familiar flutter in her heart whenever he looked at her like this, his eyes brimming with love. "Maybe that's because of last night," she murmured. "It was a wedding night to remember, wasn't it?"

"The first of many." He traced her bottom lip with his thumb, then kissed her, a slow, intoxicating kiss that sent her senses swimming. Finally, he drew away. "We'd better get to the airport."

Amy slid into the T-bird, her heart singing. Paul was right. This was their new beginning, the one they'd started planning over a year ago. With the help of Declan and Cedric—and Tammy's friends in high places—it had all come together just the way Paul had promised it would.

After her return from Mexico, Amy had gone back to New York, starting her new job as the director of the Robin Mulcahey Foundation for Abused Children, a foundation Paul had set up with the trust fund Michael had bequeathed in his will. And there, Amy Blair had met and started dating the eligible NFL football player, Paul Mulcahey. In February, after his second Pro Bowl game in Hawaii, Paul had hung up his football jersey for good. After eight years in the NFL, he'd attained a Super Bowl ring, two Pro Bowl appearances, some respectable stats, and plenty of money on which to live comfortably for at least the next decade. Not bad for a thirty-year-old professional football player. And in the fall, he'd start work at Fox doing commentary for the Giants games. All that, and a beautiful new wife.

A huge society wedding had been part of Tammy's deal. And they couldn't deny it fit with the fiction they were living as a couple who'd just met and fallen in love in the last year. A small price to pay, Amy thought, and she couldn't deny the thrill she felt at being the star of the fairy-tale wedding she'd dreamed about as a child. And it really *had* been the stuff of dreams.

Amy couldn't believe it *wasn't* a dream as she moved down the aisle toward Paul, who looked devastating in a white tux. When she reached him, his blue eyes held hers, and the love she saw in them made her catch her breath. His hands trembled as he slipped the ring upon her finger, and her throat tightened with emotion. *He really does love me. Me, Amy Shiley, the little nobody from the trailer park.*

Even the fixed smile on Tammy's flawless face and the blue ice of her eyes as she hugged her daughter-in-law hadn't taken away from Amy's joy. She knew Tammy would never like her, would never forgive her for the deception, but she could live with that. Besides, the feeling was mutual. She didn't think she could ever bring herself to forgive the woman for what she'd done to Robin.

Just graduated from Harvard, Jeff had flown in for the wedding. The pesky teen had grown into a strapping blue-eyed blond young man whose lively manner and dry sense of humor brought Robin to Amy's mind more than once. At first it was awkward between them. She saw the curiosity in his eyes, and the turmoil of wanting to ask her why she'd done what she did. But Jeff was, by nature, laid-back and easygoing, and he'd grown into a true gentleman. There was no way he'd cause a scene at her wedding. Amy had to bring it up herself, and she did so during a dance with him.

She took a deep breath, and said the words. "I'm sorry, Jeff." Her heart slammed in her chest. "I hope you'll be able to forgive me someday."

His quizzical blue eyes met hers. "I always liked you, Amy," he said after a moment. "It took me a while to accept it, and I can't begin to understand why you did it. But Paul loves you." He shook his head, and smiled. "And that's good enough for me."

He drew her back into his arms and swung her around on the dance floor, showing off for the crowd. And the subject was never mentioned again.

"All right." Paul got into the driver's seat and started the ignition. "Airport, here we come."

"Oh, wait, Paul!" Amy hastily unbuckled her seat belt and reached into the backseat for the bouquet of white and pink fairy roses. "I can't believe I almost forgot this." She scrambled out of the T-bird and hurried back to Robin's grave. Kneeling, she placed the bouquet at the foot of her tombstone.

"This would've been yours if you'd been there yesterday, Rob," she whispered. "Like I told Paul, you *would've* made a gorgeous maid of honor." She stood, smoothing her hands down her white rayon dress. "But then . . . you know that, don't you?"

It had to be her imagination, of course, but she could almost hear Robin's waterfall of laughter. See her dimple flashing. And hear her voice . . .

You know it, girlfriend. I rock!

"Yes, you do. You always did." A tear rolled down her cheek. She brushed it away, then turned to head back to Paul's car.

"You okay?" he asked, peering at her closely as she got in.

She smiled at him. "I'm perfect."